WHEN WE
Break

New York Times and *USA Today* Bestselling Author
KRISTEN PROBY

&
AMPERSAND
PUBLISHING, INC.

When We Break

THE BLACKWELLS OF MONTANA

KRISTEN PROBY

&
AMPERSAND
PUBLISHING, INC.

This is for anyone who needs some pampering, some kindness, and their hair pulled while being called a good fucking girl.
Beckett's got you covered.

Spicy Girls Book Club

TBR

Reading List:

Dom by S.J. Tilly (The book Skyla and Beckett read together)
You Were Never Not Mine by Monica Murphy
Beautiful Exile by Catherine Cowles
Wolf.e by Paisley Hope
Lights Out by Navessa Allen
Where We Started by Ashley Munoz
Beautiful Beast by Neva Altaj
Runaway Love by Melanie Harlow
Rival Hearts by Maggie Rawdon
Love, Utley by S.J. Tilly

Content Warnings

You can find a comprehensive content warning list at the following link:

https://www.kristenprobyauthor.com/potential-trigger-content-warnings

Kristen

Prologue

SKYLA

"I have to go." I shake my head as I shove a jumper into my suitcase as both men who mean the most to me watch. Connor, my older brother, leans against the doorjamb of my bedroom, broodily glaring at me through his black-rimmed glasses, while Mikhail, my dance partner and best friend of ten years, paces in front of my bed.

"You do not have to go," Mik insists, his voice thick with emotion and the Russian accent he never lost even though he's lived in New York City since he was fifteen. "Dammit, we will send him to jail."

I scoff at that and shake my head, then reach over and scratch Riley's belly before I return to my closet to grab more clothes.

"He always skirts just on this side of the law," I remind them as if we could forget. "But he scares me. I can't dance professionally anyway, Mik. Not anymore."

He snorts and shakes his head stubbornly. "You'll recover."

God, I love this handsome Russian. We've danced together since we were sixteen, and he's always been loyal and stubborn.

"I'm not going to recover from this one." I reach out and take his hand, then give it a squeeze. "We both know it. We've had our last curtain call."

My emotional Russian shakes his head again, and Connor rakes his hand through his hair in agitation.

I think this whole situation is worse on my big brother. He's beyond wealthy, he's powerful, and he's strong.

And even he can't fix this.

"Where will you go?" Mik doesn't meet my eyes, but he pulls me into his arms and hugs me, kissing the top of my head.

"Montana."

Mik gasps and pulls away. Connor scowls.

"What the feck?" Connor asks, his Irish distinct when he gets upset. "Bloody why?"

"Because I like it there." I shrug and toss another jumper in the bag. It's cold in Montana, so I'll definitely take all my jumpers. The rest can be shipped to me later. "And no one would think to look for me in a small town."

"Skyla." My friend shakes his head, obviously not happy with this news. "What happens when you are ready to dance again?"

"Mik." I sigh and sit on the edge of the bed, facing them both. "Dancing is over for me."

Mik mumbles some swear words in Russian and paces away.

"It's been ruined. But my *life* isn't over, so I'm taking it back. I'm going to Montana, where I'll settle in and open a dance studio. I'll teach."

"You are not a fucking teacher," Mik insists, practically spitting out that last word. "You are a *prima ballerina*. You've danced as Giselle and Kitri. You are not some small-town dance teacher. I won't allow it, malishka."

I glance over at Connor, who's stayed quiet, observing us.

"You're too quiet over there."

"You know my feelings on the matter," my brother replies with a shrug. "It's pissed I am that you're running away, but more than that, I'm fecking furious that this bleeding arsehole won't leave you be. I've threatened him. I've done everything I can legally do, and you won't let me—"

"No." I shake my head, swallowing hard. "I won't let you *call someone* to have him dealt with."

I couldn't live with having a person's life ended on my account.

Even if that arsehole has tormented me every day for the past two years.

"You have an expensive, well-trained dog," Mik reminds me, eyeing Riley, who watches us from the middle of the bed.

"Not the one I wanted to buy her," Connor adds, and I sigh once again. "We should have gotten the one that's trained to attack. To kill."

"I didn't want that. I want a dog that looks intimidating, is well trained and alert, and is also my best friend. Riley helps me feel better. I don't want to deal with an aggressive dog." I lift my chin, and neither has a comeback for that. "I'm going to Montana. You're always welcome there, but I won't ever return to New York."

"I wish you'd go to Ireland," Connor says. "You'd be safe with Ma and Da. Lewis wouldn't find you there."

"We don't say that arsehole's name in my house." I narrow my eyes at my brother, and he rubs his hand over his forehead in agitation before pushing his glasses up his nose.

"Go to Ma and Da," he repeats.

"I'm not a child." Shaking my head, I walk into my brother's arms and hold on tight, soaking him in. "Besides, you'll come see me all the time. You'll fly out in your fancy jet and stay with me."

"As often as I can," he confirms, hugging me close. "But running away doesn't erase what's happened."

"He won't leave New York." I sound surer than I feel, but I need to believe that. Because if I'm wrong, I won't be safe anywhere. "I'm actually excited for this new adventure. To start fresh somewhere new, to make friends, to teach."

Mik scoffs, still pacing angrily.

My Russian friend has a hot temper.

"You go then," he says, flailing his arm dramatically

4

my way, yet still looking so graceful as he does. "You go *teach* and leave me here to pick up the pieces."

"I have an understudy," I remind him. "And she's been filling in for me for three months."

Three brutal, agonizing months.

"She's not you."

Mik frames my face in his big hands, and as usual, I feel so loved. These incredible men have my back, and I know I'm lucky to have these guys in my corner.

"I'll miss you too, *a stór*."

His lips tremble. "I cannot leave as often as Connor can, but I will come visit."

"Good." I grin at him. "Bring Benji with you."

"Like he would let me go without him." Mik shakes his head. I know what he's thinking. We've always been able to read each other's minds.

This is the end of an era.

But if I'm going to live—*and have a chance to live a good life*—I have to do this.

"Connor will fly you there?" Mik asks us.

"Of course," my brother replies.

"No."

"You won't fecking argue with me on this," Connor insists.

I sigh. "Fine. You'll fly me."

To my new start. To my safe place.

Please, God, let it be safe.

Chapter One

SKYLA

"What are you doing right now?"

I pinch my phone between my ear and shoulder and open my car door, ushering Riley into the back seat. I had to buy a huge car for my huge dog.

"I'm on my way to an appointment," I inform my brother. "What are *you* doing right now?"

"I'm between meetings." I can hear the exhaustion in Connor's voice. "Thought I'd check in with you. Any news?"

"No." I start the engine and wait for my phone to connect to the car. "I haven't heard anything in months, so that's encouraging. You know, you don't have to call me every day to ask me if my stalker has found me."

"That's not the only reason I call, and you know it."

"But it's the first thing you ask me. Don't worry, I haven't dropped my guard, but it's been nice to have some peace and quiet."

"It's relieved I am that you feel safe there. That's what you wanted, that's what you got, and that's all that matters. I'll be in town next week."

I frown out the windscreen. "Really? Why's that?"

"A potential investment opportunity. And to check in on my favorite sister."

"Only sister," I remind him with a smile even though he can't see me. "Good, you'll be here for our spring recital. I'll save you a seat."

"Sky—"

"Ah, ah, ah. If you're coming to town, you'll watch my recital. No amount of money you have will get you out of it."

"Fine." He sighs heavily. "I'll watch the bleeding recital. But you'll owe me some meat pies in exchange."

"I can handle that. What day will you be here?"

"I'll know for sure in a day or so. I'll keep you posted."

"See that you do. I'd better go, but I'll talk to you later."

We end the call, and I drive Riley and me from our adorable house to the doctor's office on the edge of town.

When we walk inside, Riley is at my side in his handsome red service-dog harness, and we're greeted with a smile.

"Hello, Skyla. I have you all checked in. You can have a seat, and someone will be out for you shortly."

"Thank you." With a nod, I lead Riley to the end of a row so he can lie down next to me.

I'm obsessed with Bitterroot Valley, which has mountains and a quaint downtown full of shops and restaurants I love. So many sweet people have welcomed me here. It couldn't be more different from New York City, which I also loved, but this small town has quickly become home in the eight months I've lived here. I have friends and a feeling of belonging that I was afraid I wouldn't find outside my ballet family in New York.

But I've found it here, and I'm so grateful.

"Skyla."

The nurse grins and gestures for me to follow her. Riley is at my side, walking with me.

"How are you today?" she asks.

"I'm doing well. And how are you?"

"It's been a good day around here so far." She winks. "Let's get some vitals on you."

After I've been weighed and my temperature and blood pressure are logged, the nurse hustles out, assuring me that Dr. Blackwell will be here shortly.

Riley lets out a huff from his spot on the floor.

"I hear you."

Not long after, Dr. Blackwell bustles into the room, holding his laptop. He smiles at me and then at my dog. He's a handsome man, that's for certain. He's a mountain next to me, but then, most men are. At five foot five and lean from years of dancing, I'm used to feeling petite. *Some take advantage of that.* The doctor is broad and muscular, with dark hair and dark, kind eyes. I'm sure most of his female patients flirt with him endlessly. There's no spark, but he's certainly nice to look at while I'm here.

"Hello, you two," he says as he sits on the stool next to me and types on the keyboard.

"Hi, Dr. Blackwell."

"Just call me Blake. How's that ankle been feeling, Skyla?"

"Not normal," I reply.

He frowns. "Okay, can you be more specific?"

The usual frustration sets in. "It's not *normal*. Not how it was before it was injured."

Before it ended my bloody career.

"Well, that's not unusual. But you've done everything right. You did PT for longer than was necessary, and looking at this MRI from last week, the injury has completely healed. I would give you the clearance to dance right this minute if that's what you wanted to do."

"But I *can't*." I shake my head. "Of course, I don't plan to return to New York to resume my professional career. That's not possible. But even when I dance for pleasure in my studio, it's not the same. The range of motion, the force it can handle when I jeté—"

He lifts an eyebrow.

"When I leap or jump," I clarify, "and land on it. There's *no way* I'd be able to put in fourteen-hour practice and rehearsal days."

"And you don't have to," he reminds me gently. "It's my understanding that such rigorous days aren't a part of your lifestyle anymore."

"But I should be able to if I had to." I lift my chin. "I hate that it doesn't feel normal."

Dr. Blackwell sets his computer aside to give me his undivided attention.

"Skyla, ankle sprains are sometimes worse than fractures. They heal slowly, and occasionally, the full range of motion doesn't return. But you're a strong and gifted athlete, and I think that with time and practice, you'll feel more and more normal."

"Ankles are important in ballet," I mutter.

"I know." He nods and glances at Riley, who hasn't taken his eyes off the doctor. "Strength training, stretches —all the exercises you did in PT will help."

I nod, feeling defeated all over again. "That's all we can do?"

"I'm afraid so. Dancers' bodies take a beating, Skyla. I'm surprised you're not more beat up than this."

"You don't even want to see my feet." I laugh. "They're not pretty."

He chuckles, makes some notes on his computer, and my appointment is finished. Riley and I leave the office and walk out to the car, and he jumps into the back seat.

I'm not quite ready to go home, so we stop at my new favorite place, Billie's Books. I've become good friends with the owner, Billie Blackwell, who happens to be Dr. Blackwell's sister. We share a love of romance books, and our monthly book club is the highlight of my schedule.

"Hey, girl." Bee waves as she rings up a customer's purchase. "That new Monica Murphy book is on the shelf there."

With a grin, I find the paperback and hug it to my

chest. Monica Murphy is one of my favorites, and I've been waiting for this one. Of course, I have it on my e-reader, but I'm also a paperback collector.

I turned one of my guest rooms into a library. It might not be the size of Belle's in *Beauty and the Beast*, but it's mine, and I love filling it up.

Taking my purchase to the counter, I smile at my friend as she rings up my purchase. Bee's a gorgeous girl with dark hair perfectly styled in long, beachy waves around her shoulders. She's in a smart gray suit today, and *as usual*, her makeup is perfect.

This woman knows fashion, and I love it.

"How's it going?" Bee asks.

"I'm better now that I have this beauty for my shelves." I swipe my card and shake my head when she offers me a bag. "Do you mind if I sit in one of your cozy chairs and read for a bit?"

"That's what the chairs are for," she reminds me. "Since it's quiet in here, I'm going to run next door for a coffee. Would you like one?"

"Just a black Earl Grey tea would be lovely. Thank you."

"You got it. Back in a few."

Riley and I settle in our favorite spot. The purple chair is deep and cozy, and Bee added a dog bed next to it just for Riley. He turns in a circle and lies down, but he's still on alert.

"Good boy." I rub his head before I open the book and get sucked into this talented author's words.

Bee drops off the tea, then bustles back to work. I

enjoy an hour by the window, reading and relaxing, until I finally decide to head over to the studio to prepare for my afternoon class. It was a good choice to come to Bitterroot Valley. My ankle might not have full range of motion, but I'm strangely content and at peace.

So bloody thankful.

Chapter Two

"Tell me you hired him," Brad, my foreman, declares when I walk into the milking barn after waving off the applicant I just interviewed.

"I hired him." I nod, pushing my hat off my forehead. "And I hired the two from yesterday."

"We won't know what to do with a fully staffed team." He grins. "But I'm damn happy about it. You need some time off."

"We all need fucking time off," I reply. "And I'm grateful you guys have put in extra hours and all your hard-ass work through the winter."

"You gave us bonuses," Brad points out, "and you didn't have to. Hopefully, the load lightens up as we get closer to summer."

I nod, but I'm not hopeful. The new guest ranch side of things is going to send me to an early grave.

Someone should have beat me with a bullwhip when

I came up with the idea of building guest cabins. I've had enough on my plate with dairy operations that run pretty much twenty-four seven. I didn't need the added work of tourists.

I was naive and didn't expect they'd be so ... needy.

"I have the afternoon milking." Brad shoos me off. "And the cleanup."

"I'll go check on the calves. Jack and Ham will work on the evening feeding."

Brad nods, and we're off to handle our chores.

Before I head to the house for the night, I check on the cottage cheese and other projects in the processing barn, and when I'm satisfied, I pull out my phone and send a group text to my brothers.

> Me: I'm actually done at a decent time this evening, and I need a beer. Let's go to the Wolf Den. Dinner's on me.

I walk into the farmhouse I grew up in, shed my dirty boots and jacket in the mudroom, then snag a banana on my way through the kitchen to the stairs leading up to my bedroom.

I inherited the ranch from my parents when they retired to Florida a few years ago. I'm not the eldest brother, that's Brooks's job, but I'm the one who's worked the farm and loved this place since I was a kid.

My phone vibrates with incoming messages.

> Brooks: One hour?

Blake: I'm in.

Bridger: I'll be there.

I grin and hit reply.

Me: See you in one hour.

The parking lot isn't even half full, filling me with satisfaction. Even though my new business thrives off the busy winter and summer tourist seasons, my favorite time is always the shoulder season. Bitterroot Valley is less crowded now before the hustle and bustle of summer, with the gorgeous weather and a plethora of outdoor activities to keep people busy.

Right now, the ground is muddy, the trees are just budding, and although the sun does peek out once in a while, it's still on the chilly side.

Perfect.

I pull in next to Blake, who gets out of his SUV and meets me at the rear of his vehicle.

"No ER tonight?" I ask my brother.

He shakes his head. "I was in the clinic today. I'm off duty and ready for a beer. Or three."

Bridger, the fire chief, pulls in and parks across from us, and Brooks joins us, walking from the direction of his auto repair shop a couple of blocks down.

"Holy shit, you left the ranch," Bridger says, pulling me in for a hug. "We haven't seen much of you since the holidays."

"Work's been insane," I reply. "There's no time to leave the ranch."

"Call us to help," Brooks says. "We all grew up there. We know what we're doing. I can guarantee you that not one of us has forgotten how to milk a cow or feed the chickens."

"Yeah, and you all have jobs," I remind him as we walk toward the pub entrance. "I just hired some more guys, so we're covered for the summer. I shouldn't have added the additional two cows. More cows mean more work."

"Come on." Blake pats me on the shoulder. "Let's get some beer in you. Maybe a burger."

"I'll take it."

The Wolf Den is one of my favorite places in town. The pub has some of the best food, with local beers on tap, pool tables at one end, and a generally fun atmosphere.

Walking through the door, I allow my eyes time to adjust to the darker room and scan the faces. I know half of them.

Brooks leads us to a table along the wall, and when I sit, I realize we lost Blake.

I spot Blake talking to a big black hulk of a dog while scanning the room as if he's searching for someone. He's always been a sucker for animals. If he wasn't a human doctor, he would have been a veterinarian.

"What's he doing?" Brooks asks.

"Flirting," I reply with a laugh as the server approaches and takes our drink orders. I order Blake the same beer as mine.

If he doesn't like it, he shouldn't have gone over to flirt with the dog. A dog that's currently following Blake back to our table and jumps onto the bench next to us.

"Uh, who's your new date, Blake?" I ask him.

"I know this dog." My brother looks defensive, which only makes me smirk. "He belongs to a patient of mine."

"Where's his owner?" Bridger asks.

"No idea, and that's odd because this guy is a service dog."

My humor leaves, and I frown at the dog. "That's not a good sign."

"No, it's not," Blake agrees, frowning with worry. "You're a good boy, Riley. Where's your mama, huh? Is she around here somewhere?"

"I ordered you a beer," I inform my brother, who nods.

"Thanks."

"How's married life?" I ask Bridger. He married our longtime friend Dani over the holidays. "I figured you'd be rushing home to her."

"She'll be there when I get there." He winks. "And married life is damn good. Dani and Birdie are decorating the house for spring tonight, so this was good timing."

"What, you don't want to help decorate?" Brooks asks, making us all smirk.

"I'll leave that to my girls," Bridger replies. "And I think they enjoy having something to do that's just for them. They pretty much kicked me out of the house and told me it would be a surprise when I got home."

Movement has me glancing to my right, and my breath catches in my lungs at the sight of her. The gorgeous redhead I saw in the bookstore all those months ago. She's marching our way, and from the look on her stunning face, I'd say she's good and pissed off. Then she opens her delectable little mouth and shocks the shit out of me.

"What in the bleeding hell is happening over here? You've broken my dog!"

Chapter Three

SKYLA

"There you are," Blake Blackwell says with a charming smile. "I found Riley by himself, and I was worried."

"I was *training* him." I narrow my eyes and prop my hands on my hips. "It was an exercise for him."

"Oops," the one with the beard says, cringing. "You messed up, bro."

"I apologize, Skyla," Blake says, shaking his head.

"Did he just follow you over here?" I'm eyeing Riley, who won't look me in the eyes because he knows he's in deep shite.

"Yeah," Blake says. "He did."

"You and I are going to have a long conversation," I inform the dog, who whines and lowers his head.

"He knows," Beard says with a grin. "Hi, I'm Beckett."

"Skyla," I reply and accept his offered hand. A zing moves up my arm at the contact, and Beckett's eyes narrow slightly as he examines me. He's impressive, I'll give him that. Even though he's sitting, I can see that he's tall and muscular with dark hair and eyes, and that beard isn't too long, trimmed nicely, and would feel so good ...

Whoa, we're not going there.

"That's Bridger," Blake says, pointing at a man on the other side of the table wearing a Bitterroot Valley Fire Department shirt.

"Dani's husband?" I ask.

"That's me," Bridger replies with a grin. "Dani talks about you all the time."

"I'm so sorry I had to miss the wedding." I frown when Beckett reaches out and pets Riley, and Riley *lets him.*

This dog is in trouble.

"The photos are beautiful, and it's pleased I am for both of you. I'm sorry I couldn't be there."

"Thanks," Bridger says with a smile. My friend's right. Her husband is swoony.

"And I'm Brooks. The oldest and best looking." Brooks stands and reaches over to shake my hand, making me smile.

"So connecting the dots, you're Billie's brothers, then?" I ask as I make Riley get off the bench. He still won't look me in the eyes, but he sits dutifully at my side. These Blackwells have incredibly gorgeous genes to be sure. They all resemble each other, and the brothers are all handsome as sin.

When Beckett shifts in his chair to face me and give me his attention, it makes my lady bits take notice.

They're indeed all ridiculously good-looking, but this bearded man sets my body on fire.

"We are," Beckett replies with that deep timbre that just begs for me to shiver.

"I've heard a few stories from Billie. She's one of my very good mates here in Montana."

"You're welcome to join us." Blake gestures to the empty seat between him and Beckett, but I shake my head. "We can call Billie and have her join us, too."

"I won't interrupt your brothers' night out. It's grateful I am that you broke my very expensive, supposedly trained dog." I laugh as I pull away. "Good night to you."

I spare Riley a glance.

"Heel," I tell him, and he follows me dutifully out of the pub toward my car. "I can't believe you went with Blake. You know better than that, Riley Gallagher. You can't just follow handsome men around, you know. And we can't tell Uncle Connor about it, or he'll be surely good and pissed."

He stops abruptly and turns, alerting me to footsteps behind me. He lets out a low growl as I turn to see Beckett approaching. Okay, so my dog is still doing his job.

Beckett stops short and holds his hands up. "He's trained after all."

"Quite well," I agree and hold my hand up, giving Riley the sign to stand down. Immediately, my boy stops growling and sits next to me. Maybe we'll get some training tonight despite how the evening ended.

"I didn't mean to startle you." His eyes fall to where I've fisted my hand at my side, and I intentionally loosen those muscles before he pins me in his gaze again. "I wanted to ask for your phone number when my nosy-as-hell brothers aren't listening in. I don't want them watching while I try to charm a beautiful woman."

My brows rise in surprise. Beckett is not simply handsome. That's much too drab of a word for this man. He's ... powerful. His jawline is sharp beneath that beard, and his dark eyes look lighter, almost like whiskey out here in the soft glow of the car park lights.

And when he smiles at me, it moves through me like molasses, from my head to my toes. I want more of those smiles. *Even if I know I won't allow myself to indulge in that pleasure.*

Beckett Blackwell is sadly a person I'll need to avoid. I'm not entirely sure I'll ever be willing to be vulnerable to a man again.

Not yet anyway.

"Thank you for asking," I finally reply when he shoves his hands in his pockets, waiting and watching. "But I'll have to decline."

Those whiskey eyes narrow on me, and I almost want to take the words back.

"It's nothing personal," I rush on to assure him. If I were anyone else, if I didn't have such a fecked-up past, I'd absolutely date Beckett Blackwell. "I'm sure you're a lovely man."

"Yeah." He nods, then chuckles, running his hand

through his hair. "That's how I've been described often. Lovely."

I laugh with him and shrug a shoulder. "I'm simply not on the market."

All humor leaves his face. "I apologize. I didn't realize that you had someone."

"Oh, I don't." I shake my head and notice that his shoulders relax. Great, so he's sexy as sin *and* a nice person. "And I'm not looking for a ... someone."

"Fair enough." He takes a step back, and I breathe a little easier. "Have a nice evening."

When he turns to walk back into the pub, I have a moment of regret.

Perhaps it would be nice to get to know someone like Beckett. There's no denying that I'm attracted to him. A woman would have to have no pulse to ignore the charisma and sex appeal this man exudes.

But I was also attracted to *the arsehole*, and that ended in a nightmare.

Feeling slight melancholy and definite disappointment—*I hate this so much*—I watch Beckett go back inside and lead Riley to the car.

"This is for the best," I say to both of us before I close the door and climb into the driver's seat. After starting the vehicle and pulling out to head home, I eye the dog in the mirror. "Now, you do realize that you failed that training, right? I can't believe you went with Blake. You know better than that."

Riley lies down with a huff, and I shake my head.

"We'll try that one again soon."

Tonight is my favorite night of the month.

Spicy Girls Book Club.

Bee hosts it at her bookshop, and we're up to about fifteen members now, which is a lot of fun. But I've grown closest to the original members.

Bee and Dani are my tightest friends. Dani's twin sister, Alex, and Millie Wild, the owner of the coffee shop next door, are also wonderful.

But I enjoy all of the ladies who have joined. So many of them have known each other most of their lives, thanks to living in a small town, but that didn't stop them from graciously welcoming me into their fold and making me feel right at home.

"I brought chocolate cupcakes," Jackie, the owner of The Sugar Studio, announces as she walks through the door. "And I actually read the book this time."

With a laugh, we all gather around to talk about this month's book club read, *Love, Utley* by S.J. Tilly. We started reading a mafia series by the same author last winter and loved her so much that we decided to keep going. I'm *so* glad we did.

"This book was a masterpiece," I tell the group. "It was so heart-wrenching and sexy, all at the same time. But my favorite bit was early in the book when she had the wee fender bender after lunch with her coworkers. She's frightened and having a moment, and Maddox doesn't even look her way. He simply puts his hand out for hers, and she slides her palm into his. My heart gave such a heavy sigh at that moment."

"Hot as hell," Bee agrees, as the others nod. "We love a man who takes charge. Who knows what he wants and doesn't play any bullshit games."

As long as it's consensual, yes.

But I don't say that out loud.

We spend the next hour discussing the book and eating cupcakes. It's always so wonderful to spend time with these girls.

As is typical, once most of the other members have left, our group remains for any last-minute gossip.

"I have some news." I smile when I see that I have everyone's attention.

"Tell us," Alex says, leaning toward me. "Don't leave anything out."

"I had an interesting encounter the other night." I briefly tell them about meeting the Blackwell brothers. "You have an impressive family, Bee."

"They're all a major pain in the ass," Bee replies.

"Hey, one of those is my husband," Dani reminds her.

"I stand behind my statement." Bee shrugs.

"Well, Beckett asked for my number." I press my lips together, and I can feel my face flush as the others watch me.

"Did you give it to him?" Millie asks. "Do you have a date? Oh my God, we need details."

"No, I turned him down." I shake my head, still feeling the regret in my chest.

"Why?" Dani asks.

Even though this amazing group of women has been my friends for so many months, I haven't confided in them about what happened in New York City. Maybe now is a good time to share a few details because I need some bloody advice.

"You all know that I used to be a dancer in New York City." It still stings to use those words. *Used to be.* "Well, it's true that I can't dance anymore, professionally anyway, because of my ankle. But I also left because I had, well, a situation."

"What kind of a situation?" Bee draws her eyebrows together.

"A stalker. An unhinged man, who I dated *very* briefly. When I told him it wasn't going to work for us, he wouldn't take no for an answer. He's unstable but smart enough not to break any laws."

"For fuck's sake." Millie scowls. "What a piece of shit."

"Yes, he is. I haven't heard a word from him since I got here, so I hope that's a good omen."

"But what does that have to do with Beckett?" Alex asks.

"My instincts for choosing men are broken." I reach down to pet Riley, who nudges my hand. "I'm a bad judge of character, obviously. That experience did a number on me, so in addition to not choosing good men, I can't imagine anyone wanting to take on my baggage. Baggage I won't bore you with here, but let's just say it's hard-sided luggage you have to pay extra for because it's always over the weight limit."

Baggage that includes nightmares and a fear of being in the dark so badly that I need an emotional support dog to help me through.

They're quiet for a moment, then Bee says, "Well, I can tell you for certain that Beck isn't an asshole. If you tell him no, the answer's no, and that's the end of it."

The others nod in agreement.

"I'm sure he's not a certifiable stalker," I reply. "But I just don't trust myself. Or men, for that matter. There's an attraction there, don't misunderstand. He's handsome, and he was kind to me."

"But?" This comes from Dani, who's watching me with eyes full of concern.

"But I don't think it's a good idea even though he's the first man I've been attracted to in *any* way for the better part of three bloody years."

"Then the answer's no." Alex nods. "You have to be comfortable, babe. That's the bottom line."

"It doesn't hurt my feelings," Bee says, pushing her pretty hair over her shoulder. "My brothers tend to be on the alpha side. Bossy. Take charge."

Oh, I don't think I'd mind that so much. It's when they go too far, when it isn't consensual, that I have a problem.

"Then again," Bee continues, "I've found alpha men do give some good orgasms."

"Like your foreigner last winter?" Dani asks with a grin, and we all nod, enjoying this story. Bee had a one-night stand with a handsome tourist last year. She never exchanged names with him, so we don't know who it was, but from what she's told us, it was *hot*.

Clearly, because it's still on her mind.

"I mean," Bee adds, "he *was* pretty take-charge and alpha, and I have no complaints about that."

"Thanks for listening to me." I smile at my new friends. "I needed to talk it out. Not because I thought I made a mistake, but I did have a moment of regret as Beckett walked away. He was the first man I'd even partially considered wanting to try with, you know? But I just couldn't."

I trusted him. That's what surprised me. Yes, there was an attraction there, but I simply trusted him.

"He was kind. Handsome." *Tempting.*

"He's both of those things," Millie agrees. "But Alex is right. If it doesn't feel right to you, then you did the right thing. And the beautiful thing is, he lives here, so if you change your mind, any one of us can give you his number."

"I hadn't thought of that." I bite my lower lip, pondering that idea. "It's good to have as a backup plan, just in case. Also, don't forget the recital in just three days. Most of you have little ones who will want to see you there."

"We wouldn't miss it," Millie declares. "When do we get to see *you* dance?"

I shake my head. "Those days have passed. But maybe sometime I can demonstrate what I used to do."

"We would *love* that," Dani says. "Please do."

There's a car in my driveway when Riley and I get home. A black SUV with tinted windows and an armed man standing next to the driver's door, hands crossed at his waist, blank expression on his face.

"Riley, Uncle Connor's here!"

I jump out of the driver's side and let Riley out, smiling at the bodyguard as I walk past.

"Hi, Miller," I say. "And how are you then?"

"Just fine, miss. The boss is inside."

The door is unlocked when I push through, running past the living room to the kitchen, where my brother sits at the island, eating a bowl of my stew. He's in black slacks and a black dress shirt, sleeves rolled up, the top button undone at his neck. His suit coat and tie are draped over the back of my couch.

"I didn't know you were coming to town already."

"Yet you had the stew on for me, I see." His green eyes are full of mischief as he pops a spoonful in his mouth. I run around to give him a proper hug. "Where were you tonight, *a stór*?"

"My book club meeting," I reply as I pull away and grab myself some water. "It's monthly, and I enjoy it."

"Good. It's glad I am that you're making friends." He finishes his stew and sets the bowl in the sink. "Your alarm passcode needs to be reset."

"Why?" I frown up at him as I dish myself a small ladle of the stew.

"Because it's the same as the last time I was in town, so it needs to be changed."

"You're so bossy." I sit on a stool and eat. "I shouldn't have this. I had a chocolate cupcake at the club meeting."

"You can eat whatever you want now," he reminds me.

"No more maintaining a certain weight," I agree. "No more going hungry. But if Mik saw me, he'd tell me to take off ten pounds."

"And you can tell Mik to go feck himself," Connor replies easily as he types something on his phone.

"You like Mik."

"I do, yes. Very much. But he's not the boss of your body."

"I know." Despite how he used to nag me about my weight, I miss my friend. It's the first time we've been apart from each other in a decade. Phone calls never seem like enough. "Anyway, how long will you be here? At least three days because of the recital." I narrow my eyes at him, daring him to tell me he'll miss it.

"Why do I have to go to the recital to see a bunch of children who aren't mine twirl and fling themselves about?"

"Because it's your sister who's taught them to do those twirls and that flinging, and I'll be there, too. Plus, you're an investor, so you should see what I'm doing there."

"You're teaching dance, Skyla."

I let out a gusty, dramatic sigh. "Connor."

"Fine. I'm going." He leans against the counter and crosses his arms over his chest. "I came here from Galway. Ma and Da send their love."

"Is everything all right there?"

"They're fine. I just wanted to pop in and see them. I had business in Dublin anyway."

My brother never sits still. "Do you ever actually *see* the inside of your penthouse in New York City?"

Connor pushes his hand through his hair. He doesn't love being called out on his habits, but despite being so much younger than him, I worry about him. "I haven't been there in more than three months."

I stop chewing and frown at him. "What? Why not?"

"Because I've been busy."

Connor is a hotelier, the third generation in our family to head Gallagher Hotels and Resorts. Because of this, he's constantly on the go, from location to location, to oversee renovations or new builds and make sure things are running smoothly. But I hate that he doesn't have roots anywhere, that he doesn't really have a *home*.

"You could hire someone for a lot of what you do. You need to learn to delegate."

"No." He shakes his head in that stubborn way he's done since we were kids and pushes his glasses up his nose. "I want to be a hands-on CEO."

"At the expense of literally never being at home?"

He shrugs. "What do I have to go home to?"

I blink at him and feel guilt set in.

"No, don't you dare go there," he says, then swears

under his breath and paces the kitchen. "It's not because of you that I'm never in New York."

"It partially is," I counter. "Because you'd typically spend time in New York to see my shows and check in on me. Because you're really old, and you still think of me as a baby."

His eyes narrow, and his lips quirk up into a smile he can't fight off, making me laugh. Making my big brother smile is my favorite thing.

"I'm not fecking old. I also have four resorts in that city," he reminds me. "So you're not the only reason to go there."

I shrug. "You're right. But now, instead of going *home*, you come here to check on me. Hey, what's the investment opportunity you mentioned on the phone?"

My brother shakes his head. "I don't want to discuss it until I know with certainty that it will happen. I should know soon."

"So mysterious." I set my bowl in the sink, and Riley raises his head from his bed in the corner of the room.

I'm not going to tell Connor about Riley's escapade the other night at the pub. It'll only make him angry, and he'll remind me that I should have chosen a different dog.

"Where are you staying? Here? My guest room's ready for you."

"I have a place."

I frown at him. "Where? The resort burned down." My eyes widen. "Hey, are you going to rebuild the resort? Oh, you absolutely *should*. That would be bloody brilliant, Connor!"

The ski resort burned down last Thanksgiving, and it's been empty ever since. The old owners didn't want to rebuild, so it would make sense that my brother would take on that project. Something like this is what he's most passionate about. He would rock it.

"I didn't say I was going to do any of that."

"I'm not an idiot, you know."

"I bought a house," he says, not commenting on my idiot claim.

"You *bought* a house? Connor Gallagher, you're going to rebuild that resort, and you're going to live here while you do it. Just admit it."

"I love you, *a stór*." He kisses me on the head. "I'll take you out for breakfast in the morning."

"We're not done talking about this."

"Aye, we are. For now." He winks at me as he grabs his jacket to leave.

"Do you want to take some stew for Miller and anyone else you have with you?"

"They've been fed," he states as he walks through my house. "Sleep well. Change the alarm code."

"Yes, sir," I call back after him, and I can hear him chuckle as he closes the door.

Chapter Four

LEWIS

A.K.A. "The Arsehole"

I've been out of the country for the better part of a year. It couldn't be avoided, and I hated every minute that I couldn't be near my tiny dancer.

My sweet little dancer.

But I'm home now, so I'll make it up to her. She'll be so excited to see me. I can picture the way her gorgeous face will light up as she enfolds me into her arms and holds on tight. I can almost feel her delicate fingers in my hair.

I sent flowers this morning to let her know I'm home and will see her soon. Pink roses are her favorite.

I'll send them to her every day.

Our home will be stuffed with the fragrant, delicate blooms, reminding her how much I adore her.

How perfect she is.

The phone at my elbow vibrates with an incoming call, and I accept.

"Hello, sir, this is Molly at *Blooms* in Manhattan. I'm sorry to have to tell you that we tried to deliver your order, but we were told that Miss Gallagher is no longer with the New York City Ballet. Would you like us to try to deliver somewhere else?"

I sit back in my desk chair and frown at the windows of my office that look out onto Wall Street. "There must be some mistake."

"No, sir. I went myself and asked to speak with a manager. I was told the same thing."

"You keep the flowers for your trouble," I tell her, then hang up and make a call to the ballet myself.

"New York City Ballet, how can I direct your call?" a woman answers.

"Hello, I was wondering if I could interrupt Skyla Gallagher's rehearsal for a family emergency?"

"I'm sorry, Skyla hasn't danced here in quite a while now. God, I hope her family's okay."

"Yes, they will be. I just need to reach her. Has she gone to a different dance company in the city?"

She must have switched to a more prominent company. What a brilliant woman my tiny dancer is. I'm so proud of her.

"You know, I'm not sure. I lost touch with her, to be honest. It's just been really busy around here, you know?"

"I understand completely. Thank you for your help."

After hanging up, I stand and walk to the windows, shove my hands in my pockets, and frown.

Where is my girl?

She needs me. She couldn't have coped well without me all this time.

I have to find her.

Immediately.

Chapter Five

BECKETT

"Jesus, people are filthy." Grimly, I turn to Abbi Wild, who I hired to clean my vacation rentals. Well, I hired her company. She usually sends other teams out to do the actual cleaning, but she came today, and she's as unhappy about the state of cabin number three as I am.

"This one only sleeps two, right?" she asks.

"That's right. So how did two people make this kind of a mess during a two-night stay?" I shake my head as I take in the amount of trash, the linens strewn all over the cabin, and the broken glass on the floor.

"At least the windows aren't broken," Abbi says, then shrugs when I stare at her. "I've seen it."

"Jesus, why did I think this was a good idea?"

"It *is* a good idea," Abbi assures me. "How much is your security and cleaning deposit on these rentals?"

"I just do a cleaning fee."

Abbi shakes her head. "You need to add a *consider-*

able security deposit, and I suspect you need to increase the cleaning fee. If people have a bunch of money to lose, they're less likely to act like this. You need a manager."

"I know, and I have my eye on one, but she's not available for a few months. She's finishing a contract in Aspen, so I'll have to figure it out in the meantime."

"You can do that. And don't worry, this isn't as bad as I've seen in some other rentals. I'm going to call in another team to help me out here, though. Also, you need to add to your rental agreement that you will press charges if they destroy property. Even if you really *won't*, the threat of it is there."

"Hey, I like that. I'll add it. Thanks, Abbi."

"You bet."

As she pulls her phone out of her pocket to call in some help, I make my way through the other two cabins vacated this morning. Thankfully, nothing is out of the ordinary in either of those.

Admittedly, I see trashed cabins like that one about once a month, which could be worse, but it still pisses me off and shreds all hope I have for humanity.

With that handled, I head back for the main house and the barns. I need to look in on the ice cream we're producing and check the spring calves.

There's never a dull moment at the Double B Ranch.

Just as I walk into the processing building, my phone rings, and I see it's Abbi.

"What did we miss?" I ask by greeting.

"Uh, Beckett, there's a cat in the bathroom."

I scowl and stare blindly ahead. "A *what*?"

"A cat. Are you missing a barn cat?"

"How the hell should I know? Jesus, just let it outside. Sorry, Abbi."

I hang up and stomp into the barn, where Brad's seeing to one of our cows that's had an infection.

"Are we missing one of the barn cats?" I ask him.

"I haven't seen Morris in a few days," Brad says. "Figured he was off hunting somewhere."

"The assholes in cabin three had him. *In the fucking cabin.*"

Brad blinks and then laughs. "Poor Morris. He's never been inside anything other than a barn in his whole life. Probably scared the shit out of him."

"Let's hope not because that'll be one more fucking thing I have to pay to have cleaned up."

Brad's practically doubled over in hilarity, and I glare at the man.

"It's not funny."

"It's hilarious." He's holding his side, trying to catch his breath. "I'm just picturing the look on that poor cat's face. *Let me out! Let me out!*"

Okay, so it's slightly funny.

I kick Brad out to feed the calves and see to Bessy myself. I can tell she's hurting.

"I'm sorry, girl. We'll get you fixed up."

"Your brother's here, boss," Brad says from the doorway of the milking barn, pointing over his shoulder.

"Which one?"

"Me." Blake walks into the barn and frowns at me. "You're not ready to go."

"Ready to go *where*?"

"To Birdie's dance recital, dumbass." Blake shakes his head at me. "Go get changed. We have to go."

"Blake, I have too much shit to do—"

"Nope," Brad says with a grin. "We've got this. Go see that baby's show. She'll be sad if you don't, and then we all will kick your ass for disappointing the peanut."

Literally everyone connected with our family has a soft spot for Bridger's daughter, Birdie. And who can blame them? She's the best kid there is.

"Hurry up," Blake adds, walking beside me to the house.

"I don't need help changing my clothes," I remind him.

He smirks. "And I'm grateful for that. I'll wait on the porch."

Twenty minutes later, we're driving into town. "Did you come all the way out to the farm just to pick me up?"

"Yep. Because I knew that otherwise, you'd make an excuse not to go. Like your man said, that would crush our niece. So you're going."

"I'm here, aren't I?" I rub my hand over my face.

"I saw you followed Skyla out of the bar the other night."

I sigh, roll my eyes, and stare at my brother. "Seriously? You want to gossip?"

I'd rather not discuss the details of getting turned down by the sexiest woman I've ever seen.

"Are you going to call her or what?"

"No. She didn't give me her number." Even I hear

the growl in my voice, but my brother doesn't think twice about pressing my buttons.

"Seriously? Interesting."

"If you want to date her, you call her." My hands ball into fists at the idea.

"I don't want to date *anyone*," he reminds me. "Doctors aren't a good bet. I'm never home."

"Ah yes, ever the consummate bachelor."

"Jesus, you're a fucking prick tonight." Blake laughs and shakes his head. "Such a joy to have in my car."

"I could have driven myself and saved my sanity from the interrogation."

"Hey, I was just asking. Skyla's a nice girl. She's pretty."

"I didn't notice."

Blake tosses his head back and laughs, then the fucker smirks at me. "Right, you didn't notice the hot little redhead who sounds like music when she talks? Jesus, you followed her out of that bar like a puppy."

"Fuck you. I did not."

Okay, I did. Who the fuck cares?

He looks like he wants to say more, but we're already at the dance studio just one street down from Main Street. I jump out of Blake's fancy car, ready to take my mind off the fact that the gorgeous redhead with the voice that makes my body sit up and listen wants nothing to do with me.

I've thought about her all goddamn week. I can't get her out of my head, and that pretty much irritates the hell out of me. I don't have time to think about a woman who already told me no. I don't have time for *any* woman, but one who clearly isn't interested? Absolutely not.

"Come on, grumpy ass." Blake holds the door open, clapping me on the shoulder as I pass. "Let's go see Birdie. That'll cheer you up."

He's right, it will make me smile. She's the best thing that's ever happened to our family.

White folding chairs have been set up for families and friends to sit in for the show, and I scowl. These chairs will be damn uncomfortable for men our size for any length of time. But before I can say I'll duck out, I hear my favorite voice.

"Uncle Beck!"

"Hey, peanut." I squat next to her and kiss her cheek. "Aren't you beautiful in your pink tutu?"

She does a quick spin, her cheeks rosy with happiness. With her dark hair up in a bun and her brown eyes shining with excitement, she's the most beautiful thing in my world. She never fails to brighten my day.

"I'm so happy you're here," she says, and just like that, I'd gladly sit in this fucking chair for the rest of my life if it means keeping this girl happy.

"Me, too. Where are your mom and dad?"

"Right here," Dani says with her sweet smile, and I stand to kiss her on the cheek. "Bridger's on his way from the fire station."

"He had to work," Birdie informs me. "But he's still coming."

"Of course, he is," Dani assures her. "In fact, I just saw him parking his truck."

"You're going to be awesome," I tell her.

"I know. I know the routine perfectly, and we've practiced a lot." She moves on to Blake, who's already grinning at her.

"You're the most beautiful girl I've ever seen, cupcake."

"She's adorable," Bee says as she steps up next to me, but something across the room catches my eye, and my heart stutters. Skyla is talking with Erin Wild, laughing at something the other woman says, and my world tilts sideways. "There's Skyla. I was just looking for her. She looks so calm and collected."

"Does she have kids?" I ask my sister, not daring to take my eyes off the woman for fear that she'll disappear. I wish I could hear what she's saying. Shit, she could recite her grocery list, and I'd hang on every word.

"No, why?"

"Why would she be here if she doesn't have kids?" I can't fucking look away from her. She's laughing, her stunning face lighting up, and I'm jealous.

I'm fucking jealous because I want that laugh.

What the hell is wrong with me?

Bee props her hands on her hips. "Really? For fuck's sake, do you *ever* listen to me? I told you that Skyla runs this dance school. She owns it. She was a ballerina in New York City for a really long time, Beckett. I don't even want to know what you don't hear me say. It's like talking to a damn wall."

Did my sister tell me that, and I didn't hear her? Very possibly. Bee talks about a lot of things often. I've grown accustomed to drowning her out half the time.

Not that I'd ever tell her that. I value my life.

"You tell me a lot of things," I reply, and I can feel Bee roll her eyes next to me.

Now, I'm damn glad that Blake made sure I came today.

Skyla's red hair falls in soft, sleek curls around her shoulders. She's wearing a green dress almost the same color as her eyes, and I feel pulled to her in ways I've never experienced with anyone else before.

Sure, I want to get my hands on her, feel her beneath me, soak myself in her, but I want to talk to her. Listen to that amazing lilt in her voice. Ask questions and find out what makes this incredible woman tick. But also, how in the hell did a New York City Ballet dancer end up in our small town?

"She's pretty," Bee says softly. I can feel her eyes on me.

"Understatement." I cross my arms and watch Skyla laugh again, and I feel it in my gut. Now I can see that she has a dancer's lithe body. She's stunning. "But she said no, so the answer is no."

"She told me."

I glare down at my sister, who hums, still watching her friend. "She needed advice. She has reasons, Beck, but I can tell she likes you, so maybe don't give up, okay? You'll have to be patient with her."

I can be fucking patient if she's the reward at the end of it.

We take our seats, and as we quiet down, Skyla takes her place on the small stage and smiles at all of us. She's rocking back and forth on the balls of her feet in that way I've noticed that she does as if she's moving to music in her head.

She's adorable.

"Hello, friends," she begins. She has an incredible smile. Her eyes skim the crowd and find me, and that smile doesn't falter, but I see the surprise in those green orbs before she moves her gaze away.

She has reasons, Beck, but I can tell she likes you, so maybe don't give up, okay? You'll have to be patient with her.

She's not immune to me. I can work with that.

"It's pleased I am that you've come for our first recital of the year. Your wee ones have done such a good job this spring of learning new routines, new steps, and how to feel the music."

She tucks her hair behind her ear and glances backstage, nodding.

"For our first number, we have our three-year-olds performing, and I think it's going to fill your hearts with joy to see the sweetness we have in store for you."

She chuckles before moving to the side of the makeshift stage. Eight little girls walk out, eyes wide, terrified.

But they are sweet, I'll give her that.

I can't take my eyes off the woman who coaches the

little ones from the side. Finally, it's Birdie's turn, so I shift my attention to my niece, grinning from ear to ear at her excited smile and pure self-confidence as she moves across that stage. Birdie loves being the center of attention, so this is right up her alley.

We sit for an hour, and except for the five minutes when Birdie dances, I haven't taken my eyes off Skyla. I've caught her eyes seeking mine as she's sneaked peeks at the crowd, and each time, she's blushed before returning her attention to the kids.

Bee's right. She likes me.

So yeah, I can be patient.

Chapter Six

SKYLA

I love recital night.

Granted, there will never be anything that compares to dancing with Mikhail after months and months of grueling work on a world-class New York City stage in front of a sold-out auditorium. That's something I'll miss forever and will live in my heart until I take my last breath.

But seeing all of these wee darlings in their pretty costumes excited to dance for their loved ones takes second place.

Some of them freeze up on stage and don't do anything at all, and others—like Bee's niece, Birdie—know every single step and keep the crowd spellbound.

Honestly, I never know how the evening will go, but it's never boring.

Now that the show is over, parents are grouped in the studio, chatting with friends about their children's dance, school, or what's happening in town. I've spent time answering questions but want to check on Riley backstage.

"You didn't even sit with the audience," I say to Connor as I find my brother standing beside Riley.

"Riley needed company." He shrugs. "And I could see everything from back here. Not to mention, every chair was taken, which is a good thing. It means business is good."

Okay, he has a point. All the seats were filled, and that made me happy.

"Still. It wouldn't have killed you to stand in the back."

"I own this place, too, you know. I can stand wherever I bloody like."

"Right." I roll my eyes. "Would you like a plaque on the bleeding door announcing that you own the building?"

He tips his head to the side, considering it. "Actually, yes. I would like that."

"Skyla, I just wanted to chat for a second before I head out—"

That's Bee's voice, but before I turn to greet my friend, Connor's eyes narrow behind his glasses, taking in the woman behind me.

And when I turn around, I see that Bee has gone sheet white.

Holy shite, her mystery man really was *my brother.* I had a feeling, but Connor had left town before their night together.

Or so I thought.

49

I need information.

"Bee …" I take her hand in mine, linking our fingers, but her hazel eyes are round and cling to Connor's face. "This is my older brother, Connor. He came in from Ireland to see the show. Connor, this is Billie, my very good friend. She's bloody brilliant."

"Connor." Her cheeks have flushed, and now her eyes don't look surprised.

They look a little angry.

"Hello," Connor says, keeping his voice mild. But I saw the look on his face when he first saw her, so I know he's not unaffected. "Excuse us, Skyla. I'd like to have a word with your friend."

"I'm just—"

"Come." He takes her by the elbow and leads her out the back door. Before I can run after them, I hear someone clear their throat behind me.

And I can feel his gaze.

His.

Beckett's. The man who sat in a seat too small for him and watched his niece with the sweetest, softest smile on his face, then watched me for the rest of the performance. His eyes on me felt like a warm blanket, cuddling me close, if that blanket was plugged into an outlet and firing off sparks.

The man who's lived in my daydreams and regular dreams, if I'm being honest, all week.

I turn, and the smile that comes is easy because Beckett Blackwell is every cowboy fantasy I've ever had. Not that I really considered having cowboy fantasies before I moved to Montana. And when he smiles back at me, I fear I'll pass out. I swear to the gods that he pulled all the oxygen from the room.

"It's good to see you again," he says. It seems that my tongue has been glued to the roof of my mouth. He steps closer, not close enough to let me feel his warmth, but I have to tip my head back to see his handsome face.

I want to push my fingers through his whiskers. They look soft, and my skin itches to feel his face, but I ball my hands into fists at my sides and keep my smile, trying to remain professional while praying that he can't see that my nipples are suddenly as hard as bloody stone.

"I know Birdie was excited that the whole family came, along with her friends and their parents as well."

Beckett nods slowly and firms his jaw. "Does that mean it's *not* good to see me again?"

Of course, he paid me a compliment, and I replied with something about his niece.

I'm not good at this.

With a frown, I drop my gaze to his chest, which is eye level to me, and feel my heart skip a beat. He's a damn brick wall. So wide and hard and I'm sure the muscles beneath that black Henley are impressive.

I can see the outline of them through the soft cotton, and I want to touch him.

I've never wanted to get my hands on a man the way I do *this* man.

The Arsehole was sexy, too, you idiot.

"It *is* nice to see you," I reply and press my lips

together. "I was happy when I spotted you in the audience."

"I was honestly surprised when I discovered you own this place." He shoves his hands into his pockets. "It was a good surprise. Birdie loves you. She talks about her dance class all the time."

"She's a beautiful girl," I reply with a small laugh. "So full of energy. I enjoy her very much, and she's an excellent dancer."

"I know there are other people here for you to talk to," he says after his eyes take a journey over my face as if he's memorizing me. "I won't monopolize your time. But I will put myself out there again and ask for your number."

Beckett is tempting. Handsome. Sinfully sexy. And if I'm being honest with myself, I want nothing more than to spend time with him. But ...

"And you're going to say no," he continues before I can answer him. "I can see it written all over your pretty face."

"Beckett, I—"

Before I can complete that thought, Bee comes storming through, her face flushed and eyes bright. She doesn't make eye contact or say a word as she stomps past us, through the studio, and right out the front door.

"Uh, I'd better go see if my sister's okay." Beckett frowns. Then his gaze shifts just over my shoulder, and his eyes narrow. "And you are?"

"Connor." I step aside so my brother can offer his hand to shake. "Skyla's brother."

Beckett takes Connor's hand, but his jaw is tight. "You the reason my sister looks like she's ready to punch her fist through the wall?"

"It's likely."

What in the world?

"Do I need to punch *you*?" Beckett asks.

"I appreciate the sentiment because I'd feel the same in your shoes, but no."

Beckett nods, and his eyes fall to mine. "Skyla."

"Beckett."

And with that, he turns to follow Bee.

"What did you do?" I ask, immediately turning to my brother and poking him in the chest, making him scowl at me. "Wait. I know what you did. I've heard stories."

"Really? Do tell." His lips curl up into a satisfied grin, and I shake my head.

"Absolutely not because now I know they're about *you*." Ugh. That makes me a little nauseous. "If you fucked up my friendship with that woman, I'll never forgive you, Connor Declan Gallagher. She's a good person, and she's been kind to me, and I care about her deeply."

"Nothing's fucked up," he assures me. "Well, between you two, anyway."

"I can't believe you."

Connor shakes his head, seemingly unfazed by my wrath. "Go finish up with the parents so we can get out of here."

"You can go. I have Riley."

"And I have a security detail with weapons. That trumps Riley. I'll wait."

I blow out a breath, then return to mingle with the remaining parents.

No, this was definitely not a boring recital night.

"Have a good flight." I hug Connor, then wave to Miller, who's standing by the open back door of the black SUV waiting to take my brother to the airport.

He scratches Riley behind the ears, then grabs his briefcase. Connor usually wears slacks and a button-down, if not a whole suit, but he's in jeans and a T-shirt today, which throws me off a bit.

"Why are you so casual, by the way?"

He lifts an eyebrow. "It's a flight, not a board meeting."

"You usually wear clothes that would fit a board meeting."

He smirks. "Because I'm usually coming from one. Today's casual."

"And you *are* leaving town, right? You're not off to whisk my best friend off for some ... I can't even complete that sentence."

"I'm leaving." He narrows his eyes. "And the rest is none of your concern, Skyla Maeve Gallagher."

"She's—"

"None of your business. I mean it."

I huff, but he stalks off to the car. Riley and I watch as he climbs inside, and I wave as the car drives away.

"None of my business, my arse," I mutter to Riley, who watches me with his expressive, seemingly concerned eyes. "She's our best mate in this town, so that means it's my business. We'll stop by the bookshop on our way to the studio."

I want to dance today. I don't always anymore. Not only did I dance every day before, but I also danced for eight to ten hours a day while gearing up for a specific performance.

These days, I dance a few times a week. It's a great workout, and I want to make sure that my muscle memory doesn't fade. I know I don't need it for anything specific, but it's mine all the same, so I'll hang on to it for as long as I can, even if my ankle doesn't want to cooperate.

Will I ever let the anger go regarding my injury? The circumstances surrounding it? The bitterness and help-lessness that I still feel deep down in my soul?

I don't know.

"Let's not dwell, Riley." I grab my handbag and set the alarm system on the house, using the new code Connor insisted I implement. Then Riley and I head into town. I park at my studio and walk the few blocks over to the bookshop, where I'm sure to find Bee.

And sure enough, she's stocking copies of the new Catherine Cowles novel on a shelf.

I'll be picking up one of those before I leave.

Billie looks lost in thought, her brows pulled together

in a frown. She always dresses as if she's ready for a killer date or an important meeting, and today, she's in a red dress with black heels that could likely maim a man. Her hair is twisted back in a braid, and she's wearing a pretty necklace that falls between her breasts.

I'd kill for this woman's breasts. Billie has curves in all the right places, and I have a ballerina's body. Painfully slim, and no boobs to speak of.

"Hey there," I say softly and still manage to startle the poor woman, who drops a book, then cringes when she sees the cover got bent. "Sorry, I'll buy that copy. I was going to buy one anyway."

"No, it's my fault for not paying attention." She slides the book on the shelf with the others. "It's been slow in here today, so I'm just restocking and tidying up."

"I like the new display by the front door."

She nods, lets out a gusty breath, then props her hands on her curvy hips. "I don't want things between us to be awkward."

"It's glad I am to hear you say that because I don't want that either. It would be the worst thing ever. Do you need me to disown him? I could probably piss him off somehow. Make life hard for him, at the very least."

She smiles, and her shoulders sag in relief. Then she lets out a big laugh and pulls me in for a hug, and I know that everything will be okay.

"The moment I saw him at the recital was maybe one of the most surreal moments of my life," she admits as we walk over to my favorite chairs and take a seat. Riley curls up on the dog bed next to me. "I kind of wanted the floor to open up and swallow me."

"I can only imagine. I suspected when you first told us about it that it could be Connor from the way you described him, but I swear to you, Bee, as far as I knew, he'd left that previous afternoon."

"I think he was supposed to, but then we got that snowstorm, and he ended up staying another day." She bites her lower lip and stares outside.

"Was he an arse when he pulled you outside?"

She doesn't immediately answer. Instead, she looks down at her hands, then over at me, and her cheeks flush again.

"I don't want to know this, do I?"

Bee laughs. "I'm absolutely *not* starting something with your brother."

Bristling at that, I square my shoulders. "Now, why not? He's handsome, and successful, and you said the sex was decent—"

"Not decent." She shakes her head. "I think he pulled my soul out of my vagina."

I press my lips together, then double over laughing. "That paints a picture."

"I kind of like keeping him in that little one-night bubble. A happy memory that I can pull out and look at once in a while, then tuck back away. I have a business, and a family, and all kinds of things to see to here, and while your brother is all of the things you described, he's also not *here*."

Connor never confirmed to me whether he was going

to buy the ski resort to rebuild, so I don't want to say anything out of turn to my friend.

"He's not here," I confirm.

"So now I just know who it was." She shrugs and changes the subject. "Now, tell me about you and Beck."

"There's nothing to tell."

"And what's wrong with *my* brother?"

An image of Beckett and his lust-filled eyes dropping down to my mouth fills my mind, and the zing zips down my spine, just as it's done the previous million times I've thought of it.

"I don't know him at all, but from what I can see, there's nothing wrong with him."

"I know him *very* well," she says. "And aside from being a little—and by a little, I mean a lot—alpha and bossy, he's a catch. Then again, he has to be bossy because he owns the ranch, runs a dairy farm, and has guest cabins. It's good he's an expert in controlling things."

I nod, taking that in. "A dairy farm, is it then?"

"Yep."

"Does he get up and milk the cows while sitting on a stool in the wee hours of the morning?"

"No." Bee laughs at that and tucks a stray lock of hair behind her ear. "It's a modern operation with milking equipment. But if that breaks down for any reason, he does do the milking by hand. Or he has his employees do it. He supplies Millie with all of her cow and goat milk for the coffee shop, and you can buy it, along with ice cream, cottage cheese, and sour cream at the local grocery stores."

"That's fascinating." I mean it. I don't think I've ever met anyone who owns a dairy farm. "No cheese?"

"Not enough cows for the cheese. And he'd need a bigger processing system." Billie uncrosses and recrosses her legs. "Now, I won't push Beck on you ever again. But he likes you."

She winks at me, and my cheeks heat.

Because the truth of it is, I like him, too.

I need to dance. I have an hour before my first class for the afternoon, so with Riley on his bed by the door, I cue up my favorite music from *Giselle* and begin stretching. Using the barre, I dip into a plié and sigh when my body loosens. The muscles take over as if they have a mind of their own. Pulling my leg up until I'm one smooth, vertical line, I point my toes and stand here for a few long seconds.

Lost to the music, I move, watching myself in the mirror. I need to raise my chin and straighten my left arm a little more.

I'm so out of practice.

Mik would be disgusted.

This is when he'd lift me, my arms would wrap around his shoulders, and our mouths would be just inches apart, as if in a lovers' embrace. This dance is passionate and intimate.

Romantic.

No one in that audience would believe Mik didn't love me with the fire of a thousand suns. He's such a talented performer.

I can almost hear the applause from the audience, the gasp when he lifts me high, and then the emotion radiated back to us when the song ends, and we're locked in an embrace.

I run the music back and do it again and again until I feel loose and my form is perfect. My feet don't love the new blisters, but that's part of the art of it.

For the next hour, I can get lost in this piece of myself that I love so much. I can pretend that I'm still a prima ballerina, that I live in New York and see Mik every day. I can eat at my favorite restaurants, and I don't have a crazy man determined to keep me terror-stricken.

Everything is as it was *before*, when I escape into the movement. God, I love it.

I jolt awake.

Something doesn't feel right.

Is there someone in the flat? Connor's in Milan.

I reach for my phone. "Oh, feck, where is it?"

Slam.

"Oh God ..."

And I'd do anything to have it back, just for one day. For one performance.

For one moment.

Chapter Seven

BECKETT

I'm going to give this one more shot because I can't get Skyla Gallagher out of my head, and I have a feeling I'll regret it if I don't do everything I can to get to know her better.

Those alluring eyes.

That thick red hair.

That voice that slips its way under my skin and heats me from the inside out.

I need to at least try because something tells me that she's definitely worth the effort.

The bell above the door of Paula's Poseys rings as I push through and see the owner, Summer Wild, fussing with a bouquet at the front counter.

"Hey, Beckett," she says with a smile. "How can I help you today?"

"I need flowers, but I'm not sure what kind."

"That's what you have me for." She sets her bouquet

aside and gives me her undivided attention. "Who are they for?"

"Skyla Gallagher."

Her eyebrow lifts, and her lips tip up in a smile. "I like where this is going. Is it for an occasion?"

I could tell Summer it's to congratulate Skyla on her first recital, but let's face it, this is a small town. Summer's friends with my sister, so honesty is the only option.

"Yeah, it's for *please give me your number so I can take you out.*"

Summer laughs now and nods. "We're going to make this happen, my friend. Give me five minutes to do a little research, and I'll put together something beautiful."

"Have at it." I grin at her and hear the bell over the door ring.

"Hey, blondie," Chase says to his wife as he walks in. "Beck."

"Hi, Chase." I shake the man's hand. Chase and I have known each other since we were kids, and I consider him a good friend. Our ranches aren't too far apart, and our families have always been close. "Any crime to report out there today?"

He rests his hands on his policeman belt and shrugs a shoulder. "Nothing to speak of. How's the milk business treating you?"

"I can't complain."

"I got it!" Summer exclaims as she rushes out of her walk-in cooler, carrying a bouquet.

"You're fast."

She grins at me. "I know my flowers. Okay, so Skyla is Irish. I don't have any shamrocks or anything like that around here, but I *do* have ranunculus, which are a part of the buttercup family and grow in Ireland."

"Wow, I just wanted pretty flowers, Summer."

Chase laughs and runs his hands down his face. "It's never *just* pretty flowers, man."

"I guess not. Those look great, and I'm sure she'll love them."

"I hope they do the trick." She wraps them up in pretty paper with a green bow and rings me up. Once I've paid, I make my way out of the store and walk the couple of blocks over to Skyla's studio.

The door's unlocked, so I step inside and pet Riley's head when he perks up, but I don't make any noise because ... the woman is dancing, and all of the air has been stolen from my lungs.

She's fucking *spectacular*.

I don't know how her body can do what she's doing. Up on tiptoes, jumping effortlessly into the air, her legs so high above her head.

I've never seen anything like it. She's graceful and confident. So goddamn strong. Her muscles flex, and it's clear that she works hard to be in such good shape with that much flexibility. So talented.

Skyla is exquisite. I've never been one to fantasize about what the perfect woman would be, especially not for me. In the back of my mind, I figured I'd be with someone who loves the land, who loves small-town life. Someone strong, both physically and mentally. Because let's face it, I don't want or need a doormat. Never have. But Skyla Gallagher has somehow crushed through those thoughts and has completely captivated me. *She's like a dream come true even though I've never dreamed of her.*

When the music fades away, Skyla stops in place, breathing hard and in a pose that would probably put my back out and send me to the hospital. I'm so moved by what I just saw that I don't want to break the spell.

I don't want to ruin it.

"Alexa, stop music," she says, and the room goes silent, except for Skyla's gasping breath. She opens her eyes and sees me standing behind her in the mirror and shrieks before covering her chest with her hand. "Bloody shit, you scared me."

"I'm sorry, I didn't mean to. I didn't want to interrupt because I think I just witnessed the most beautiful thing I've ever seen in my life."

Her face softens, and she licks her lips. Noticing her water bottle on a table near me, I fetch it and take it to her, and she accepts. She's breathing fast as she drinks, her bright eyes on me.

"Thanks," she says.

"These are for you." I offer her the flowers, and she smiles softly. "Summer helped me, and I think she did a good job."

"They're beautiful. I love ranunculus." She accepts them and leans in to fuss over a bloom. "You shouldn't have."

"No, I really should have." With my hands empty, I shove them into my pockets and rock back on my heels. "I feel like I interrupted something personal, but I'm not sorry because watching you dance is breathtaking, Skyla."

She frowns down into the flowers before answering. "Thank you. It is personal, always. But I don't mind sharing it. I performed on a stage for far too long not to enjoy an audience."

I want to ask so many questions. I *need* to know everything there is to know about this woman.

"Are you going to ask for my number again, Mr. Blackwell?"

I could try to turn on the charm or be funny, but something tells me that isn't what this woman wants or needs.

So I go with flat-out honesty.

"Yeah, Ms. Gallagher. I am."

Her brows pull into a frown, and I want to reach out and smooth the pad of my thumb over the lines between them, but I keep my hands in my pockets.

"Am I so out of practice, having spent far too long with only cows and chickens, that I'm fucking this up so bad?"

She simply raises an eyebrow, her chest still heaving from her dance.

"Cows. Bessy's pretty, but she doesn't respond to adult conversation all that well."

That earns me a smile, and a wrinkle of the nose that is fucking *adorable*.

I'm already obsessed with this woman.

"One date, Skyla. Let me take you to dinner, converse, and be near you for one evening, and if you decide that I'm a complete idiot, I won't ask again."

Those mossy eyes watch me for a moment as if she's trying to solve a puzzle.

"I have character references," I add. "And I can give you a background check if you want. I don't have any arrests in my past unless you count the time when I got caught toilet-papering the math teacher's house when I was sixteen. My dad made me sit in jail overnight just to teach me a lesson."

"And did it work?" she asks.

"Hell yes, it worked. I'm not cut out for prison."

She laughs again, and I can see the moment she softens. "Dinner sounds nice."

"Are you free this evening?"

"That quick, is it?"

I grin at her and can't resist reaching out to tuck a lock of that gorgeous red hair behind her ear. She doesn't pull away.

"My luck just changed, and I'm going to take full advantage. I don't want you to change your mind and break my heart."

"Hmm." She swallows and glances at the clock on the wall. "I have a class coming in fifteen minutes, and I'll be done for the day at six."

"Pick you up at seven?"

Skyla bites that lower lip, then nods. I wisely hold back my fist pump. "Seven it is. But I can meet you."

"That's not a date, Skyla. I'm a gentleman. I'll pick you up and drop you off when the evening is over."

She lets out a chuckle. "You're good at pushing, aren't you then?"

"I know what I want. You'll need to send me your address. And to do that, you'll need to give me your number."

"Pushy cowboy," she mutters as she crosses to a table, sets down the flowers, and retrieves her phone. "All right then, it's my number you're getting out of me, Beckett Blackwell."

It's about fucking time.

I give her my phone after unlocking it. "Go ahead and text yourself."

She does, and when her phone buzzes with a notification, she passes me back my cell, opens her phone, and shows it to me.

"There, was that so hard?"

"We'll talk about it later," she says and lifts her gaze to mine. Jesus, I want to pull her in and kiss the fuck out of her. Push my hands in that thick hair and hold on tight as my mouth memorizes hers.

I want to lose myself in her. Fuck her so hard that she'll forget anyone who came before me, then I want to talk to her for days.

"Thank you," I say.

"For what, exactly?"

"Saying yes. I'll make sure you won't regret it."

Her smile lights up the whole room, but then a car

door slams out front, signaling the first of her class to arrive, and cueing my time to leave.

"I'll see you at seven." I lean in to kiss her cheek and breathe in her soft lavender scent before I pull away and walk to the door.

I have to go get ready for a date.

Because she *finally* said yes.

At seven on the dot, I pull up in front of the house in a neighborhood I don't know all that well. It's a newer subdivision with larger lots, so she's not close to her neighbors. A wrought iron fence, at least eight feet tall, surrounds the property, and she even has a gate and cameras. Her security system is impressive.

When I press the button, there's only a slight pause before Skyla answers.

"It's Beckett," I say to her.

"Drive on through," she replies, and the gate swings open, allowing me to pass.

The house isn't huge. My farmhouse likely has more square footage, but Skyla's home is newer, and I can see it's well taken care of, with tulips blooming along the side of the porch and shrubberies perfectly groomed.

After parking, I walk up to the front door and ring the bell. I hear Riley bark only once as if he's letting his human know someone's at the door.

And when said door swings open, my jaw drops.

Skyla's dressed casually, but that doesn't mean she's not dressed to kill.

And kill me she just might.

Her jeans fit her waist and ass perfectly, and her soft pink sweater falls off one shoulder, showing me creamy white skin and even more freckles that I want to trace with my tongue.

Her hair is loose and straight, falling almost to her waist.

But those alluring eyes currently taking a tour of my body hypnotize me.

"You're so fucking beautiful," I breathe, unable to hold the words in, and Skyla's gaze snaps up to mine. Her cheeks darken as she bites her lower lip.

"So are you," she whispers before clearing her throat and turning her attention to Riley. "I prefer to take him."

"Of course." I'm glad I thought ahead about her mountain of a dog. "I called ahead and made sure he could come with. We're just going to Old Town Pizza, and Heather, the owner, said it's no trouble at all for him to join us."

Skyla blinks up at me. "You included Riley in the reservation?"

"Well, yeah. I noticed that you take him everywhere and that he sometimes wears a service-dog vest, so I thought you'd want him along."

"Wow, thank you for thinking of him."

"It's no trouble. He should fit in the back seat of my truck."

"Why don't we take my SUV?" she asks, pointing

toward the garage. "I bought it just to accommodate this big boy. Don't worry, you can drive, so it still feels like a proper date."

I grin at her and nod. "So I've brought you over to the real date side."

Skyla laughs that infectious laugh and leads me through her house to the garage where her vehicle is. We get Riley situated and climb in, then I start it up.

"This is a nice car," I comment as I push the seat back to allow for my long legs.

"I like it. Without the dog, I don't need anything this big, but my boy weighs over one hundred and fifty pounds, and he needs something comfy."

The gate opens for us, and I drive us through, surprised that I feel so comfortable driving her vehicle. I wonder if some men might take issue with her request, but I'm quickly figuring out that I'll do anything to accommodate this woman's needs.

Including calling Heather about Riley.

"Have you had him long?"

"Riley?"

"Yeah. He's a great dog."

"Thank you." She grins back at the enormous canine. "I've had him for about a year now and can't imagine my life without him. Do you have any dogs at the ranch?"

"I don't have one right now, but my manager, Brad, has a lab named Sadie. She had puppies last year."

"You didn't snag one?" she asks. "You seem like the dog type. Riley's taken with you."

Here's to hoping his owner is just as taken with me by the end of this date.

"No time for a puppy right now. I hope you like pizza." I frown over at her once I've parked. "I should have asked."

"Are there people who *don't* enjoy pizza?" She grins and moves to open the door, but I stop her.

"Wait for me."

Pushing out of the car, I walk around and open her door, reach across her to unbuckle her belt, and take her hand to help her out of the tall SUV.

Once we have Riley on his leash, we walk inside and are quickly shown to our table on the rooftop.

"Down," Skyla says to Riley, and he lies under the table at her feet.

I have so many questions about the dog, but I'm going to hold those until later.

Instead, we order drinks, Guinness for both of us, and settle in with the menu.

"What do you like on your pizza?" I ask.

"I lived in New York City for a decade, so I'm pretty much a pepperoni kind of girl, but I'm open to suggestions."

"Works for me."

"Bee tells me that you own a dairy farm," she says, sipping the beer placed in front of her. "Ah, I get one of these a year, and it's bloody fantastic."

"Just one? And you're using that one on me?"

Skyla winks at me over the rim. "That I am. Now, tell me about your farm."

"Tell me why you only get one beer a year."

"Because it has a lot of extra calories, and dancers stay away from those. Maybe now that I'm not dancing professionally anymore, I could have it twice a year."

Yeah, I have a million questions.

"The farm?" she prompts me.

"Yes, I run a dairy farm I inherited from my parents. I also have a fairly new guest ranch that's a pain in my ass."

"Yes, guests can be difficult. My family owns hotels."

Gallagher Resorts. Everyone in the world recognizes that name, even if they don't travel often. It's as recognizable as Hilton or Ritz-Carlton.

"Honey, your family owns an empire."

Her cheeks darken, and she shrugs a shoulder. "Yes, well, that's true enough. I grew up in hotels all over the world, and I can tell you that whether you're a small operation or a large one, patrons can be difficult."

"You didn't want to go into the family business?"

We're interrupted by the server who takes our order, then Skyla leans her elbows on the table.

"I didn't want to work for my family, no. I've been a dancer since I was old enough to walk. I moved to New York City to dance when I was just sixteen."

I lift an eyebrow. "I assume your parents went with you?"

"My mother did for a while. Then they'd send a nanny or my brother. I always had someone with me to help, but I was so focused on the work that it didn't matter who was there. I was too busy working my way up through the ranks until I finally secured a prima ballerina position. It's all I wanted. And I worked my arse off for it."

"I believe it. I only saw you dance for a few minutes, but it was pure magic."

"I know that it was meant to be a private moment, but it's glad I am that you saw me dance, so you have an idea of what it looks like."

"It looks like art."

"And it is art, yes. I loved it."

"Why did you stop?"

A shadow moves over her face as the pizza is set down between us. When we're alone again, I reach across the table to take her hand.

"Hey, Irish. You don't have to talk about that. Forget I asked, okay?"

"I don't mind," she admits, but doesn't let go of my hand right away. "But maybe we'll talk more about it after dinner, okay?"

"Sure." Reluctantly, I pull my hand away, and we dish up slices of the pie and take a bite. "Mmm, fucking good pizza."

She nods, then wipes her mouth with a napkin. "It reminds me of a favorite spot of mine in New York. Anyway, tell me more about your dairy farm. How many cows do you have that produce milk for you?"

I frown as I swallow a bite. "Do you really want to know about this stuff?"

"Of course. It's what you do, where you live. The purpose of a date is to get to know each other better. I want to know everything."

It's been my experience that women don't want anything at all to do with my ranch, least of all the farm side of it.

Tori couldn't get out of there fast enough. It almost gave me whiplash.

"I have six milking cows," I explain. "They're milked twice a day."

"But not with a stool and your own two hands," she says with a grin.

"Not anymore, no. We have machines for it that are faster, but sometimes a cow needs to be milked by hand. We're a small dairy, not a huge corporation, so if a cow needs a little TLC, we can give it to her."

"I've milked a cow, you know." Her eyes shine as she bites into her crust.

"Tell me more." I lean back in my chair and cross my arms over my chest. The way her eyes flick down to my biceps isn't lost on me. It almost makes me want to flex. "I find it surprising that a hotel heiress has had an occasion to milk a cow."

"I'll have you know that my best friend as a girl, Bridget Mary O'Reilly, had a farm, and they milked the cows for their own milk, and whenever I spent time there, I was permitted to milk them myself."

I raise an eyebrow. "You squatted on a stool and milked a cow?"

"Well, to be fair, I was a wee girl, so I didn't have to squat. I sat." She grins and sits back, mirroring me. "And I'll also have you know that I was quite good at it. Someday, you'll take me out and introduce me to Bessy, and I'll show you what I'm about."

Jesus, I'll take her there right now and keep her there.

"You've got a date. You're welcome out there anytime, and you don't even have to milk anything."

She chuckles and takes a bite of her pizza. "Billie said you make ice cream. What flavors do you offer?"

I can't help but grin at her. "Are you an ice cream fan?"

"It's a weakness, but I don't indulge often. Tell me you make peppermint ice cream, and I might try to sweet-talk you into a pint."

"During the holidays, we do. Mostly, we specialize in the typical vanilla, chocolate, huckleberry, and strawberry. But we add one or two flavors with the different seasons."

"I haven't had huckleberry ice cream yet," she says, wiping her mouth with her napkin. "I didn't even know what a huckleberry was until I moved here last year. I was too late to pick some of my own."

"I will have plenty growing on the ranch this summer. You can pick all you want."

Her smile is so wide, I feel like I just won the lottery.

"How often do you get back to Ireland?" I ask.

"Typically just once a year, during the holidays. Maybe now that I'm not dancing, I can try to get over there for a couple of weeks in the summer as well."

"Do you miss it?"

She tips her head to the side as she finishes her crust as if she's giving it some thought. "I miss my parents, and yes, there's plenty about Ireland to love, but I adapted well to living in the States. How long has your family owned the ranch?"

"My parents bought it when Brooks was a baby, and the rest of us were all born there. Home births."

"You were *born* in the house you still live in?" She blinks at me in surprise. "That's amazing, Beck. And quite unusual these days."

"My mom was afraid of hospitals," I reply. "I find it ironic that one of her kids is now a doctor and spends most of his time in one."

"That *is* funny." The conversation continues to flow as we eat. Not only does Skyla ask intelligent questions but she also seems interested in the answers.

When we've finished our dinner and the server approaches, I'm surprised to discover we've been here for over an hour.

"Can I get you two any dessert?" the server asks, and we shake our heads. I pay the bill, and my jaw tightens because I don't want to simply drop her off and leave.

There's still so much to talk about.

And I've quickly become addicted to being in her company.

"I should get Riley home," Skyla says quietly.

With a nod, I stand and offer her my hand, helping her to her feet. Before letting her go, I pull her fingers to my lips and press a kiss against her knuckles.

I'd never stop touching her if I thought she'd let me.

We're quiet on our way back to her place. When we reach the gate, I look her way.

I have to punch in a code to get us in, and she worries her bottom lip before saying softly, "Six one nine four."

I'm quite sure that telling me the code to her gate was a big deal for her, and I won't let her regret it.

The gate swings open, and I park her SUV in the garage, where she had it before. However, she turns to me in the darkness before we can get out.

"Why don't you come inside for some tea?"

Thank Christ.

Chapter Eight

SKYLA

The truth is, I'm not ready for him to leave. I've never felt so comfortable talking to a man in my life. Certainly not one I'm attracted to.

Connor and Mik don't count.

"I'm just going to quickly let Riley outside, then I'll put the kettle on."

Beckett smiles in that soft, patient way he does, which immediately puts me at ease. I love how calm and patient he is. And that face of his makes me ache. I so want to run my fingers through his whiskers. "I can put the kettle on," he says and drags his hand from my shoulder to my hand, sending shivers through me. "Take care of your boy, Irish."

Irish.

That's the second time he's called me that, and I don't hate it. I've had many nicknames over the years, but nothing sounds quite as sexy as Beckett saying that one simple word.

With a nod, I motion for Riley to follow me out the back door, and he knows that it's time for him to do his business.

Glancing back at the house, I can see Beckett moving about my kitchen. His broad shoulders in that bloody *hot* gray button-down might be enough to make a girl pregnant.

And don't even get me started on his arms. The way his biceps fill out those sleeves pushed up, and his forearms flex and move, showing off muscles and veins when he drives or eats or *anything*. Beckett Blackwell is a large, imposing man, yet I don't know that I've ever felt safer.

Which is daft because I barely know him.

And my instincts have been wrong before.

However, I know his sister very well, and I believe in my heart of hearts that if there was anything to worry about, physically, where this man is concerned, Bee and our friends would have warned me.

Because they've come to be as close to me as family, and I trust them.

"That's a good boy," I croon to Riley when he's finished and we go back inside.

Beckett's leaning against my counter, his ankles crossed, and his arms folded over his chest, showing off more of those arms.

"I have Earl Grey or Irish breakfast tea," I inform Beckett as the water in the kettle boils. "Do you have a preference?"

"I'll have whatever you're having," he says, watching

me as I prepare our tea. He hasn't moved from his position at the counter. "Are you nervous?"

Tilting my head to the side as I ponder that question, I pull down the tea bags and put one in each mug, then pour the hot water.

"Perhaps a little, if I'm being honest."

"Always be honest," he says and nods when I hold up the honey, wordlessly asking him if he'd like some.

So I doctor his up the same way I do mine, and then we take our mugs into the living room and sit on my overstuffed sofa.

"I'm not nervous in the sense that I'm uncomfortable with you," I inform him as I set my tea aside to cool. "But I don't date, so having *any* man who isn't my brother or Mik in my house is unsettling."

"Who's Mik?" He sips his tea, yet doesn't seem jealous or angry with the question, which is a good thing. *The Arsehole* had a creepy fixation on Mik, and I won't let another man threaten my dearest friend ever again.

"Mikhail was my dance partner. Every major performance I've ever danced since I was sixteen has included him as my co-lead."

"That's a tight bond," he replies. "Sometimes those relationships turn into romantic ones."

Grinning at him over the rim of my cup, I take a sip of my tea, then set it aside and kick my shoes off, but before I can pull my legs up under me, Beckett tugs them into his lap and rests his hand on my shin. I don't mind the physical contact at all. In fact, his touch is nice, igniting something in me that's been long dormant.

"Sometimes it does, yes. But not for us. He's like a brother to me, and his husband might take issue with Mik and I starting something up."

"Ah." Beckett nods thoughtfully. "How deep can my questions get here tonight, Irish?"

"You're in my home, holding on to my legs, drinking tea. I'd say you can ask me pretty much whatever you like."

Whether or not I answer every question with the full truth remains to be seen. I do feel safe with this man, and I trust him—surprisingly, given we've spent so little time together.

Do I want him to know all my secrets? I guess I'll see how this goes, and if I tell him, I tell him.

"I'd like to know more about Riley and why you need a service dog."

Nodding, I finish my tea and turn in my seat, facing him more fully. "To answer that, I need to back it up to why I no longer dance, as they're linked. But I'll warn you, it's a long tale."

"I have all night. Actually, hold that thought."

Holding up a finger, he digs his phone out of his pocket and, rather than send a text, he taps the screen, sets it on speaker, and someone answers, "Hey, boss."

"Hi, Brad. I need a favor. I know you took care of everything this evening, and I appreciate it. I need someone to look after things in the morning as well. I might be back in time, but I don't want to rush."

"No worries, we'll handle things. Good night, boss."

"Thanks." He hangs up, stuffs his phone back in his pocket, and grins at me. "There. *Now* I have all night."

"Did you just blow off your duties for me?"

"I don't think you realize what I'd be willing to do for you, Skyla. But I think you'll learn. Talk to me. What happened?"

I haven't told *anyone* the entire story except for Connor. Not even Mik knows everything. Certainly no one here in my new town knows what I worry about daily.

He watches me so patiently, with those beautiful, kind eyes, and his hand is warm on my skin.

"I don't think you realize what I'd be willing to do for you, Skyla."

He's serious. And I know this isn't just about getting in my pants. He wants to know me. When was the last time I felt so ... revered? And that's when it clicks. If I choose to date this man, which is becoming painfully clear that I want to do, he needs to know this part of my history.

And I want to talk to him.

I don't want to hold anything back.

If this is too much for him, it's good to find out now before we invest more time and become attached. Because I could absolutely see myself becoming attached to this sexy, sweet man.

"Almost three years ago, I met a man."

Beckett's eyes narrow. "Is this story going to piss me off?"

"Probably. It makes me bloody irate on the daily. But

there's no way of sugarcoating it, so if you'd rather not hear it, I don't have to tell it."

He lifts his hand from my leg and links our fingers together.

"Don't sugarcoat it and tell me everything."

"Okay then. I met Lewis—and that's the only time I'll ever speak his name again—about three years ago. He'd been to a few of my performances, had some strings to pull, and ended up backstage to introduce himself to me. He was charming and handsome, and I agreed to go out with him. We saw each other for roughly a month's time, Beckett. It was nothing serious, and I never slept with him. I never let him into my flat, and I never went to his. It was only ever dinner or drink dates. We took a walk through Central Park once, but that's it."

"Okay, casually dating the dude. Got it."

"Exactly. Very casual. I was so busy that carving out time to foster any kind of romantic relationship was difficult. But I would have, for the right person. The Arsehole, as I'll now forever refer to him, was not the right person."

"All of this sounds pretty normal so far."

"And that's where the normalcy ends." I lean my cheek on the back of the sofa, enjoying the way Becket's thumb makes circles on the backs of my knuckles. It feels good to be touched, to have this handsome man *listen*.

Without any judgment in his eyes.

"He would do weird, controlling things when we were out, like not even let me look at a menu but just order for me. He didn't ask if I had allergies or if I actually *wanted* something. He simply decided for me. I didn't like that."

"So he's a dick."

I chuckle and nod in agreement. "He'd make comments about my weight."

Beckett's eyes narrow menacingly.

"He'd remind me that I was a *tiny dancer*, and that I should have a certain diet as if I hadn't been a professional dancer for most of my life and knew exactly what was required to maintain the physical shape needed. He was condescending and not any fun at all. So on the walk through the park, I told him that I appreciated his time, but that it wasn't going to work out for me, and I wished him well."

Beckett shifts on the sofa, still facing me, still holding my hand.

"Let me guess. He didn't like that."

"At that moment, he was calm and said he understood and also wished me well. I thought nothing of it when I left and returned to work that afternoon. I was relieved that it went as well as it could, and honestly, I forgot about it. For about two weeks. And that's when it all went to shite."

Pulling out of his grasp, I stand and walk to the kitchen, grab two bottles of water, and return, offering him one. When he takes it, I sit where I was before, and Beckett takes my hand again as if he simply has to touch me, and I'm grateful.

I do enjoy his touch.

"He never did anything that was technically against the law or that I could *prove* was against the law."

His eyes narrow, his hand tightens on mine, and for the first time in my life, I want to move over and put myself in a man's lap. "Explain, please."

"He'd call but not incessantly. He'd send me flowers. Pink roses." I shiver at that and shake my head. "Ugh, if I never see another pink rose, it'll be too soon."

"Noted."

"He kept inserting himself into my life even though I'd told him to stop. And when I stopped answering him, he got agitated."

"How long did this go on, Skyla?"

I chew on my bottom lip, doing the math. "Almost two years."

He pulls his hand away and leans forward, those amber eyes full of anger. "*Two fucking years?*"

I nod. "Yes. Remember, I'd call the police, and they'd tell me that he hadn't done anything wrong. That he wasn't bothering me to the point of it actually being considered stalking or *harassment*. And there were times when he'd go months without reaching out to me. And just as I'd start to feel secure, believing that he'd finally moved on, something would happen. It was enough to keep me on edge and in a constant state of worry but not enough to get him into trouble."

"Fucking asshole."

"Quite, yes. One night, I woke up in the middle of the night, and I *knew* I wasn't alone."

Beckett stands and starts to pace, so angry that he can't sit still.

"I'm sorry, I'll stop telling you. I just have to explain this to get to Riley and—"

"I want to hear it," he says, shaking his head. "And I want to kill him, all at the same time."

But he sits, drags his hand down his face, then holds my hand once more.

"Are you okay?" My question is a whisper, and instead of answering, he simply tugs me into his lap, wraps his arms around me, and buries his face in my neck. I've never felt anything better in my life. My stomach quivers, my lady bits come fully awake, and it's clear to me, right here and now, that being in Beckett's arms is my favorite place to be. If I'm wrong about this man, it will devastate me because every molecule in my body screams that I can trust him.

And gods, how I want to trust him.

"This is better," he murmurs, dragging one hand down my spine. "Are you okay with this?"

"Yes." Wrapping my arms around his shoulders, I slide my fingers into his hair and hold on. I am so much more than okay with this. "Yes, this is lovely."

"We need a minute." He presses his lips to my skin, where my neck meets my shoulder, and I take a deep breath, soaking in this moment.

This is what it must feel like to be treasured.

And he hasn't even kissed me.

"Okay." He pulls back and loosens his hold on me but keeps me in his lap. "Go on."

I've wanted to touch his beard since the first moment I saw this man. If he can tug me onto his lap, I can do this.

My hand drifts down his face, into those whiskers, and I was right. They're soft and feel amazing against my palm. And when I use my nails to scratch his cheek, he groans.

"Keep doing that, Irish, and we won't make it through this conversation, and I think we *need* to finish this."

"You're right, but I've wanted to touch you like this since I saw you at that pub."

His eyebrows climb. "Is that right?"

"Yes. Your beard is sexy."

"Then I'll keep the beard." He pulls my hand away and kisses my palm. "Now, keep talking, sweetheart."

I lick my lips and frown, trying to remember where I left off.

"Middle of the night. You're not alone," he reminds me.

"Ah yes. I didn't have Riley yet, but I also lived in a building with great security. I might have been considered a starving dancer, but my family certainly wasn't starving, so my parents bought me an amazing flat in a safe building."

"I understand." He dances his fingers down my face, and I take a deep breath.

"If I can't touch, you can't touch. Those are the rules."

His lips twitch as he drops his hand, and instead of touching my face, he grips my hip.

"I panicked." My heart leaps with the memory, and Beckett's hold on me tightens.

"You're okay, Irish."

I lick my lips. "My phone wasn't by the bed. It had been moved. And from what I've pieced together, when I woke up, it scared The Arsehole because I heard my front door shut. I flew out of bed and fell, spraining my ankle something fierce. I didn't know for sure if he'd left. But I knew who it was. I knew."

"Of course, you knew."

"I crawled—"

He growls at that. Actually *growls*.

"Into the living room and found my phone on the coffee table. It had been unlocked, and he'd been going through it. Not that he would have found anything, but still, it was an invasion of privacy. Connor was out of the country at a property in Milan, so I called Mik, and he and Benji rushed right over. They took me to an emergency clinic, where I was told that I sprained my ankle so badly that it would have been better if it had broken. It would have been easier because torn ligaments take longer to repair."

"Shit." He's touching me again, running his hands up and down my back, soothing me. "I'm so sorry, Skyla."

"I couldn't dance, of course. And when I saw my regular physician, he didn't mince words. I likely wouldn't be able to dance professionally anymore. But I waited in New York for three months. I went to physical therapy and got a second, then third opinion. I did everything I could to salvage my career, but they told me it was unlikely.

"Then I got an email from The Arsehole, letting me know that he'd have to leave the country for a little while but not to worry because he'd be home soon, and we'd resume our romance."

That email has been burned into my retinas. I can't unsee it.

"He's a delusional fuckface," Beckett says, scowling.

"Absolutely, yes. But more than that, his calm exterior terrified me. He was unpredictable, and I'd become scared of living on my own. I ended up staying with Connor after that night. I was afraid of *everything*, and I hated it so much. So I decided to move." His eyebrows climb in surprise.

"Just like that?"

"Just like that. He took away everything I had sacrificed my life for. Dancing was the very essence of me, Beckett. Every element of my life was wrapped up in that world and those routines. I loved it. And he took it away. I couldn't ... I couldn't stay. I couldn't live so close to what I used to have and what I'd never have again. *He'd won.* But I refused to give him that victory. How could I stay if he could still find me?"

"Oh, Irish. Sweetheart, I'm so sorry." And the pain in his voice is evident. *This man is one of the good ones.*

"Don't be. This town has been a balm for me. I'm healing. Growing confident again."

"What made you decide to move here?"

"I'd been here a few years prior with some friends for a winter getaway. We couldn't ski because it was in our contracts that we couldn't do anything that might break bones, but we came out to enjoy the snow, and I loved it here. It stayed with me. And when I realized I had to leave New York, Bitterroot Valley immediately came to mind.

"Connor wanted me to go back to Ireland, and Mik is still in denial and thinks I'll be back in New York any day now to resume my place as prima ballerina, but they're both wrong. This is where I want to be."

"And Riley?"

"Oh yes, I almost forgot. Well, after the middle-of-the-night incident, Connor wanted to get me one of those attack dogs that cost hundreds of thousands of dollars, that aren't to be pets, but only fierce guard dogs, like for presidents and such."

"I might have had the same reaction," he admits with a grin.

"I didn't want that. If I have an animal living in my home, I want them to also be my friend, and I want to be able to trust them with children and other animals. So we compromised. Riley is a Bouvier. He's been highly trained as an alert dog, so if someone approaches me from behind like you did after the pub that night, he'll alert me. He's always on the lookout. I don't typically let people pet him because he has to be aware that most people aren't to be trusted. I work on his training every day. But in return, he's sweet and good company for me, and we trust each other. I got him just before I moved out of New York."

"I'm glad you have him, Irish. That was a good decision. Since you've been here, has The Asshole reached out to you?" he asks.

"No. But I changed my email address, my phone number, everything. I didn't leave a forwarding address with the ballet company or with my building. Mik or Connor would see to having anything sent to me, and it's been long enough that nothing really comes to me through New York anymore. I'm not hiding here. I haven't changed my name or anything, but I didn't make it easy for someone to find me, either. Who would think to look for me in Montana? No one."

"I'm glad you're here." He brushes my hair behind my ear, and his fingertips drift down my jawline to my neck. "And now I know why you didn't want to give me your number. I'm sorry if I made you uncomfortable when I didn't take no for an answer, and if you want me to go, I will."

"You didn't make me uncomfortable. Trust me, if I'd been angry or put off, I would have told you to go feck yourself without thinking twice about it. I'm not shy in that regard, not anymore."

"Good girl," he murmurs, and those two words might have just made my ovaries explode.

I glance over at where Riley's lying on his bed. He's sleeping soundly, which is unusual for him when anyone other than the two of us is in the house. *Dogs see more than humans, so if Riley trusts this man, that's almost all the reassurance I need.*

"Looks like he's off duty," Beckett says.

"He's always on duty. If I have a nightmare, he knows to turn the lights on for me. It's one of the things he was trained to do."

He takes my chin in his fingers and turns me to look at him. His eyes are narrowed and intense, and I swallow hard.

"It's probably not sexy to be afraid of the dark, is it?"

"Every single thing about you is sexy, Irish."

"Should I get out of your lap?"

"Not on my account." His mouth tips up in a half smile. "But if you don't want me to kiss you, you might want to move."

Oh, I want him to kiss me. I've dreamed about him kissing me for a while now.

When I don't move, his eyes dip to my mouth, and I lick my lips. He cups my neck and jaw, his thumb brushes over my cheek, and he closes the gap between us and takes my mouth with his.

It's so much more than I imagined.

His whiskers rasp against my skin, and he licks my bottom lip, making my stomach quiver. When my mouth opens to him, he sinks in.

This man kisses me like he was born for it, and it's everything I never knew I needed.

But it's over too quickly, and when he pulls away, we're both breathing hard and fast.

"Wow," I whisper.

"There are two things I'm not going to do tonight," he tells me and swallows hard.

"Okay, what are they, then?"

"One, I'm not going to fuck you. Even though I want to with every goddamn fiber of my body, I'm not going to take it any further tonight."

Well, that's a shame.

"And the second?"

"I'm also not going home. I'm going to stay here, and we're going to talk, and I'm going to hold you until we fall asleep. Unless you kick me out because you're the boss, Irish."

"I'm not for kicking you out, Beckett."

He presses his lips to mine again, but this kiss is softer. Gentler. And then he pulls back and settles me against him so my head rests on his chest, under his chin, and he's holding me close.

This feels so right.

He could have run away, thinking that I came with too much baggage. Yet he kissed me and promised me a night of comfort and friendship. And even though I'm feeling a little raw from speaking about *him*, I also feel content. At peace somehow.

I know some things about the Blackwell family because of Bee and Dani, but I want to know more from Beck's perspective. Now feels like the time to ask him.

"Where are your parents?"

"Florida," he replies and kisses the top of my head. "They moved down there when they retired, but they come up often. They don't want to miss too much of Birdie's life. They just hate the snow."

"I love the snow." I also love the sound of Beckett's heartbeat against my ear. "Are you the eldest sibling?"

"No, that's Brooks."

"That's right, he told me that when I met you all at the pub. Where do you fall in line?"

"I'm actually the second youngest, just before Billie. But there's a bit of a gap between us. She's twenty-seven, and I'm thirty-one. Billie was a happy surprise."

"I like that. A happy surprise. Connor is almost forty, and I'm nearly twenty-eight. I was also a surprise. Ma and Da didn't think they could have more children."

"You are absolutely a happy surprise, sweetheart." He kisses the top of my head, and I melt further into him.

So are you, Beckett Blackwell. So are you.

Chapter Nine
BECKETT

Something wet pressing against my face pulls me out of a dead sleep, and when I crack open an eye, I find Riley staring back at me.

I'm lying flat on my back on the couch, and Skyla, the woman I can't get enough of, is draped over me, her head on my chest and arms wrapped around me, sleeping sweetly.

Riley lets out a little whine, telling me that he needs to go outside, so I gently roll the beauty in my arms to the side and prop a throw pillow against her chest. She immediately wraps herself around the pillow, and I stand and head for the kitchen.

Opening the back door, I let Riley slip outside, then I get to work making coffee. I can tell it's still early since the sky is just starting to lighten, but the sun isn't up yet.

It's probably not quite six, and I've usually been up and working for an hour by now.

Does Riley always get his human up this early?

Just as I get the water in the coffee maker, Riley's back at the door, so I let him in and stand at the sink, staring out the window to the backyard with my arms crossed as I wait for the coffee to brew.

"He's always on duty. If I have a nightmare, he knows to turn the lights on for me. It's one of the things he was trained for."

Fuck. She has a dog trained to respond to her nightmares, and she somehow thought that would detract from her attractiveness. *She's so fucking wrong.* Skyla Gallagher is one of the strongest people I know. To have to pivot her life's trajectory so significantly ... *It's so wrong.* She lost her dream.

Now I understand more about why her brother, Connor, was a hard-ass. He isn't just an overbearing older brother. He has good reason to be wary.

This thing—whatever it is—between Skyla and me has progressed a shit ton in the past twenty-four hours. We went from *I hope she'll give me her number* to *snuggle and talk the night away* in the blink of an eye.

I'm so fucking grateful that my feelings aren't one-sided. The way she touched me and smiled at me and confided in me last night tells me that she's as into me as I am her.

Thank fuck.

It pisses me off that some deranged asshole almost ruined what could be the best thing in my life because she was scared to trust her own instincts where I'm concerned. She didn't say that out loud, but it doesn't take a psychologist to see that.

No matter what happens between us, he'll never get near her again. I'll fucking make sure of it.

The coffee's finished brewing, and when I check the fridge, I find some coffee creamer and doctor up a mug for both of us. I assume she takes the creamer since it was in her fridge.

When I return to the living room, Skyla's awake but hasn't sat up. She's fucking gorgeous in the morning, with sleepy moss-green eyes and messy hair. Having her tucked against me all night long was a slice of heaven. We couldn't be more different, size-wise. I'm well over six foot four and more than two hundred pounds, and this whisp of a woman is a foot shorter and a hundred pounds lighter, but she fits against me like a missing puzzle piece.

"I smelled the coffee," she says with a grin as she stretches. "And hoped you'd share."

"Always, sweetheart."

She sits up and takes the mug, gives it a smell and closes her eyes, then takes a sip. "I was never a coffee drinker until I moved to the States. Now I don't know what I'd do without it."

Sitting next to her, I take a sip from my own mug. "I let Riley out."

"I appreciate that. Also, I can't believe I forgot to set the alarm last night. I must have been preoccupied with good conversation because I *never* forget the alarm. Connor would be livid."

"You had both Riley and me here." I reach over to

smooth her hair over her shoulder, then let my thumb brush over her bare skin. "You're safe."

Her brows pull into a slight frown before she takes another sip, and she sets the mug aside, then pulls her legs up under her, shifting just out of my reach. Just like that, a wall goes up.

Fuck that.

"What's wrong, Irish?"

She bites the lower lip that I've learned is my favorite thing to taste and lets out a sigh.

"I might have divulged too much last night. It was a lot to dump on you all at once, and, well"—she clears her throat and pushes her hair behind her ear—"it's sorry I am for making you uncomfortable."

I lift an eyebrow and move closer to her so I can touch her, run my hand down her thigh. "Do I look uncomfortable?"

"I don't think I know you well enough to know if this is your uncomfortable look."

"Trust me, it's not. I asked you to tell me, remember?" My knuckles drift down her cheek, over the freckles there. "You didn't say anything that made me want to run away. If that were the case, I wouldn't have stayed, Skyla."

She nods once and links her hands in her lap nervously, and I don't like it one fucking bit. "Beckett … I'm a lot."

"You slept on me all night, so you won't pull away from me now unless you're telling me that I'm completely off base and last night didn't affect you the way it did me, in which case I'll apologize, and I won't bother you again."

"That's not what I mean."

"Good." Reaching for her, I cup her cheek and brush my thumb over her skin. "You're not too much for me, Irish. You had something really shitty happen to you, and you want to make sure you're safe. *I* want to make sure you're safe. That's not a lot or too much, but even if it was, I can handle just about anything you throw at me. Let's not end this before it begins just because of The Asshole. He doesn't have any power in this."

She swallows hard and closes her eyes. The next thing I know, she's crawled into my lap and wrapped herself around me, almost desperately.

"I was afraid you'd come to your senses this morning and decide I'm not worth the trouble."

"You're worth a whole lot of trouble." That makes her chuckle, which is what I wanted. "But what you shared with me last night isn't trouble, sweetheart. It's simple honesty."

"Okay." She rubs my beard in that way that makes my cock sit up and beg.

"Are you hungry?" I ask.

"I'm always hungry in the morning." She pulls back far enough to smile at me.

"Fuck me, you're beautiful," I whisper before brushing my lips across hers. "It's a punch in the gut every time you look at me."

"You say lovely things, Beckett Blackwell."

"Just being honest. Now, let me take you to breakfast

before I haul you off to bed because we're not doing that on this date."

My cock is *not* in favor of that declaration, but I'm not going to rush this with her and fuck everything up.

I can be patient. I can earn her trust.

An hour later, after Skyla changed clothes and gave me a toothbrush to use, the three of us walk into Kay's Diner and are shown to a booth by the windows.

Kay's is newer to town and is a typical 1950s-style diner with old rock-and-roll decor, black-and-white-checked floors, and red vinyl seats. There's even a jukebox that's always pumping out music. Today, it seems to be an old Prince song.

It's fun, and breakfast here is delicious.

"Have you had the crepes here?" Skyla asks me as she dances in her seat.

"No, ma'am. Are they a must try?"

"If you enjoy crepes, you'll like these," she says, and when the server comes around to take our order, I go for the crepes.

Skyla orders bacon and eggs.

"No crepes for you?" I ask with a raised eyebrow.

"I admit, I have a plan." She grins and leans forward as if she's going to tell me a secret. "You ordered them, so I can have a bite of yours and eat something else as well. Best of both worlds."

"And if I don't want to share?"

She bats those eyelashes at me and bites her lower lip —and yes, I'd give this woman anything she wanted. Crepes. A car. A kidney.

She wants it, she gets it.

"Yeah, okay, I'll share my crepes."

"That was simple." She twists her legs up under her and sips the coffee that the server just dropped off for us. "I'll share my bacon with you."

"I'll let you."

"Do you have chickens on your farm?"

"About a dozen or so, yeah."

"And do they produce eggs for you?"

"Plenty. If you ever want some, let me know."

"I absolutely want some. Farm-fresh eggs are the best."

"When are you free to come out? You can choose your own eggs and anything else you want."

"I can shop right on the farm?" Her eyes light up at the idea, and I feel like I just won an award or something. "I'll take you up on that. Let's see, I have classes this afternoon, and I'm sure you have plenty of work to catch up on since I've monopolized the better part of the past twenty-four hours."

Worth it.

"What about tomorrow?" she asks. "Is that too soon?"

"It's not too soon. Will Riley be okay around the animals?"

Skyla nods and sits back as our food is delivered. "Yes,

he's well trained and will listen to any command I give him. He'll be curious, but he won't attack any of the animals. If you'd rather I leave him at home, though, I will."

I frown over at her. "But you always take him with you."

"It's true that I do always have him with me, but ..." She shrugs and reaches over to take a bite of my crepe, and it makes me grin. Fuck yes, I'll share my breakfast with her. "I think I'm safe with you out at the farm."

"You're safe with me anywhere, Irish." When she holds her bacon up and offers me a bite, I take it and wink at her. "But Riley isn't a problem, so if you want him on the ranch, he's welcome."

"I'll decide tomorrow, then." She scoops some eggs onto a piece of toast and takes a bite. I love her appetite. She's not afraid to eat. "What *do* you have to do today? I'm curious."

"I'll take over the afternoon milking and feeding," I reply, thinking it over. "I need to check on the rentals. I'll probably saddle up a horse and check some fence line to make sure nothing needs to be mended or replaced. There's always a list of chores that needs to get done."

"And what time do you typically start in the morning?"

I offer her the last bite of crepe, and she accepts it, popping it in her mouth with a happy sigh.

"Around five," I reply. She chokes on her food, then reaches for a glass of water. "Not a morning person?"

"*Five*? Ugh, that's early. I used to start dance practice

at seven, so I'd be up at six, and it felt like I was being punished for something I'd done in a past life."

"You were up early this morning," I remind her.

"I was sleeping on a man, on the couch, so it was a little different." She stops to think about that and chuckles. "A lot different, actually."

Her phone rings from inside her bag, and she frowns, licks her lips, and digs the phone out of her bag.

"Sorry, it's Mik."

"Take it."

She answers but doesn't leave the table. "I thought for sure you'd be in practice right now. What are you about?"

She listens, and I can't take my eyes off her. She's quick to smile, to laugh, to offer a kind word. She's not only beautiful on the outside but on the inside, too.

"Mik, that's wonderful. Congratulations. Of course, I'd love to see that performance, but you know I can't— yes, I know. I'm so proud of you. I love you, too. Come see me soon. Bye now."

With a sigh, she drops the phone back in her bag.

"He secured the lead in a performance we'd been working on for years," she says softly. "And I'm so proud of him. He deserves that role."

"And he wants you to come watch it. Of course, he does. You should."

Skyla shakes her head. "I won't ever go back to New York. I just can't. But it'll be filmed, and I'll watch it from here."

"Wait." I reach over and take her hand in mine. "Are some of your performances available to watch online?"

"Many are, yes." She nods and wrinkles her nose. "You want to watch them?"

"Fuck yes, I want to watch them."

"Don't watch them with me," she insists. "Because I'll be annoying and give you all the commentary you didn't ask for. And I'll critique myself endlessly. I'm not a good audience for myself."

"You're not invited, then." I laugh when she frowns. "You just said I shouldn't watch with you."

"I thought you'd try a little harder than that."

"Okay." I pull my card out and offer it to the server. "Let me watch it with you so you can teach me something. Maybe tell me what you were thinking when you were performing."

"I knew you'd be good at the convincing. All right then, I'll watch with you sometime."

I like that we continue to make plans.

After I drive Skyla and Riley home and get her car stowed away in the garage, I walk through the house with her, and she joins me on the porch.

"That was the longest date of my life," she says, checking her watch. "Fifteen hours sets a record."

In answer, I take her chin in my fingers and tilt her face up so I can nip at her lips before sinking in and dragging my tongue along the seam of her mouth. She opens up for me and groans as her hands fist in my shirt. I slip my free hand over her hip and around to her ass, pulling her against me.

When I pull my lips from hers, I gaze down into emerald pools and feel my heart stutter. "I'll see you tomorrow. I'll pick you up."

"You don't have to—"

"I'll pick you up, Irish." I kiss her once more, and then tear myself away before I lift her up and carry her back inside, straight to her bedroom, and lose myself in her for the rest of the day. "Have a good afternoon."

"You too." Her fingers are on her lips as she watches me climb in my truck, and just as I'm about to pull away, I see her in the rearview mirror, standing there, and I can't resist her.

I throw the truck in park, push out of the vehicle, and march up to her. As I approach, her arms open wide, as if she already knew what I was going to do. With my hands planted on her ass, I lift her, and she wraps those strong legs around my waist, her hands dive into my beard, and I kiss the fuck out of her.

She moans, and my dick hardens. Jesus Christ, I want her more than my next breath.

"Beck," she whispers against my lips.

"Yeah, Irish?"

"Tomorrow feels far away."

I grin and nip at her lips once more, and she moans, pressing herself closer to me as she wraps her long arms around my neck, holding on tight. I bury my face in her neck, hugging her close.

"I know. It's already killing me. What time are you done with classes?"

"Four," she says against my skin.

"I'll be there at three fifty-five."

Skyla nods, and I release her, letting her slide down my body to her feet. Her eyebrow quirks at my hardness pressed against her.

"I've been touching you for fifteen hours," I remind her. "It's fucking torture, but it's worth it."

She laughs and leans in to kiss my chest, right over my heart. "Drive safely, Mr. Blackwell."

"Have a good day, Ms. Gallagher."

I return to my truck and pull away from the house, sure not to look in the rearview, so I'm not tempted to stay with her. I have too much to do at the farm, and I can already tell that twenty-four hours are going to be too many without her.

Before I head home, I stop at a tractor supply store and load up on things I'll need for Riley if they spend a significant amount of time at my place. It may be presumptuous, but dammit, I want them at the farm with me as much as possible.

And so, with all of the gear Riley could need loaded up in the truck, I set off for home.

Chapter Ten

SKYLA

"Well, this is unexpected, my friend." I usher Riley inside and close the door behind us, setting the alarm. "I think I have a huge crush on my best friend's brother."

I wrinkle my nose at that, then let out a little laugh. Riley stomps his feet as if he thinks it's funny, too.

"You like him. You're relaxed with him here, and that's very telling." I lean down and kiss the top of Riley's head, then give him scratches behind his ears. "You were a very good boy in those restaurants. That means you get a special treat."

His ears perk up at that, and I gasp as if I'm excited, too.

"Yes, you do. What a good boy." Riley follows me into the pantry, and I get him one of the chews that he loves. It only takes him fifteen minutes to devour it, but he still loves them all the same, and with it proudly in his mouth, Riley scampers off to his favorite bed to enjoy his treat.

With thoughts of a shower in my mind, I walk down the hallway to my bedroom, and Riley follows, then curls up on his bedroom bed to continue working on his chew.

He's been trained to always stick close to me, and I love that I have him nearby. He's like a security blanket.

Before I can take my shirt off, my phone rings, and I smile.

"Where are you, and what time is it there?" I ask Connor.

"I'm in Paris, and it's late. What are you doing?"

I bite my lip, wondering if I should tell him about my date.

"Skyla?"

"Well, I was just going to take a shower. I had a date last night—slash—today." I bite my lip again as silence descends over the line.

"With whom?" he asks, his voice hard.

"Stop it. I'm great. I had a nice evening with a nice guy, who isn't a psychopath, thank you very much."

"How do you *know*?"

"How do *you* know that the women you sleep with aren't psychopaths? Christ, not that I slept with him. But you know what I mean."

"Skyla, I'm in no mood for this. Who the feck is he?"

"For the love of all the saints, Connor, it was just Beckett Blackwell. Billie's *brother*. Stop being a shite and tell me why you're calling me from Paris. Also, how pretty is it there right now? Are the trees blooming then?"

"Aye, they are," he says. "You should come with me next time."

"I have a business here," I remind him. "Tell me what you're about."

"I want you to change the codes on the doors again, and I'm going to hire security detail for your house."

"No." I shake my head and sit on the side of my bed. Immediately, Riley rushes to me and lays his head in my lap. He can tell I'm agitated. "I don't want strangers wandering around my property, Connor."

"I don't bloody care."

"What's brought this on?"

"The Arsehole is back in the States, *a stór*. And he's been googling you."

I lean forward, burying my face in Riley's neck.

"But he's in New York City," I reply, my voice a little muffled.

"For now, yes."

"And he can't find where I am. This house is owned by the corporation. My business is owned by an LLC that doesn't circle back to the family in any way." I lift my face and sigh. "I'm safe here, Connor."

"I still want you to change the code."

"What good does that do?" I demand as I stand to pace my bedroom. "If he can figure out a six-digit alarm code, it shouldn't matter how often I change it."

"Let me hire the men," he says, softening his voice

because he knows I'll react better if he's not demanding. "At least until he leaves the country again."

"He may never leave the country again," I remind him.

"Yes, he will. I don't like that he's looking for you."

I'm suddenly so tired of all of this bullshite. "I'm *fine*, Connor. I have Riley, a bloody secure house, and I'm in a small town. I don't want strangers walking around my property, and that's that. I know you'll be keeping an eye on if he leaves New York and where he goes, so unless he's bought an airline ticket out West, I'm keeping things the way they are. You can't just lock me down all of the bloody time. I'm going to live my life."

The tension crackles through the phone.

"I don't like it," he says.

"Well, I'm an adult, and this is how it's going to be for now. If he leaves New York and heads this way, we'll hire the men."

"Fine. Are you going to see more of this Blackwell?"

"I'll say that's none of your business because that's what you said to *me* about Bee, and that still makes me mad."

"It's not the same thing."

I laugh, and I can almost hear Connor gnashing his teeth together.

"Oh, Brother, it's exactly the same thing. I'm not in any danger with Beckett."

"I'm running a background check."

"Fine. Do that. In the meantime, I need a shower. I love you, *a stór*. Enjoy Paris."

"I love you as well."

Connor ends the call, and I blow out a breath but then smile when I see a text from Beckett come through.

> Beckett: *Sends photo of a cow* This is Bessy. She says hello.

Grinning, I pull my shirt off and pad into the bathroom, turn on the spray in the shower to heat it, and then set the phone down while I take the rest of my clothes off.

> Me: Bessy is beautiful. Is she milked and happy, then?

The bubbles bounce on my screen as I twist my hair into a bun on the top of my head.

> Beckett: Bessy and the other ladies are happy. What are you up to?

Glancing around, I grab a towel and wrap it around me, then turn so the shower is in the background and take a selfie.

> Me: *Sends selfie* I'm about to enjoy this hot shower.

I let the water run as I wait for his reply. The bubbles appear but then disappear again. This goes on for several minutes before a reply finally comes through.

> Beckett: Fucking hell, Irish.

I start to giggle, but then my phone rings through with a video call from Beckett.

"I like you, but I'm not going to get naked on a video call," I inform him.

"Are you trying to kill me?" he demands.

"If I kill you, I don't get to enjoy you, and I plan to do plenty of enjoying you, Mr. Blackwell." I grin when his eyes narrow on me. "Why are you calling me so soon after leaving here?"

"I texted you a photo of a cow, and you replied with *that*. Why do you think I'm calling?"

I snort and shake my head. "I need to get in the shower before all the hot water is gone. Go away."

"Do not hang up—"

But I do hang up and leave the phone on the counter as I get in the shower and do my business. I can hear it buzzing with another call but ignore it because the water feels too good.

Last night was better than I could have imagined. I love that Beckett seems to be physically affectionate because I am, too, and it's something that I've never really had in a partner.

Not that I've had many serious relationships. There was never time, and then The Arsehole happened.

So to be held by Beckett's strong arms, to feel his lips on my skin, and see how much my story affected him made me feel warm inside.

Yes, I'll be seeing much more of Beckett.

And *yes*, the thought of The Arsehole being back in New York does scare me. But I worked hard to ensure

I'm safe here in Bitterroot Valley. He can't get to me here.

I'm safe.

He's three thousand miles away, and Connor will be alerted if he leaves New York City.

There's nothing to worry about.

"My mom's here," Birdie says when the door to the studio opens, and Dani Blackwell steps inside, hugging Birdie to her in greeting.

"Hey, pumpkin. How was dance?"

"The best," Birdie replies, making me feel good. I love that this wee girl loves my class so much.

"And how are you?" I ask Dani.

"Glad it's Friday," she replies with a tired smile. "What are your weekend plans?"

Before I can answer, Beckett himself walks in with intense eyes aimed at me.

"Well, well, well," Dani murmurs, grinning widely.

"Uncle Beck," Birdie exclaims.

"Hey, peanut," Beckett replies, and kisses her on the head. Then he moves straight for me, cups my face in his hands, and presses his lips to mine, making my toes curl.

"Uncle Beck is kissing Miss Skyla," Birdie says in a loud whisper, making me laugh against Beck's mouth.

When he pulls back, his whiskey eyes are on fire, and I have to clear my throat.

"Well, it's good to see you as well."

Dani laughs at that, and Beckett finally looks away from me.

"It looks like I'm the last one to collect my kiddo," Dani says, taking Birdie's hand in hers. "So we'll head on home. It's our night to take dinner to the fire station."

"We take Daddy dinner," Birdie informs us. "It's extra special. Tonight is taco night."

"Have fun with that," I reply as I walk them to the door. Birdie runs back and gives her uncle a quick hug, and he holds her close, his eyes shut. *How this big man loves his wee niece.*

"Bye, Uncle Beck," Birdie says.

"See you later, peanut. Be good."

"I'm *always* good," she answers, then runs to Dani.

When they're gone, I lock up behind them and turn to the sexy man watching me from across the room. "Hi."

His lips twitch, and I slowly walk back to him, taking him in. His beard has been trimmed since yesterday, but it's still just begging for my fingers. He's in a red Henley, with the sleeves pulled up his forearms, showing off muscles and veins that make me go weak in the knees.

His jeans envelop his muscled thighs perfectly, and based on the way his hands flex in and out of fists at his sides and his hot gaze as he watches me, I'd say he wants to get those sexy hands on me.

And I wouldn't tell him no.

"Stay the weekend with me at my farm." His voice is

rough as I close the distance between us and push my fingers into that beard.

"I don't have an overnight bag."

"We'll stop and get your things," he replies, his mouth hovering over mine. "Say yes, Irish."

I'd say yes to just about anything when he calls me that.

"We'd like that."

He brushes his lips over mine, gently this time. His hands land on my shoulders, then ghost up to frame my neck, his fingers in my hair, and it feels like little tiny fireworks explode up and down my skin.

"We'd better go," he whispers against my lips.

"Okay."

Beck follows me home, and the three of us bustle inside so I can pack up Riley's and my things.

I only pack casual clothes and a few things that I don't mind if they get dirty, given that we'll be out in barns and on the ranch. With my bag packed, I take it to the living room and pass it to Beckett.

"I just have to gather Riley's food and a bed and—"

"I already have that out there," he informs me.

"You have his *food*?"

He shrugs. "I noticed which brand you fed him and picked some up on my way home yesterday. I also grabbed him a bed, bowls, and toys. He should be good to go."

My mouth opens but then closes again because I'm not sure what to say.

"I know, it's pushy." His knuckle drifts down my

cheek. "And if this weekend goes badly, you can take it all home with you and keep it. But I'm hoping you'll want to spend a good amount of time out there with me."

"I don't think it's going to go badly."

He kisses my forehead, igniting more fireworks down my body.

"I don't either. Let's go, you two. I'm making dinner tonight."

I look at Riley and give him the hand command to follow me.

"Do you want to take my SUV again for Riley?" I ask.

"Come see if what I did to the truck will work," Beck replies, holding the door open for me.

I follow him down the steps, and when he opens the back door, my stomach clenches, and tears fill my eyes as I clamp my hand over my mouth.

"Beck."

He's taken the back seats out of the truck entirely, and in their place are two thick, plush industrial dog beds, side by side, so Riley will have a soft place to ride.

"Will this work?"

Before I can reply, Riley jumps into the truck, turns a circle, and then lies down in the middle of the space, letting out a satisfied huff.

"I guess it will, yes." I shake my head and look up into his gaze. "Thank you."

"I need our guy to be comfy." He shuts the door, but before he opens my passenger door, he reaches up and brushes his thumb down my neck. "I need *you* to be comfortable, Irish."

"I'm more comfortable by the minute."

He winks and opens my door, then helps to boost me into the truck. He doesn't shut the door right away. No, this cowboy buckles me into the seat belt, kisses my cheek, then shuts the door. He circles the hood and gets into the driver's seat.

I let out a long breath, willing the butterflies in my stomach to calm the hell down.

I can't help glancing over my shoulder to where Riley's curled up, already snoring, in the back of the truck.

"I need our guy to be comfy."

I shake my head. One date. We've spent such a short time together, yet he's gone out of his way to ensure I feel safe. That my dog feels safe and welcome. It's surreal and so unexpected.

"That might be the nicest thing anyone has ever done for me."

He takes my hand and lifts it to his lips. I love how his whiskers feel against my skin as he presses soft kisses on my knuckles.

"Riley and I are buddies," he says. "We have to look out for each other."

I let him keep my hand as he drives us out of town to his property, and when he has to put a code in, and we wait for a gate to open, some of the tension leaves my shoulders.

"*The Arsehole is back in the States,* a stór. *And he's been googling you.*"

"You have security."

"I do," he says with a nod. "I have quite a lot to protect out here. Does this make you feel more at ease?"

"Honestly, yes."

"Good. You're safe out here. Nothing will hurt you." He drives down a gravel road and pulls up to a stunning farmhouse you'd expect to see in a movie.

The two-story charmer has a deep, wraparound porch complete with hanging swings and furniture that looks like you could nap away an entire summer afternoon in the soft cushions.

"Beckett, this is beautiful. Homey. How many naps have you taken on that porch?"

He blinks over at me. "None."

"What? That's criminal. It's begging for naps."

He laughs and kisses my hand again. "Do you nap often?"

"No, but I'm telling you right now that this porch was made for lazy summer afternoons, with a cool drink, a book, a breeze, and a refreshing sleep."

He follows my gaze. "When you put it that way, I can picture it. I'll give you a tour of the rest of the ranch tomorrow since it's about to get dark."

I hop out of the truck. Beck lets Riley out and leads us up the porch steps to the front door. He opens one side of the double door, and I can't help but grin.

"Are those cows etched in the glass?" I ask, nodding to the frosted glass in the door.

He nods and grins.

"Of course. Welcome," he says before he picks up my bag and follows us in. "Nothing in this house is off-limits to you, so make yourself at home. I mean that."

"Thank you."

He sets my bag at the bottom of the stairs, then takes my hand and leads me back to the kitchen. The house is beautiful, with vintage and modern touches that make it feel like a home.

When I see that Beck not only bought Riley's food but also bought him a raised feeder with big bowls for food and water, my heart catches.

Across the room, there's another new bed, similar to the ones in the truck, and Riley stomps over after getting a big drink of water, making a mess on the floor, and curls up on the bed.

"Well, Riley's made himself at home." I laugh and grab a towel off the countertop so I can wipe up my dog's mess.

"Good. That was my plan." Beckett wraps his arms around me from behind and brushes my hair to the side so he can press his mouth to the crook of my neck. "Thank you for being here."

"Thank you for inviting us." I lean back against him, soaking in his strength, his warmth. He feels so damn good, I could stand here like this all night long. "Can I help you make dinner?"

"No, ma'am." He kisses me once more, then leads me to the island, pulls out a stool, and helps me onto it. "You sit here and talk to me while I cook."

"What are you making?"

Beckett grabs a clean towel out of a drawer by the sink, tosses it over his shoulder, and then pulls a knife out of a block and fetches vegetables out of the refrigerator.

"Wait, before I start, *do* you have any allergies?" He leans against the counter, watching me.

"No. No allergies. I don't like mussels, but aside from that, I'll eat just about anything."

"How does roasted chicken with asparagus, carrots, and rice sound?"

"Like I'm at a restaurant." I grin at him. "Seriously, what can I do to help? I'm not too bad in the kitchen myself."

He narrows his eyes at me, making me shiver. Between everything he's generously bought for Riley, his soft kisses, and now beckoning me with a wicked gleam in his eye, I'm a mess of need.

"Come here, Irish."

With pleasure, Beckett.

Chapter Eleven

BECKETT

She circles the island, her lips curved in a sassy smile that has my cock twitching.

"Tell me how I can help. I don't want to sit over there and watch. Let me in on the action."

I tip up an eyebrow and brush my fingers through her thick, red hair. "Oh, I plan to give you some action, Irish."

She laughs, wrinkles her nose, then bounces on her feet. Unable to resist her, I lean in and kiss her on the head before I cross to the fridge.

"I have the chicken ready for the oven, so that part is easy." I even had the oven warming while I went into town to get her, so I take the pot out of the fridge and slip it into the waiting oven.

"I love a man who plans ahead."

"If I don't plan, I don't eat. Because by the time I get back from working a full day on this farm, nothing would be ready. Now, we just need to get the vegetables and rice going while that cooks."

"I'm excellent with a knife."

"Okay, you chop, then." I pass Skyla the knife. Our fingers brush as she takes it from me and bites that plump lower lip. "I'd like a bite of that."

"Of wha—"

I swoop down and kiss her, pull her lower lip between my teeth, then soothe it with my tongue and kiss her some more.

"Mmm, delicious."

"What brought that on?"

"I'm a jealous man, Irish. You bit that lip, and I needed my share."

With her eyes on mine, she swipes her tongue over that lip and hums as if she can still taste me there.

Christ, at this rate, we won't make it through dinner.

"Why don't you have any music on in here?" she asks, turning her attention to cutting the tie off the bunch of asparagus.

"We can do music, but I just never think of it. Birdie left a Bluetooth speaker on the windowsill a few weeks ago. Feel free to use it."

"I will," she says, and gets busy pairing her phone to the little speaker. "Do you have a music preference?"

"Guest's choice." I wink at her and lean against the countertop, my arms crossed, enjoying her while she chooses something on her phone, and then a song I recognize begins to play.

"I love P!nk," she says with a grin, and her hips start

to move with the music. "Have you ever seen this woman in concert?"

"No, have you?"

"Aye, I have, and it's brilliant. She's such an incredible athlete. She dances, yes, but she also *flies.* She's an aerialist, and seeing her in action is just incredible. Whenever she came to New York City, Mik and I were sure to go see her. She's also incredibly kind. I was once lucky enough to meet her."

"I bet you've met all kinds of interesting people."

Walking past her, I brush my hand over her lower back and watch with satisfaction when she curls into the touch. Jesus, I can't keep my hands to myself, and she doesn't seem to mind.

"Many," she agrees. "We've danced for celebrities, royalty, politicians. And most want to meet us after the shows, which is always an honor. I need to wash these."

She's already cut the stems off the asparagus, and as she turns toward the sink, she pauses and kisses my arm right over the bicep since that's as high as she can reach, and it makes me still.

I want to pull her to me and devour her.

"I'm sorry," she says with a frown. "Should I not have done that? You stiffened up. I don't want to make you uncomfortable, but you've been touching me, so I assumed—"

"Whoa." I take the vegetables out of her hands and set them aside, and then lift Skyla and set her on the counter opposite where we're working. "You can touch me anytime, anywhere. I'm free game for you, sweetheart."

She narrows her eyes as if she's searching my face to make sure I'm telling the truth, so I take her hands and put them on my chest.

"Touch me."

Her hands ghost up to my face, to my beard, and I grin at her.

"You like the beard."

"I really do." She wrinkles that nose, and I lean in to kiss it. "It's sexy."

I'll never shave it off for as long as I live if it means I get to have this amazing woman around.

"Beck."

"Yeah?"

"I have to wash the vegetables. I'm a hungry girl."

Grinning, I help her to her feet. "Then we'd better feed you."

Back to work, we move side by side, and it seems so ... effortless. She brushes my arm with her shoulder, and I kiss the top of her head as I walk past. The music brings noise into my often-quiet kitchen, but Skyla brings life. Energy.

How is it possible to feel so at ease with someone so quickly?

Skyla starts to dance to another P!nk song, and I twirl her into my arms and dance with her, making her face light up.

"You have *moves*, Mr. Blackwell."

"That's how you get the pretty girls." I wink at her,

spin her out away from me, and then back in, twirling us around the kitchen. "My mom used to enjoy dancing like this when we were kids."

"And that might be the sweetest thing I've ever heard."

With a laugh, I dip her back, and the buzzer on the oven sounds.

"Good timing." I press a kiss to her lips and release her.

We work together as if we've done it for years. She opens cupboards until she finds plates, and I gather the silverware after pouring some food into Riley's bowl for his dinner.

Before long, we're at the table, our plates full, candles lit, and I tap my wineglass to hers.

"How were your classes today?" I ask.

"They were great. I think I'm going to start offering a barre class for women, and I might even start a modern dance class for women as well. I've had some of the moms tell me that they'd be interested, and I think it would be fun."

"So it's not only ballet that you do?"

Skyla shakes her head, then tips it side to side as if contemplating her answer while eating.

"Ballet is the only dance I've done professionally," she says. "But I've taken so many classes over the years. Jazz, tap, modern, you name it. It's all fun. But ballet is rigorous in different ways than the others. That's not to say that the others aren't difficult or beautiful."

"I get it. Explain what you mean by more rigorous."

She licks her lips and steals a carrot from my plate even though she has plenty on her own plate, and it makes me smile.

She likes to share.

"Well, as a ballerina, I have to contort my body in ways that aren't natural. When I was young, I had a foot stretcher."

I lift an eyebrow at that.

"Yep, it's what it sounds like. You know how we arch our feet and walk on our toes?"

"Sure." I take a bite of my food and grin when she reaches for a piece of my chicken. From now on, we'll eat off one plate.

"I need my feet to arch much farther than what comes naturally."

"That sounds painful."

"Definitely." She nods and eats her own rice. "It's agony, and it never stops. It's not unusual to always be bruised, sore, hurting. My feet are horrible."

"You have cute feet."

"You've only seen them in socks," she reminds me. "And if I have my way, that's the only way you'll ever see them."

I narrow my eyes at her. "No."

"They bleed, or they did, when I danced every day. The toenails are almost completely gone now. I'll never be a woman who comfortably wears a cute peep-toe heel. And that's okay."

"How does your ankle feel?"

That question has her eyes sobering. "It's the same.

Not normal. But I can dance for fun, and I guess that has to be good enough. As I age, my back will hurt, and my knees will ache. It's the price a dancer pays. I'm actually lucky that I didn't get more beat up than I am because of the way Mik would fling me about. He's not gentle."

With my plate cleared, I lean back in the chair. "Is it gentle you want, Irish?"

"I'm not fragile," she says with a chuckle. "And I ate half of your dinner."

"I don't mind. Do you want more?"

"No, I'm full, but you might need a second helping to make up for what I took. Some people get cranky about sharing their food."

I chuckle but shake my head. "I don't. There are far more important things to get cranky about."

"Such as?"

"Hungry children. Oppression. Stalkers."

She snorts. "You're not wrong about that. Also, what about the fact that neither the cereal companies nor the chip companies can get in bed with the Ziploc people? Isn't that a simple phone call?"

Laughing, I thread our fingers together. "You'd think that someone could make that happen."

"It's time to clean up."

"I can do it," I reply, but she's already shaking her head and standing.

"No, we'll get it done faster if we just dig in and do it together. This was delicious. You're an excellent cook."

I'd rather she didn't clean up. Not because I think she's incapable but because I want her to relax. If I've

127

learned anything about this woman over the past few days, she won't take no for an answer, so we clear the table together.

"I like this shirt," she says as she drags her hand down my arm, from shoulder to elbow. "It hugs you in all the right places."

The flirting, the touching, the fucking allure of her all evening has kept my blood simmering, and she continues the teasing while we clean up.

And I fucking *want her.*

She's at the sink, rinsing dishes for the dishwasher, and I walk up behind her, brush her hair aside, and plant my lips on her neck, just below her ear.

"I'm fucking obsessed with this thick, gorgeous hair, Irish."

"Mmm." She tips her head back, leaning against me. "It's a fine spot you've found there."

"Your voice," I whisper against her, "is going to be my undoing."

"It's a cliché to be attracted to the accent, you know."

"It's not just that." I drag my lips to her shoulder and tighten my arms around her. "It's the tone. A little raspy, as if you've just rolled out of bed after a night of fucking. Add in the accent, and you keep me permanently hard."

Her breath catches, and her hands clutch mine. After kicking the dishwasher door closed, I turn Skyla in my arms to look at her stunning face and drag my knuckles down her cheek. I'm trying to be a gentleman and let her set the pace.

"You look conflicted," she whispers.

"I'm trying to go easy. It's only our second date, so if you tell me you want to sleep in the guest room, I'll be fine with that, Irish. You're the boss, but fuck me if I don't want you."

She takes a deep breath, and as her eyes drop to my mouth, she bites that pillow of a lip, and it's almost my undoing.

"Beck." My name on her lips is all I can take.

"Fuck it," I growl, and cupping her face, I cover her mouth with mine. She grips my arms, not pushing me away, and I'm already consumed by her. Planting my hands on the globes of her ass, I lift her. She wraps her long legs around my waist, and I easily carry her through the house. Before ascending the stairs, I pick up her bag.

"You're fecking strong," she says against my lips.

"You're small, baby." I nibble the side of her mouth. "I could carry you around like this all damn day."

When I reach the bedroom, I drop her bag on the floor and carry her to the bed.

"Legs."

She releases me, and when I sit on the edge of the bed, she straddles me and brushes her fingers through my beard, kissing me for all she's worth. She settles her core against my already hard cock, rocking back and forth.

Out of the corner of my eye, I see Riley walk into the room, and he lies on the bed I bought for him.

"You got him *another* bed?"

"He needs one for the bedroom," I reply, then lift her off my lap and to her feet so I can undress her. "Tell me now if you don't want this, Irish."

"If you stop now, I'll be for slashing your tires, Beck."

Gripping the hem of her sweater, I urge it over her head, then cast it aside, and she's left in leggings and a pretty blue lace bra against creamy skin peppered with freckles.

"You're fucking beautiful."

She presses her lips into a line, and her cheeks darken. I push my fingers into the leggings, urging them down her hips and legs, and she steps out of them, leaving her socks on.

But they'll be gone soon.

"I'm going to kiss every freckle."

Her eyebrows climb. "We'll be here for a while, as I've a lot of them."

"I have time." Leaning forward, I kiss her sternum, just between her breasts, then down to her navel. Her hands thread through my hair, holding on as I grip her ass and hips, my big hands spanning her entire backside. She's so small next to me. "I don't want to hurt you."

"Not fragile, remember?" She kisses the top of my head. "You won't hurt me."

"I'm going to devour you." I brush my nose over the front of her pubis, and she moans. "You smell so fucking good, Irish."

My hands are everywhere. I want to touch her all over, all at once, and taste every bit of her. I unclasp her bra, and she lets it fall. My mouth closes around a tight nipple, making her moan again.

Her tits.

They're made for me. Small, perky, and gorgeous.

130

"Love these, Irish," I say reverently.

"They're dancer's breasts," she moans out.

"Perfect, sweetheart." *And I'll keep showing her until she believes me.*

I hook my fingers in her panties and draw them down her legs, but when she steps out of them, I don't cast them aside.

I lift them to my face and inhale.

"Holy feck," she whispers, still gripping my hair in her fist.

"I'm going to kneel in front of you and eat you until you can't fucking remember how to breathe."

Without waiting for a comment, I hit my knees and lift her leg onto my shoulder. I wrap one arm around her waist to hold her steady and drag my nose over her bundle of nerves.

"Beck."

"Hmm?"

I start lightly tonguing her folds, already so wet and ready for me, just ghosting against her skin. Her hips start to move, silently begging me to give her more.

But I want to make this last.

I want to make her go out of her mind.

With one hand braced around her thigh and the other around her waist, I pull her closer and bury my face in her heat, eating as if I'm starved.

"Beckett." Her breathing is hard, her voice rougher than usual, and her core shivers under my mouth. "Please."

"What do you need?"

"Please."

I kiss the inside of her thigh and look up into eyes so bright, I'd swear they were emeralds.

"Tell me what you need."

"Inside me. Fingers, tongue, I don't care."

"Good girl." I bite that soft flesh before I push two fingers inside her, and she cries out. Her muscles contract around my fingers as I press my tongue against her clit, swirling it around, and she comes in a gorgeous wave that leaves me breathless. "God, you're beautiful."

Kissing my way up her body, I lift her onto the bed, but when I move to crawl over her, she shakes her head.

"You get naked," she instructs me.

"Irish—"

"Don't you *Irish* me. I need to see the muscles under that bloody shirt, Beck. Right now."

I quirk up an eyebrow, and she catches her forefinger in her teeth.

"Please."

I cover her without stripping off the clothes and kiss her cheek and her chin. When she closes her eyes, I whisper, "Eyes on me, beautiful girl."

When she obeys, I reward her with a kiss while my hand slides down her side to her hip.

"I'll take my clothes off since you asked nicely, but I don't want you to get this twisted, Irish. I'm in charge in this bedroom."

"Dominant side much?"

"You have no idea. If that's a problem, you need to say so."

She swallows hard, but she's not afraid, and that's *exactly* the reaction I want.

"No problem for me."

"Just tell me if there *is* a problem. I want your words."

"I can do that."

With a nod, I kiss down her body, circle my nose around her navel, and then press a hard, sucking kiss over her pussy before I stand and reach over my head to pull my shirt off.

Her eyes go glassy as they journey down my torso, taking in every inch of muscle and spattering of hair. While she's distracted, I pull her socks off.

"Beck—"

"I want all of you," I reply, lifting one foot to press a kiss in the center of the arch. They definitely show signs of years of hard work, and when I see the embarrassment move through her eyes, I kiss her ankle and then the front of her shin. "You're beautiful, baby. You worked hard, and your feet are the evidence of that. They're your battle scars, and I will kiss every bit of them."

She wrinkles her nose, but she doesn't look embarrassed anymore.

"You want my pants off?"

"Of *course*, I want your pants off."

With a smirk, I unfasten the jeans, push them down my hips, and step out of them. Then I pull my briefs off and stand before her. The way her eyes light up and she bites that lip is a great boost to my fucking ego.

"You might break me after all," she says, her gaze pinned to my cock.

"No way." I fist it, give it a tug, and then crawl back on the bed with her. "You're so wet, baby, you'll take me. But there's no rush."

"Except I want you, Beck. So yeah, there's a rush."

I wrap my lips around her nipple, pluck it through my teeth, and push two fingers inside, and she moans.

"You know," I whisper against her ear, "I used to think your laugh was my favorite sound you make. But then I discovered that fucking amazing moan of yours, and *that* is my favorite sound."

"You're going to ruin me for all men, aren't you?"

I grin, lick up the side of her throat, and nudge my way between her thighs.

"Hell yes, that's exactly what I'm going to do."

Because I've found my way to heaven, and I don't think I'll ever want to let it go.

Chapter Twelve

SKYLA

No one has ever, in my entire life, looked at me the way Beckett is looking at me right now. As if I'm every desire he's ever had in bodily form, and he's going to permanently mark me as his.

And yes, this may be our second date, but I'm not at all against that idea.

I already found him attractive and sexy, but it's also his genuine generosity that has sucked me into his orbit. He bought four beds for my bloody dog, for feck's sake. Who does that? He offered me the spare bedroom ... He's such a good man. And the way he takes control of my body so respectfully? So attentively? I didn't know this level of sexy and gallantry was possible. He's every fantasy I've ever had. I don't know if I'll recover from him.

"Your body is beautiful," he murmurs as he kisses down my neck and over my chest. "If I'm too much, just say so. We'll take it slow."

I moan, but it almost sounds like a whine because I

don't *want* to take it slow. I want him inside me, fucking me into this mattress like a man should.

But I simply bite my lip.

"Say it."

"Why is it that you can read my mind?"

His lips quirk as he takes his cock in his hand and nudges the head through my wetness, up and down, making my hips move with him.

"I can see when you want to say something. Say it. Always. Don't hold back with me, Irish."

"I don't want you to go slow." His eyes narrow, and I swallow hard. "See? You don't want to hear that."

He grips the hair at the back of my neck, and I groan. He presses just the broad tip of his cock into me, then leans forward to whisper in my ear.

"I want your words," he says, exciting me. "Doesn't mean you'll always get what you want, not until I'm ready to give it to you, but I need to know what you need because your pleasure is the only thing that matters to me. For this first time, I have to go slow, baby. I don't want to hurt you."

He kisses me softly, and I melt into the bed. His kisses are like a warm summer day, and I would be perfectly content to have his lips on me all the time.

He grabs a condom from the bedside table and quickly sheaths himself. When he starts to push forward, he doesn't miss my sharp inhale at the sting of him stretching me despite how sopping wet I am.

"That's why," he murmurs, nuzzling my neck. "Trust me, I want to fuck you hard and fast because you feel so damn amazing, but I refuse to hurt you. We have to get you used to me, baby."

"You're incredible." I push my fingers through his hair, down to his beard, and guide his mouth to mine.

I can't get enough of his kisses, of how his whiskers feel on my skin. And as he sinks farther into me, brushing my tongue with his own, he presses deeper down below. My muscles relax, letting him in until finally, he's seated fully, and we're both struggling to breathe.

"You're so damn tight." His voice is thick and rough as he rests his forehead on mine.

"You're so damn *big*." I grip his arse hard. "Please, Beck."

"Tell me." He brushes his nose back and forth against my own. "What do you need?"

"Please *fuck me*."

He grins and starts to move. Not little pulses, but long, firm strokes, and his crown massages my walls. It's the most fulfilling, mesmerizing sensation I've ever felt.

"You're perfect for me," he says, picking up the pace. His hand fists the bedsheets by my head, and his other hand pushes into my hair once more. He's tugging deliciously, and it's commanding. *Claiming.*

It's everything I never knew I needed, and I can't look away from how his muscles move and contract above me. How he looks with that light sheen of sweat covering his tanned skin. He's so *gorgeous.*

Every inch of him is pure male perfection.

I reach down between us and press my finger to my

clit, and he growls. "Yes, baby. Fuck, you clenched even tighter. Touch yourself."

I keep going a little harder. He closes his eyes and grits his teeth, and I can feel him swell inside me. It makes me feel powerful to know that I have this effect on him, and I squeeze him a little harder.

"Christ. Skyla."

"Beck."

"I want you to come for me. Come all over this cock, Irish. Make a mess, sweetheart."

His words, his *voice*, his hand in my hair, and the way his cock fills me leave me no choice. My back bows off the bed, and every muscle in my body contracts as I come apart beneath him.

Beckett roars above me, and then he's coming, filling the condom. He pumps his hips through it all, sending me into another orgasm that has me digging my heels into his arse and my toes curling.

"Bloody shite," I grind out before biting his shoulder.

He's kissing me. My neck, my chin, my chest, and he's pushed his arms under me, holding me to him so tenderly, such a stark contrast to the incredible way he just fucked me, that it brings tears to my eyes.

"Shit, did I hurt you, baby?" He kisses my forehead and down to my cheek.

"No." I shake my head and touch his beard. "No, you didn't hurt me. It might have been just a wee bit intense, that's all."

"Yeah, it was fucking intense." He brushes a piece of

hair off my face, then strokes my cheek with his knuckles. "Are you okay?"

"I'm amazing, Beck." It's been ... a long time since I've had sex. But that? Nothing has ever felt that amazing.

"Good. I'm going to take care of the condom, then I'll take care of you." I frown, but before I can say anything, he kisses me, and he's gone, walking into the en suite bathroom. I hear the toilet flush, then the water running, and he's back with a washcloth. Without a word, he uses the warm cloth to clean me, and then he lifts me, holding me to his chest while he peels the comforter off the bed. He replaces it with a clean one he pulls from a chest at the end of the bed, all while I'm wrapped around him, naked flesh to naked flesh.

"You don't have to carry me." I kiss his cheek, and he simply grunts. So I stay quiet while he covers the bed with the blanket, then tucks us both under it, cradling me to him. "This is nice. Thank you."

"I'm going to check in with you again, and I'll do that often. I can get way more fucking intense than what just happened a minute ago, and it's important to me that you feel safe and cared for. How do you feel, Irish?"

I know he doesn't want to hear *I'm okay.* So I nuzzle his bare chest and take in a deep breath, taking stock of my body.

"I'll be a little sore, but it's nothing I can't handle. My skin feels like it's buzzing. All in all, I'm pretty blissed out."

I feel him grin against my hair, and he tightens his hold on me.

"Those are good things."

I boost up on my elbow so I can see his face. "I don't mind intense, rough sex. Although I can't say that I've ever had it."

His eyes narrow on me.

"Um, I don't think you want to know—"

"I want to know." His thumb brushes over my lips.

"My experiences are pretty vanilla. Soft. Like I'm fragile. But I'm not."

He smiles and licks his lips, and I wonder if he can still taste me there. "No. You're not fragile."

"But I don't want to call you sir if it's all the same to you."

That makes him laugh, and he rolls me onto my back, where he rakes his fingers through my hair. "No, I'm not *a* Dominant. I just have controlling tendencies in the bedroom. I like to be the one in charge. And yeah, sometimes I like it rough."

"Brilliant."

I'm awake. The sun isn't up yet, but Beckett moves behind me. He's still wrapped around me, his front to my back, and he's holding me as if he's afraid I'll disappear, but he's awake.

He brushes his lips against the back of my head, takes a deep breath, and tightens his arms around me in a hug.

Then he's gone.

He rolls away and pads into the attached bathroom, silently closing the door before the light comes on.

I take a look at the time and see that it's before five. My gods, we were up well into the night, talking and having all kinds of intense, amazing sex, so how his internal clock woke him up this early, I'll never know.

It's soothing to listen to Beckett go through his morning routine. I hear the water run, the toilet flush, and then the light goes out, and he crosses the room to what I assume is the closet.

I can see him from the ambient light of the moon coming through the windows, and a few moments later, he emerges in jeans and a clean black T-shirt.

"It's early," I say. He stops in his tracks, then immediately climbs onto the bed behind me and wraps me tightly in his arms once more.

God, nothing in the world feels this good. I'm not entirely sure it should be legal to feel like this.

"I have to go to the barn for a while," he whispers, brushing his lips against my ear and sending a shiver down my spine.

"You didn't get much sleep."

"You're worth every second, baby." He kisses my neck, then my cheek. "Go back to sleep for a while. I'll make breakfast when I get back. I won't be more than a couple of hours."

I twist around so I can see his face and wrap my arms around him.

"Your bed is comfortable. I suppose I could sleep some more."

"Good." He presses a sweet kiss to my lips and nudges my nose with his. "Rest. Stay cozy. I'll see you in a bit."

But he doesn't leave. He tucks my head under his chin and hugs me close, and I can't help but moan at how good it feels to be in this warm bed with Beckett wrapped around me.

"I thought you had to work."

He chuckles, making his chest shake against my cheek. "I do. I'm going."

With one last kiss on my head, he rolls away and strolls out the door. When I hear the back door downstairs open and close, I get up to use the bathroom myself, then hurry back to bed. Riley follows, jumps up, and snuggles me, and I slip back to sleep.

When I wake again, the sun is up, and I stretch over to check the time.

I got another hour and a half of sleep.

"We should get up," I say to Riley as I scratch him on the head. "Come on, big boy. Did you sleep well, then? You sure did snore your heart out."

I climb out of bed and slip on some clean jeans and a jumper, twist my hair back into a long braid, then lead Riley downstairs.

"You stay close," I warn him as I let him out the back door to do his business. I watch him closely, making sure he doesn't venture too far or get distracted by wildlife. He never has before, but these are new surroundings for him.

But my boy is solid, coming right back to me after relieving himself, and we return to the kitchen.

"Beck had to go to work early, so we should make him breakfast," I inform the canine as I fill his food dish and set it out for him. Then I take stock of what Beck has in the fridge and pantry.

The man has a little bit of everything. This isn't a bachelor's kitchen, with just beer and chips. He obviously cooks for himself often.

So I pull out the farm-fresh eggs—I could hear the hens when I took Riley out, and I can't wait to meet them later—and get to work chopping vegetables for an omelet.

It's not what I'd typically eat before I came to the States, but I can see the appeal. Loaded with veggies, eggs, and cheese, it's a filling breakfast rich in protein and nutrients. Ma used to have Chef make this with sausage, bacon or beans, and black pudding, all separated rather than combined, but I've adapted to this as a fairly quick alternative.

As I'm grating a potato for hash browns, my phone rings, startling me.

"Hey, Mik." I set it to speakerphone and go back to grating. "And how are you this fine morning?"

He's silent for a moment. "And who is this man that has you sounding this way?"

I smirk. "I don't know what you're talking about."

"I know you, and I know this voice. Tell me."

"You haven't come to visit me, so you wouldn't know him," I remind Mik. "But he's someone new in my life, and I'm quite smitten. That's all I'll say. Now, what are you about?"

"We need to talk." I pause in my grating and frown.

"About what?"

"I want you to listen to me, and do not interrupt, and do not tell me no until you've heard what I have to say. Promise me, Skyla."

"Now you're making me nervous."

"Promise."

"Yes, fine, I promise. Now, talk before I have an anxiety attack."

He takes a deep breath, and I frown as I cross to the sink, where I can look outside. The mountains look beautiful out here, and I can see chickens walking around the yard. *And to think Beck gets to see this every day.* It makes me a wee bit jealous.

"We've been asked to dance *one performance* of *Giselle* in London for the coronation of King Frederick."

I scowl at the poor chickens. "That's ridiculous. Why wouldn't The London Ballet Company be asked to do that?"

"Because we are the best, of course. And because he saw us perform it once, and he loved it and wants us."

"*Us*, as in, you and me?"

"Of course. There is no one else."

I sigh and close my eyes. "Mik. I love you so much, and I won't lie and say that I don't miss dancing with you because you know I do. But I *can't.* My ankle isn't where it should be."

"It's been almost a year since your injury," he says,

frustration heavy in his voice. "No doctor will tell you that you can't dance."

"No, in fact, I've been given clearance to dance, but that doesn't mean that the joint is strong enough for what I'd have to put it through to get into shape for a performance like this. Mik, I've gained weight."

"How much weight?"

"Ten pounds."

"Psh, you can take that off. Rehearsal alone will take that right off you, and you know it. Tighten up your diet, malishka."

Restrict my diet again. Go hungry again. Hate every extra pound, all over again.

"Mik—"

"I said don't say no. It is *one* performance, Skyla. I am not asking you to move back to New York City and pick up where you left off. It is one night."

"Sure, one night that will require weeks of work, and you know I won't go to the city to rehearse with you. I will *not* do it. I live here. My business is here."

"And your man is there," he finishes for me.

"Yes. Frankly, my entire life is here, and if you'd move here, my life would be complete."

He scoffs at that. We both know that Mik will never leave New York City.

"What if I come there for rehearsal?"

I blink, staring blindly out the window. "You'd do that?"

"This is important. We never got to say goodbye,

malishka. We never had our final curtain call, our moment together."

No, because we didn't know that that last night would be the end of it. We had no way of knowing.

Water fills my eyes as I take a shaky breath.

"After more than a decade of work together, we deserve this. We *both* deserve it."

"When do I have to let you know?"

"The sooner, the better. The performance will be in June."

"*Mik.*" I shake my head. "We'd have to start rehearsals in just a few weeks."

"That is why you need to let me know. I will hound you about it. It is happening."

"You know I don't like being handled, Mikhail."

"Yes, you do. I have to go. And seriously, malishka, please consider it. We need it."

He hangs up, and I lean on the countertop, still looking outside.

"You should do it."

With a gasp, I whirl around and clutch my hand to my chest, then scowl down at Riley.

"You're supposed to warn me of these things."

"You were pretty deep in thought," Beck says. He's leaning against the wall across the room, his arms crossed over his chest, watching me.

"How much did you hear?"

"Most of it," he admits, and I get back to work on breakfast.

"I hope you don't mind that I took over your kitchen."

"I don't mind at all." He crosses the room and leans on the island across from me, watching as I grate the last of the potato. "What are your hesitations when it comes to this? Let's talk about it."

Blowing out a breath, I pour some oil in a pan and set it on the stove. I light the burner, glad I have something to do with my hands while I talk.

"My ankle, for starters."

"You mentioned that it's healed."

"Yeah, but like I told you last night, it's not the same. I've done the stretches and exercises, but it'll never be as strong as it was. When I jeté, it feels like it might twist out from under me. That makes me uncertain, and there's no room for that in a performance."

"Okay." I feel him round the island so he's facing me while I work at the stove. "What else?"

"I really don't want to admit this to you."

He's quiet, so I glance over and see him watching, waiting, with an eyebrow raised.

"I've gained weight."

He shakes his head, ready to dismiss that, but I continue.

"Look, I know I'm a thin woman, but my body isn't professional dancer-ready anymore. I don't restrict my eating. I don't go hungry to keep the extra pounds off."

His hand slides across my lower back, and that simple touch makes my shoulders drop, taking away some of the tension.

"Eating disorders run rampant in show business. That's no secret. Mine was never as bad as it could have been because I'm naturally long and lean, but some women *killed themselves* to be the shape of a ballerina. It's disgusting, but it's part of the business. Anyway, I've enjoyed eating mostly what I want without worrying if Mik would feel it later when he had to lift me."

"It's ten pounds," he says, but I shake my head again.

"It might as well be fifty." With the potatoes almost done, I crack eggs and whip them up for the omelet. "Physically, this will be grueling. Emotionally, it'll be a strain. I don't know if I want to put myself through it again."

"But part of you wants to."

Glancing up, I stare into his eyes and feel my chest warm. "I miss it so much."

"You should at least try," he says and leans in to kiss my forehead. "Because he's right. You didn't get to say goodbye properly to something you love so much. Take this for you. Take it, and go out on *your* terms, not what was given to you by The Asshole."

I bite my lip as I work the eggs in the pan. "I'll think about it. If he wasn't willing to come here, it would be an immediate no."

"But he's willing." His hand glides from the back of my neck, down my spine, to my arse. "Because he needs it too. But don't do it for anyone but you. Selfishly, I'd love to see you dance."

I grin, and when he wraps his arms around me from behind, I sigh with happiness. I'd love for Beckett to see me dance too. Does that mean he'd want to fly to London to see that, though? What we have is so new, and like I said, the rehearsals alone will be time-consuming and grueling. Do I want to add that to this new relationship? *If that's what we're calling this?*

But then I think about Mik's plea. *Giselle* in front of King Frederick. That's ... such an honor. I understand his desire to do this. And he's not wrong about how we finished. We didn't get to say goodbye to years of dedication, sweat, tears, and joy. That, too, was stolen from us.

And then there's Beckett's insight.

"Because he's right. You didn't get to say goodbye properly to something you love so much. Take this for you. Take it, and go out on your terms ..."

He's surprisingly wise about something he potentially has no experience with, and that makes me appreciate his words more. I need to think on it, though. I fear risking an additional injury, and there really is no place in professional dancing for uncertainty. For now, though, I want to feed the beautiful man beside me. *That* I can do.

"Breakfast is ready."

"Good. I'm starved, and we have lots to see today."

Chapter Thirteen

BECKETT

Several hours later, I lead Skyla to the horse barn, the final stop on the farm tour. I hang back as she immediately walks over to my horse, Maverick, and pets him on the nose.

"What's your name?"

"That's Maverick," I tell her. "He's mine."

"How many horses do you have?"

"About ten."

I've never been as fucking attracted to a woman as I am to *this* woman. She's been excited all morning, asking intelligent questions about milk and processing and the animals themselves. She loves the chickens and asked if she could check for eggs whenever she was here.

I don't think I'll ever have it in me to ever tell her no. She can hunt for eggs all day long if it makes her happy.

"Have you ever ridden a horse?" I ask.

"When I was a girl," she says, nodding as she rubs her hand down Maverick's neck. "I'd be rusty. When I was under contract, I wasn't allowed to ride or do anything that might cause an injury."

"I'm surprised they didn't insist that you walk around in bubble wrap."

She snorts and wrinkles her nose, and I can't keep away from her anymore, so I cross to her and grab her braid, loving how soft her hair feels under my palm.

"They probably would have loved that idea," she agrees, leaning back into my touch.

"It's sexy as fuck having you on my farm, Irish."

She turns away from the horse and loops her arms around my waist, staring up at me with happy eyes and lips that I could lose myself in.

"I enjoy being here," she says softly. "We should probably go back to the house and check on Riley."

She requested that we leave the dog at the house so she didn't have to worry about him and could fully enjoy the tour. It surprised me and made me feel good because that meant she trusted her safety with me.

"In a minute. First, I think I'll fuck you in this barn."

Her jaw drops, her pupils dilate, and her arms tighten around me in response.

"Don't hate that idea, do you?"

"No, I don't hate it," she admits, "but someone could walk in. You have employees all over the place."

I gave explicit instructions for everyone to steer clear of this barn for the next hour, but I don't tell her that.

Instead, I grin down at her.

"Then you'd better be quiet, Irish."

She hums deep in her throat as I lower my mouth to

hers, her lips already open and ready for me. She purrs—*fucking purrs*—and grips my shirt with her fists before gliding them around to the front of my jeans, and I steal both hands in mine, then kiss them.

"If you touch me," I growl against her neck as I keep her hands in mine between us, "I'll lose control, and I'm doing my best to keep it together here."

"Well, damn," she whispers, making me grin against her skin. I nibble her pulse point and glide my tongue up to the shell of her ear.

"You smell so fucking good."

Skyla whimpers, and it makes my cock twitch in my jeans.

"I'm going to make you come undone. I'm going to make you feel things that you never have before. Keep your hands at your sides."

Letting her hands go, I frame her face so I can kiss her, but her sweet little hands land on my stomach, and it makes me feral.

Jesus, just one touch from this woman, and I want to wreck her in the most carnal, delicious ways. But I don't want to send her running for the hills.

"Nope." After having her hands removed once more, Skyla pouts, sticking out her lower lip, and I bite it. "Since you won't follow directions, I'm going to restrain you."

I'm staring into her lust-filled eyes to get her reaction, and she bites that pillow of a bottom lip as her eyes widen.

"If you ever want me to stop, you say so, and it immediately ends. Understand?"

"Yes, Beckett."

Jesus fucking Christ on a stick.

My eyes slowly close as my blood heats, and I blindly reach out for a leather horse lead and guide Skyla over to a pole in the middle of the room.

"Grab the pole."

She frowns, her eyes bouncing between me and the rough wood. "How?"

I move up behind her and let my hand drift over her hip and up her side, and she trembles under my hand. "I want you to bend over and grab that pole for me."

"I still have my jeans on."

Grinning against her neck, I drag my nose back and forth over her skin, making it pebble up in goose bumps.

"I don't fucking care, Irish."

Letting out a shaky breath, she leans forward, sticking her perfect peach of an ass out, and grabs the pole.

"I'm going to tie you there," I inform her. "Okay?"

"Yes." There's no hesitation in her breathless response, so I wrap the thin leather around her wrists in a figure eight before securing it around the pole. I check to make sure that she can't slip out of it but also that it's not cutting off her blood flow.

"Good girl," I murmur, leaning in to kiss her shoulder. I love that I have control of her. That I can pleasure and enjoy her until I'm ready for her to return the favor.

Her sweatshirt has ridden up, exposing the smooth

flesh of her lower back, and I press wet kisses there, making her moan. Reaching around, I unfasten her jeans and work them over her ass and down her hips to mid-thigh, where I'll leave them.

"The air feels cool," she says, her voice thick with arousal.

"I'm going to warm you up." I press more wet kisses over her ass cheeks on both sides, then squat behind her, spread her open, and push my face into the sweetest pussy I've ever fucking tasted.

"Oh feck," she groans, her hips moving against me.

"Stay still," I warn her and grin when she stills. I lick her from her clit to that small puckered muscle at the top and back down again. Her head hangs down, her finger-tips white against the pole. "You're already soaked for me, Irish."

"I know. Christ Jesus, Beck, I've never ... Oh God." My tongue is inside her now, lapping and pushing.

"You've never what?"

"Felt anything like you."

"Mmm." Pushing one finger inside her, I suck on her hard clit, and her hips start to move again, earning her a slap on one side of her ass. Not hard enough to hurt but hard enough to get her attention.

Skyla gasps and tries to look back at me as I soothe the skin with my palm.

"*Beckett.*"

"I warned you to stay still," I remind her and go back to sucking on her, feeling the rush of wetness coming from her pussy. "You're unbelievable. So fucking beautiful. Your body was made for me."

I stand, two fingers inside her now, so I can check in on her. She's biting that lip, her eyes are closed, and she's so damn gorgeous, I know I can't hold back much longer.

Quickly, I unfasten and unzip my jeans and pull my already hard and weeping cock out, brush it up and down through her soaking wet folds, and she moans again.

"Yes," she says over and over again. "Yes. Please."

"I fucking love it when you ask for it." I'm gripping her hips so tightly that there will be bruises later. I push inside her until I'm bottomed out, and we're both moaning in pleasure. "Do you know how perfect you are?"

With a whimper, she drops her head again.

"It's so good, Beck."

Her voice and her tight little pussy are more than I can take. I'm pushing in and out of her so hard and fast, I'm surprised the pole doesn't give out and make the barn collapse. Reaching up, I pull the hair tie free and loosen her hair, then fist the strands at the nape of her neck and tug, making us both groan.

"I love your hair."

"Harder," she whispers, surprising me.

"You want me to fuck you harder, Irish?"

"Aye, fuck me harder." The accent is thicker with her arousal, pushing me closer to my climax. Shit, I need her to come.

With one hand still in her hair, I reach around with my other hand and press my fingertips to her clit, and she shudders around me, making my eyes roll back.

"Oh God. Beck. Fuck, just like that."

"Come all over me, baby. Go over. Let go."

Her entire amazing body tightens, clenching around me, and her walls ripple around my cock. Just as she's coming down from her climax, I pull out, fist my cock, and walk around to her face.

"Open that pretty little mouth, and let me fill it up."

Without hesitation, she follows direction and greedily wraps her gorgeous lips around the crown, sucking, and my balls lift and tighten. The next thing I know, I'm erupting inside her mouth, and she's moaning happily, taking every last drop down her throat.

"You're such a good girl." My hand is fisted in the back of her hair again, but I'm not pushing hard. I don't want to choke her.

As she's licking my shaft, I'm untying her with one hand, and when she's free, she immediately wraps her hands around my cock. I swear to God, I've died and gone to heaven.

With my knuckle under her chin, I guide her up to standing and pull her jeans up, kissing her with all I have.

"You're incredible," I whisper against her lips.

"I was about to say the same to you." She's grinning, those lust-filled eyes shining as I tuck myself back into my pants and help her fasten hers. "Well, that was a lovely way to end the tour."

She rubs at her wrists, and I gently take them in my hands, frowning down at the red marks from the leather.

"Let's go back to the house." I kiss her wrists gently and pull her to me in a big hug. "I need to take care of you."

"I believe you just did."

I laugh at that, then kiss the top of her head. "I'll feel better if I get you in a shower and get some salve on these marks."

"They're not so bad." She stops talking when I scowl at her. "Okay. Please take care of me."

She pushes her fingers into my beard, and I lean into her.

"You *need* that, don't you?" Her voice is gentle as she scratches my whiskers, and now I'm the one who wants to purr.

"What?"

"The aftercare part."

"Yeah, Irish." I kiss her nose, then her lips before leading her out of the barn. "I need it."

Just as I requested, no one is around as we head to the farmhouse. Riley's asleep on one of his beds, but he greets us at the back door.

"I'll let him out really quick," Skyla says, and we wait together as the dog does his business. She makes a face. "My scalp is sweaty. I feel bad that you had your hands on it."

"I got you that way." I smirk at her and shake my head. "Nothing about that isn't sexy, but we'll get you in the shower and clean us both up."

When Riley's done, he lumbers back inside, and I lead Skyla upstairs. Riley lies on his bed, and I move into the bathroom to start the shower so it has time to warm.

"How do you feel?" I ask Skyla as I join her in the bedroom. I take the hem of her sweatshirt and pull it over her head.

"I'm great. You?"

"Never better." I kiss the ball of her shoulder and continue undressing her.

"Can I touch you now?"

Smiling down at her, I nod, and she starts to pull my shirt out of my jeans, returning the favor of getting me naked. I love the fact that she knows to wait, knows to ask. I'd never demean her or take advantage of that trust. And I'll never deny her unless I'm in the middle of drawing out her pleasure. When was the last time I found someone so sexually compatible? *I doubt I have, if I'm honest.*

Once our clothes are shed, we get into the shower, and I get to work.

I need to take care of her. Make sure she knows that she's always the focus. Her needs. Her pleasure. Her satisfaction.

"You're very good with your hands," she says with a sigh as I rub a sudsy washcloth over her body.

"I'm touching you," I reply, using the cloth to quickly wash myself. Then I can move on to what I *really* want to do. "Now, back up to the spray. I'm going to wash your hair."

"Oh, that sounds brilliant." She doesn't hesitate to tip her head back to get her long red hair wet.

I take my time massaging the shampoo into her thick strands and scalp. Her hands land on my sides, anchoring her so she doesn't wobble.

Her touch sets me on fire as if she's branding me.

"I'm going to say it again because it's worth repeating. You're *excellent* with your hands, Beck."

I lean down to kiss her chin, then urge her back again so I can rinse the shampoo from her hair. I repeat the process with the conditioner. It's not easy to get all the soap out of her long and thick hair when there's so much of it.

Once we're both clean, I turn off the water, then grab a towel to wrap her hair in before using another to dry us both off.

"First thing's first," I murmur, loving the softness of her skin beneath my fingertips. "I want you to put on the comfiest clothes you have with you. If you need to borrow a shirt of mine, that's okay, too."

"I wouldn't pass it up."

She pads to the bag at the end of the bed and pulls on clean underwear and some leggings, and I walk into the closet to grab her one of my old T-shirts, which, by the look of sheer joy on her gorgeous face, I'd say makes her happy. She immediately pulls it over her head and grins.

"It's soft, and it smells like you."

"Comfy?"

"Aye."

"Good. Come on." Taking her hand, I lace our

fingers and lead her back into the bathroom. There's a vanity space with a stool that I only use when Birdie's staying the night because my niece thinks it's fancy. I pull out the stool, and gesture for Skyla to take a seat. Then I move to the medicine cabinet and grab the ointment I need for her wrists.

"Oh, I don't need that." She shakes her head. "These will be gone by morning. It wasn't that tight."

"You'll heal better with this." I kiss her forehead and dab some of the ointment on my fingers, then soothe them over the small friction burns. "I'm sorry I left marks on you."

"I'm not." She bites that plump lower lip and grins. "Not at all. That was bloody hot."

With a chuckle, I set the ointment aside, then tip her face up to kiss her.

"Yes, it was fucking hot. You're not ready to run yet?"

"Why would I do that? I'd miss out on all of the sexy fun."

I search her eyes, but I can see that she means it, so I take her shoulders in my hands and turn her to face the mirror.

It only takes me a moment to grab some earbuds and the blow-dryer, along with a comb. I tuck the earbuds in her ears, causing her to look at me with surprise.

"You should relax and listen to whatever you want. They're paired to my phone." I open the phone and hand it to her. "Play whatever you're in the mood for. Music, podcasts, videos, I don't care."

"Beckett." The word is quiet as she looks up at me in the mirror.

"Go ahead." As she lowers her gaze to my phone and starts to thumb through the music app, I take her hair out of the towel and comb it through, making sure there aren't any snags. I clip half of its weight to the top of her head, then flip on the blow-dryer to start on the bottom portion.

Skyla's hair is *thick*. Heavy. And so fucking soft, I'll enjoy every minute of drying it for her.

She must have found something she wants to listen to because she sets the phone down and sits quietly, watching me in the mirror as I carefully run my fingers through the strands, blowing it dry before I pull more sections down and continue the same steps.

I've never done this before. Sure, I've blow-dried Birdie's hair when she's stayed over, but I've never been so invested in a partner to want to blow-dry her hair. *Why Skyla?* What is it about this woman that has me pulling out all the stops, so keen for her to want more of me?

I've no idea, but I do know that I want to keep her here, and I've never felt that before. She's so ... perfect for me. For this farm. Not that I'll tell her that, as I'm sure that would send her running. I'll keep that to myself for now.

When it's all finished, Skyla tugs the earbuds out of her ears, places them in the case, and stands. She loops her arms around me and hugs me close. I'm still watching in the mirror. She fits perfectly against me, her head not quite meeting my chin and her cheek resting just over my heart.

"Thank you," she murmurs. "That felt *incredible*. You can do that every week when I wash my hair if you want."

"You wash your hair once a week?"

She nods against me. "Yep. If you want a new hobby, you've got it."

I smirk and plant my lips on the top of her head, breathing her in. I fucking love that she intends to keep me around long enough to pamper her week after week. "I would love that, actually."

She jolts back and frowns up at me.

"I was kidding. Of course, I don't expect you to do that all the time."

"I'll do it anyway." I shrug and kiss her lips. "Come on, let's make some dinner, then cuddle up for the evening."

"Can we watch reality TV?"

She walks out of the bathroom ahead of me, and I laugh as I follow her. "Absolutely not. What's wrong with an action movie?"

"One action movie for every two episodes of *Love is Blind*."

I narrow my eyes at her. "What is that?"

"Trust me, you'll love it."

Chapter Fourteen

SKYLA

The movie he chose isn't horrible. There's a lot of gratuitous blood and a lot of running, but the hero is handsome, so there's that.

We had another delicious meal of leftovers from last night, keeping it simple, and we've been curled up on his sectional couch with pillows and blankets, watching TV for the better part of an hour. It's already dark outside, but Beckett closed the blinds, so it feels like we're in a cozy cocoon.

My scalp still practically tingles with joy from the way he tenderly washed and dried my hair for me. It felt a million times better than going to a salon, and from the look on his face while he did it, I'd say that he might have enjoyed it more than I did.

And that's saying something because I wasn't joking when I said he could do that as often as he wants.

I lean further into Beck's side, nuzzling his chest

against my cheek. I love how solid he feels against me, how warm and strong, and he smells *so fecking good*.

His lips are planted in my hair, and there's an explosion on the screen when suddenly, everything goes black. We're shrouded in immediate silence and darkness, and my heart kicks up as panic settles over my nerves.

"Shit," Beckett mutters as he stands, probably to check what happened.

It's so dark.

It feels like an elephant is sitting on my chest, and my side, where he was, is now ice-cold without his warmth. I start to shake, and the breath leaves my lungs.

Riley starts to whine.

"It's okay, boy," Beck says from across the room.

"He's looking for the lights." I swallow hard. My voice sounds thready. "He thinks he has to turn on the lights."

"Can you call him to you?" he asks, and I can hear the concern in his deep voice.

"Riley, come."

The dog jumps onto the couch and covers my lap. He's a huge, heavy dog, but I need him right now because this absolute darkness ...

I bolt upright in bed. What's that noise? "Feck, where's my bloody phone?"

There's no light. I can't see my hand in front of my face, and I am not okay. I. Need. Light.

Is someone in my apartment?

"It's okay, Irish," Beckett says, keeping his voice calm. "I'm grabbing candles right now. Take a deep breath."

But I can't. I can't fecking breathe, and I need lights. I need to be able to see.

Someone is there with me. Hovering in the darkness. Oh God, someone is here. That scent. I know that cologne.

"Hey, talk to me," Beck says. I wish I could see him.

"Can't." I try to suck in air. Riley whines and shoves his head in my chest.

Finally, there's the flicker of a lighter, and a candle is lit. Beckett lights at least half a dozen more and sets them around the room, casting a soft glow, and then crosses back to me and sits beside me, but he doesn't pull me to him. He takes my hand in his, squeezing it tight.

"I need you to breathe, Irish." His eyes are pinned to mine, and he takes a deep inhale. I know I'm supposed to mimic him, but my lungs just don't want to fill. "Tell me three things you see, Skyla."

I frown but look around. "The pillow."

"Good."

I lick my lips. "That plant."

"One more." He's rubbing his free hand up and down my arm.

"A book."

"Good. Three things you can feel."

"Scared."

"No, baby, physical things. Do you feel the couch under you?"

I swallow hard and nod. "The couch. Riley shaking. Your hands."

"Good girl." He leans in and kisses my cheek. "Breathe, baby. Take a deep breath for me, okay?"

KRISTEN PROBY

Finally, I'm able to fill my lungs with a shaky breath.

"That's my girl. Tell me three things you can hear."

I close my eyes and listen. "The wicks burning in the candles. The wind outside. Oh God, is that why the power is out?"

"One more thing, beautiful girl. Tell me one more thing."

"Your voice."

"Excellent. Another deep breath for me."

He's really good at this. At calming me down.

"Look in my eyes, Skyla."

Following his orders, I gaze into his eyes, and feel my heart start to slow down just as my eyes fill with tears.

"Hey, hey, hey." Beck takes my face in his hands and leans in to press his lips to my cheek, simply holding me there. "It's okay."

"I'm so embarrassed."

"Shh. No, Irish. Don't be. You already told me about this. You're doing so great."

"I'm a fecking mess."

"You're gorgeous." He brushes his fingers through my hair and tips his forehead against mine. "Take another deep breath."

We do it together, sucking in a long breath, and when I exhale it all out, I'm no longer shaking.

I rub Riley and hold him against me in a hug as Beckett pulls back just a bit.

"You're a good boy." I kiss Riley's cheek and rub his sides, and he calms down, too.

166

"I'm getting a fucking generator," Beckett says, his voice a little harder now that I'm calming down.

"You don't have to—"

"It's happening." He shakes his head, and when Riley moves off my lap, Beckett pulls me into his, holding me tight. "I'm so sorry you were scared."

"It's not your fault." Brushing my fingertips through his whiskers, I kiss him gently, feeling like I need to soothe him the way he is me. "It's my own PTSD from a terrifying, life-altering night, Beck. This was not as bad as it could have been."

His eyes close as he wraps his arms tightly around me and holds me to him in a hug that has me calming.

The way this man touches me is extraordinary. We've only just started seeing each other, yet I feel so connected to him, I can't imagine not being here like this.

Is it love at first sight? Is it just sexual chemistry? I have no idea, but I'm thankful. Few men would do what Beckett just did. Few men would know how to reach someone in the middle of a panic attack.

Few men are like Beckett Blackwell.

"Okay, we can't watch TV," Beck says as he kisses my neck. "I'll read to you if you want. Did you bring a paperback or one of those doodads with e-books on them?"

Pulling back, I stare at him in surprise. "You will?"

"Sure. Why not?"

A thrill zips up my spine, and I bite my lip in anticipation. "Wow, okay. You're going to *read to me*?"

"Don't look now, but I think that turns you on, Irish."

"Oh, it absolutely, without a doubt, turns me on. I did bring my Kindle, and it's upstairs in my bag."

He kisses me before setting me on the couch, and then he's jogging through the house and up the stairs, and I have to take a second to pull in another deep breath. The candles make the room look romantic, with the flicker of the flames, and now it doesn't seem scary at all. It feels sweet and soft, and with the promise of Beckett reading me a spicy book, I'm completely content.

I hear his footsteps coming down the stairs, and he returns with the device in his hand. He turns it over and grins at the back.

"*Beg, Baby Girl*," he says, reading one of the stickers aloud, and then raises an eyebrow and looks up at me.

Pressing my lips together, I shrug. "I told you I like spicy books."

"Mm-hmm." He sits next to me and pulls me against his side, then passes me the Kindle so I can wake it up for him.

"You can start this book from the beginning if you want, but I'm not too far in yet."

"I'm fine. Give me a quick report of what's happened so far. Also, I like that this screen lights up. Makes it less dark in here for you."

I kiss his biceps as warmth moves through me. Being taken care of feels good.

"It's called *Dom* by S.J. Tilly. Mafia romance. The hero's name is Dominic, and hers is Valentine. Val for short. They met in an airport, happened to be on the same flight, and sat next to each other."

"Handy," he says, making me laugh.

"And entertaining, I might add. The whole flight has basically been foreplay, the sexual tension is *thick*, and now they're in the next airport, and he just took her into a breastfeeding pod."

Beckett frowns down at me. "Is she a mom?"

"No." I bite my lip and shake my head, and I want to smile because I know exactly what's about to happen.

"Then why ... oh."

"Yeah. That's as far as I got."

"Irish, are you telling me that I'm diving right into a sex scene?"

"I don't know, I haven't read it yet." I giggle when he pins me in a stare that clearly says *you have got to be kidding me.* He clears his throat and starts to read.

The main characters, Dom and Val, go into the pod, and they are so bloody attracted to each other, it's palpable. She gives him permission to touch her. They come together, kissing and making out, and it's hot.

Beckett squirms and has to clear his throat again, and I lean my cheek against his biceps and close my eyes, imagining this intimate scene. Beckett's voice is far sexier than what I'd been hearing in my head for Dom. It slides over me like warm molasses as he reads aloud. *Imagine if he was a book narrator. Women would not be able to put the book down.*

Listening to him describe the bench inside the room, her naked body as she straddles Dom, what she's experiencing while he's suckling her nipples is enough to make my breath catch. I feel like I'm there as Dom makes them both crazy with his attention to her breasts. Beckett's almost growling out the words as she unfastens his shirt so she can see his tattoos.

The hero is *hot*. Covered in tattoos that I can clearly see in my head as Beckett reads. And then it starts to get *really good* and Beck's voice gets rougher.

Dom strokes one finger up the length of my slit but doesn't push in.

"I can't wait to be inside you." His finger slides the length again.

I pull his belt free from the buckle.

"I'm so tempted …" The first inch of his finger presses inside me. But he pulls it back out.

I whimper while I undo the button on his pants.

"But if I start now, you'll be coming on my hand." He traces his finger back up toward my clit.

I pull his zipper down.

"And I want you coming on my cock."

I pull down the top of his boxers, and his dick pops free.

It's so big and thick that it audibly slaps up against his hard stomach.

Beckett stops and stares down at me. "Really?"

"Hey, yours is that big," I remind him. His eyes narrow on me, and his jaw tightens. I glide my hand over his rippling abs and feel them tense under my touch. "And your stomach is hard."

He smirks and then continues.

Dom slides his other hand down my back, down the crease of my ass, and keeps going until his fingertips touch below me. One hand in front and one behind.

"Hold my cock steady," Dom demands as he lifts me.
He lifts me off his lap.

"Hmm, nice," I murmur and wiggle in my seat. "We love a strong man."

"If you keep talking like that, Irish ..."

"Read." I kiss his biceps, and he shifts his attention back to the book.

His thighs are so thick, and I'm so much shorter, that even on my knees, I can't get the height I need to get his dick inside me.

So he's lifting me. By the vagina. One hand on either side of my entrance, holding me open.

"Enough." Beckett tosses the Kindle aside. He pulls me over his lap until I'm straddling him, and his hands are firm on my arse, holding me against him.

His cock is *hard* in his sweats, and I grind down on him as he pushes his hips up and groans in my mouth.

"You'll have to finish reading to me later," I whisper against his lips. "If this is what happens."

"It's your sweet little body pressed against me, and the way you're squirming ... and I heard you licking your lips. Fuck me, Irish, you'd tempt a fucking saint, and I never claimed to be a saint. I need to be inside you more than I need to breathe."

He rips my leggings so effortlessly that it makes me gasp.

"Take my cock out, baby."

I bite my lip and do as I'm told, pushing the elastic of his sweats down and revealing his hard, thick cock. I can't help but chuckle when it does, indeed, slap against his hard abs.

"Told you," I mutter as he lifts me and pulls my panties to the side to rub his fingertips over my opening.

"Fuck, you're wet."

"I want you. It's as simple as that," I reply, but then he's swearing under me. "What's wrong?"

"I don't have a condom down here."

Earlier, he simply came in my mouth. And that was bloody sexy as hell. No one has ever done that before.

"I'm on birth control," I inform him and bite my lip, suddenly feeling shy. "And it had been *years* before you."

He sits up and cups my face, kissing me deeply. "Are you sure, baby?"

"Yes, Beck."

Without another word, he presses his cock against me, and I'm so bloody wet that he slides right in. The stretch is delicious now and doesn't sting like it did last night, and I can't help the moan that comes out of my mouth as I sink over him.

"God, you take me so well," he groans, and I clench around him. "So damn tight."

I start to move, and I realize that this is the first time that we've been together and I've had any sort of physical control, so I take advantage of it. I roll my hips, grab the couch behind him for leverage, and start to move faster, up and down.

"Listen to that," he murmurs before lifting my shirt and tossing it aside, then licking one of my tight nipples. "You're goddamn delicious."

The next thing I know, he's looped his arm around my waist, and I'm on my back, my legs pushed up, my knees into my chest, with Beck's face in my core, and an orgasm is *right there,* ready to consume me.

"Beck!"

"That's right." He licks and sucks, and I thrash my head from side to side. "God, you're so fucking wet for me. You taste incredible."

His mouth is going to be my undoing.

"You're not going to come on my face, Irish."

I hate to break it to him, but it sure feels like I am.

"You're going to come on my cock."

"Beck."

I'm tugging on his shoulders, needing him to move up and push inside me. He hears my unspoken request and kisses his way up my body. He bites a nipple, then has my legs over his shoulders, and he's inside me again, kissing me.

"Taste yourself. I want you to taste how incredible you are, baby."

It's too much. His words, his cock, and the taste of myself overwhelm me, and I swear that I explode into a million pieces, seeing stars and feeling like I'm breaking apart.

With a roar, Beck follows me over, rocking through his climax, and then we're a tangled, heaving, spent beautiful mess.

And when he raises his head to smile down at me, my heart catches.

"If you're trying to kill me"—I have to swallow hard —"you're doing a good job of it, *a ghrá.*"

He smirks and drags his nose down my jawline, making me shiver. "What did that mean?"

I swallow hard again and frown. I didn't mean to say that out loud.

"It's just an Irish term of endearment."

He growls against my skin. "Did you know that your accent gets heavier when you're turned on?"

I smirk and hug him to me as another shiver rolls through me. "Doesn't surprise me."

"Are you cold?" he asks.

"No, those are post-orgasmic tremors."

He snorts and sucks on my neck, and that only makes my core tighten again.

"Beck."

"Yes, Irish?"

"You're heavy."

He doesn't pull away, but he does brace himself on his elbows to take some of his weight off me.

And then, like magic, the power comes back on again. I hear the fridge kick on in the kitchen, and the hum of electricity settles around us. Beck lifts his face to look at me.

"Our sexy bubble is over," I whisper, feeling disappointed as I drag my fingers through his whiskers.

"I'm just happy you're okay."

"I don't know if I've ever been better, and that's the truth." But I wiggle beneath him. "I could, however, use some water and the bathroom."

"You can have whatever you want."

He lifts himself off me, pulls up the sweats, and takes my hand to help me up. And then, I remember that my leggings are ruined.

"I guess I should change clothes, too." I pull his shirt over my head and inhale, enjoying having his scent wrapped around me. "Since these pants are ruined."

"I'll buy you more."

I shake my head and walk toward the stairs. "I have more up in my bag."

I'm a mess as I climb the stairs, and I wrinkle my nose at how sticky and dirty I feel. Honestly, I could use another quick shower just to rinse off, so I do that.

And when I emerge from the bathroom in clean clothes and feeling refreshed, Beck is waiting for me with a glass of water.

"I was messy," I inform him.

"Not sorry," he replies with a chuckle and kisses my forehead. "Come on, let's go finish that movie."

"Or that scene in my book."

He narrows his eyes at me. "Do you just want me to be permanently inside you all weekend, Irish?"

"Wouldn't be the worst thing that's ever happened to me." I bat my eyelashes at him and take a sip of the cool water. "Besides, you know you like the book."

"Come on, then. Let's go see what kind of trouble Dom and Val get into."

Chapter Fifteen

LEWIS A.K.A. THE ARSEHOLE

Where is my tiny dancer?

Since I've been back in New York City, I've discovered that not only did she leave her dance company but she also no longer lives in her apartment.

That's unacceptable.

That apartment is in the most secure building in the city, and I should know. I bought the fucking building as soon as I met her. I need her to be safe, especially when I'm out of the country for months at a time. What was she thinking, moving without giving me the courtesy of finding a new home for her?

Scratch that. She should be living in *my* home.

In *our* home.

Our bed.

I've never had a problem finding her before. An easy Google search usually tells me when her next performance will be, and even what her rehearsal schedule is.

My beautiful girl is a public figure, someone who others admire.

And she's all mine.

It didn't bother me when she said she needed to take a step back from us. I know that her career is important to her, and with my own schedule so busy with travel, it made sense to take a break. Of course, I had to go see her before I left the country.

My tiny dancer is gorgeous when she sleeps.

But now, when I google her, I find nothing recent. There's no mention of her in recent or upcoming performances.

"Where did you go, my love?"

I don't prefer to ask for help, but it seems this time, I don't have a choice. I'll call her former dance partner, Mikhail.

I never liked him. The way he looked at my girl sets my teeth on edge, but he's her friend, after all, and I have to be tolerant of certain things.

Of course, once she's truly mine, he'll be out of the picture.

The phone doesn't ring or go to voicemail.

He blocked me?

Anger tickles the back of my throat as I swallow hard and decide to make another phone call. One that I only use in emergencies.

After just two rings, the call is answered.

"I have a job for you."

Chapter Sixteen

SKYLA

I t's only been two days since I said goodbye to Beckett and his amazing farm, but it feels like it's been weeks.

I miss him.

"And isn't that ridiculous?" I ask the dog, who lifts his head from his bed and tilts it to the side. "It's only been two days, and I've had plenty to keep me busy, haven't I?"

In fact, right now, I'm alone in my studio after two back-to-back modern dance classes that went *so well*. I haven't even advertised them yet. I simply mentioned them to a few of the mums after rehearsal, and they jumped on it. We laughed and moved and enjoyed the music, and I think these classes will be a highlight of my week.

"I have plenty to occupy my time, and I don't have to be with a certain dirty farmer every minute of the bleeding day."

I jump when my phone pings with an incoming text.

> Beckett: I can't stop thinking about you.

I sag in relief. Thank the gods that I'm not the only one feeling this way.

> Me: What are you doing right now?

> Beckett: Does that mean you're not thinking about me?

> Me: Of course, I'm thinking about you. You're texting me.

> Beckett: *pouty emoji*

> Me: If you must know, I miss you, too. I was just telling Riley about it, actually.

> Beckett: You're talking about me?

Laughing, I walk to my water dispenser and fill my bottle as another text comes in.

> Beckett: *photo of chickens* I was just collecting the eggs from the girls.

> Me: And how many did you get?

> Beckett: About a dozen. How is your day going, Irish?

My skin tingles every time he calls me that.

> Me: It's been a good day. New dance classes with the mums! Hard workouts but fun.

> Beckett: Good. I have to go deal with a sick cow, but I'll talk to you later.

> Me: *kissy face emoji*

> Me: What are you doing right now?

It's Wednesday night. I've just finished putting the dishes away after dinner, and I'm curled up on the couch with Riley by my side, ready to read more Dom, but I'm missing Beckett. He replies faster than I expected.

> Beckett: *photo of himself, no shirt, with a paperback copy of Dom open and lying on his stomach*

I drop my phone with a gasp.
"Holy fecking hell."

> Me: Did you seriously just send me a thirst trap photo?

> Beckett: What's a thirst trap photo?

> Me: Exactly what you just sent me!
> Jesus, warn a girl, Beck.

> Beckett: So you're saying that you like
> my ... book?

He's funny. With a laugh, I settle deeper into the couch.

> Me: Yeah, I like your ... book. You
> bought it?

> Beckett: Yes, from Bee. Are you still
> reading it?

> Me: Of course. What part are you on?

I take a drink of sparkling water as the bubbles bounce on my screen.

> Beckett: They're married and at his
> penthouse. And it's the following
> morning, and she just woke up.

He's not too far behind me.

> Me: Poor Val. He tricked her!

> Beckett: Yeah, kind of an asshole
> move.

I smirk and sip more water.

> **Me:** Would you ever tattoo your name on someone while they're out cold because you drugged them?

> **Beckett:** I'm intense, but I'm not THAT intense, Irish.

> **Me:** THANK FUCK! Talk about red flags. I do like your level of intensity, though.

> **Beckett:** I'm relieved to hear that. I'll show you more intensity as soon as possible.

> **Me:** Okay, you go read, and I will, too.

> **Beckett:** Good night, beautiful.

> **Me:** Good night.

"Well, don't you look ... happy." Bee smirks at me and bites her lip, and I can feel my cheeks darken.

"Why wouldn't I be happy, then?"

"Oh, I'm sure you're thrilled, friend. Beckett looked pleased with himself when I saw him, too."

"You saw him? Oh right, when he bought the book."

Bee pauses, then lets out a laugh. "Yeah, when he

bought the *spicy romance book* that my friend recommended to him."

"We're both reading it." I shrug as if it's no big deal, but it's a big fecking deal. My phone pings in my pocket, and I pull it out immediately and read the text from Beckett.

> Beckett: Tell me something good.

I grin. Dom sends the same text to Val in the book.

> Me: I'm hanging out with your sister right now.

"Come here," I say to Bee as I open my camera. "Selfie time."

She wraps her arm around my shoulders, we tip our heads together, and I snap the photo.

"I'm sending this to Beck."

She's quiet as I type the message.

> Me: *sends selfie* She says hi!

When I glance up, Bee's staring at me.

"What?"

"So you guys are definitely a thing now, huh?"

Nibbling my lip, I fiddle with the stickers she's organizing on the counter. "Yes. As far as I'm concerned, we definitely are a thing. I spent last weekend with him."

Her eyebrows climb as another text comes in.

> Beckett: You're so fucking beautiful, Irish.

I show her the message, and she smiles.

"Okay, that's swoony."

"I know."

"You know, my brother doesn't invite girls to the farm. Ever."

"Ever?"

"No. Well, he did once, and that turned into a disaster, so he's always avoided it. The fact that he took you there means it's serious for him, too." She wiggles her eyebrows. "And he's reading spicy books for you."

"He read *to* me last weekend."

"Now, I hate you."

> Beckett: I'm sorry we can't spend the weekend together, baby.

I sigh and set my Kindle aside. It's Friday night, one week since I first went with Beck to his place. I haven't seen him all week, and I know he's had a rough time of it with work.

> Me: I don't expect an invitation every weekend.

Beckett: You should. I think I've
turned the corner with this sick cow.
It's been rough for her.

Me: I'm sorry. What do you do while
you sit with her?

Beckett: I read. Text you. Do
paperwork. The part when Dom
punched his way through that guy's
chest …

Me: Stop! I'm not that far yet! You
read ahead of me.

Beckett: Oops. Better catch up, Irish.

Suddenly, the phone rings, but it's not Beckett. It's my mother.

"Hello?"

"Hullo, darlin'," she says. "And what are you about this evening?"

"Wait. It's the middle of the night for you. What are *you* about? Is Da all right?"

"He's fine, and he's snoring in his bed. I couldn't sleep," she admits with a soft sigh. "Are you ready for the benefit dinner in LA next week?"

Scowling, I pick at a string on my leggings. "I'm not going to a benefit dinner."

"Aye, you are. Your father emailed you about it a month ago."

"Ma, I can't just leave. I have a business."

"It's only for two days, Skyla. You need to go. Now that you're not dancing, you can have a bigger presence regarding the charities we're involved in—especially this one. Dreams for Kids was your idea in the first place, so you should be there. We'll be raising a lot of money."

"When next week?" I close my eyes, resigned to having to leave for this. "And can I take Riley?"

"We'll be in the private jet, so of course you can. It's next Friday night. We'll pick you up Friday morning and take you home on Saturday. Connor will be with us, of course."

"I'll think about it."

"You'll go. I already have an haute couture dress from Dior for you," Ma says, leaving no room to argue, and I admit, the idea of a custom dress sends a zip through me. "And it's happy I am that I get to see my girl. It's been too long, my darlin'."

"I know. I miss you guys, too. Go get some sleep, Ma. Kiss Da for me."

"I'll try, and I will. See you soon, *a stór*."

She hangs up, and I see that I have seven texts from Beckett.

> Beckett: How was your day?

> Beckett: Do you believe in aliens?

> Beckett: There's a position described in this book that I want to try ASAP. With some modifications, of course.

> Beckett: Blink twice if you're okay.

> Beckett: Irish, don't make me come over there.

> Beckett: Are you okay? I'm actually worried that you fell and hit your head. Or, you've decided to ghost me.

> Beckett: I will spank your ass if you don't answer me.

I've just finished reading the last message when my phone rings.

"Hey, sorry about that. I'm not ghosting you."

"You're okay?"

"Yeah, my mum called right in the middle of texting with you. I didn't mean to make you worry."

"Okay, good. As long as you're safe, that's all that matters. How's your mom?"

"She couldn't sleep, so she was calling me. I guess there's a charity benefit dinner that I have to go to next week in LA."

He's quiet for a minute.

"Did I lose you?"

"No, just processing that you'll be out of town for a few days."

I grin and pet Riley's back. "You could go with us. It's only one night. And it's for a children's charity."

He's quiet again, and I realize I'm a bloody idiot.

"Forget I said that. Christ, we've only just started

seeing each other. You don't need to meet my family and go to a bloody charity event with me. I'm just going to go jump off a bridge now. It was nice knowing you, Mr. Blackwell."

He's laughing in my ear, and I cover my face with my hand.

"Take a breath, Irish."

"I'd like to die now."

"If you die, I won't have a beautiful date for a fancy dinner thing next week."

My eyes snap open in surprise. "You'd actually go with me?"

"Are you under the impression that I can say no to you about literally anything? If you want me there, I'll be there."

"I'd love for you to go, but only if you feel comfortable. And if you can get away from the farm."

"I can. I have enough help." He sighs on the other end of the line. "I miss you, Skyla."

"I can come out there if you'd like. Riley and I could wait for you at the house."

"I'll be out here all night. I have the night shift with Bessy. But I'd like to take you out for dinner tomorrow night."

"What if Bessy isn't feeling better?"

"We're not putting that out into the universe. She's going to feel like a champ, and I'm going to hang out with my girl."

My girl.

"Yes, please."

"Good. I'll pick you up at six."

"Beck, do you need anything? I know it's been a rough week. I could bring something out and drop it off to you. How can I help?"

He sighs, and I can hear the weariness in it. I want to wrap myself around him and hug him close, push my fingers in his whiskers.

I want to comfort him.

"You're helping. Trust me on that, okay?"

"Okay then. I'll see you tomorrow."

"Sleep well, baby."

Chapter Seventeen

BECKETT

"Hey, boss," Brad says as he walks into the barn. It's barely daybreak, and I'm ready for some fucking sleep. "How's our girl?"

"She's a lot better this morning," I reply as we check Bessy over. "She's turned the corner, which is good. I was afraid we might lose her for a couple of days there."

"Me, too." Brad nods and reaches out to pet Bessy's cheek. "We'll keep her on the antibiotics for a couple of weeks, which means we can't use her milk for a while."

"No, you'll have to toss it," I agree. "But she'll be okay, and that's what matters. I'm going to get a few hours of sleep, then I'll be away from the ranch most of the day."

"Good. We've got everything handled here."

"I feel a little guilty." I drag my hand down my face, and Brad scowls at me.

"Why?"

"Because I've had you guys handling a lot more than usual lately. I've been less hands-on."

"You have a full crew of guys right now," he reminds me. "It's our job to do this so you don't have to. Beck, you're entitled to a life, just the same as anyone else. Being in this barn twenty-four hours a day isn't healthy."

"You're out here more than I am."

"It isn't healthy for most people," he replies with a grin. "Skyla seems really nice. She's beautiful."

I narrow my eyes at him, and he laughs and holds his hands up in surrender. "I'm not being a dick, I'm just stating the obvious. When I met her last weekend, she seemed interested in what we do, and she looked at you like you hung the fucking moon."

I cross my arms over my chest. "I'm so glad you watched her so closely."

Brad laughs again and pats me on the shoulder. "Go get some sleep, boss. We've got things handled out here. I'll see you tomorrow."

"Yeah, okay. Oh, before I forget, I'll be out of town for two days late next week."

"Got it. No problem."

I can tell by his tone that he means that, but it doesn't quell my guilt that I'm not out here as much as I should be.

"You're not a one-man show," he says, obviously reading my mind. "You're the boss. A good one, by the way. Now, go get some sleep. This is under control."

"Thanks, Brad."

Walking toward the house, I pull my phone out of

my pocket. I'm *so* tired, and I need a solid six hours of sleep, but I also need to touch base with Skyla.

I haven't seen her all fucking week. Texts and brief calls just aren't enough. I want to see her, hold her, lose myself inside her.

It turns out that I'm an impatient man where Skyla's concerned.

It's still early, so I type out a quick text to her.

> Me: Good morning, Irish. I hope you slept well. I can't wait to see you tonight. x

My feet feel like lead as I trudge up the back steps and into the house. I should eat, but I'm just too tired.

And that's when I see it.

On the counter is a brown paper bag with a note beside it. Eagerly, I snatch up the piece of paper and scan the pretty handwriting.

Beck,

I hope you don't mind that I let myself in. Your back door wasn't locked. I know that you won't want to fix yourself something to eat before you sleep this morning, so I've grabbed a few pastries from The Sweet Shop for you. A small selection because I'm not sure what you prefer. Please, have a little something before you sleep.

I will see you tonight.
heart Irish

"Fuck me." I read the note three more times before I set it on the counter and open the bag. There's a muffin, a scone, and what looks like a whole loaf of some kind of bread. Without thinking, I take a bite of the muffin and moan.

Huckleberry lemon. So fucking good.

I wish she'd stayed. However, if I'd found the most beautiful woman in the world standing in my kitchen this morning, I never would have slept because I would have fucked the hell out of her all day long.

It's probably best this way.

I type out another quick text as I take the stairs up to my bedroom.

> Me: Thank you for breakfast. It was perfect. Sad I missed you.

With the muffin in my teeth, I strip out of my clothes and pad into the bathroom, turn on the shower, and then finish the treat in two more bites. The shower is short and sweet, and after drying off, I don't bother to put on any clothes before I tumble into bed. I don't even give a shit that the sun shines right in the window.

It won't matter.

With thoughts of a redheaded Irish girl, I fall to sleep.

After a solid sleep, I feel human again and roll out of bed. It's early afternoon, so I didn't sleep the whole day away. I have plenty of time before I pick Skyla up.

I call Brooks.

"Yo," he says.

"That's a professional way to answer the phone at your place of business." I grin and tie my shoe.

"You called my cell, asshole. What's up?"

"My truck needs a quick oil change. Do you have any time this afternoon for me to stop by?"

"I actually do. Swing in, and I'll handle it."

"Be there soon."

I hang up, grab my jacket, and head to the truck. I haven't seen Brooks or any of my family in more than a week. We usually have family day on Sunday out at the ranch, but with Bessy sick and time with Skyla, we haven't scheduled it.

Maybe next week, I'll have everyone over, as well as my girl, and she can see what it's like out there when we're all in one place.

If she can survive that chaos, she's up for anything.

I pull in behind one of the garage doors at Brooks's garage, and it opens. Brooks waves me inside, and tells me when to come to a stop, and then I hop out of the vehicle.

He presses a button, and the truck starts rising in the air.

"You know, the saying is true," I say when I walk over to stand next to him. "It's not what you know, it's who you know."

"You're lucky I finished another project this afternoon. We're booked up a month in advance."

"I know." I grin and stand back, watching as Brooks goes about his routine. "How are you doing? What's new in your world, man?"

"I'm fine, and nothing's new." Brooks is a broody bastard. "I work a lot of hours, and that's about it."

"Not dating anyone?"

He scowls at me from under my truck. "Just because you're suddenly all aflutter over some broad doesn't mean the rest of us will follow. Jesus, you sound like Bridger."

Okay, so I admit that it wasn't all that long ago that Bridger fell for Dani, one of our lifelong friends, and told me that I needed to get a life.

But this isn't the same thing.

"I'm just making conversation, you know. Have you heard from Juliet lately?"

His whole body stiffens, but he doesn't look at me. He just keeps working.

"That's none of your fucking business. If you're going to annoy the fuck out of me, go sit in the waiting room."

"I'm not trying to annoy you."

"Yet it's happening."

"Why are you so touchy today?"

"Okay, let me ask you this. Have you heard from *Tori* lately?"

I scowl, and my brother nods. I never want to think about that nightmare or how she screwed me over again.

"Exactly. When was your last oil change? This shit is like sludge."

"You'd know better than me."

"Jesus, Beck."

"I've been a little busy, you know?" I lean back against his workbench, cross my ankles, and tell him all about Bessy being sick, the newest mess with the rentals, and all of the other shit that happened this week.

By the time I've wrapped up my story, he's finished with the oil change and is lowering the truck. He wipes his hands on a rag and crosses to me.

"What do I owe you?"

"I don't want your money, but I'll tell you what I do want. Never mention Juliet's name to me again. Ever. Because the answer will always be no, I haven't talked to her."

"Brooks." I sigh, but he shakes his head.

"No. It's not up for discussion. Keep her name out of your mouth."

"Jesus." I scrub my fingers through my hair. "Okay. I won't bring it up again."

"Good. Now, get in here for an oil change before it looks like your engine might seize up."

"Now you're being dramatic. That wasn't going to happen."

"You're such a pain in the ass," he replies. "Always have been. Always will be."

"Hey, at least I'm consistent." I grin at him, and then I pull him in for a hug, which I can tell surprises him, but he pats me on the back. "Don't stay pissed at me."

"Whatever. Go away."

I grin and hop in the truck, and with a wave, I pull out of the garage.

Skyla opens her front door, and I move in to seal my lips over hers. She lets out a little gasp, then her hands are in my hair, pulling me to her, pressing that long, lean body against me. I walk her backward and nudge the door closed.

Riley barks once and nudges my leg, making Skyla laugh.

"He's happy to see you," she says against my lips.

"What about you?" My nose drifts up her jawline, breathing her in. "Fuck, you smell good, baby."

"As do you." She pulls back just a little so she can smile at me, and I swear to God, her smile steals the breath from my lungs. "It's happy I am to see you, Mr. Blackwell."

Skyla rubs her thumb over my lips.

"I was wearing lipstick." She grins up at me. "I don't think I'll bother reapplying it."

"Waste of time," I agree, and then take her in. She's

wearing a black top that falls over one shoulder and blue jeans with wide legs that make her legs look a mile long. "You're a fucking heartbreaker, Irish."

She smirks and turns to walk away, but I cup her cheek and pull her back to me.

"You're the most beautiful thing I've ever seen in my life."

Her eyes soften, and she leans in to hug me, wraps those arms around me, and rests her face on my chest, then takes a nice, long breath.

"I'm so very glad you're here," she says. "And I'm starving. Where are we going for dinner?"

"Ciao, if you're okay with Italian."

"Oh, I've heard such great things about that place. I'd love it. I'm leaving Riley here tonight. He's been fed and gone outside, so he'll be fine for a couple of hours."

I tip up an eyebrow. "Are you sure?"

"I feel safe with you."

She turns away, and I rub my chest over my heart. *She trusts me.* After all she went through and the necessity to have Riley, she trusts me. I know that's a significant thing for her. Not only that but she also cared for me in a practical and thoughtful way this morning. I'm still slightly awestruck that she said yes to dating me. I have never felt this strongly about a woman ... *ever.*

Jesus, I'm falling in love with this woman.

"Hey, come back here really quick." I catch her hand and tug her back into my arms and kiss her again until we're both out of breath.

"What was that for?" she asks.

"My breakfast surprise."

Her smile lights up the room. "I'm glad you enjoyed it. I was up early and couldn't sleep, so Riley and I decided to take a little adventure. Did you notice I also fetched the eggs from the hens this morning?"

My eyebrows shoot up into my hairline. "No, I forgot to check the chickens today."

"Well, it's done." She grabs her bag and gives Riley a kiss on the head, and he lets out a little whine. "It's okay, big guy. I'll be fine. I won't be long."

She locks up the house behind us, setting the alarm, and I hold the truck door for her. After she's climbed inside, I buckle her belt, kiss her cheek, then round the hood to the driver's side.

"Thank you for the eggs."

"I admit, it was for purely selfish reasons. I love those chickens, Beck. I had no idea that I'd enjoy them so much, but they're so cute, and they work so hard for those eggs. Oh, and Riley came out with me, and he didn't try any funny business."

"Now I'm pissed that I missed this adventure."

She laughs and reaches over to pat my hand. "Don't worry, I'm sure it'll happen again."

I glance over when she goes silent and notice her cheeks are flushed.

"What's wrong?"

"I mean, if invited, I'd spend time with the chickens."

"Okay, let's clear the air here, Irish. You're welcome at my ranch any minute of any day. You want to come over in the dead of night? Come on the fuck over, I'll be waiting at the door. You want to be there in the morning to search for eggs? Spend the night. There's never a time when you're not welcome in my home. You have the code to the gate, and hell, I'll give you a key."

When I look her way again, she's looking at me with wide eyes and her jaw dropped.

"Does that clear it up, baby?"

"So this is serious."

I frown over at her. "As a heart attack."

"We're ... monogamous."

Without hesitation, I pull the truck to the side of the road in a residential area of town, unbuckle us both, and pull my girl onto my lap. She's so small, I don't even have to put the seat back.

Her eyes are wide with surprise, and I cup her cheek, brushing my thumb over her smooth skin.

"No one exists but you, Irish. You are under my skin and in my head, and I can't imagine being with anyone else. Yeah, we're serious, and we're monogamous. Unless you tell me that you've had your eye on someone else, in which case I'll take care of him."

She swallows hard as her eyes fall to my mouth.

"Eyes on me, baby."

"No. That's not what I meant, Beck. I don't fancy anyone else. I think I wanted to make sure that we're on the same page, so I'm not for making a fool of myself when you tell me that this isn't what I thought or hoped that it is."

"Good. Same page, then." I kiss her quickly before helping her back over to her seat. "Let's eat."

If I didn't move her over, I would have fucked her right here in front of Mrs. Martin's house from high school, and that isn't a great idea.

When we reach the restaurant, we're shown to our table, and a server named Kyle writes his name with a crayon on the white paper that covers the table.

"Hi, folks, I'm Kyle. I'll be your server this evening. Can I start you off with something to drink?"

"Water for me," Skyla says as she looks at the menu.

"Same, thanks."

"Okay, I'll get those waters. You take your time with the menu. If you're looking for recommendations, I'm partial to the lasagna and the pasta ravenna. But you really can't go wrong with anything on the menu."

He walks away, and Skyla smiles over at me. "He's very enthusiastic."

With a smirk, I reach over and take her hand in mine, rubbing my thumb over her knuckles, and set my menu aside.

I'll get the lasagna.

"Tell me about this charity function next week."

Before she can say anything, Kyle's back with waters and garlic bread, then he takes our orders and is off again.

"I don't think I should eat that," Skyla says, staring at the bread.

"Why not?"

"Because I won't be able to stop."

With a laugh, I cut her a piece and pass it to her, then do the same for me and bite in.

"Jesus, that's good."

"I could have just had this for dinner." She chews and moans, and my dick immediately comes to attention and bitches me out for not fucking her earlier. It's *very* aware that it's been a week since I've been inside her. *Fuck, I've missed her. And her delectable body.* "Okay, so the charity is called Dreams for Kids, and it's something my family started about ten years ago or so. I'd been working with a summer dance program for children in New York City, and a couple of girls were terminally ill but wanted to be treated as normal kids. They just wanted to learn how to dance, wear pretty clothes, and perform for their parents. So we modified things and made sure they were able to do that."

She's fucking amazing.

"I decided to use my privilege for something magical for these wee ones who struggled with something I can't imagine going through. I guess you could say we grant wishes. If a little boy wants to meet his sports hero, or a girl wants to meet a pop star, or whatever it might be, we make it happen at no cost to the parents."

"That's an incredible idea."

"Well, I can't take all the credit. Sure, the idea was mine, but I don't have a ton to do with the foundation, mostly because I've always been so busy with work. But now that I'm no longer performing, I can at least go to fundraisers and be more of a face for the organization. I don't honestly mind going. I just wish that I'd had more notice."

"This is a last-minute dinner?"

"No, but I didn't read my father's email about it last

month." She presses her lips together, then shrugs a shoulder. "He's always trying to get me more involved with the business, and I don't want to. It's just not what I'm meant to do with my life. That's all Connor. So if Da sends something that looks professional, I delete it right away and get on with my day."

I can't help but laugh as our meals are set in front of us.

"And," she continues, "now that you're going, I'm excited for it."

"Good. I'm looking forward to it." I take a bite of lasagna, my eyes pinned to her pink lips as she chews her food. Jesus, I've missed those lips this week. She reaches across the table and takes a bite of my lasagna and nods in appreciation. "Did you finish the book?"

"Yes." Her eyes shine as a smile spreads over her face, and she offers me a bite of her meal, which I take. "You?"

"Of course, I did. And I'm about to go back to the beginning and buy books one and two from Bee."

"You don't have to. I own them on paperback as well as e-book because I'm obsessed. You can borrow them. Just don't break the spines."

"I'm not an animal. Of course I won't break the spines."

She laughs and takes another bite off my plate. "Did you enjoy the rest of the story, then?"

"I really did. There was action, sex, a little mushy stuff, but the action made up for it. What did you think of it?"

"I think it's my favorite of the series so far although

it's hard to choose." She pulls another piece of bread onto her plate.

"And what is it about these books that you love so much?"

She takes a bite of her pasta and squints her eyes, thinking. After swallowing, she says, "It's several things. Yes, I enjoy the spice, but without the chemistry and the connection between the characters, the spice doesn't matter. I like watching a relationship build, and I love it when friend groups are involved or family that scoops up a character and says, *'You're one of us now.'* I enjoy banter and humor. Like in Dom, when they go to the mountain house with Val's brother and his friends, and the guys are *so funny* together, I was rolling with laughter."

"So you like the relationships in general."

"Aye, I do. I want to see it all unfold. Maybe I'm nosy." She shrugs that bare shoulder and takes another bite. "What did you like about it?"

I grin at her. "The sex and the action."

She laughs and picks up her water glass. "To sex and action."

Chapter Eighteen

SKYLA

"Miller will arrive in five minutes to get us and take us to the airport," I inform Beckett. He's sitting calmly in the chair in the corner of my bedroom, watching me as I bustle around packing up anything last minute that I might need. I'm glad he's here because my stomach is out of control with nerves. "Did I grab my curling iron?"

"Yes, and then you double-checked it," he says with a chuckle. "Why are you so nervous? This is a one-night trip."

"I'm not nervous," I lie, shaking my head, unable to meet his eyes because he'll see right through me. "Shite, did I grab Riley's favorite chews?"

"We have all of Riley's things ready to go," Beck confirms. Standing from the chair, he crosses to me, takes my shoulders in his hands, and kisses my forehead. It's amazing how just one touch from this man calms my nervous system right down. "Breathe, Irish."

"I don't want to forget anything."

"We're going to LA, not the tundra of Siberia. If we forget something, we can find it there as long as we have our phones and a wallet."

"I know, but—"

His lips press to mine, effectively shutting me up, and I melt into him. He wraps his strong arms around me, hugging me while he kisses me, and it's just the comfort I need right now.

"Talk to me, baby. What's wrong? What do you need?"

I tip my forehead against his sternum and close my eyes. *What do you need?* This man is incredible. "I don't know why I'm anxious, other than I haven't traveled since I moved here last year, and you're going to meet my family, and what if you don't like them?"

"What if they don't like *me*?"

I tip my head back and frown up at him as if that's the stupidest thing I've ever heard. "Well, that's ridiculous. They're going to love you."

"Then there's no problem." He smiles and frames my face in those big hands before sealing his lips to mine again, and I whimper against his mouth. "I wish we had time for me to bend you over that bed."

"You were inside me less than an hour ago."

"Too long." He rubs his nose against mine as he trails his hands down my back, sending a shiver through me. "What else are you worried about, baby?"

"Riley." I bite my lip and glance over at the dog, who's watching us. "My mother's assistant is joining us, and during the fundraiser itself, she'll stay at the hotel with Riley, but I hate leaving him with a stranger."

"He's going to be great, Irish. But if you freak out, he will, too. You know that. I have no doubt he'll be just fine with your mom's assistant. If it bothers you that much to leave him, we'll take him to dinner with us."

I frown and shake my head. "No, he'll stay back. It's too many people for him, but I love that you suggested it. Thank you."

Beck's hands and his deep voice have soothed me, and I take a deep breath, then let it out slowly.

"Okay, you're right. I have everything I need. Ma's bringing my fancy dress with her, so I don't have anything else to pack."

"Good." He zips up my suitcase and carries it to the front door just as Miller pulls to a stop in the driveway. "He has the code to your gate?"

"He does, aye. Connor comes and goes from here as he pleases, and Miller is his driver and personal security."

Beckett nods and opens the door, then carries our suitcases out to Miller, who's already standing at the back of the vehicle, ready to load our things. The two men shake hands and nod at each other. Miller's a massive man—bigger than Beckett—and that's saying a lot, given how tall and broad my man is. Miller can be intimidating, which is the whole point, I suppose, but he's always been kind to me, and I feel safe with him.

After grabbing Riley's things, I lock the house, set the alarm, and we all pile into the giant SUV.

"How are you, Miller?" I ask as he pulls away from the house.

"I'm fine, miss. And yourself?"

"I'm well, thank you. How is my family? Everyone okay, then?"

Miller glances over at me. I'm in the passenger seat, and my two big boys are in the back.

"Everyone seems to be just fine."

Beckett leans forward, and his hand is suddenly on my shoulder, grounding me. Honestly, I don't know why I'm so out of sorts today. I want to see my family, and I'm content with introducing them to Beckett. I think they'll like each other. So that's not what's bothering me about this trip.

I'm not a nervous flier. And although I don't love that Riley will be alone with a stranger for part of tonight, I know he'll be safe with Sally, Ma's assistant. I like her very much.

There's no good reason for my anxiety, but I can't seem to calm myself down.

Miller drives onto a back road at the airport, then onto the tarmac, where the family jet awaits us with the door open.

"I'll get your things," Miller says with a nod, and before we get onto the plane, I join Beckett and Riley at the front of the car.

Beck holds his hand out, and I slide my palm into his.

"It's going to be great," he says with an encouraging smile, and I lead him to the steps that Riley's already taken onto the plane.

"Good boy," Connor says as I step inside. My eyes scan everyone, and the anxiety is already lifting as I see my family. Then my gaze lands on a smiling, smug face that makes my heart explode.

"Mik!" I run into my partner's arms, and he lifts me off the ground, turning a circle as he hugs me close. "You're here! What are you doing here? Why didn't you tell me you were coming along?"

"Surprise, malishka," he says into my ear as my eyes fill with happy tears. "It has been too many months."

"And who is this, then?" Ma asks, and I pull away from Mik to introduce everyone to Beckett. "It's a handsome guest you have here, *a stór*."

"Oh, I'm so sorry. This is Beckett Blackwell, and he is my date this weekend. Beck, this is Mik, my ma and da, Maeve and Patrick, and of course, you've briefly met my brother, Connor."

Beck's already shaking everyone's hands, and I'm taken aback again by how handsome he is in his simple blue button-down shirt and jeans, his sleeves rolled up his forearms. He trimmed his beard and must have gotten a haircut this past week.

He looks sexy, like he could milk a cow or walk a runway.

"More surprises," Ma says as she smiles at my man. "And a happy one at that. Welcome, Beckett."

"Thank you, Mrs. Gallagher," Beck says.

"Oh, we're not formal here. Please, I'm Maeve."

Beck nods, and I take his hand in mine. He gives it a squeeze as we find seats next to each other.

"Where's Benji?" I ask Mik as we all get buckled in and ready for takeoff.

"He had to work this weekend," Mik replies with a shrug. "But he sends love."

"We'll video call him so he doesn't feel left out," I reply.

"How's the ankle?" Mik asks, his blue eyes narrowing. Nothing about him has changed. He's still lean and fit and beautiful. So painfully beautiful.

"It's as good as it's going to get," I reply simply and shrug. I know he wants to know what my answer will be about London and dancing *Giselle*, but I'm still unsure. It's so good to see him, though.

Ma and Da are listening but unusually quiet as they hold hands and watch the rest of us. Connor reads something on his phone, as he usually does.

Miller and Sally are in the back of the plane, and Riley's lying at my feet.

It's a full plane.

"You're not in shape," Mik says in that honest way he has that no longer offends me.

Beckett's hold on my hand tightens. It seems Mik *does* offend my man.

"I think you look beautiful, *a stór*," Da says with a wink. "You look happy."

"Thanks, Da. I am happy. And no"—I turn to Mik —"I'm not in professional dancing shape. I already told you that when you called and demanded that I do this performance with you."

"What performance?" Connor asks, lifting his perceptive gaze at us.

"It's one night," Mik says, and outlines what he told me to my family. "It's not in New York, it's in London. For one performance. And yes, you'll have to lose the fifteen pounds you gained, malishka. Not ten. Fifteen."

"Keep talking to her like that and you and I are going to have a problem," Beckett says, his voice harder than I've ever heard it, and I tighten my hand in his once more.

"He's right," I tell Beckett, as the two men have a stare down. "I'll have to get into shape."

"Oh, I hope the dress I brought with me fits," Ma says with a concerned furrow of her brow. "I used your older measurements for it, not taking into consideration that you haven't been dancing. I'm sure we can make it work. Maybe we can let it out at the hotel. Although it's couture, so altering it would be a shame."

"Well, I can't lose the fifteen pounds by this evening," I reply, immediately feeling bad for the snarky tone. "I'm sorry, I'm sure it'll be just fine. I'm still in the same sizes."

"Not your costume sizes," Mik says, and Connor sighs heavily, rolling his eyes.

"With all due respect," Beckett says to my mother as he leans forward in his seat, "what in the hell is wrong with all of you? Skyla's absolutely stunning, just as she is."

"Beck," I say softly, rubbing my hand up and down his spine. "It's all right."

"No." He shakes his head and looks over at me, his dark eyes full of indignation. "It's not okay for anyone to comment on your or anyone's size, Irish."

"Irish?" Connor asks, but we all ignore him.

"I'm the one who has to lift her in the air," Mik insists, his stubborn face in a scowl.

"Then I guess you'd better hit the gym because I have no trouble at all lifting her and carrying her wherever the hell she wants to go."

Da's eyebrows wing up. Ma presses her lips together, trying not to smile.

And Connor laughs.

"I've been saying this shite for years," my brother says, running his hand down his face. "Finally, someone agrees with me."

"I get that you have a job to do," Beckett says to Mik as the two men glare at each other. Ma winks at me. I can tell she likes my man. "But it's not *her* job, not anymore. I won't have her hungry, or starving herself, or hating any inch of her gorgeous body because she feels loyal to you and obligated to perform with you one last time. You'll speak to her with respect, or you won't speak to her at all."

The plane is utterly silent as Mik glares at Beckett, then he turns to me.

"I like him."

Da laughs and leans over to pat Beck on the shoulder. "Aye, as do I. What do you do, Beckett?"

Beckett tells my family about his dairy operation, his guest ranch, and how his family has been a mainstay in

Bitterroot Valley for so long. My parents listen, interested, and it makes me proud that they don't for even one minute insinuate that Beckett might not be good enough for me, simply because he doesn't come from the same economic background as my family.

"I respect a family-run business backed by a strong work ethic," Da says when Beckett pauses. "Tell me more about the guest homes you rent."

Even Connor leans in, listening. Ever the businessman.

When anyone discusses hospitality around my family, that's all they want to talk about. And honestly, I don't mind because I'm proud of Beckett.

"I have to interrupt," I say, and when I turn to Beckett, he nods. "Beck has shown them to me, and I have to say that they're just brilliant. Eight tiny A-frame homes face the most gorgeous view of the mountains. Honestly, if I stayed there, I'd never leave to do other activities because he's had them decorated so sweetly, such that they're cozy and luxurious, and with that view, he can't go wrong."

"You should be in charge of all of my marketing, Irish," Beck says before planting a kiss on my temple.

"Oh, I'd love to see them," Ma says. "We've been to Bitterroot Valley a couple of times to see Skyla, of course, but we haven't been able to get out to see the scenery. Perhaps we'll have to rent one of those cabins the next time we're in the area."

The thought of that excites me.

"You should. And he has chickens."

Connor blinks at me. "So?"

"I love the chickens."

Beckett's laughing beside me. "Out of all the animals on my ranch, I think it's hilarious that you love those chickens so much."

"They're hard workers," I insist, lifting my chin. "And the eggs are delicious."

Mik's eyes are narrowed on me as he listens.

"My malishka is no longer a city girl."

Lifting an eyebrow, I tip my head to the side. "No, I guess I'm not."

"And one day," Da says, "you'll tell us the real reason you left the city. I know it's not just because of your ankle, *a stór*."

I feel Beckett's eyes on me as I nibble on my lower lip.

"I can't dance," I reply with a shrug. "And I was tired of the city."

"We're beginning our descent into Los Angeles," the pilot says through the speakers, interrupting the conversation and taking the pressure off me.

No, I never told my parents about The Arsehole.

There's no reason for them to worry. They were so far away, and there was nothing for them to do.

"What are you working on next, Connor? Are you still in the middle of the rehab project in Paris?"

"That's wrapping up," my brother says. "I have a few things happening. After this trip, I'll be in Miami for a few weeks, then back to Dublin for a bit."

"And when will you be rebuilding the ski resort in Bitterroot Valley?"

My brother's eyes narrow on me, but I flash him a bright smile.

"I never said I'd be doing that, and you know it."

"You didn't have to tell me. I know you. It's exactly the kind of project that Gallagher Hotels would take on. Also, as long as you promise not to be a complete shite, you could date Billie. You bought your own house and everything."

"What?" Beckett asks as Connor growls and runs his hand down his face.

"I'm just saying it's something to think about."

"Who's Billie, then?" Ma asks.

"Beckett's sister, and she's one of my best mates," I reply, still holding Connor's gaze. "She's gorgeous and smart and lovely, and she owns the bookshop that recently opened."

"Why couldn't I have been an only child?" Connor asks my parents, who both chuckle in response.

"Now, where would the fun be in that?" Ma asks him, reaching over to ruffle his hair. She doesn't care that he's almost forty. "It seems I need to spend more time in Montana."

"No," Connor says, shaking his head. "Not on my account."

I narrow my eyes at him, but he doesn't back down.

Not that he ever would anyway.

"Do I need to have a conversation with you?" Beckett asks Connor.

"No."

Grinning, I sit back in my seat as the plane lands and

lean my head on Beckett's shoulder. I don't know what I was worried about. Beckett's won them all over without difficulty. This is already turning out to be a fun trip.

The only thing I have left to do is to put the dress on. My hair is washed and dried and curled in big waves, flowing down my back and over my shoulders. My full face of makeup is perfect, including the fake lashes. Ma offered to hire a glam squad to come into my suite and get me ready, but I did this for a living. No one did my hair and makeup when I had to get ready for a performance. It soothes me.

Besides, Beck remembered to bring a little Bluetooth speaker that he bought for me, since Birdie took hers home with her. He set me up here in this massive bathroom with my music, then left me to get ready.

I can't wait to see what he's wearing this evening. He's always beyond sexy, but seeing him in a suit might send me over the edge, and I won't want to leave this suite.

I took a peek at the gown Ma brought, and I have to admit, it's magnificent. The long, sleek column of champagne-colored lace with a high neckline and no sleeves, the dress shimmers and will make me feel amazing.

As long as it fits.

If it doesn't, I'll be going in jeans and a jumper.

"Beckett?" I call out as I fasten a gold and diamond

earring in my ear. "Do you mind helping me with this dress?"

I can hear him walking through the suite, and when he fills the doorway, I gasp.

Bloody hell. I was absolutely right.

The man fills out a black suit like it's his fecking job. And when my gaze climbs to his eyes, I find him staring at me with pure hunger.

"For fuck's sake, you have to warn me, Irish."

"Warn you of what?"

He moves to me, wraps his arms around my waist, over the belted hotel robe, and lowers his lips to press them against my forehead.

"I don't want to mess you up," he whispers, "but fuck me sideways, I want to *mess you up.*"

Grinning, I let my hands skim up his chest, along his lapels. "You're so handsome in this suit, Beck."

"No one's even going to know I'm there," he says with a grin. "And I'll be in prison before the night is over because I'll have to kill every single man who looks at you tonight."

"You haven't even seen the dress yet," I remind him. "It could look like—"

"Doesn't matter." He shakes his head, and his fingertips drift up and down my back. "You're a goddamn vision, baby. God, your hair is every fucking fantasy I've ever had in my life, and all I want to do is get my hands in it."

"It took me a long time to make it look like this," I

remind him. "So please try to restrain yourself for just a little while. Later, it's all yours."

"When we get back here"—he pulls the robe apart and presses his lips to my bare shoulder—"I'm going to fucking devour you."

"Whoa." I press my hands to his chest again. "Hold that thought. I have to get dressed, or else I won't get dressed at all, and we have to leave soon."

"Fine."

Pleased that he likes what he sees so far, I turn to the closet with a grin and pull the dress off the hanger. I return to the bathroom, where I shed the robe, step into the dress, and wiggle it over my hips.

"I hope it fits," I mutter as Beckett moves behind me to help. "The color is divine. Dior is always a good idea, and Ma never misses, but—"

"Stop worrying," he murmurs and kisses the back of my head. "Jesus, it's all buttons. No zipper."

"I know."

The entire back, from the top of my neck to just above my arse, is a row of tiny satin buttons.

"My fingers are too fucking big for this."

"No, they aren't, there's a hook."

I run back to the garment bag that the dress came in and find the hook in the bottom, then return to him.

"This helps and makes it faster. You just—"

"I see it," he murmurs, and I watch in the mirror as his eyebrows pull together in concentration. "Whoever came up with this hook thing is smart as hell."

I can feel him start to pull the loops over the buttons

from just above my arse. He brushes his knuckles over my spine, making goose pimples rise on my skin, and it suddenly feels *hot in here.*

"Mmm." He kisses my back, and I squirm. "Hold still, baby. Fuck me, I can't wait to get you out of this dress later."

"I'll be for stripping you out of that suit." I smile softly as he hooks another button, then places another kiss. Only Beckett can turn helping me with a dress into a sexy game.

"You can keep the shoes on," he says, almost conversationally as if he's not driving me mad. "And don't for a heartbeat think that I didn't notice that you're completely bare under here."

"A bra and panties would ruin the lines," I reply softly. "And there's material strategically placed to cover me up."

He's only about a third of the way up my back because he keeps pausing to kiss me and brush his fingers over me. He's driving me out of my bloody mind.

"I'm going to worship you tonight." Gods above, I love it when his voice gets rough like this. I'm already wet, and I have to survive several hours before I can come back to our suite with Beck and lose myself in him. "I'm going to feast on that beautiful pussy you just covered up. I'm going to kiss you and fuck you until your legs shake and every fucking person in this hotel knows my name."

"For feck's sake, Beck." I swallow thickly, leaning forward against the vanity. My puckered nipples are sore against the rough material of the dress, and I'm uncomfortably wet. "I can't walk around all night like this."

"Like what, Irish?"

"Wet and aching and needy."

He growls and licks the side of my neck as he continues to loop the buttons closed. "That's exactly how I want you, baby. Needy for me."

He's at my neck now, and I'm partly relieved that the dress fits, yet so turned on that I can't breathe.

"Bloody hell, the things you say."

"You're gorgeous," he says as he slips the hook on the vanity and catches my gaze in the mirror. He's so tall, so broad behind me. And his hands come around me, looping around my waist as he presses a kiss to my temple. "Now, we'd better go before I rip this expensive-as-fuck dress off your body."

"We only have to stay for a couple of hours," I promise him, but he shakes his head and grins at me.

"No, we'll stay until what you need to do is done. And then you're all mine."

I'm already his.

Chapter Nineteen

BECKETT

I've been around wealthy people before today. I've flown on a private jet before today. I'm lucky enough to have influential people in my life who I count among my friends, and I'm not a stranger to getting dressed up for fancy events.

But I don't think I've ever seen anything like this.

The ballroom of this hotel—a sister property to the one we're staying at just a few miles away—has been transformed to look like a super classy carnival. The food tables resemble carnival food trucks. Balloons and games and colors are all over the place.

And I have to admit, it's not only fun but also appropriate for a children's charity.

Despite the *fun* aspect, it still looks fancy as fuck. And security is everywhere. From what I can tell, Miller's in charge, and I know it helps put Skyla at ease, which is Connor's priority. Considering the millions of dollars in jewelry floating around this room, not to mention the clothes, security is a no-brainer.

But best of all, Skyla is in her element.

We've been here for an hour, and the woman hasn't stopped smiling and talking, greeting guests as if they're old friends. She works a room like she was born for it.

And I suppose she was. She not only comes from an affluential family but also has a dozen years' experience in performing.

My girl can work a crowd like no one else I've seen.

Her dress shimmers under the glow of the crystal chandeliers as we hold glasses of champagne that we've hardly touched and move toward the edge of the room where the silent auction is being held.

"I'm not supposed to bid on anything," Skyla says, leaning in so only I can hear. "But I'm always tempted because there's some beautiful stuff offered. Oh look, a weekend at a chalet in Colorado. Just like in that book we read."

She pauses, then looks up at me, squeezing my hand. I fucking *love* that she hasn't let go of my hand once since we walked into this room. She has no problem leaning into me, letting me touch her, and touching me in return in front of all of these people. She has no issue revealing to every person here that she's mine.

"I have a question," she says.

"Do you want *me* to bid on Colorado? I will if you have your heart set on it." Jesus, I'd do anything for her.

"No." She chuckles and shakes her head, making her red waves move around her shoulders. I can't resist setting my glass down so I can reach up with my free hand and wrap one of those curls around my finger. It's so fucking soft and so beautiful against my skin. "I was wondering if you'd ever offer a stay at your ranch for one of our auctions."

I tip up an eyebrow in surprise. "*My* ranch?"

"Of course, yours. It's a beautiful place, Beck. It would fetch a high bid. Anyone looking for a mountain getaway would love it." She smiles up at me so sweetly, it makes my heart ache. Jesus, I'm falling in love with her so fast that it makes my head spin, and I know there's no way of stopping it. Not that I want to stop it.

"If you want to offer the ranch, Irish, it's yours." Her green eyes dilate as I sweep my knuckles down her soft cheek. "Anything you want. You know that."

"It would be good advertising for you as well." Her gorgeous mossy eyes fall to my lips, and she licks her own before continuing. "Because those who don't win would likely also book a stay."

"If you say so." I want to kiss her. I want to kiss her so fucking bad. So I cup her cheek and lean down, but before I can get my lips on her, someone says my name.

"Beck? Is that you?"

I turn to look behind me and am stunned to find Ryan Wild, along with his wife, Polly, standing behind us.

"Ry?" I accept his hand and pull him in for a quick hug. "Holy shit, I know someone here."

"Same," Polly says, hugging Skyla. "Oh, you're so beautiful. Is this Dior?"

"Aye," Skyla says with a shy smile as her gaze drifts down Polly's dark blue dress. "And that's Chanel. Oh, it's just lovely, Polly."

"Thanks." Polly kisses her husband's shoulder, leaving a smear of lipstick that he doesn't seem to mind at all. "Someone spoiled me on Valentine's Day."

"I don't have any idea who that might have been," Ryan says, but then offers his wife a grin. "You deserve it."

"Oh, I know," Polly replies, making us all laugh.

"I'm so sorry," Skyla says as she frowns at someone waving her down. "It seems my mother needs me. I'd better go mingle."

"Do you want me to—"

"No, stay." She smiles up at me, then at our friends. "I wish I could stay, too. This was a lovely surprise, and I mean it. Thank you both for coming. Polly, I'll see you at our book club meeting next week?"

"Wouldn't miss it," Polly agrees before Skyla bustles off to mingle.

"So you and Skyla." Ryan sips his whiskey. "I like it."

"Do you know her well?" I ask him.

"Not well," he replies, shaking his head. "I didn't realize she'd moved to our town until Polly mentioned she went to their book club. I know Connor a bit, as I've invested in hotels in the past few years. When I was invited to this, Polly and I decided to take a couple of days away. I like her brother. And her family as a whole seems like good people."

I nod and let my eyes move over the crowd, looking

for my girl. I find her laughing with a woman, and it makes me jealous.

I want to hear her laughter.

Fuck me, I've gotten soft.

"I have to say," Polly adds with a grin. "I like the way you look at her, Beck. I've known you a long-ass time, and I've never seen you look at a woman like that. Not even Tori."

Polly and I grew up together. Her brother, Mac, is one of Ryan's and my closest friends. And, once upon a time, she was tight with my ex.

"And how do I look at Skyla?"

"Like you love her." She smiles softly and reaches out to pat my arm. "It looks good on you."

"Yeah, well, I think this weekend is teaching me that our worlds are pretty different."

"Fuck that," Ryan says, shaking his head. "Money is just money."

"Says the man with a shit ton of it."

"She came to Bitterroot Valley on her own because she likes it. Who she is has little to do with her parents' investment portfolio. Don't be a dick about it. Enjoy her. If she's the one," Ryan continues, "love her."

I blow out a breath and nod.

Ryan makes it sound simple, but it wasn't so long ago that he was a confirmed bachelor. Just as Polly said, however, love looks good on him.

Is that what I want? To love Skyla and have her love me back?

Fuck, yes.

"I'm not letting her go. I'll do charity events if she wants me to, and then I can go back to my cows. She does like the ranch, so that's something."

"Who wouldn't?" Polly laughs at that. "It's beautiful. Also, FYI, I need ice cream for all the summer parties we're about to host since we're opening the pool soon."

"I'll hook you up."

"We're having a house party in a couple of weeks," Ryan informs me. "Bring your girl."

"Sounds good, thanks. We'll be there." My eyes skim the space again, and I find Skyla talking with her father and another man who looks to be her father's age. Her body is relaxed, her mouth in a smile. She's fine. "Hey, how is the ranch merger going between the Wild River and Lexington ranches? Is it final yet?"

Ryan's family ranch borders the Lexington ranch. They were always bitter rival families, but Ryan's younger sister, Millie, married Holden last year, and they've decided to combine ranches, making them the biggest cattle ranch in Montana.

It's impressive.

"It is," Ryan says with a satisfied grin. "And so far, it's great. Everyone's happy."

"Even your father?" Everyone knows how much John Wild hated the Lexingtons.

"He's come around," Ryan says with a nod. "It's been a good thing for both families."

"I'm glad. I hear Holden broke ground on the house he's building for Millie. He showed me the plans. It's going to be an awesome house."

"Yeah, there's never a fucking dull moment." Ryan laughs and leans down to plant a kiss on his wife's head, and I search the crowd for Skyla. She's moved farther away, almost on the other side of the room, but I can feel it as soon as I spot her.

Something isn't right.

Her shoulders suddenly stiffen, her eyes go wide, and every ounce of color leaches from her face. There is no universe where my woman should look like this.

What is it, Irish?

"Excuse me," I murmur as I make my way to her.

Whoever just put that fear on my girl's face is going to fucking pay.

I move quickly through the crowd, and when I see Connor, I put my hand on his shoulder. "With me."

"Excuse me," he mutters, falling in behind me. "What's up?"

"I'm about to find the fuck out."

Chapter Twenty

SKYLA

I'm already exhausted, but tonight's going so well. Everyone seems to be having fun. I know we'll bring in a lot of money for the foundation, and that's the most important thing.

I've just moved away from a woman whose name I can't remember when, suddenly, someone's hand slips across my lower back, caressing me.

Oh God. No. It can't be.

Ice-cold fear spears through my body.

Before I can fully turn, lips are pressed to the shell of my ear.

"So good to see you, my beautiful, tiny dancer." He kisses me—*fecking kisses me!*—and then he's off, moving through the crowd.

I can't breathe.

My heart kicks up as I press my lips together, searching the crowd, and then I see him.

Beckett.

His face is murderous as he makes his way through the packed room to me. My feet won't move. My *body* won't move.

But I don't have to because then, Beck's here, and his warm hands frame my face as a sob tears from my throat.

"What is it, baby?" He presses his lips to my forehead and then stares me in the eyes. "What happened?"

"He's here." Is that rough whisper my voice?

"Who is?" That's Connor's voice, but I can't tear my gaze away from Beckett's eyes.

"L-The Arsehole."

Beckett's grip tightens on me.

"He touched me." I lick my lips. "And said it was good to see me. Called me tiny dancer. I fecking hate that name."

"We need to get out of here," Beck says to Connor, who's already nodding and motioning to someone.

"I can stay." I shake my head and take a breath. "Let me collect myself."

"No, we're leaving," Beckett insists. "Connor?"

"Sir, what's going on?" Miller joins us. He takes one look at me, and his face goes stony.

"Get us back to the hotel," Beckett says. "And find the fucker who keeps terrorizing my girl so I can have a word with him."

"Beck."

"Follow me," Miller says, and he's already speaking into his wrist, the way you see in movies. I don't know why, but that makes me laugh.

"She's going into shock." I think that's Connor's voice.

"My handbag."

"I've got your bloody handbag," Connor says. His voice is so *growly* when he's angry. "And I'll handle everything here."

My skin is crawling, and I shiver. Oh God, he had his bloody hands on me. His *mouth*. I wish I was numb. I wish this creepy sensation would go the bloody hell away.

"Beck." I can't stop saying his name.

"Can you walk?" Beckett asks me as his thumbs move over my cheeks, catching tears that I don't want anyone else to see.

"Okay."

"I will carry you out of here if I have to," Beck says in a low voice, leaning in to press his cheek against my own, "but I don't want to bring any more attention to this. Can you walk out of this room, Irish?"

I nod, but he grips more tightly.

"Skyla. Can you walk?"

"Yes. I can walk."

He nods, seemingly satisfied, and takes my hand so firmly in his, I don't think anything could tear him away from me.

And that's exactly what I want. To be with him, right next to him, from now on. I wonder if he'd let me just milk the cows with him all day, every day?

That makes me want to laugh again, so I press my lips together and nod at people as we make our way through the crowded ballroom toward a back exit.

Miller leads us to a waiting black SUV and opens the back door for us.

"I'm sorry, miss," he says, and I stop to look into his eyes.

He's so ... *angry.*

"It's not your fault."

"Yes, it fucking is," Miller growls by my ear. "It won't happen again."

Beck helps me get into the back seat. Since this dress is so tight, I can't lift my leg high enough to boost myself into the vehicle. Then he's right next to me, and we're riding to the hotel. I'm shaking so hard, my teeth chatter, and Beckett slides over so he can hold on to me.

"I've got you," he whispers as I shake.

We're quiet as a security guard I don't know drives us, giving status updates into his radio.

"Pulling into the hotel," he says, but he doesn't stop at the front entrance.

He takes us into a parking garage and escorts us to a private elevator that leads us to the suite level where we're staying.

"I'll be right outside this door," he says with a nod as Beckett gets us inside.

"My dog." I turn back to the security guard. "Riley's with Sally at the end of the hall. Can you get him for me?"

"Give us about thirty," Beckett adds.

Security nods and closes the door, and Beckett pulls me against him, wrapping his arms so tightly around me, but I wiggle away, making him scowl.

"Not yet. I need a shower." I'm shaking my head as I stomp for the bathroom, trying to will my body to stop the bloody shaking. "My skin is crawling. He touched me. He *touched me.*"

I feel Beck right behind me, and I'm trying to reach behind me to unfasten the buttons of my dress, but it's a lost cause.

There's no way.

"Get this off me."

"Do you want me to be gentle, or can I tear it off?"

"*Get this off me.*"

He grips the fabric on either side of my spine, and with one yank, buttons go flying, and I'm able to wiggle out of it. I need help with my shoe straps because my hands won't stop shaking, then Beck's turning on the water in the shower.

He sheds his jacket and shoes but doesn't bother taking anything else off before he gets us both under the hot spray. I'm seriously losing my shite now that the adrenaline is wearing off.

It's so good to see you, my beautiful, tiny dancer.

"Tell me what to do," Beck says, pain in his words, and I cover my mouth with my hands, panicked because I'm going to throw up.

He springs into action, leaving the shower to grab the garbage can, and I throw up into it, my stomach heaving as I remember how it felt to have *his* hand on me, *his* lips on my ear.

Beck's rubbing my back, murmuring soothing words until I'm done heaving, and he sets the can aside.

"Okay, baby. You're safe. I'm right here. Nothing's going to happen to you, I promise." He kisses my head, but I don't feel clean yet.

"I have to wash my ear."

"Your ear?" He frowns down at me.

"He k-kissed my ear." The tears want to come, but I swallow them down.

Beckett's jaw twitches as he grinds his molars together, but he's so gentle with me as he leads me under the water and helps me wash my hair, and I rub my soapy hands over my ear, trying to get The Arsehole off me.

When the soap's gone, Beckett moves closer and presses his own lips there.

"I'm right here, Irish," he says, immediately soothing me. "Just me. You're safe. It's my lips here now, and they're the only lips that will be here ever again. You think about that and only that."

"Thank you." I lean into his touch, pressing my hands against the sopping material of his white shirt, letting his words seep into me. *The only lips that will ever be here again.* Does he mean that, or is he simply trying to soothe me? Either way, it makes me feel better. "You're still dressed, Beck."

"Doesn't matter. The only thing that matters is you, baby."

God, he's amazing. "It's wonderful, that's what you are." I swallow as he pulls me to him, and I cling, hugging him close, burying my face in his wet chest. "You're bloody *everything*. And it's sorry I am that I've ruined our night—"

"No, baby. Shh. You didn't ruin anything. I just need to make sure you're okay and that you know that you're safe. However we need to make that happen."

I nod against him but don't let go. "This is a lot, and our relationship is so new, and if you decide that you don't want to deal with this, I understand."

"Not getting rid of me. You're not a fucking burden simply for existing, Irish."

He doesn't sound angry or frustrated. He sounds almost … bored with that comment, which makes me feel warm.

"How did he get in?" I ask at last.

"We're going to find out," he replies and buries his lips in my wet hair. "Do you want to dry off, or do you want to stay in here for a while longer?"

"You're soaked, and this can't feel good."

"Hey." He makes me look him in the eyes, and all I see there is … *love.* And it steals my breath away. "Don't worry about me. I'm just fine. I get to hold you, so don't think for a second that I'm anything but fine."

"Maybe we can get dry."

He nods, and turns off the shower before grabbing me a towel. He stands before me, this tall, strong man, soaked to the bones and still wearing his suit, which has to weigh a ton, but instead of taking it off, he's drying me, soothing me with every brush of the towel and every press of his lips on my damp skin.

"Go slip into that fluffy robe," he says as he unbuttons his shirt enough to slide it over his head, and it lands in a sloppy heap on the tile floor. "I'm right behind you. I'll leave these in here."

"Your suit is ruined."

"It's just a suit, Irish."

I chew my lip as I push my arms into the robe and watch Beck as he peels the trousers down his legs and then his socks and boxer briefs. Finally naked, he reaches for a towel and brushes the terrycloth over his skin before stepping out and pulling me against him once more.

"I'm going to order you some tea," he says, and that sweet gesture is all it takes for my eyes to fill. "You don't want tea?"

"I do. That would be lovely." I sniff and wipe a tear away. I have so much I want to say to him. I want to tell him that I love him.

Bloody hell, *I love him.*

"I just need to grab some dry clothes," he murmurs, moving into the attached closet. He pulls pajama pants and a T-shirt out of his bag and slips them on, along with a fresh pair of white socks. When he returns, he's dressed and looking so cozy, and I just want to curl into him.

But before I can, Beckett kisses my forehead, turns me away from him toward the mirror, and he picks up my comb. I look awful. My hair is a wet mess, my makeup is running all over my face, but he doesn't seem to mind.

"You don't have to dry it," I murmur as he gently makes his way through my wet hair. "I'll braid it."

"Whatever you want," he says, his voice soothing and

quiet, and I watch him work in the mirror. "Do you want your music?"

God, this man is good at taking care of me. "No, I like the quiet right now."

"Hmm." He smiles at me in the mirror and continues to work. "How do you feel?"

"I'm settling down."

"You're so fucking strong, baby."

I can't respond to that. I just watch him as he methodically combs my wet hair, and when he's finished, he doesn't give me the chance to braid it myself.

"Tip your head back for me," he says, and I immediately comply.

"How do you know how to French braid hair?" I ask him, surprised when he sections the strands and starts to weave them together.

"Birdie." He winks at me in the mirror. "She loves braids, and when Bridger was single and without child care, I'd take care of her sometimes. Billie taught us all how to braid so we could do it for her. Your hair is easier."

"It's way thicker."

"Yeah, Birdie's hair is fine, and my hands are too big. Your hair is easier for my clumsy fingers."

"Your fingers aren't clumsy. Trust me, I know."

He exhales, and when he reaches the bottom of the braid, I pass him a black tie from the counter. When it's secure, Beckett wraps his arms around me from behind and kisses my ear.

"I've fallen in love with you, Irish."

My heart stops, and my eyes flit up to his in the glass. He's so calm. His whiskey eyes are full of warmth and tenderness, and my heart starts to beat again, sending fire through my veins. It's as though he could read my mind just a few minutes ago.

"Beck." I spin in his arms to look him in the face, and my fingers instinctively reach for his whiskers. "I love you, too."

He boosts me up onto the vanity, and his lips find mine in a kiss so tender it brings tears to my eyes. But rather than deepen the kiss, he pulls back and ghosts his fingers down my cheeks.

"Where are your makeup wipes?" he asks, making me raise an eyebrow.

"In that drawer." I gesture to my left, and he opens the drawer, pulls out the blue container, and tugs out several wipes to remove my makeup. "And how do you know about makeup wipes, Mr. Blackwell?"

I slap a hand over my mouth. Of course, I'm not his first girlfriend.

"Forget I asked that."

With a shake of his head, he takes my hand away from my face and kisses it before setting it back in my lap.

"Billie used to walk around the house at the end of the day, wiping her face down. My sister is a girly-girl, so we always had to have her makeup wipes."

"Hmm." He frowns at my eyelashes, and I grin up at him. "Those are fake. You'll have to peel them off."

Taking a step back, he holds his hands up in surrender. "That's above my pay grade. Peel your own lashes off, Irish."

For the first time since we got back to the suite, I laugh. Once I've peeled off the artificial lashes, Beck steps back to me to resume wiping my face. Having my makeup removed has never felt so good.

"Can I ask some questions?"

He brushes the wipe over my eyebrow. I never knew that could feel so good.

"Shoot," he replies.

"Have you ever lived with a woman?"

Beck takes a breath and doesn't immediately say anything, giving me my answer.

"Got it."

"It's a story," he says, pausing in the makeup removal to kiss my lips softly and then brush his nose against my own. "I did live with someone, briefly. Her name is Tori, and you'll hear people talk about her once in a while, so you should hear this from me. I don't have any secrets. Not from you."

He tips my chin up with his finger and resumes taking off the makeup. He's methodical about it, working on one spot at a time before moving on to the next. I reach out and tuck my first two fingers in the waistband of his pants, anchoring myself to him.

"I'm listening."

He presses another kiss to my forehead. This man's lips are always on me, and it's heaven.

"Tori is from Bitterroot Valley. Like most people in town, I've known her a long time. She was a couple of years behind me in school, but I didn't really know her until she moved back after college. Anyway, it was the typical thing. We had mutual friends, ended up hanging out with the same people, and started seeing each other."

He discards the wipes, then turns on the tap and wets a cloth. He uses my cleanser to finish cleaning my face, moving in little circles over my skin.

"How long did you date?"

"About a year, give or take." He shrugs and rinses out the cloth, then removes the cleanser from my skin. "I invited her to live with me at the ranch."

I pull back and grab his wrists, so he's no longer touching my face, and frown up at him.

"You lived with her *at the ranch*?"

In the bloody bed that we've made love in?

I'm not okay with that.

"No." He kisses my nose, and his smile turns tender. "No, Irish, she never lived at the farmhouse."

I release his wrists and take a deep breath. He takes my hand and guides it back to his waistband, and I grab it with my fingers once more.

"All right then."

He tips his head to the side, his eyes bouncing back and forth between my own. "You don't like the idea of that."

"No, and I can't explain the why of it. I just don't like it."

Perhaps because it already feels like my *home.*

This is my man.

Those are my chickens.

Mine.

He nods and warms the cloth again before returning to his task of wiping my face.

"Fair enough. Anyway, she didn't want to live at the ranch. She wanted to be in town, so we moved into a place, and I commuted."

"What did she do for a living?" I ask, frowning. Why wouldn't she want to live at the ranch?

"She's a nurse. She had shift work at the hospital, so I figured she didn't want to have to drive back and forth in the middle of the night, and I couldn't blame her. I didn't really want her to do that either. But I put in long hours, so I'd leave well before five in the morning and not get home until close to ten at night. Sometimes later. I didn't have the staff that I have now."

Tossing the cloth aside, he reaches for my moisturizer, but I pass him the rose water spray that I use first, and close my eyes while he spritzes it on my skin.

"Now this?" he asks, and I nod as he dips his finger into the pot. "We never saw each other. I hated the drive into town every day, and she made it perfectly clear that she'd never be a ranch girl. She didn't like the animals, and honestly, I think she assumed I was wealthier because I ran a successful dairy operation."

"What do you mean?"

"She wanted me to tell her to quit her job. To do whatever she wanted. Buy whatever she wanted. And I told her that if she quit her job, we'd have to live at the farm."

"And she didn't like that."

"No." He shakes his head and shrugs. "Not long after, I walked into our place, after a long day at the ranch, and found her in bed with some tourist she'd picked up at the bar."

My eyes go wide as I stare up at him. How could anyone do something like that to *Beckett*?

"Never spoke to her again," he continues. "And it was probably telling that it didn't really break my heart. It pissed me off, don't get me wrong, but it didn't hurt me. I knew we weren't going to work out. We wanted very different things, so shoving my things in a bag and leaving that night felt really good."

I frame his face in my hands and pull him to me so I can kiss him.

"Worked out well for this Irish girl."

He laughs against my lips. "I'd say it worked out fucking fantastic. How about you? Any live-ins?"

"No. Do you have any children I should know about?"

Beckett's eyebrows climb in surprise. "Not that I'm aware of."

"Hey, you never know. A girl has to ask."

"Any kids for you?"

I laugh at that and shake my head. "No. I went years without having a period at all. Sorry, that might be TMI."

"No, it's not. Why?"

"Because when a woman's underweight and under immense stress, her body is in survival mode, and periods become irregular or go away altogether. It's common in

KRISTEN PROBY

athletes, dancers in particular. Gymnasts, too. I had intense diet restrictions, Beckett. I don't think I can adequately explain how strict my diet was, and I put my body through a lot. So it wouldn't have been possible for me to get pregnant for a long time. But I was so busy with dance that sex wasn't really something I worried about."

"Let's take this chat into the living room, and we can get Riley," he suggests, and I nod and hop off the vanity, feeling so much better.

"Do you want to change? Your family is going to end up in here soon."

"Yes, that would be better."

He nods and finds me some leggings and one of his shirts.

"Can I have the shirt you wore on the plane earlier?" I ask. He looks surprised, so I bite my lower lip. "It'll smell more like you."

His eyes soften as he reaches up to brush his thumb over the apple of my cheek before he goes back into the closet and returns with the blue button-up from the plane. I button it up, then slip on my leggings and follow Beck into the living area of the suite just as there's a knock on the door.

"Who is it?" Beckett asks.

"Sanders, Ms. Gallagher's security. I have Riley."

"Well, that was good timing," Beck says as he opens the door. Riley comes bounding in, his tongue hanging out of his mouth happily, and when he sees me, he races to me.

"Hey, beautiful boy." I kiss his head and feel so much relief having him by my side. "Were you good for Sally? I missed you."

As if he can sense that I'm not okay, he pushes his head into my stomach, trying to soothe me.

"It's okay. We're okay."

I sit on the sofa, listening to Beckett's voice. The front door closes, and then he's talking to someone else. Probably room service.

Even though I'm still in shock that The Arsehole found me—how did he know that I'd be at the fundraiser?—having Beckett here, determined to soothe and care for me, has made it all more surreal than terrifying. I have no doubt that Miller will figure this out, and Connor won't rest until all the details are gathered. And knowing Beckett loves me? Nothing has ever felt so wonderful. So despite the growing anger from seeing *him*, and especially now that I have Riley with me, I know I'll be okay.

I hated that meltdown, but I'm not alone.

Not this time.

When Beck walks into the room to join me, he picks me up, sits in the corner of the couch, and settles me in his lap, and I curl up around him, looping my arms around his neck and pressing myself to him. I sense Riley lie down in his bed next to the couch, and I sigh, truly feeling completely content since the moment The Arsehole put his hand on me.

"So," Beck says, his fingertips under my shirt,

ghosting over my skin deliciously, making me want to purr. "Sex is a higher priority now."

I smirk against his neck, nuzzling him, breathing him in. "Absolutely, as long as it's with you."

"If it's with someone else, we're going to have a problem, Irish." He chuckles and nips at my ear.

"I love you."

"Say it again," he whispers, tightening his arms around me.

"I love you, Beckett Blackwell."

He pulls back and brushes my hair back behind my ear. "I love you too, Irish."

With a grin, I press my lips to his so gently that it's barely there until he moves in and deepens the kiss, nudging my mouth open with his tongue.

He's claiming me with this kiss, the way he's done before, but there's no mistaking this feeling of belonging.

Of ownership.

From both of us.

The doorbell rings, and Riley barks, but Beck doesn't immediately pull away. He rubs his nose over mine and sighs before he sets me on the cushion next to him, then pads over to open the door. Room service rolls in a table topped with a silver tea set. They raise the edges of the table, making it round, and pull hot plates out from under it.

"Would you like me to pour the tea, sir?"

"No, thanks," Beck says with the shake of his head. "We can handle it."

He walks the man to the door, tips him, then returns to me.

"I got you some soup in case you wanted something to eat," he says as I stand. "Along with a grilled cheese sandwich."

"Are you handling me then, Mr. Blackwell?"

"I'm taking care of my girl," he replies and presses his lips to my forehead. "What would you like?"

"Tea for now, but keep the warming domes on the others because I'll probably want them in a bit."

He nods and makes my tea the way he knows I like it, then he joins me on the couch.

After I take a sip, I set the cup aside, then take his hand in mine and thread our fingers together.

"Was it too soon for declarations of love?" I can't help asking.

Beck frowns and shakes his head. "Time doesn't matter. Shit, I knew you were it for me that day that I saw you in the bookstore months ago."

"What day?" I sit forward, interested to hear about this. "I don't remember seeing you at the bookshop."

"You didn't see me." He grins and simply pulls me to him again, and I happily sit in his lap. "I was in a hurry, and you were there, reading the back of a book, and you were so fucking gorgeous, it knocked the earth off its axis."

"When was this?"

"Last winter."

I blink up at him. "*Winter*? But we just met—"

"We just met this spring," he confirms. "But I saw

you months before that. Then I had to work to get you to go out with me."

Laughing, I sag against him, nestling my head under his chin.

"I guess it's good you're a hard worker. This is nice. When do you suppose the others will get here?"

"As soon as they can. I should have checked my phone."

I don't move to get off him. "I'm so tired, Beck."

"You can go to bed, and I can handle the rest."

"No." I shake my head and drag my fingertips up and down his arm, enjoying the way his muscles feel under my touch. "I don't mean that. I'm so tired of dealing with *him*. It's gone on too long."

"We're going to figure this out, Irish. I promise. This is the last time that fucker gets close to you in any capacity."

I don't just want to believe him, I *do*. Because I know that Beckett won't let anything happen to me.

I haven't felt this safe in three years.

Chapter Twenty-One

LEWIS

A.K.A. The Arsehole

Tonight was worth every moment of planning, strategy, and money that it took to make it happen. God, the scent and softness of her lustrous skin. The feel of her slim body beneath my fingers. Absolute heaven. No doubt she's hated being away from my touch as much as I've loathed being away from her.

But not for long.

I watched her all evening, moving around the room, smiling. Laughing. Her elegance and sophistication are so effortless.

She was with a man, but when she was finally alone, I made my move, and it was everything I'd hoped for. She's gained weight, and that will have to come off, of course.

My tiny dancer has to look a certain way.

But her dress was beautiful, and when I leaned in to say hello and pressed my lips to her ear, I swear I heard her gasp with lust.

It thrilled her to see me as much as it did me to see her.

I had to rush to the men's room and lock myself in a stall and stroke myself until I came all over my hand. My attraction to her is so intense. I wish I'd had time to invite her with me, to boost her up against the wall and rut myself into her until I filled her with my release.

Next time.

And there will be a next time.

As soon as I figure out where my tiny dancer is hiding, I'll make her mine.

Chapter Twenty-Two

BECKETT

I have my lips buried in Skyla's damp hair, quietly simmering with rage. She's needed me to be gentle tonight, to care for her, to love her, and I'm happy to do that for her, but I'm ready to tear someone apart.

A specific someone.

Skyla startles when the doorbell rings, and I sweep my hand down her spine and back up again.

"That's them," I whisper and slide out from under her, then I make my way to the door and open it to find Skyla's parents, Connor, and Mik, all still dressed to the nines, all with worried scowls on their faces as they walk past me and into the suite.

"Someone's going to tell me what in the bloody hell is going on," Patrick insists, his hands fisted at his sides.

I still can't believe that her parents don't know about The Asshole. How could she keep this from them, and for all this time?

Mik crosses to Skyla and tugs her up into a hug, then pulls back and holds her face in his hands.

"Did he hurt you, malishka?" Mik asks.

"No," Skyla says, shaking her head. "No, I was creeped out, but I'm okay. And I need to tell my parents before my da has a stroke."

Maeve wrings her hands as she sits on the edge of the chair next to Skyla's.

"You're scaring me, *a stór*."

Skyla's eyes find mine, and I see the distress in them, so I cross back to her and sit next to her on the sofa. She leans into me and begins telling them the same story she told me when we started this relationship.

I keep my eyes on Patrick and Maeve, who go from scowling, to horror, to fear, and back to anger again. Maeve begins to cry, but Patrick looks like he wants to murder someone. His face is red, and his hands are fisted.

And I know how he feels.

"Tell me your men found him," I say to Connor, who's stood back with his hands in his pockets, grinding his teeth this whole time.

"No," he says quietly, and Skyla's hand tightens around mine. "Not yet, anyway."

"He was *here*," Maeve says, shaking her head. "Tonight? But we have the best security money can buy. No one not on the guest list could have gotten in."

"We're running an internal investigation," Connor says, pulling his hand down his face as his phone rings, and he answers it.

"I want to know why I'm just now hearing this tale,"

Patrick says. A vein protrudes from his temple, and his face is hard with anger. "If my fecking *daughter* has been dealing with a bloody stalker all this time, why in the name of all the saints wasn't I apprised?"

"Because I asked that you not be," Skyla says. "Because there was nothing you could do."

"Nothing I could do?" he roars. "You listen to me. I'm Patrick fucking Gallagher, and I have contacts that you've never even dreamed of, *mo mhuirnin*. I'm worth more than fifty billion euros, and I can make that piece of shite disappear from the face of this earth, and no one would ever question it."

Good. His rage matches my own.

"I can't prove that he's done anything illegal," Skyla continues. "The police told me that he's a nuisance at worst, and I should ignore him. He used to go away for months at a time. This is the first time that anything has happened since I moved to Montana. I'm not lying about that, Da. I'd hoped that he'd finally lost interest."

"But he's why you're not in New York," Maeve says. "And he's why you can't dance."

"I'm happy where I am," Skyla insists as she reaches for her mom's hand. "No, it's not how I would have chosen to leave, but I have a full life, and I'm *happy*. I just need him to stop."

"You don't have to say that for my sake," I tell her, but she turns to me and shakes her head.

"It's the truth of it, Beckett Blackwell. Bitterroot Valley is my home. I have friends and a home, and a business. And best of all, I have you. I don't want New York

City. I just want *him* to stop. I don't want his fecking hands on me."

"He touched you?" Patrick asks, his voice eerily quiet now, and I can see that *that* is what had to have terrified his competitors early in his career. Patrick Gallagher isn't a man you want to cross. "Tonight. He laid hands on you?"

"He touched my back," Skyla whispers, and I release her hand to wrap my arm around her shoulders and pull her against me. "And he whispered in my ear, which gave me the creeps, and I had to wash him off me."

"He's a dead man," Patrick says as he paces.

Mik also paces the room, looking like a pissed-off brother.

Connor's taking calls across the room and scowling, and then he hangs up and pushes his glasses up the bridge of his nose.

"I'm putting a team of four men, twenty-four hours a day, at your house," Connor announces, still looking down at his phone. "We'll add more cameras to the exterior as well."

"No."

All eyes turn to this fiery Irish girl at my side.

"What?" Connor asks, scowling.

"No, I've told you before, I don't want strange men wandering around my property. It's my *home*, and I won't have it. I won't feel like a prisoner."

"It's not to keep you bloody in," Connor says with more emotion than I've seen from him before. "It's to keep that psychopath *out*. It's not up for debate, Skyla Maeve."

"Don't think you can use my whole given name and have me folding as if I were a wee girl," she replies, getting hot now as she sits forward on the sofa, pulling out of my arms.

God, she's fucking gorgeous when she's pissed.

"You'll do what you're bloody told," Conner retorts, and I think I just saw steam come out of my girl's ears.

"He's right," Mik interrupts, speaking for the first time. "Malishka, you can't be stubborn and careless."

"Careless?" Skyla stands and stomps across the room, shaking her head. "You think I'm fecking *careless*? I moved my whole life because that arsehole threatened you. Threatened all of you. I disappeared from everything I knew and loved to keep everyone safe, and he *finally* went away. It's been almost a year without any contact of any kind, and it's been the best year I've had in so long. Everything was finally starting to feel normal again. If you call living in what might as well be Fort Knox with a highly trained attack dog *normal*."

"Back up," Connor says. "Who threatened who?"

Skyla's mossy eyes, so full of emotion, widen, and she clamps her lips closed.

Jesus, I want to hold her.

"What are you talking about, *a stór*?" Maeve asks.

"It doesn't matter."

"Yeah, it does," I reply before anyone else can. "It all matters, Irish."

She sighs and looks so weary, but then she squares her

shoulders and lifts that beautiful chin. "He made it clear that he'd get rid of everyone else in my life, so it was only him and me."

"What the fuck?" Mik asks. "You did not tell me? Malishka, between your family and mine, we just take care of him."

"Right, because I want the Russian mafia in my business," Skyla says with a huff.

"None of this matters," Connor interrupts. "You'll have protection, and that's how it's going to be."

Skyla shakes her head, and I cross to her now, taking her face in my hands.

"Baby." My voice is firm, but I'm not yelling or raising my tone. "I want you to hear me loud and clear right now. Everyone here loves you. We want you to be safe." Her eyes well as she stares up at me, and her chin wobbles.

"It's an invasion of my privacy, and I won't give him that," she says, her voice rough with emotion.

"I understand. So there's only one solution to this."

"What?" A tear falls from the corner of her eye, and I catch it with my thumb.

"You'll be moving in with me."

Her brows pull together. "In one of the rentals?"

"Fuck, no." God, she's adorable. I can't help the bark of laughter that slips out. "No, Irish, you'll be living with me. On my farm. The chickens are now your responsibility."

She catches that pillow of a lower lip in her teeth and, for the first time since everyone got here, her shoulders drop, and she lets out the breath she's been holding all evening.

"I love those chickens."

"I know."

"But not as much as I love you."

"Glad to hear it."

"What in the bloody hell is happening?" Connor asks the room at large. "You've known each other for two minutes."

"More like three and a half," I reply without looking away from my girl. "She'll be safe with me. I have security on my property, and no one can link her there."

I wrap my arm around Skyla, tuck her against my side, and turn so I can look at the others in this room, not wavering in my gaze.

If they have a problem with me, they need to speak up now.

"I don't love it," Patrick admits. "You'll need to close down your studio."

"It'll be a cold, bloody day in hell before I do that," Skyla retorts, and I tighten my hold on her. "I have students. I can't do that."

"Miller will escort you to and from work then," Connor offers, but Skyla's already shaking her head.

"No need," Mik interrupts. "I'll be with her at the studio."

"What?" My girl shakes her head. "You have a life in New York City."

"We have to rehearse," Mik says with a shrug. "I

might as well come to Montana a couple of weeks early. We will get a head start."

"What about Benji? Are you telling me your husband won't have an issue with you living across the country?"

"He'll come with me for a chunk of the time. This is the best offer you're going to get, malishka. Take it or leave it."

"I'd take it," I murmur before kissing her temple.

"I'm not pleased that those I love are being inconvenienced," she admits with a huff. *So adorable.* "But I love you all so much, and it's grateful I am that I have you. I'll live at the farm, and Mik can join me at the studio. We might very well kill each other in the first week."

"You love being with me all day, every day," Mik says with a satisfied grin. "You can't wait."

Maeve, who's been listening and fighting her own tears, crosses the room and takes her daughter into her arms.

"My darlin' babe."

I pull away and gesture for Connor to follow me out of the room. When the door's closed, I turn to him and finally let my anger show.

"I want some fucking answers."

"Aye, so do I. Just what exactly is happening between you and my sister?"

"I'm in love with her. As soon as she'll let me, I'm going to marry her. And right now, I want to know why the *fuck* you've known about this for three goddamn years, and that son of a bitch is still breathing?"

Connor's nostrils flare, but before he can reply, the

elevator dings, and Miller strides off, his face a stony mask.

"Report," Connor says as Miller approaches.

"We have him on the security footage," Miller says. "He had an invitation when he came to the door. Under what name, we don't know yet. He mingled all night, staying close to the edges of the room, and I can see that he was watching Skyla."

I push my hands through my hair. I've never been a violent man, but I want to punch a hole through the goddamn wall.

"We have him approaching her, and it all happens the way she said. Then he leaves."

"Where the fuck did he go?" I ask.

"First, he went into the restroom, and then he returned to the party, looked for Skyla, and when he didn't find her, he walked away."

"Out the front door," I mutter, shaking my head. "But he's not anonymous. You know *who* he is. So follow him to New York and take care of him."

Connor lifts a brow. "You want me to commit murder?"

"Of course not. Talk to him. Threaten him."

"Do you think I haven't tried that?" Connor demands. "Regardless of what my sister asked, of *course* I did that. I spoke with the cops. I hired a private investigator to follow him. He still follows him, but somehow, the son of a bitch lost my tail on his way here. He's slippery, and he's connected."

"To who?"

"Politicians. The chief of police of New York City. Enough people that they look the other way."

"Until he kills her."

Both of the men before me tighten their jaws.

"You know I'm right. They all look away while he terrorizes a woman and potentially hurts her. Because what is his endgame in all of this?"

"He's convinced that Skyla belongs to him."

"Yeah, well, he's dead fucking wrong." I shake my head. "If you can't figure this out, I have other contacts who can. You're not the only billionaire I know or who I have ties to."

"Are you fucking threatening me?"

"Not at all. I actually like you, so I'm telling the truth. Figure out a way to hit this asshole where it hurts. Make him lose all of his money. His home. Report something interesting to the IRS. What does he do for a living? Fuck that up, too."

"I like him," Miller says to Connor, then clears his throat when Connor glares at him. "Sir."

"There are ways to destroy a man without killing him. But rest assured, he's going to wish he were dead when we get through with him."

Connor blows out a breath. "It's been almost a year. Why is he back now?"

"It doesn't matter. He's back. And now he's done."

Chapter Twenty-Three

SKYLA

I wanted to come home. I didn't want to stay in LA for the night. All I longed for was to return to Montana with Beckett and Riley and be where I knew I was comfortable and safe.

So we all got on the plane and came to Montana.

Mik's at my house in town. Connor and my parents are at his new house, which I haven't seen yet, but I'm determined to visit as soon as possible.

And Beck and I just walked into the farmhouse.

When I turn to him, I can see the fatigue around his eyes and immediately feel regret. He didn't sleep on the plane, but he held me so I could doze in and out.

"We should have stayed in LA," I murmur. "It's sorry I am that I kept everyone up into the night."

"No, don't be sorry. The others are probably in bed by now." He pulls me to him and kisses the top of my head. He wraps those strong arms around me and holds me in a hug that I've become addicted to. "I kind of love that you wanted to come home."

I grin against his chest, then I'm suddenly in his arms, being carried up the stairs, with Riley running ahead of us, already anticipating where to go. Beckett flips off the lights as we move through the house, and then we're in the bedroom with the soft glow of a bedside lamp.

"Did you leave that on before we left town?" I ask.

"No, Billie stopped over and turned on the lights when I told her that we'd be coming home tonight."

I frown up at him after he sets me on the bed. "But that was late."

"She's my sister." He shrugs as if it's no big deal as he peels out of the T-shirt and jeans he wore on the flight.

I stayed in the leggings and his button-down that I pulled on after the shower in the hotel.

"And my girl doesn't like the dark, so you won't come home to a dark house. Ever."

My eyes fill with tears. I can't help it. Maybe it's the exhaustion, but I think it's the pure love this man shows me so effortlessly. It's as if it's his only mission in life.

Once he's fully naked, he tugs me up to my feet and removes my clothes as well, then we climb into bed and snuggle together. Beck's on his back, and my front is against his side, with one leg over his and my arm around his chest.

And for the first time since I felt *that arsehole's* hand on me, I take a long, deep breath.

"I take it back," I whisper against his skin into the

darkness that doesn't seem to bother me when I'm in his arms. "I'm not sorry. This is what I needed. Right here with you, in this bed."

I feel his lips in my hair, and then he tips my chin up so he can cover my mouth with his. With that simple caress of his lips and tongue, heat moves through me in slow, delicious waves.

"I'm suddenly not so tired anymore," I whisper against his mouth, and he grins as I move over him, resting on his chest because I can't move my mouth away from his. I'm lost in the way his mouth feels against mine.

"Jesus, I feel like I haven't had my hands on you in forever. Not like this."

"Less than a day," I murmur as I nibble the corner of his mouth, loving the way his whiskers feel against my skin.

"Too goddamn long." His fingertips skim up and down my back, and my skin erupts with goose pimples.

I want to be the one in control for a little while. I think I need it after what happened earlier. So I kiss my way down to his chest, then his hard, rippled stomach, and glory in the feel of his smooth skin. He's so ... *big*. Everywhere.

"Your body is bloody brilliant, Beck."

His chuckle turns into a moan when I drag my tongue between the hard lines of muscle, then kiss my way over to the V in his hip.

"This right here should be illegal. Or come with a warning label at the very least."

"Irish, I'm about to flip you over—"

"Let me." I lift my head and stare up at him, and I know my eyes plead with him to let me be the one to lead for a little while. "Please, *a ghrá.*"

His thumb drifts over my bottom lip, but he doesn't stop me, so I continue my exploration and slip my hand over his already hard cock, from tip to base.

He lifts and thrusts into my hand with a growl so feral it makes me grin just before I wrap my lips around the crown, tasting the essence of him already there.

"Fucking Christ, Irish," he grits out, fisting the bedsheets. His forearms flex, his veins pop, and Holy Mary, it makes my core flood with desire.

I briefly wish I hadn't had him braid my hair so he could fist his hands there.

I'm kneeling between his legs, and all I want to do is take him deep into my throat and make him go bloody crazy.

"Your pretty little mouth looks so fucking good on my cock."

He's breathing hard, moving under me, and I've never felt more powerful. I take him deep, past the back of my throat as far as I can until tears form in my eyes, and I'm certain I'm going to choke until I pass out.

But I don't.

I ease up, catch my breath, then do it again.

"Fuuuuck," he growls. "You've got three more seconds, baby, before I lose control and take you."

Satisfied, I pull up, firm my lips around him, and sink

back down again, but this time, I keep it shallow and lick over the crown, humming.

"That's it."

Beckett sits up and rolls us over so I'm on my back, and he kisses me hard and deep as if his life depends on it. His big hand drifts down my torso, then his fingers are in my already wet pussy, and I cry out against his lips.

"You're so fucking wet for me. Does sucking my cock make you wet, baby?" He kisses down my jawline to my ear as I nod. "You're gorgeous. Every inch of you. And you're mine. You hear that, Irish?"

I nod again because I'm pretty sure all of my words have left the building, but he bites my earlobe.

"Tell me."

"Yours." My voice is breathy, a little choppy. "I'm yours, *a ghrá*."

"That's right." He nudges his way between my legs, and then he's *there*. I lift my hips in invitation. "Fuck, you're warm."

He slips inside, filling me, making us both moan.

"And tight. So goddamn tight. Am I hurting you, baby?"

"Never." Cupping his cheek, I scratch my fingers in his soft whiskers. "You'd never hurt me. God, it's so bloody good, *a ghrá*."

He smiles before he kisses me and moves his hips in a circle. I'm pretty sure my soul just left my body.

He pulls my nipple into his mouth and licks the hard nub before moving to the other side to give it the same attention. My body is *on fire* for this man.

"I need to get closer," he mutters against my neck. "I can never get close enough."

"Pull my leg up," I whisper. He does, but only hooks it around his elbow, which opens me way wider. He's able to go deeper, but that's not what I meant. "More."

He frowns down at me, and it makes me grin.

"Push my knee into my shoulder, Beck."

He shakes his head. "I don't want to sit up."

"You don't have to."

I love that he doesn't want to hurt me, but I'm a ballerina.

So I show him. I pull my leg up myself, and his eyes go wide.

"Push inside me now, *a ghrá*."

He does, and now he's bottomed out, and he groans before covering my mouth with his.

"Jesus Christ, you're flexible."

"Perk of the job."

He snickers, then he's moving once more, and neither of us is laughing.

"Fuck, Irish, I need you to get there."

"I'm there." I feel the contractions start. The heat rolls through me, and it feels like my body explodes into a million pieces, with Beckett there to collect every single one and put me back together again. Is that roar the sound of my blood in my ears, or Beck falling over with me? I think it's the latter, and the next thing I know, he's reversed our positions again, and I'm lying on top of him. He's still inside me and hugging me as if his life depends on it.

"I love you," he says as he brushes loose hair off my cheeks and cups my face. "God, I fucking love you. I want you to sleep, baby."

"I love you, too."

"You've lost your bloody mind."

I'm lying flat on my back, knees bent, struggling to breathe while staring at the ceiling of my studio.

"You're being lazy." Mik stands over me, scowling.

"I am *not* lazy, Mikhail." Bloody hell, why can't I breathe? "You're a tyrant."

"Again."

"No, I'm going to lie here until I die."

"*Again*, malishka. Up."

He snatches my hand off my belly and pulls me up to my aching feet. I want to cry out, but I won't give him the satisfaction.

I have nails coming off again, blisters on my blisters, and this is my third pair of toe shoes this week.

And we've only been practicing for nine days.

"It never used to be this hard." I hang my head and wish for a nap. "Or hurt this bad."

"Yes, it was, and it did," he says, but he doesn't soften his voice. Mik's always been a pain in the arse. "But you've been away so long, you've forgotten."

"I'd like to keep forgetting."

He shakes his head and gestures for me to return to

the middle of the floor so we can start from the top of the scene.

Of course, the king wants to see the most emotional, most difficult scene of the entire show for his inauguration. It's ten minutes of torture.

"I need a break," I tell him.

"No. You need to keep going."

"Jesus, babe, give her a break."

I let the smile come as Mik's head whips around to the door where Benji's standing. Beck's right behind him. I knew Benji was flying in today, and Beck offered to pick him up from the airport and surprise Mik at the studio.

The timing couldn't be better. I really *do* need a break.

Mik runs to his man, and they embrace. My romantic heart sighs as they kiss as if they haven't seen each other in months.

"Okay, tyrant, stand aside. I haven't seen your man in too long, and I need a hug."

I push Mik out of the way and am swallowed up in Benji's hug. He's a tall, lean man without an ounce of fat on him. He wears glasses, and he has the start of a five o'clock shadow on his handsome face.

"Hey, pretty girl," he murmurs and kisses my head. "Are you keeping him in line?"

"He's abusing me. That's what he's doing," I say, giving Mik an evil grin. "He's really mean to me, Benji. Make him pay. No sex. No cuddles. No murder documentaries."

"Wow, you're gonna make me pay too, huh?" Benji

gives me one more squeeze before he lets me go, and I'm suddenly surrounded by my man, who's hugging me from behind.

"Surprise," I say to Mik, who's hugging his guy once again. "*Now* will you give me a break?"

"We'll come back to it tomorrow." He narrows his eyes at me. "You need to stretch, and you need to soak those feet. You've been stumbling and hobbling around here."

"It's grateful I am that you're so good for my ego, Mikhail." I roll my eyes. "Do you two want to have dinner tonight?"

"No," they say in unison, making me cackle.

"Ew. Okay then. How long are you here, Benji?"

"As long as he is," he replies, kissing Mik's forehead. "I'll work from here. Are you sure you want us living in your house?"

"I'm at the ranch with Beckett, so yes, please live in my house. Make yourself at home there, and let us know if you need anything."

"We're leaving," Mik announces, pulling on his shoes. "I'll see you in the morning."

"You're welcome," I call out to Mik, who just sends me a wave, not even looking back at me. "Love you, too!"

I'm laughing as the door closes behind them, then I spin around and hug Beck.

"That went well."

"Benji seems like a nice guy," Beck says, trailing his fingertips down my cheek.

"Oh, he's way nicer than Mik." Pulling back with a

laugh, I sit on the floor so I can unlace my toe shoes, wincing with every movement. "Benji is the sunshine to Mik's grumpy. They're good together."

"How long have they been married?" Beck shoves his hands in his pockets, but his jaw clenches when he sees the state of my foot. "Fucking hell, Irish."

"I know, they're bad." I sigh and cringe as I wiggle my poor toes. "They've been married for about five years, give or take, but together for almost ten. Benji's a total nerd. He's a book editor, which means he and I have a ton in common since I'm also a book lover. Mik hates to read. They met through mutual friends. Mik finally got up the courage to ask Benji out on a date, and they've been pretty much attached at the hip ever since. This is probably the longest they've been separated, so it's glad I am that Benji can work here."

I peel the other shoe off and moan at the blood seeping out of my middle toes.

"You're not putting shoes on those feet, Skyla."

"I can't walk around barefoot."

"That's exactly what you're going to do." The look in his eyes says that there's no room for argument. "I'm taking you home, and we're going to put your feet in to soak."

Okay, that's exactly what I was hoping to do, so I won't argue with him.

"I still have to get home," I remind him. "But I do have flip-flops with me. I invested in some, but I refuse to wear them in public because only you're allowed to see me like this."

"I'll carry you."

I smirk up at him.

"Hold on, I need five seconds to turn off lights and lock up. And I really do need to stretch."

"Stay." He points at me and walks to the back. I can hear him rustling around, and then the overhead lights go out. I quickly go through some stretches as Beck moves about the area.

Even Riley watches intently as Beck comes back to me and passes me my handbag.

"Thanks."

"You're welcome."

He offers me his hand, but instead of just pulling me to my feet, he lifts me onto his shoulder and gives Riley the command to follow us.

When the door is locked, he carries me to his truck, opens the back for Riley, then sets me in the passenger seat.

"Well, that was ... nauseating." I let out a laugh. "I don't think I enjoy the shoulder carry. Hello, motion sickness."

"So noted." He buckles me in, kisses my cheek, then walks around to climb into the driver's side.

He holds my hand all the way out to the ranch, and once he's parked in front of the house, he lets Riley out, who quickly relieves himself in the grass. Beck carries me inside and up the stairs to the bedroom.

"I'll get the Epsom salts," he says as he sets me on the vanity. "I want you to soak those feet."

"I will. That sounds nice, actually. Do you have to go back to work then?"

"No, I'm going to stay with you."

He turns on the water in the sink, and when it's the temperature he likes, he pulls the stopper to keep the water in and pours in a handful of salts.

This is how I prefer to soak my feet. Sitting on the bathroom vanity with my feet in the sink. It's easiest.

And when I slowly lower my poor feet into the warm water, I sigh. It hurts at first, but then it starts to soothe.

"Is this going to be how it is until this performance is over?" Beckett asks as he leans on the counter and pulls me into him, hugging me to him and brushing his lips over the top of my head.

"It'll get better. I don't have any calluses anymore. Just when my feet adjust, it'll be time for the performance, then it'll all be over."

"Hmm." He kisses my temple. "What can I make you to eat?"

I let this sweet moment soak into my pores as I lean against him. I do believe that Beckett's love language is acts of service. He's constantly caring for me and pampering me. His aftercare once we've finished making love is next-level brilliant. He's always making sure I'm comfortable and never hungry.

It's no wonder that I fell in love with him so quickly.

"I should probably have a protein smoothie and some chicken."

"What do you *want*, baby?" He's still peppering my head with kisses.

"A cheeseburger." I laugh against him, and he tightens his arms around me. "But I can't do that. I'm working too hard. The protein is good for me. Maybe we can have pasta for dinner. I could use the carbs, too. I'm burning a lot of calories right now."

"You can have whatever you want."

"You say that to me often, Mr. Blackwell."

"Because it's true." He buries his lips in my hair. "Why don't we curl up for a while and read when you're done here?"

"Wow, you're really spoiling me today."

"Get used to it, baby."

I'm definitely getting used to it. It's been nine days of being spoiled, of living here at the farm, and aside from some bad dreams and waking up in a cold sweat because of everything The Arsehole has done to me, I've mostly felt at peace. All because of this man.

I'm not simply used to it. I'm keeping him if it's the last thing I do.

Chapter Twenty-Four

BECKETT

"I can walk, Beck." Skyla's arms are curled around my neck as I carry her out of the bathroom.

"No." After kissing her temple, I snatch her reading device off the bedside table and carry my girl downstairs to the living room.

We like to curl up in the corner of the sectional to read together. It's become a routine in the evenings, one of my favorite things to do with her.

I enjoy the stories, but mostly, I just like being with *her*. With the woman of my dreams, curled up to my side, hugging me as we read to each other.

I know my brothers would give me shit for it but fuck that. I like it. Looks like Bridger was right after all. Not that I'd tell him that.

After I get Skyla settled under a blanket, I kiss her head. "Want some tea?"

"No." She shakes her head. "I want you to sit with me."

"I'm getting you water, then."

Riley follows me into the kitchen and indicates he wants to go out, so I open the door for him, and he bounds out to do his thing. Skyla prefers her water with lemon in it, so by the time I fill a glass with ice, water, and the fresh lemon, Riley's ready to come back in.

"A bottle of water would have been just fine," she says when I pass her the glass, and Riley curls up on his bed.

"You like it this way, so you'll have it this way." I catch her chin in my fingers and kiss her sweet lips. "Ready to read?"

"Hmm." She wakes up the device and passes it to me, which makes my lips curl up in a smile. Although we typically take turns reading, she prefers it when I read to her. We started a book last night about a motorcycle club president and a girl who just moved back to her home-town after being dumped by her stupid boyfriend.

Mafia to motorcycle clubs. Who knew this would be my life?

It's not long before said president has the girl alone, in his bedroom, and up against the wall.

I glance down, and Skyla has that lower lip trapped in her teeth. Her hand squeezes my bicep, and I decide to have a little fun.

"Here, Irish. Your turn to read."

My girl frowns up at me. "You're tired already?"

"Not tired." I shake my head and insist she take the device. "Just keep reading."

"If you have to go to the bathroom, I can wait—"

I cut her off with my mouth on hers. "Just read, baby."

She shrugs, skims the page, then picks up where I left off as I kneel on the floor between her legs. I tuck my fingers in the waistband of her leggings and tug them down her hips, legs, and then off completely, tossing them aside along with her panties. Skyla gasps, watching me.

"Read." My voice is hard, and her pupils blow wide at the command, but she keeps watching me, so I push up and frame her face in my hands, kiss her hard, and pull back. "Read to me, gorgeous. Don't stop. If you stop reading, you don't get to come."

"Beckett."

"No, I think his name is Wolf." I smirk and kiss her neck before I make my way back south. "Do it."

She licks her lips, clears her throat, and starts to read again while I get to work.

"My gods, he just quoted *The Great Gatsby* to her," Skyla says, then sighs when I kiss the inside of her thigh. "Beck—"

"Nope. I have this handled. You read."

The man in the book has the woman by the throat, and it makes Skyla's voice turn breathy. It has to be that because I don't have a finger on her yet.

So my hand drifts up her leg, up her torso over her shirt, and I loosely hold on to her throat, and her words stumble to a halt.

"You like that, baby?"

"In theory." She licks her lips, not looking away from the book. "But I like it better when you pull my hair."

Fuck me.

"That's my girl."

She clears her throat and keeps reading, and I slide the tip of my finger through her already wet slit, making her stammer.

But she doesn't stop.

And I reward her with a light lick over her clit.

"Oh, feck," she whispers.

"Is that in the book?"

She shakes her head, and I pull away, making her groan in frustration.

"I warned you about what would happen if you stopped."

She glares at me, but she begins reading again, and I return to the task at hand. Her pussy is already swollen with arousal, and I can't resist her. Leaning in, I bury my face in her, lapping and nibbling, making her hips rotate and her voice shake.

But she doesn't stop.

Her feet are sore, and I don't want her digging into my back or the cushion, so I brace her legs over my arms so her feet dangle to the side. I open her wider, still kissing her core.

My girl continues to read without missing a beat but manages to get her shirt over her head and casts it aside. The clothing against my own skin is too much, and I pull back long enough to yank off my T-shirt, unfasten my jeans, and release my aching dick. I'm surprised there isn't a permanent imprint from my zipper up my shaft since I'm so fucking hard for her.

Skyla lets out a gasp of surprise when I tug her down and flip her over so she's bent over the seat of the sofa. I pull the tie off the end of her braid, loosening her soft red strands so I can dig my fingers in. She moans, drops her forehead to the seat, and I back away.

"Beckett!"

"I didn't say you could stop reading, Irish."

She whimpers but then pushes up onto her elbows and grabs the device. Her voice is smoky, full of lust and need as she reads, and I lean in to pepper kisses on her back and over her sexy freckles, making her whimper again.

But she doesn't stop.

From behind, I press my two middle fingers into her and feel her tighten around me.

"So fucking wet," I growl against her shoulder blade as my thumb brushes over her hard clit, making her hips buck against my hand.

And she doesn't stop reading.

Kissing and nibbling my way up to her ear, I press my lips to the shell of that gorgeous, freckled ear and whisper, "Good girl."

Her pussy clenches around my fingers, making me chuckle.

But she doesn't stop.

I drag my whiskers down her spine, and her flesh erupts with goose bumps as I kiss the top of her ass, just above that little puckered muscle. I bring her right leg up, resting her knee on the cushion.

I fucking *love* how flexible she is.

Just as the woman in the book reaches her climax, I take my fingers from her pussy, lick them clean, and push my dick inside her. I bury myself balls deep and fist my hand in that gorgeous-as-fuck hair, tugging her head back.

"Beck."

I pause but let her speak.

"Please."

"Please what, Irish?"

"Please, can I stop?"

Grinning, so fucking pleased with her, I reach around to press my fingertip to her hard, pulsing clit.

"Yes, baby, you can stop now."

"Thank Christ," she mutters and lets her head fall, but my grip on her hair keeps her from collapsing onto the sofa. "Oh my God, I've never—"

She can't complete the sentence as I push hard, over and over again, into her sweet, tight pussy.

"Never what?" I demand.

She tries to shake her head, but I hold firm.

"Never what, Irish? I won't ask again."

"I've never felt anything like this." She groans as her contractions start, and I know she's *right there*.

"Come, beautiful. Come all over me. God, you're making such a beautiful mess. I fucking love it."

"Beckett," she cries out, pushing against me. "Harder."

I raise an eyebrow in surprise but don't need her to repeat herself. My hand in her hair tightens, and I slam into her, and she yells out, falling apart.

Her pussy milks me so hard, I can't help but follow her over, and I swear I must black out because the next thing I know, I'm folded over her back, panting, kissing her shoulders.

"Jesus, Mary, and Joseph, are you trying to kill me, then?" she asks with a laugh in her voice.

"God, baby." I can't stop touching her soft-as-fuck skin. My hand drags down the long curve of her spine, and she purrs. "You're every fantasy brought to life."

"That's you." She shakes her head, and when I release her hair, she falls to the sofa, trying to catch her breath.

I pull out of her and take in the mess we made—I wasn't exaggerating. She made a fucking *mess*—and I decide, fuck it. I lift her in my arms, sit with her in my lap, and reach for her water to offer it to her.

"You need this, Irish."

Her eyelids are heavy, and she looks so blissed out. It makes me proud.

"Thanks."

She wraps both hands around the glass and sips.

"I'll clean us up in just a minute." I kiss her forehead. "Are you okay?"

"Aside from the fact that my brain is numb?" Her smile is soft, and I love the way she wrinkles up her nose when she rubs her fingers in my whiskers. "I'm bloody fantastic, *a ghrá*. And how are you, then? What can I do for you?"

"You can tell me what *a ghrá* means."

Her lips twitch into a soft smile, and she runs her fingertips down my face and into my whiskers.

"It means *my love*."

She blows me away every day. I don't need anything from her when she's in my arms like this. Nothing at all.

"This. This is all you need to do for me, and I'll take care of the rest."

She sighs. "I do love the way you take care of me, Mr. Blackwell."

"I wanted the rentals to be far enough away from the dairy operation and my house that I don't get unwanted visitors," I inform Connor as I drive him in the side-by-side on the path toward the cabins. "We get a few wanderers now and then, but they're quickly directed back to where they need to be. There's a separate gated entrance onto the property for guests."

He nods, taking in the scenery around us.

It's a Sunday, which means that all of my siblings are here for the day, to play or work, whatever they want to do. We also invited Connor, Mik, and Benji out, and they took us up on the offer. Skyla has Mik and Benji out at the horse barn.

Connor wanted a tour of the guest cabins, which didn't surprise any of us.

"Do you have accommodations for meals?" he asks me.

"No, I don't have a communal space for a kitchen, or lounging. Each cabin has its own kitchen. I've thought of adding a lodge-type building with single rooms or suites and a commercial kitchen, so it becomes more like a bed and breakfast, but for now, I'm a one-man show, and I'd need much more staff for that, not to mention money."

He nods again. "My sister was right. It's beautiful out here, Beckett."

"This whole area is amazing," I agree. "But I like to think there's something extra special about this property. The views from the cabins are the best out there. Before my parents retired and I took over the farmhouse, I thought about building my own house out here. When I didn't need to do that, I wanted to do something special instead. You should see the alpenglow on those mountains when the sun is setting. It's ridiculous."

I turn the bend on the path, and the trees magically part, showing off a stunning mountain range and pasture full of wildflowers. To my delight, a family of moose gathers about fifty yards away.

"Bloody hell," Connor breathes, and I can't resist looking over at him. His eyes are wide, and he's slack-jawed as he takes it in. "Did you pay those moose to be here?"

"I wish it were that easy. You should hear the complaints from guests who thought they'd have grizzly bears outside their front door every morning, didn't, and then left me a one-star because of it."

"Wait. They *wanted* a grizzly to be waiting for them?"

"They're stupid, man." I shrug and pull up in front of one of the empty cabins, cut the engine. "This one is clean and empty. Let's have a look."

But when I turn back, Connor's standing with his back to me, his hands on his hips, staring at the mountains. At the moose. At the pasture.

So I wait.

Because I get it. Montana will wrap itself around your throat and squeeze when you least expect it.

Finally, he takes a deep breath and then turns to me with a nod.

After punching in the code for the door, I open it up and step aside, gesturing for him to go in ahead of me.

I don't join him for a minute. I give him time to look without me hovering, but the truth is, I'm fucking nervous.

I like Connor, but he's a third-generation hotelier. Hospitality is in his blood. I just have eight rental cabins with a view.

"I have questions," he says, so I step inside.

"Shoot."

"Are all of these the same size?" he asks.

"No. This one sleeps four. I have a few that sleep two and one that sleeps up to six."

He nods and leans on the marble countertop of the island.

"How much do you have invested in these?"

I narrow my eyes on him.

"I'm just curious."

"About two million."

He nods slowly. "You did a good job with these, Beckett. Skyla was right. They feel luxurious and would bring in clientele from all walks of life."

"Would *you* stay here?" I ask him, crossing my arms over my chest. "You say all walks of life, but you're telling me a billionaire would rent this place?"

"I wouldn't hesitate because of the accommodations," he replies. "But *I* wouldn't stay here because you don't have a lodge that offers room service and concierge services. Staying in this cabin, for example, would be perfectly acceptable to me if I want to go camping."

I snort out a laugh, and he shrugs.

"I'm not kidding. *This* would be like camping for me, or as close to it as I'd want to get. But again, that's just me. I know plenty of very wealthy people who'd snatch this up in a heartbeat because they don't give a shite about room service. They prefer to be left alone. They may ask you to stock the kitchen for them, but that would be that."

I nod, thinking it over. "Makes sense."

My phone rings in my pocket, and I scowl when I check the screen.

"Uh, sorry, I have to take this."

"No problem."

I step outside and accept the call. "Hello?"

"Um, hi, Beckett, this is Juliet. Brooks's ex."

The hell? Why is my brother's ex-girlfriend calling me?

"Of course, I know who you are, Jules. I'd be lying if I said I wasn't surprised to hear from you."

Brooks is going to blow a gasket when I tell him.

"Yeah, I know, and I hope I'm not making this too awkward, but I have a couple of questions for you."

"Okay." I shove my free hand in my pocket and stare at the moose still standing in the field. "What's up?"

I have no idea why she'd be calling *me*. We weren't particularly close when she and Brooks were together, and when they broke up, there was no question as to where our loyalties lay.

And it wasn't with her.

"Well, I'm going to be opening a new eatery in Bitterroot Valley, and my specialty is going to be farm-to-table food. Organic, gluten-free, with a clean kitchen."

"Shouldn't all kitchens be clean? I mean, I'm no restaurant expert, but—"

She chuckles. "I mean that it will be safe for people with food sensitivities like celiac disease."

That grabs my interest. Does she know that Birdie was diagnosed with celiac earlier this year?

"I want to use as much local food as I can," she continues. "And I'm making a list of vendors to buy from. I'd like to buy all of my dairy products from you."

"I don't see why that would be a problem." I always have enough on hand for new customers, and with enough notice, I can adjust accordingly.

She's quiet for a moment, then lets out a gusty sigh. "You don't think Brooks would freak out if my restaurant serves Blackwell Dairy products?"

"Brooks is a grown man, Jules."

There's another pause.

"How is he, Beck?"

I remember how angry Brooks got at his garage when I mentioned her.

You'll keep her name out of your mouth.

He's not okay where she's concerned, but that's not my story to tell.

"Brooks is great," I reply because aside from the shit that went down between them, it's not a lie. "But I won't tell him you said hi. When are you moving back to town?"

"In a few months. I need to come home."

"Well, good luck with the new business. When you can, let's meet up and work out quantities and delivery schedules and all that stuff. My guess is that you'd need to give about a thirty-day heads-up so I can have everything you need on hand. But we can fine-tune that when we get closer."

"I can do that. Thanks, Beckett. I'll see you later."

"Bye, Jules."

I hang up and let out a breath. Jesus, Brooks is going to be a dick about this, but I have to let him know.

Today.

At dinner.

Fucking awesome.

"Who the feck is Jules?" Connor asks as he steps out of the cabin behind me. "And do I have to break your legs?"

I shake my head and push my phone into my pocket.

"Fuck, no. Jules is my brother's ex, and she's going to open a new restaurant in town. She wanted to know if she could buy her dairy from me. I don't see a problem with that, but I'll have to tell Brooks."

"I take it that they didn't end as friends."

"Fucking understatement of the year. He won't be happy. About what you said, though, you don't have to worry about me fucking around on Irish. That's not my style."

He nods and shoves his hands in his pockets, mirroring me.

"I can see that you love her. Your house is outfitted for a dog as if Riley has lived there since he was a puppy."

"She loves that dog," I reply. "And so do I. He's a good boy. He should be as comfortable as we are. And if you're wondering what my *intentions* are with your sister, well, like I told you in LA, I'm going to marry her. I'm going to worship her for the rest of my life because there is no one else for me. She's everything good in this world, and I don't care if that sounds ... whatever. I love her."

"Good." He claps me on the shoulder. "Don't fuck it up."

With a laugh, I move toward the side-by-side. "We'd better head back."

On route to the house, I glance at the other man again.

"Before we're with the others, is there any news on The Asshole?"

Connor blows out a breath. "There's no evidence

that he ever left New York. No flight booked, commercial or private, under his name."

"How the fuck did he manage that?"

Connor shakes his head. "He's so fecking dirty, who knows."

"Does he have mafia ties?" I ask him, and his head jerks as he scowls at me. "I'm serious. Does he?"

"Not that I know of."

"I don't know anything about that world," I continue, "but it seems to me that he has an awful lot of people in his pocket and magic tricks up his sleeve for a run-of-the-mill rich guy."

Connor's hands ball into fists.

"I'll make some calls," he says quietly, effectively ending that conversation. We're at the house now, anyway.

When we walk inside, I see that everyone is already here. Dani and Skyla, along with Blake and Birdie, are in the kitchen, and everyone else is gathered close, at the far side of the island or the breakfast nook, chatting and laughing.

Gatherings just like this are what this house was built for. It's way too big just for me, but for family gatherings, it's perfect. And as my eyes find Skyla, as if they can't stay away from her, a level of contentment envelops me. *She* is the reason this house has become an even better place to come home to each day. As Connor said, Riley seems to have lived here since he was a puppy. But she made these walls a home, almost effortlessly.

"Uncle Beck," Birdie says, waving from the kitchen. "We're making s'getti with meatballs."

"Sounds good enough to eat." I bury my face in Birdie's neck and blow a raspberry, making her giggle. "How are you, peanut? Feeling okay?"

"Yep. We have gluten-free noodles for me," she says with a smile. "And they don't taste too bad."

"Well, good. I'll eat them with you if you want."

"No, they're for *me*."

"Fine, keep them, then." I turn to Skyla, who's grinning at me, and I wrap my arms around her shoulders and kiss her, right here in front of everyone.

"Get a room," Blake says as he walks by.

"Go away," I reply without looking at my brother. "How are you, Irish?"

"Happy you're here."

Chapter Twenty-Five

SKYLA

"I'm happy to see you, too," Beckett says before kissing me again. "Brooks, I need to talk to you."

He squeezes me, then lets go and turns to his eldest brother, and I see Brooks's eyebrow cocked in curiosity.

"Okay, talk," Brooks says and pops an olive off the charcuterie board into his mouth.

"We should do it privately," Beck says, and Brooks shakes his head.

"We don't have secrets," Brooks replies, not even caring that I'm here, along with Mik, Benji, and Connor. "Just tell me what you have to say."

"Juliet called me."

The room goes dead quiet. Bee, who just walked into the room from outside with some fresh eggs, stumbles to a stop.

"Juliet?" Bee asks.

Brooks immediately scowls.

I sidle up to my best mate. "Who's Juliet?" I whisper.

"Brooks's ex," she whispers back.

"She said—"

"I don't want to know," Brooks replies, shaking his head, his face grim.

"Maybe it's important," Blake says, but even I can tell by the stubborn look on Brooks's face that he won't budge.

"It's not life-threatening. She just—"

"No." Brooks's voice is hard and firm, and Beck holds his hands up in surrender.

"Okay. Forget I said anything. It smells good in here. What's for dessert?"

"I made some pies," Dani says, pointing at the pies she brought. "Peach and huckleberry, because I still had hucks in the freezer from last year, and they needed to get used. But the crusts are gluten-free, so Birdie can have some, too."

"Yum," Benji says, winking at Birdie, who bats her eyelashes at him.

This little girl is a flirt. And she has all of us wrapped around her wee finger.

"When is the big performance?" Blake asks, and I glance at where Mik and Benji sit at the nearby breakfast table.

"In about a month," I reply.

"How does your ankle feel?" Blake asks. "Be honest, Skyla. Don't just say *fine.*"

"I have moments when I feel like it wants to give, but I've learned to adjust my stance or the way I land, and so far, it feels good."

Blake nods. "Are you wearing a brace?"

"I haven't needed to."

"That's good news."

"Where are you going to dance?" Birdie wants to know.

"London," Mik says to her. Even Mik loves Birdie, and he usually stays away from kids. "We're going to perform for the new king and queen."

Birdie's eyes go round. "Wow. I want to go watch."

"London is far away, peanut," Bridger says, shaking his head. "And we haven't been invited."

"If you all want to go," Connor says before anyone else can speak, "I'll take you in the jet. There's room for everyone."

I *love* my brother. I know he's broody and can be intense, but he's also generous, and the fact that he'd offer to take this family to London shows me that he accepts them. And that means the world to me.

"Are you sure?" Bridger asks with a frown. "That's a lot, Connor."

But my brother simply shakes his head. "It's nothing."

"It's not nothing," Billie replies with a frown. "Don't be a stubborn ass, and let people thank you once in a while."

Connor's eyes zero in on Bee, but everyone else is

already talking about plans to travel to Europe, and I'm soon scooped up in a hug from Dani.

"What do I wear to something like this? I'll have to call Polly," she says.

"Oh, yes, Polly will have something brilliant," I reply with a nod. I absolutely adore Polly Wild's dress shop downtown and have bought a lot of my things there.

"Are you okay with this?" Beckett asks me, his mouth near my ear as he slips his arms around my waist, hugging me to him. "With everyone coming? We can whittle it down to a few, Irish. There are a lot of us."

"I want all of you there if you're willing to come." I bite my lip and stare up at him. "It's nervous I am for this performance, and I didn't want to ask you to come, but—"

"I wouldn't miss it," he replies, his chest rumbling against me. "I'm so fucking proud of you." He kisses me before he moves away, and I take a moment to breathe this all in. Apparently, Beckett and his family spend most of their Sundays like this. All together, out here at the ranch. I absolutely love it.

I hope we continue doing it often because this gorgeous farmhouse needs this. *Family. Laughter.* It reminds me of back home in Ireland before I left for the States. Even though it's only Connor and me in our family, our parents come from large families, and they regularly get together for someone's birthday, Easter, or anything to celebrate. I hadn't realized how much I'd missed that essence of a large family until this moment. I love that Bridger and Brooks are chatting with Benji and Mik as if they're old friends. Beckett is now sitting with Birdie, watching something on his phone with her on his lap, laughing. That I'm in the kitchen with Dani and Blake, making a meal for all of these wonderful people.

It feels like family.

It feels like *home*.

I glance around, wondering where Connor and Bee went. I'm about to go looking when Bee walks into the room, her hair mussed, her lips a little pink and swollen, and her pretty hazel eyes bright.

My brother walks in not far behind her, looking cool and calm, but I notice the way his hand lingers at the small of Bee's back as he passes by, and her cheeks flush.

Well, look at that. Maybe these two will make their way to each other after all.

Blake's phone rings, and Birdie scowls.

"Are you being called to the hospital?" the little girl demands, clearly not pleased with that idea.

"No, peanut," Blake replies as he declines the call but sends a text. A second later, they must reply because he smiles. "But I have a date later."

"A *date*," Bee demands, her hands on her hips, clearly recovered from whatever she and my brother were up to. "With who? I didn't know you were seeing someone."

"You're so fu-freaking nosy," Blake says, eyeing his niece. "You don't know her."

"Oh, I bet that's a big, fat lie, Blake Adam Blackwell," Bee says. "I know everyone in this town. Who is she?"

"Now I know why Skyla fits in so well here," Mik says loud enough for us all to hear. "She's as much a busybody as Billie is."

"Hey." I toss a hard noodle at my best friend, hitting him in the forehead and making him roar with laughter, which Mik doesn't do. He's never *roared* in his life. "Be nice."

"It doesn't matter who she is," Blake says with a shrug as he shoves his phone in his pocket and returns to stirring the sauce. I may be madly in love with my Beckett, but I'm not blind, and all of these brothers are *handsome*. With a capital H. "She won't be around long."

"He's so romantic," Bee says, shaking her head. "I'm so proud of his playboy ways."

Connor smirks at that, and I blink at him. My brother doesn't laugh at much. He's always so serious. I love that the Blackwells bring out the humor in all of us. They're good for us.

"And what did you think of the cabins then, Connor?" I ask him.

"You were right, they're beautiful. That view is ... bloody amazing. And I've been thinking about an idea."

Beckett's eyebrows climb. "Okay."

"You and Skyla have both mentioned that it hasn't been easy for you with destructive and annoying guests. That's going to happen, but I'm sure you feel it harder with only having a few rentals."

"Go on," Beck replies, crossing his arms over his chest.

"Something that we've wanted to do with Dreams

for Kids is have a place, like this if I'm being honest, where families can come to decompress. To play. To spend time together and enjoy something that they wouldn't normally be able to, especially before their wee one passes away."

My heart flutters. Oh, this would be the perfect spot for this idea.

"What if, instead of continuing to rent your cabins out to anyone and everyone, you contracted with Dreams for Kids and other similar charities?"

Beckett frowns, dragging his hand over his beard, clearly thinking it over.

"I can't honestly afford to give them away for free. A few weeks a year, sure, but I depend on the income from those units."

"I'm sorry," Connor replies, shaking his head. "I'm not suggesting you should offer them for free. The foundations would pay you the nightly rates. It would be free for the families, but you would still be paid."

"And he could do that year-round?" Billie asks, tapping her lips with her finger. "Do you think there would be that much interest?"

"I can guarantee you'd have a waiting list," Connor replies, holding Billie's gaze for a few seconds longer than necessary.

Is it a wee bit hot in here, or is it just me?

It's not just me because I notice Bee's blushing, too.

"If these are sick children," Blake cuts in, leaning against the counter, "they may need medical care while they're here. Would you have a team for that? Do they have hospice doctors and nurses who travel with them?"

I love that all of Beck's family is here to ask these questions, and I know there will be more, but there's no one better than my brother to answer.

"Some travel with their own care team," Connor replies. My brother's *super* casual today, in jeans and a T-shirt, and I like seeing him like this. It's rare. "Some may need emergency care here, but there's a hospital in town."

Blake hums, and I can see the wheels turning in his head.

"It's an idea I thought I'd toss out there." Connor shrugs. "I know that you've not enjoyed the guest side of things, Beckett. This could be an answer to that."

"I definitely want to think on this more." Beckett nods. "Because it could be something great. We could probably hire a couple of guys to offer horseback rides, and if the families are interested, we could give them a tour of the dairy side."

"Beckett, this could be exactly what it was meant to be all along." I nod as the idea takes root in my mind. "What a special thing to offer people who desperately need something happy in their lives. There's nothing like that view."

He's already nodding, giving me that special smile. "Yeah. We'll talk, Irish."

"Connor," I say, leaning on the counter, "how long are you in town for this time?"

"After I wrap things up in Miami and Dublin? Indefinitely."

My jaw drops, but Billie goes pale, and her body jerks in surprise.

"Really? Don't you have properties in Bermuda to oversee or something?" I ask.

"Not right now." My brother shakes his head. "Now that the sale has gone through, I can tell you that I bought the ski resort. We'll be tearing everything down and building from the ground up. It'll be a Gallagher resort."

I clap my hands, so excited by this news. "That's *brilliant*. I knew that it would be perfect for you. So you'll be here to oversee the whole build?"

"Aye, I will," he says with a nod, and I'm pleased to see that everyone here looks happy by the news. "And I can talk with you, Beckett, about your cabins."

I should say that everyone looks happy except Bee.

"How long will the build take, do you think?" I ask Connor, not taking my eyes off my best friend.

"From start to finish, probably two years," Connor says, and Bee slowly shakes her head. "It's a big resort, and it's going to be top of the line in luxury."

"Two years," Billie whispers, then takes a breath.

Connor's gaze finds hers and narrows. Billie shifts back and forth on her feet, bites her lip, and finally tears her gaze from his. There's so much sexual chemistry you could cut it with a knife.

But Billie finally scowls, shakes her head, and turns to me. "Give me a job. What can I do?"

I quickly glance around. "You can make the salad."

"Done."

Connor looks like he wants to say something, but he firms his jaw and remains unusually quiet. *Gods, this could be a tricky situation.*

And I'm here for it.

I notice that the group in the kitchen nook is still chattering away and that dinner is just about ready, so I let it go. But I wish I knew what was happening between them.

"It only took a month for my feet to callous up a bit and my body to remember how to do this correctly." I have Riley on his leash, and Mik and I are walking down the footpath, away from my studio and toward the coffee shop. We decided to end rehearsal early and take a walk in the sunshine.

Spring has exploded in Montana, and it's the loveliest thing. It reminds me of Ireland, with the greenest trees, flowers spilling out of baskets, and air so fragrant, I can't get enough of it.

"Hey, Skyla," Jackie, the owner of The Sugar Studio, says with a wave as we walk past her.

"It's a lovely day, Jackie," I reply with a smile.

"You've become part of this community," Mik says quietly.

"Aye, I have. And I love it, Mik."

"But, malishka, you are wasting your talent here. Now that you're back in shape and no longer rusty, you are as good as you were before. Maybe stronger. You should come back and dance with me."

"I love you." I take his hand and hold on tight. "And I will *always* love you, Mik, but my life is here now. I love these people and the mountains, and I enjoy my wee studio. Even you said yourself that my kids' classes are fun."

"They're tolerable," he grumbles.

"Your exact words were *'This is more fun than I thought it would be.'* See? Fun."

I wave back at Polly, who's stepped out to write something on her wee board in front of her shop.

Mik halts me, and Riley comes to a stop at my hip. Mik takes my shoulders in his hands.

"I love you, too, my malishka. I am selfish, and I know this. But I miss you. No one dances with me like you do. No one ever will. This one performance won't be enough for me."

"I know." He takes my face in his hands, and I lean into him. "I know, my sweet Russian. And it's sorry I am that I left you, especially in the way that it happened. We both deserved so much better. I miss you, too. Every day, and I'm not lying about that, Mik."

His eyes, those beautiful eyes, are full of torment as he watches me.

"But you're not going to come back to me."

"No." It's a whisper, and I clear my throat. "I can't.

This is my home now. Maybe, one day, when you've retired, you and Benji could live here."

"I hate snow," he says.

"But you love me, and I'm your family."

He huffs out a breath and leans in to kiss my forehead. "Benji loves it here. And I've grown fond of the Blackwells, too. They're good people. Your Beckett will likely marry you."

My heart jolts at that thought, and I can't stop the smile that spreads over my face.

"I'd like that."

"You are so special, malishka, and not just for your dancing. Although I've never seen another dancer like you."

I can't hold the tears that drip onto my cheeks.

"But because of your heart. Your sweetness. You make me a better person because you're my best friend. So because I love you, I will consider moving to the frozen Siberia of North America when I finish my dance and am one hundred years old."

I laugh and wrap my arms around him, hugging him close. "Good. In the meantime, you can visit me between projects."

"Yes, yes. Now, buy me coffee."

With his hand in mine once more, we walk into the coffee shop, but rather than walk up to the counter, Mik leads me through the archway that leads to Billie's Books.

"I thought you wanted coff—" I cut off, stunned. Mik and I stand side by side, and finally, I snort. "Hey, Benji."

Mik's husband blinks behind his glasses. He has a pen clenched in his teeth. His blond hair stands on end as if he's run his fingers through it a million times. But the best part is the array of mostly empty drinks sitting before him on the small table. There are seven of them—some were iced coffees, some were hot. There's a bottle of water and an empty cup, aside from the teabag in the bottom.

"Hi. Hey." Benji blinks some more and then takes his glasses off to rub his eyes.

"What are you doing?" Mik asks.

"The house was too quiet," Benji replies. "I'm used to a loud city, so I decided to come work here. Billie set me up, and Millie kept bringing me drinks."

Mik and I share a look, then he takes his husband's hand and pulls him to his feet, planting a kiss on Benji's forehead.

"Let's get you home, and I'll feed you."

"Yeah." Benji grins and cups Mik's cheek tenderly. I love their love so much. "I guess I'm hungry. How did you two do today?"

"It was a good rehearsal," I reply. "We're ready for next week."

I didn't think we'd ever be ready. The rehearsals and getting back in shape were much harder than I remember. But it's also been magical to dance with Mik again, so I've savored every moment.

I'll be as sad as he is when it's all said and done.

"Of course you are," Benji says as he throws his

empties away. "You two are the best there is. Do you guys want something from next door?"

"Yeah, I want an iced coffee," I reply and wave at Billie, who's busy ringing up customers. It's crowded in here today.

Mik and I order an iced Americano, then the three of us walk back to the studio with Riley still at my side. My phone rings.

"This is Beckett," I inform them and answer. "Hello there, handsome."

"Hey, gorgeous. I'm so sorry, but I can't come to town to pick you up. We discovered some fence down, and I'm dealing with a grizzly bear."

My eyebrows wing up. "Wait, you're dealing with a grizzly bear *right now*?"

"No, I have a call out to Fish and Wildlife. Usually, it wouldn't be a big deal, but it's too close to my cabins, and I don't need anyone getting hurt. So I can't get away, baby."

"It's okay." I turn to the boys. "Can you two give me a lift home?"

"Of course," Benji replies.

"I have a ride. You take care of what you have going on out there, and I'll see you in a bit."

"Thanks, baby. I love you."

"I love you, too." I hang up and see both of the boys watching me. "What?"

"You're so lovesick." Benji shakes his head.

"Uh, hello. Do you even see the way you two look at each other? It's borderline disgusting most of the time."

"Touché." Benji laughs. "Come on, let's get your stuff and get you home."

"Hey, Miss Gallagher," Brad says when I walk into the horse barn an hour later. After getting home, I changed clothes, got Riley some dinner, and decided to see if I could find my man.

Not the bear.

"Hello, Brad. I don't suppose Beckett's back yet?"

"No, ma'am." He grins when his dog, Sadie, hurries over to say hello to Riley. "Those two are good friends. If you ever need anyone to watch over Riley for you, I'm happy to do it."

My jaw drops in surprise. I'm still getting used to this small-town hospitality.

"Really?"

"Sure. Riley's the best-trained dog I've ever met, and Sadie loves him. He's welcome at our place."

"You know, we're all going to London next week for the coronation, and I'd rather not take Riley. It's a tough trip for him."

"Don't even worry about it," Brad says, shaking his head. "He'll be here with us."

That's a weight off my shoulders that I didn't realize I was carrying. "Thank you so much."

"Beck should be back in a few. He was heading this way about ten minutes ago." He smiles at me, then whistles for Sadie to follow him, and the golden lab follows her master, but Riley looks up at me with sad brown eyes.

"Aw, did your friend have to go home?" I rub him behind his ears and bend down to kiss him. "It's okay. You'll see her soon."

I hear the clop of horse hooves and see Beckett riding this way. Bloody hell, he looks good on a horse. He's wearing riding chaps over his jeans, along with brown leather gloves and his cowboy hat, and my core tightens.

"Well, shite, Riley. He's a sight for sore eyes, isn't he? Look at how he fills out those jeans." Beckett swings off the horse, giving us a view of his arse, and I bite my lip. "Oh gods, that butt. And the shoulders. Have you ever seen a man so ... *big*? He's bloody huge, Riley."

I've buried my face in the dog's neck, hugging him as I talk.

"I fucking love that dirty mouth of yours."

I don't pull away. I smile against Riley and let out a little giggle. Then his hands are on me, pulling me up and against him so he can hug me.

"I hope you were talking about me," he growls against my ear as his gloveless hand drifts down my hair.

"You're the only sexy cowboy I know."

Beckett kisses my temple, then my forehead. "Good answer. I'm sorry I couldn't come to town, Irish."

"Hey, you're busy. I get it. The boys didn't mind giving me a ride. Now." I snatch his hat off his head and settle it on mine. "I think we should get you inside and directly into the shower. You're filthy."

His slow and sexy smile makes my nipples harden.

"Is that right?"

"It is, Mr. Blackwell."

"I might need some help reaching all the nooks and crannies."

"I am a capable shower attendant," I inform him, squeaking in surprise when he easily lifts me into his arms. Riley barks and hurries after us. "Why are you carrying me?"

"I have to dirty you up, too, Irish. It's only fair."

Chapter Twenty-Six

LEWIS A.K.A. THE ARSEHOLE

She's in *Montana*?

Scowling, I stare at the photos on my screen. Surely, the love of my life, my tiny dancer, would never live in barbaric Montana.

It's unthinkable.

It's ridiculous.

But as I read the report, it seems that it's true. My tiny dancer moved to Montana and opened a ... *dance school?*

No.

I shake my head and sit back, staring in disbelief as I hit play on a video and watch my girl through the front windows of a building, teaching little brats to dance.

"She left me for *that*?"

There are more images. Skyla in a bookstore, in a coffee shop, and buying groceries. But the next to last image has my blood boiling and the red haze of fury moving over my eyes.

She's in the arms of that man from the charity dinner. She's laughing and staring up at him like he hung the goddamn moon.

And in the very last image, he's kissing her.

"No."

I close the laptop and tap my fingers on it before I yank it up and throw it against the wall, breaking it in half.

After everything I've done for her, this is what she does? I stand and cross to the windows, shove my hands in my pockets, and stare outside.

It seems I'll be going to Montana.

And my tiny dancer will pay for every mile she put between us. She's going to pay for every minute I've been without her.

And that fucker who has his hands on her is going to die.

Chapter Twenty-Seven

SKYLA

"I can't believe it's time for you to go to London already," Erin Wild says as her little girl, Holly, twirls around my floor with her friends. "The past month *flew* by."

"I can't believe how fast the time has gone," I agree and smile at Dani as she joins us. She wraps her arm around my waist and gives me a wee hug. "You know, I rarely get nervous before a performance, but I can admit that I'm terrified this time."

"Don't be," Erin assures me as she rubs her hand up and down my back. Aye, I love this community I've found myself in. "You're a brilliant performer. I saw you once in New York City when I went with my family on vacation."

I blink at her in surprise. "You never told me that."

"I didn't want to make it weird." She shrugs. "I come from a famous family, and I know that sometimes people say awkward things. But I can confidently tell you that

I've seen you in action, and you have *nothing* to worry about, my friend."

I'm reminded almost daily how wonderful it is to be a part of Bitterroot Valley and the friends I've made here.

"Thank you." I take a deep breath. "We leave tomorrow."

"Dani said that the whole family is going?" Erin asks, and Dani nods.

"They are, yes. I was afraid to ask it of them, if I'm being honest. I knew I wanted Beck there. Having the rest of his family would have been a dream, but asking it of them felt like an imposition."

"Yeah, going to Europe to watch my insanely talented friend dance for the freaking *king and queen* is a huge pain in our ass." Dani shakes her head at me. "Honey, we love you. You're part of us now. If Beckett loses his mind and ever lets you go, we're keeping *you* and sending him out to pasture."

Okay, that makes me giggle.

"I love all of you, too," I reply and lean over to kiss her cheek.

"How are things with Beck?" Erin asks.

"They're amazing. We're in love. I never would have expected that I'd have to move all the way to Montana to find the man I'm supposed to be with, but that's what happened."

"It's romantic," Erin replies. "And I'm so happy for you. We'll be watching you here, I promise. We're all rooting for you. Don't stress, it's going to be amazing.

And when you get home, we'll have a big party to celebrate."

Home. When I get home.

Because Bitterroot Valley is absolutely my home.

"Thank you."

Erin smiles and then gathers her daughter and the two of them leave.

"Birdie and I are headed out, too," Dani says. "I have to finish packing. We're meeting at the airport at eight?"

"Last I heard, yes."

"I've never flown on a private plane before. It can get us all the way to London?"

"It's the largest plane in the fleet," I reply. "It's so big, we won't even have to stop anywhere for fuel."

"Crazy," she says, shaking her head. "Thank you again for including us. And I want to make it very clear to you that I'm friends with you, I *love* you because of who you are as a human, Skyla. It has absolutely nothing to do with your money or this trip."

I blink at the tears that want to form and yank her into a tight hug. "I know it."

"I'm sure that people have tried to use you or been manipulative—"

"Hey." I pull back and brush my hand down her pretty dark hair. "Aye, they've done all of those things, but I'm good at choosing the right people to have in my life. You've been my friend since I came to town and no one knew anything about me. You just welcomed me into your friend group, and made me feel like I belong here."

"You *do* belong here," Dani insists.

"I want you to come to London because you're my support system. You and Bee are my best friends in the whole world. Don't tell Mik."

Dani laughs at that.

"It's handy that my family has more money than God Himself, and all I have to do is say the word to have you all with me. I know that I'm a lucky girl. And I'm so grateful that you're coming because I'm going to need a pep talk before that performance."

"I'll give you all of the pep talks you need. I'll have snacks on hand and a Taylor Swift and P!nk playlist already curated for this occasion. We've got this, babe."

"See? You get me, Dani Blackwell."

Maybe someday, Dani and Bee will be my sisters-in-law. That would be *incredible.*

"I absolutely get you."

"Mama, I'm hungry," Birdie says, slipping her hand into her mother's.

"I know, pumpkin. We're going." Dani kisses my cheek. "See you in the morning. I might FaceTime you later to go over what I'm packing."

"Do it. I want to see it all, and it'll keep my mind occupied with something other than being nervous." I walk them to the door and then sigh when it's just Riley and me left.

After tonight, my studio will be closed for the next ten days.

We'll be in London tomorrow, but the performance is five days after that. Mik and I want to make sure we're through the jet lag and in peak condition before we perform, then we'll take a couple of days to decompress before we come home.

Although it's true that I'm nervous, I'm also excited. My parents will meet us there, and I'll have everyone that I cherish most in this world with me for ten whole days. Not to mention, I get to dance with my partner. The rehearsals have been rigorous, but we're ready, and I'm so grateful that we have this opportunity to dance together one more time. To finish our career together on *our* terms.

"It's going to be fun, Riley, and I promise you'll have a grand time with Brad and Sadie. You won't even know that I'm gone." Riley's lying on his bed, watching me intently. "Beck should be here shortly. Let's head to the back and start shutting everything down."

Riley leaves his bed at my command, and we walk into the back room so I can type some notes on my computer, reply to a couple of emails, and use the bathroom.

With a frown, I check the time. Beck should be here by now.

"He probably lost track of time," I tell Riley as the bell above the front door dings. "There he is. I'll be right out!"

I turn to grab my handbag and the light jumper I brought for this evening. The spring days have been warm, but it's still brisk after the sun goes down.

Suddenly, Riley starts to growl.

"Hey, what's gotten into you?" I rub his neck, but he doesn't stop. "It's just Beckett, baby. Come on, let's go."

But when I step around the wall that separates the office from the studio, I stop, and my blood runs cold.

Riley barks.

Lewis's gaze flicks down to my dog, then back to me. He pastes on a fake, smarmy smile.

"Hello, tiny dancer." *Oh God. How did he find me? Why is he here?*

Bile rises in the back of my throat. God, I fecking hate that name.

Riley's snarling now, gnashing his teeth. I didn't even have to give him a signal. It's as if he just *knows*.

But I do give him the signal to intimidate.

"Shut him up," Lewis snarls.

I simply shake my head and pray that Beckett's almost here. Why did I let my guard down? Why didn't I lock the door behind Dani?

Lewis takes a step forward, and Riley loses his mind. He's always so mellow and sweet that I forget that he also has this fierce side. He's so well trained—*thank the gods*—and knows to protect me with his life if need be.

Come on, Beck. Please get here now. Please.

Suddenly, Lewis takes a gun from his pocket and aims it at my dog, and I shout, "No!"

"If you don't want me to kill him, shut him the fuck up, Skyla."

"Riley." My voice shakes, but it's hard. "Calm."

He follows my command but whines and shifts back

312

and forth on his feet in agitation. He *knows* this situation isn't right.

"Now, leave the dog and come with me."

"Lewis." God, I hate saying that name. "I can't go with you."

"You can, and you will. I don't know what you were trying to prove by moving *here* of all places, but I'm taking you home where you belong."

"I am home." I swallow hard when his face goes beet red. How did I ever think this man was handsome? "I *am* home, Lewis."

"No." He shakes his head and steps toward me, and it excites Riley again, making him bark and snarl and lunge at Lewis. Lewis hits Riley on the head with the butt of his gun, knocking my poor boy out. "Riley!"

I fall to my knees at his side, my heart breaking. *No. Not Riley.* There's so much blood. I can't lose him.

"Oh, my baby."

"Enough," Lewis snaps. He grips my upper arm and yanks me to my feet, almost pulling my arm out of the socket. I cry out in pain, but he doesn't seem to notice as he pulls me along out of the building and toward a black Mercedes parked at the curb.

I know without a doubt that I absolutely should *not* get into that car.

"Help!" I scream, but then his hand is over my mouth. He simply lifts me off my feet and tosses me into the back seat of the car before he runs around and climbs into the driver's seat and peels away.

"You're going to learn to do what you're told, tiny dancer."

"Don't call me that." The words are out before I can stop them, and Lewis glares at me in the rearview mirror.

"I'll call you whatever I want. Right now, I want to call you *whore*. How *dare* you cheat on me with that redneck cowboy? I saw the pictures, Skyla. I know he had his hands on you, and I will not tolerate infidelity. I would never do that to you."

Jesus God, he's crazier than I thought.

"Lewis, this isn't going to work."

"Shut up."

"You and I, we just aren't meant for each other. I think you're a lovely man." I have to swallow the bile that comes up with that lie and work to keep the panic from rising so I can get more words out. "And I know you're perfect for someone else. I'm simply not that someone."

"I said shut up!" He's gripping the steering wheel so tightly, his knuckles are white.

"Lewis, you should stay in town for a few days. It's really a lovely place. I think you'd like it here."

"I'm going to forget you said that to me," he says, and now that his voice is calm, it scares me even more. Jesus, what's he going to do? "You belong in the city with me. We're soulmates."

I want to throw up and cry at the same time.

"I can visit the city another time, but I have—"

"I am going to shut your cunt mouth up with my cock as soon as we get out of this car, tiny dancer."

He turns a corner, and my already cold blood goes even colder.

Because he's just turned into the airport, and he's headed for a private plane. *Oh God. No.*

Chapter Twenty-Eight

BECKETT

"I have to go, Brad. Skyla's waiting for me."

"Sorry, boss, I just had to get this handled before you go. One more thing—"

"No. Call me if there are issues, but you know this as well as I do. I have to *go.*"

He nods, and I wave, hurrying to my truck. The last class ends in fifteen minutes, and it'll take me at least that long to get there. I don't want my girl alone for even a minute. There's no evidence that The Asshole has left Manhattan, but I'm not taking any chances with her safety.

Every day for the past month, she's had someone, if not me, collect her from the dance studio. Family members have stepped in when I've been busy, or Benji has driven her home on the rare days that none of us are available. I hate that we don't know where the fucker is or what his motives are. Does he know where she is?

Hopefully not, but we've stayed vigilant, and this delay has me feeling on edge.

I'm making decent time into town when I come upon an accident and have to slow way down until I crawl to a stop.

Chase Wild holds up a hand, then crosses to my window, and I roll it down.

"What's up?" I ask him.

"Fatality," he says grimly. "They were going too fast around the bend. Hit a deer."

"Shit." I tighten my hand on the wheel. "Anyone we know?"

"No. Tourist. It's going to take about ten more minutes to get the ambulance out of there and the vehicle moved."

"Skyla's alone at the studio," I reply in agitation. "It makes me nervous."

"Call her and check in," he advises. Connor reached out to the Bitterroot Valley Police Department after the incident in LA, just in case we had any surprises, and I'm glad he did. I've known Chase all my life and trust him implicitly. "I'll get you through here as soon as I can."

With a nod, I pick up my phone and dial her number, but it goes to voicemail after the fourth ring.

With a scowl, I press the call button again but get the same result.

"Fuck," I growl. It's likely that she's just in the restroom or neglected to turn her ringer back on after her class, but I have a sick feeling in the pit of my stomach.

So I call Connor.

"Gallagher," he says.

"It's Beck. I'm stuck behind an accident on the highway, and I'm late getting to Skyla. She's not answering her phone. How far away from the studio are you?"

"Closer than you. I'll head over."

"Appreciate it," I reply, and he ends the call. I need to know that she's okay. I hate being late in getting her. It doesn't happen often, and after today, I'll make sure it doesn't happen again.

Nothing is more important than Irish.

Finally, the ambulance leaves the scene, and Chase waves his hand at me, indicating that I should drive through. With a relieved sigh, I do just that, nodding at my friend as I pass by.

When I'm sure I'm past the wreck, I floor it.

I pull up to the studio and see that I have beat Connor here. I'm about to call him back to tell him that I have this under control when my eyes spot a black mass on the studio floor.

Riley.

Something is *not fucking right.*

Running out of my truck, I push through the door and scream my girl's name.

"Skyla! Baby, where are you?"

There's no answer. It's silent in the studio as I run through checking every room, but I know I won't find her.

She's not here.

And she'd never leave Riley.

I fall to my knees beside the dog, my heart in my

throat and blood roaring through my head as I press my hand to his side.

He's breathing.

But he's hurt.

He has blood on his head, and his eyes are rolled back.

The bell dings as Connor comes inside.

"What the fucking hell?"

"She's not here. Riley's hurt and needs help." Jesus, I don't know what to do. "He's got her. That's the only way she'd ever leave Riley like this."

"Call your sister to help with him," Connor says as he pulls his phone out of his pocket. "Miller."

He talks to his security man, and I call Bee.

"Hey," she says.

"I need you at the studio. Riley's hurt. Call a vet or something. We don't know where Skyla is."

Those last six words almost kill me.

"On it," she replies and ends the call.

What feels like hours later, Bee rushes inside and runs over, dropping to her knees beside me.

"The vet's on her way," she says, and I can tell she's struggling to keep her voice calm. "I have this handled. Where is she?"

I shake my head as terror wants to take over, but Bee lays her hand on my shoulder.

"Stop. No panicking. Do you hear me? No. Panicking."

I swallow, push the terror back, and nod. "We don't know. She was gone, and I found Riley like this."

More people rush inside. The vet, more security. Even Chase, whose eyes narrow on me in an unspoken question.

What the fuck?

I shake my head. I don't know what's fucking happening, and it's tearing me apart inside.

"Go," Bee says, placing her hands on the dog. "I've got him. You find your girl."

Just as I cross to Connor, Miller pushes inside, his face grim.

"Airport," he says before we all run outside and climb into Miller's waiting black SUV. Chase is behind us, the lights on his car and siren on, and then more cop cars join us. It looks like something out of an action movie.

"What in the actual fuck is happening?" Connor demands.

"There was no record of Lewis leaving New York, but there *was* a record of him landing here this morning. He has a private jet, and it's parked on standby. Engines are running, boss."

"Explain why the feck you didn't know he left New York," Connor snarls.

"There was literally no flight record," Miller replies. "He doctored the flight logs. Or it wasn't logged at all, but he doesn't have anyone paid off here to do the same."

"He's trying to fucking *take her*?" I shake my head and answer my phone when I see Bee's name.

"Riley's okay," she says immediately. "We're taking him to the hospital for X-rays and stuff, but the vet says he's going to be fine."

"Thanks, Billie. I'll be in touch."

I hang up and notice Connor fisted his hand when he heard me say my sister's name, but I don't have time to address that right now.

Right now, I need to get to my girl.

"If he's so much as given her a goddamn papercut, I'll end him," I say.

"He's not making it out of here alive," Connor says, catching Miller's gaze in the mirror. Miller nods.

It seems we're all on the same page.

"The gate's already up," Connor says when we turn toward the private plane area of the tarmac. The four cop cars follow us through, but they've cut the sirens.

"Chase must have called ahead," I reply, and then my eyes narrow.

Because there's Lewis, pulling Irish out of the back seat of a sedan, his hand fisted in her hair, yanking her.

He's going to suffer for that alone.

Lewis must hear us coming because he starts to pull her faster, and when Miller stops at the base of the steps of the plane, I push out, running toward them.

But Lewis turns around and presses the barrel of his pistol against her head.

"Jesus fuck," I mutter as Skyla's terrified gaze finds mine.

Intentionally, I let my shoulders drop and keep the fear out of my face.

Her lip trembles.

"*I got you, baby.*" I mouth the words, and she gives me a tiny nod.

"Drop the fucking gun," Miller growls out, but Lewis sneers.

"I'm taking what's mine," Lewis yells back. "She belongs with me."

A tear falls down Skyla's cheek, and now I hear running footsteps as Chase and the other police join us.

"Bitterroot Valley PD. You heard the man," Chase calls out calmly. "Lower your weapon. No one needs to get hurt. You know that we're not going to allow you to leave. You're not taking her anywhere."

Lewis laughs and yanks on Skyla's hair again, making her yelp.

"I can't get a shot," Miller mutters next to me. "I won't risk hitting her. I need her to fall. To drop, so his head isn't hiding behind her."

"If you kill my girl, I'll kill *you*."

Miller doesn't waver. "I won't hit her."

Jesus. I have to trust this man that I barely know with Skyla's life. *He'd better not be wrong.*

Her gaze is still pinned to mine, almost desperately.

"*Fall*," I mouth to her. "*Drop down.*"

"Stop that!" Lewis screams, pointing the gun at me. I'd rather it was pointed at me than at my girl. "Don't you fucking talk to my tiny dancer. Don't you even *look at her!* She's mine. She's my love."

Skyla frowns. Then it's like a light bulb goes off, and her eyes widen. His grip on her has loosened during his tirade.

"Get ready," I tell Miller just as Skyla lets her legs relax, and she slumps down. The arm Lewis has wrapped around her middle doesn't let her fall to the ground, but it's enough that his head is clear from her body, and Miller, along with several cops by the sound of gunfire around me, immediately take their shot.

Lewis's body jerks as the bullets hit his forehead, his chest, his neck, all miraculously missing my girl, and I leap forward as the man slumps and Skyla falls back with him. Thank God she doesn't take a nosedive forward off the steps.

She's pushing his arm off her as I reach her and tug her into my arms, lifting her against me and walking down the steps so the cops can do whatever they need to do with the dead piece of shit behind me.

Skyla's face is pressed to my neck, and she's crying. Shaking.

"Riley," she says. "He killed Riley."

"No, baby. Riley's going to be okay." I kiss her head, her temple, hold her so close to me, I never want to let her go. I'm *never* letting her go again. "Billie's with him. He's going to be fine, my love."

She gulps, and those huge emerald eyes look up at me. "You're sure?"

"I'm sure." I set her on the back seat of the SUV and turn her so I can cup her face and kiss her lips, her cheeks, and her nose, then take her in. "Are you hurt?"

"No." She shakes her head. "Well, just my scalp because he pulled my hair."

I growl and reach out for her, not giving a shit that she's got some blood spatter on her. I'm surprised there's not more. There would be if she'd been behind him.

323

"Fuck, Irish. That took ten years off my life."

"How did you find me?" She sniffs, and she keeps her eyes on mine as if she can't bring herself to look away.

"Miller," I reply. "He did whatever he does and knew you'd be here. Thank fuck you weren't on that plane yet."

"I kept trying to talk to him," she says, swiping at her tears. "Tried to reason with him, to have a conversation, to just bloody stall him."

"It worked. My clever girl."

She's shaking more now, and I can see the shock setting in.

"He's ... dead?"

"Yes, baby." I pepper more kisses on her face. "He's gone. It's over."

She nods, and her teeth start to chatter.

"Hey, look at me. Give me your eyes, Irish."

Those beautiful orbs fill with water again as she raises them to mine. "I n-never wanted anyone to die."

"I know." I don't tell her that I regret that it wasn't my own hand that killed him. That I didn't get to make him hurt for every moment of agony that he put my girl through. "But he wouldn't have stopped, baby. And he has too many people in his pocket that would have let him go free. Not to mention, he had a gun pressed to your fucking head. So yeah, he had to die today."

She blows out a breath and curls into me.

"I'm going to have questions." I didn't even hear Chase walk up behind me. "But they can wait for later."

"We leave for London tomorrow," I reply.

He nods. "That's what Connor said, too. I can ask my questions when you get back from that trip. It won't change what happened here today."

"No, I'll answer you now." Skyla squares her shoulders. "I don't want any part of this hanging over my head while I'm in London. I need it over."

"Are you sure?" I hold her face in my hands, and she smiles up at me.

"Yeah. Let's finish this."

With a nod, I step back, and Chase addresses Skyla.

"Can you state the victim's full name? We will, of course, confirm identity," Chase adds.

"Of course." Skyla swallows hard. "His full name is Lewis Spangler. I don't know his middle name."

"There will be an investigation into which bullet was the kill shot and whose gun it discharged from," Chase says. "Just letting you know."

"Makes sense." I nod but look at him. "You okay?"

"Needed to be done. He had a gun pressed to her head and then turned it on all of us." He holds my gaze for a moment before turning to Skyla. "Let's make this quick so you can go home, okay?"

"Aye, please."

I stand nearby as Skyla tells Chase about waiting at the studio for me, going into the back room and hearing the door, thinking I was there to get her.

Jesus, if I'd just been there, none of this would have happened.

She cries when she tells us about Lewis hitting Riley, and it splits my heart in two.

"And then he put me in his car, and made me leave my boy, and brought me here. I tried to distract him, to slow him down, but I didn't know if you knew where I was. You know the rest."

"I'm sorry to ask this, but can you tell me why he abducted you? He's a long way from home, and I'd like to get an idea of motive," Chase says. Skyla swallows hard. *Fuck, I hate this for her.*

"A few years ago, we dated very, very briefly. I called it off and thought he'd been okay with that. Turns out he wasn't, and then the stalking started." She looks down, and I can see how hard this is for her. I'm about to tell Chase she's done when her eyes flick, and I see pure strength in her face. "He was incredibly clever to taunt me but never do anything, or rather be seen to be doing anything illegal."

"We'll search his apartment in New York City. If there's evidence of stalking, we'll ensure it's destroyed in due course, Skyla. No one will get access to evidence."

"Thank you. I appreciate it."

"Do you have any records of the deceased reaching you by phone or email?"

"No, I've deleted everything. I never thought it would get to this ... level of depravity." *That's one word for it.*

Chase nods, then looks over at me. "That's all I need. Have a safe trip."

He pats my shoulder and walks away as Conner and Miller approach us.

"We'll wait a day to go to London," Connor says, but

Skyla's already shaking her head as Connor wraps her in a blanket from the back of the SUV.

I need to get these clothes off her and get her in the shower to rinse his blood away.

"No. We won't wait, and that's final. He doesn't get to feck up my life anymore, not for one more minute. I'm mostly packed and ready for tomorrow. Oh God, I have to tell Mik."

"I called him," Connor says, then blows out a breath. "Jesus Christ, I've never been so scared."

He tugs his sister into his arms and hugs her close.

"It's all over," she says, patting Connor's back. "It's all over now. I need to go home and shower, Connor. I feel dirty."

Because that son of a bitch had his hands on her, just like before. I'd like to bring him back to life so I can tear the flesh from his body.

"I'll make sure your truck gets returned to you," Connor tells me. "Miller will drop it off at the ranch. You take this SUV, and we'll switch them out after we handle everything here."

"I appreciate it. Billie's with Riley," I remind him.

"I'll deal with that too," Connor replies. "And I'll call you or have Billie reach out when I've checked in on them."

"Thank you." After I shake his hand, I get Skyla situated in the vehicle, then we're on the way to the ranch. My girl pulls my hand into hers, lacing our fingers, holding on almost desperately.

"I wish I could sit in your lap," she murmurs. "Can I crawl over and cling to you?"

"I want you safe in that belt, baby. Don't worry, I'll have my hands on you all night. I'm not going to let go of you."

She bites her lip and nods, then looks out the passenger window.

We ride in silence. My heart is still hammering. Christ, I almost lost her today. I could have fucking lost her. I wouldn't survive her being ripped away from me like that. She's my entire world, and losing her at the hands of a fucking madman wasn't an option. Losing her, period, isn't a goddamn option.

When we arrive at the farmhouse, I guide Skyla out of the vehicle. With her hand in mine, we walk into the house, and she turns into me, clinging to me.

"Let's get you in the shower," I say as I lead her to the stairs. My emotions are all over the place. I want to get her clean, to get the blood and gunk from The Asshole off her, and get him gone for good. To take care of her.

To worship her.

"Beck, let's sit." She points in the other direction, toward the couch.

"You need a shower, baby. Let me take care of you."

"Soon. First, I need you to sit with me." Her voice is even now, and there are no tears in her eyes. No sign of distress. In fact, she looks ... *calm*.

I walk to the couch with her, and when I sit, she straddles me, and her fingers dive into my beard as she tips her forehead against mine.

"Talk to me," she whispers. "You're so quiet, *a ghrá*."

I'm so fucking angry. With him. With myself for not being there. And I won't take that out on her.

"Just tell me what you need, Irish."

She frowns and settles more against me, then wraps her arms around my neck and hugs me close.

"I need you," she murmurs against my skin, and my heart thumps. "Just you. Please hug me back, Beck."

I crush her to me, my arms wound tightly around her, and bury my face in her shoulder. I breathe her in, and it all starts to pour out of me. I couldn't stop it if I wanted to.

"I'm so sorry." I choke out the words as my hands move up and down her slim back. "I failed you today. I wasn't there to protect you and Riley, and I'm so fucking mad at myself. You shouldn't have gone through that. None of what happened tonight should have happened, and it's my fault."

"Hey, hey," she says, kissing my neck. "No, Beckett, don't you dare do that to yourself. Everything that happened this evening is *his* fault. Not yours. Not mine. It's all on him. You got to me as quickly as you could, and at that moment, when I was on those steps with him, you were the only thing that kept me sane. Your eyes. You telling me that you had me. You, Beckett."

I can't get fucking close enough to her. She's clutching me to her, kissing my neck, and I know she's safe here with me, yet my hands are still unsteady when I reach up to trace her cheek with my knuckles.

"I could have lost you tonight." My voice is rough. My stomach is in knots. "I can't lose you, Irish."

"I'm right here, and I'm not going anywhere. You'll have to serve me with an eviction notice if you want me out of this farmhouse, *a ghrá*, because I love you." She smooths her nose up the side of my neck and then along my jawline until her lips hover over mine. "So much that it makes my chest ache."

"I love you. And no, I'm never asking you to move out of this house. Move the rest of your shit in, Irish. You're mine, and you can stay forever if that's what you want." With a soft kiss, I stand to carry her upstairs, but my phone rings, and I frown. "I'd normally tell whoever is on the phone to fuck off, but this is Billie."

She bites her lip and nods.

"Hello?"

"Hey, it's me," Billie says. "Riley's great. He'll probably have a headache from the bump on his head and maybe a concussion, but there's no break in his skull, and he's not injured anywhere else. They're going to keep him for a few days to monitor him. What should we do while we're in London? Do you want me to stay behind to take care of him?"

"No," Skyla says, obviously able to hear my sister. "Brad's going to take care of him, and I think that'll still be just fine. But I'll want to see Riley before we leave in the morning."

"The vet said you can come in anytime," Billie says. "Are you all okay?"

"Yeah." After our moment on the couch, I'm steadier

as I look down at my girl. I need to take care of her. "We're okay. We'll see you in the morning."

"Okay. I love you both. Good night."

"Love you," Skyla says into the phone before I hang up. "Bee's the best."

"She's okay."

Skyla grins and pushes her fingers through my beard. "The *best*, Mr. Blackwell. Now, I'll take that shower, and then I'm going to get naked with my man."

I raise an eyebrow as I climb the steps toward our bedroom. *Our bedroom.* "You're remarkably calm after what you've been through tonight."

She lays her head on my shoulder as I climb the stairs. "Now that the initial adrenaline has worn off, it feels different than it did in LA because I know he's gone. He can't hurt me or taunt me or upset me ever again. It's over. And I'm here with you, where I always feel the safest."

"I'm going to fucking worship you tonight."

She grins, wrinkling her nose in that way that makes my cock twitch. "I'll never say no to that."

Chapter Twenty-Nine

SKYLA

"I can wash my own face," I remind Beckett as he gently smooths the warm cloth over my skin, wiping away the cleanser he used.

"I know you can," he replies as his eyes track the movement of the cloth. "But so can I, and I need to pamper you tonight."

My sigh is one of contentment. He's certainly in his aftercare mode. The shower was long and hot and luxurious. He took his time washing my body, and he was careful with my hair because my scalp was sore from where The Arsehole yanked on it. Beck made me feel so treasured, it almost brought tears to my eyes.

And now, not unlike when we were in LA, I'm sitting on the bathroom vanity, wrapped in a towel, my wet hair woven into a braid, and he's taking care of my skin.

He reaches for my rose water, and I close my eyes as

he spritzes it over my face, and then his fingers gently massage my moisturizer into my skin.

"Don't make me get too accustomed to this, Mr. Blackwell."

"Why not?" His voice is soft as if his movements have mesmerized him as much as they have me.

"Because I'll grow to crave it, and then you'll be on the hook for this treatment every day."

The corners of his lips tip up and his warm hazel eyes smile down at me, and heat pools in my belly. The love and care he shows me is as intoxicating and sensual as everything else about him. He makes my body hum with desire.

"I'll do this for you every day if that's what you want me to do." He kisses my forehead as he sets the tub of moisturizer aside, then he steps between my knees, wraps his arms around my shoulders, and pulls me to him.

He's also only wrapped in a towel that matches mine. Needing to feel his flesh in my grip, I pull the terry cloth loose and let the towel fall to the floor, then tighten my hand on his arse.

"Have I ever told you what a mighty fine arse you have?"

I feel his chuckle against my cheek. "I don't think you have."

"Well, that's a shame because for the love of all the gods, Beckett, your arse could end wars."

He barks out a laugh and tugs my towel free, then carries me to our bed, where he gently lowers me to the mattress and crawls over me, hovering. His face is suddenly so serious I can't resist brushing my fingers through his hair.

"What is it?" I ask softly.

"You're surprisingly calm. I know I said it before, but baby, tonight was intense."

I nod, watching my fingers as they comb through his dark strands. "I started to break apart," I admit softly. "When I was finally in your arms, and I knew that *he* couldn't hurt me anymore, I started to feel the way I did in LA. I was shaking, and I was panicking."

He lowers to his elbows and gently pushes his fingers into my hair, listening intently.

"I know some of that is adrenaline because, God, *a ghrá*, I was terrified, but then I remembered that when we break, you're always there to put us back together. No matter what I need, even when I don't *know* what I need, *you* know. Your touch, your voice, your love are all I need to feel safe."

"Baby." He closes his eyes and lowers his forehead to mine. Then his lips are on me, kissing me softly and nibbling at the side of my mouth. I raise my legs onto his hips, and I can feel the hard length of him move against my slit, sending a zing through me. I'm already so wet for him, needing him inside me, but when I move my hips, urging him to push inside, he growls against my lips.

"I'll come in three seconds if I move in now," he warns me as he nibbles down my neck to my collarbone. "And I told you that I'm going to worship you tonight."

"That's what you've been doing, Beck." I bite my lip

when his mouth latches on to my nipple, sucking hard. "Ah, hell, that's bloody good."

"What else do you need?" He kisses over to the other breast and skims his teeth over my sensitive flesh before moving lower. "Tell me, baby."

"Your mouth." My voice is breathy, and I can't keep my hands out of his hair. "On me."

"It's on you," he reminds me before leaving a wet kiss just below my navel. "Be more specific."

I whimper, but he doesn't move lower.

Because he wants me to ask for it.

"I want your mouth"—I have to pause to lick my lips —"on my pussy. Please."

With a growl, he shoulders his way between my thighs. Before licking me, he takes a deep inhale, breathing me in.

If it wasn't so bloody sexy, I'd almost be embarrassed.

"This pussy is goddamn incredible," he murmurs before he licks me from my entrance to my clit. My hips buck up off the bed, so he loops his arm over my stomach to hold me in place. "And all mine. You're such a good fucking girl, Irish."

I flush with his praise, and I feel him chuckle against me before he pushes two fingers inside me. My walls contract around him, making us both groan.

"Ah, Jesus." I thrash my head back and forth, my breath heaving on the cusp of an incredible climax.

"Do not come," he warns me, and I lift my head and stare down at him.

"What?"

"Not yet." He shakes his head, pulling me closer to the edge. "I mean it, Irish. You can hold out."

"For feck's sake, Beck." My hands clench around the bedsheets. I bite my lip. "I can't."

"Listen to me, beautiful girl." I shake my head, but he keeps going. "Take a breath."

"Let me come."

He smiles against me, and I've a mind to squish him with my thighs.

"Beckett."

He quickly pulls his fingers out of me, and I feel so empty, but then he climbs over me and slams his cock inside me.

"Now," he growls against my lips. "Come for me, baby."

There's no way I can stop it. My back arches, my arms and legs clutch him to me, and I scream his name as I break apart.

"Yes, that's it," he says, and then he tenses and follows me over, rocking into me through his own orgasm, whispering words of love to me. "You're so perfect. You're everything, Irish. So fucking amazing."

I couldn't hold the tears back if I tried. They spill down my temples, and he leans down to kiss me.

"Don't cry, baby."

"I just love you so bloody hard, Beckett Blackwell."

He sighs and brushes my nose with his. "I love you too, Irish."

"Thanks for the ride," Beckett says to Brad, who's driving us to the airport, but first, we need to stop in to check on my boy. "This is easier than leaving my truck at the airport."

"It's no trouble," Brad says. "Besides, I need to talk with the vet to make sure I have everything ready to bring our boy home with me."

"I so appreciate this," I add, twisting my hands in my lap.

I'm anxious to see Riley and make sure he's really going to be okay.

I'm the first one out of the truck and running to the door of the clinic, where the vet is waiting for us.

"Where is he?" I ask right away.

"This way," she says, gesturing for us to follow her. "He did so well through the night. He'd probably be okay to go home today, but I don't think it's a bad idea for us to monitor him for one more day."

Finally, we're taken into the back, where many kennels are set up but only a few are occupied, and I see my boy.

He whines when he sees me. Tears fill my eyes when she opens the door, and I'm able to get on the floor and climb in with him.

Riley is big, which means his kennel is, too. And I'm a small girl.

"Hello, my sweet boy," I croon as I take his face in my hands. "I'm okay, baby."

He cries, resting his head on my shoulder, and I can't help but cry with him.

"I know, you had to be so scared. I'm sorry that you were hurt. But I'm just fine, sweet boy."

He whines again and licks my tears away.

"We're okay," I repeat, resting my forehead against his neck. I can hear the vet talking to Brad about his care once he goes home tomorrow.

Part of me wants to tell everyone that I'll take him to London with me, but I know that's not what's best for Riley. The trip over is rough on him when he's healthy. It would be agony when he doesn't feel well.

"I love you so much," I whisper to him. "You were so brave. You scared that horrible man, and that's exactly what you were supposed to do. I'm proud of you, baby."

When I look over my shoulder, I see Beckett squat next to me and reach in to pet Riley's neck.

"You guys okay?" Beck asks softly.

"We are. Happy to see each other."

"I can see that," Beck replies with a smile in his voice. "Are you sure you still want to leave today, Irish? No one will mind if you need a day to regroup."

Part of me wants to say yes, but it's time for me to go to work.

"No. We'll go." I take Riley's face in my hands. "I have to go for a little while. You're going to stay with Brad and Sadie while I'm gone."

Riley tilts his head to the side, listening. He's such a smart boy.

"Don't worry about me, okay? I'll be home before you know it. You be good."

He whines again and rests the full weight of his head in my hands as if he's hugging me, and my eyes fill with tears once more.

"I'll miss you, too."

"Irish, you're breaking my heart over here." Beck's voice is rough, and he's rubbing circles on my back. "Fuck the performance. We don't have to go at all."

I smile at that and wipe my tears away.

"Yes, we do. I'm just not good at leaving my boy behind." I kiss him once more and then nod at the doctor. "Thank you for everything. I can pay you before we leave."

"It's been taken care of," she says, shaking her head. I don't miss the look she shares with Beckett, and I turn my attention to him in surprise.

"You didn't have to—"

"You don't have to worry about anything," he says, pulling me into his arms. "Not one thing, baby."

Brad makes plans to pick up Riley the following morning, and then we're back in the truck, headed for the airport, and the nerves settle in again. I'm not excited to be back here, where the worst moments of my life took place just hours ago, but when we arrive, I see my family's jet waiting for us. *Gallagher Resorts* is written across the side, and even that is a comfort to me. I'm willing my brain not to think about anything that happened here last night.

I refuse to give *him* any more real estate in my mind.

He's gone. He'll never get near me again. No more taunts. No more messages. No more touches.

Beck and Brad meet the grounds crew with our luggage so they can stow it inside the plane, and I thank Brad before I climb the stairs of the jet. I know that everyone's already here waiting for us, but when I turn to look at all of the faces, tears form again.

Connor's watching me through his glasses; he's so stoic and strong the way he always is.

Dani and Billie are grinning, almost dancing in their seats.

Beckett's brothers look so solemn, and I feel Beckett behind me. His arms wrap around my shoulders as I find Mik's gaze, and I smile at him. He's holding Benji's hand tightly.

"You are all right then, malishka?" he asks me.

With a nod, I skim my gaze over everyone here. "Yes. I'm fine and well, and grateful that you're all here for this."

"Look at this cool airplane!" Birdie exclaims, making us all laugh. "There are snacks and everything."

"She's never going to want to travel any other way," Dani adds, brushing her hand over Birdie's hair. Bridger leans in to kiss her temple.

"Let's do this." Beckett kisses my head.

"I love you all," I say before anyone looks away from

me. "Every single one of you is important to me, and it's a lucky girl that I am that you're all here with me."

"There's nowhere else we'd rather be," Blake says with that devastating grin. "We're proud of you, Skyla."

My gaze finds Connor's again, and he's almost smiling now, which has me blinking in surprise.

"Let's go," he says, gesturing for us to sit. "My sister has a date with the king."

Chapter Thirty

BECKETT

"Again!"

I hate it when Mik yells at my girl like that. They're rehearsing, *again*, and I'm standing off to the side, watching.

I haven't made it a habit of hovering during the past few days of rehearsals here in London. In fact, I've spent most of my time with my family, doing the tourist thing, while Skyla and Mik work their asses off for tomorrow night's performance. Earlier in the day, they'll meet Their Majesties in a private reception.

Skyla's still trying to get me to join them, and although the thought of meeting royalty gives me hives, I'd do pretty much anything she asked of me.

"Again, malishka!"

"For feck's sake, Mik, stop tossing me around like that. It's not me who's messing this up."

Good girl. Stand up for yourself, Irish.

I turn when I feel a hand on my shoulder and look into the same green eyes as Skyla's.

"Mr. Gallagher," I say with a nod.

"That's Patrick to you," he reminds me. "They're going to be at this for a long while. Let's go to the pub and have a drink."

I look back at my girl and see her arguing with Mik, then I nod at Patrick. "I could use one."

He grins, and we walk side by side out of the large ballroom that Mik and Skyla have taken over at the London Gallagher Hotel for their rehearsal space and down the long hallway to the hotel bar.

This property is opulent. There's no other way to describe it. I know that Gallagher Resorts and Hotels has a reputation for being fancy. Luxurious.

And this one is no different.

Our suite is bigger than an average house, and it's not even the biggest on the property. I'm pretty sure that Patrick and Maeve are in that one.

As they should be.

The dark pub has a long, polished bar and gold-and-navy wallpaper. The pillows and cushions are also in golds and blues, and look comfortable.

"Two glasses of the Macallan," Patrick says to the bartender as we pass by and take a table in the back corner.

This man should intimidate the fuck out of me. He's powerful, wealthy, and he's the father of the woman I love more than anything.

But he doesn't scare me.

I've already faced my biggest fear and made it out to the other side.

My girl, at gunpoint, with a fucking monster holding on to her.

It'll be in my nightmares for the rest of my life.

Patrick and I take our seats, and seconds later, the bartender delivers our drinks, and we take a sip.

"Do you think they're ready for tomorrow, then?" he asks.

"Yes. I think they're over-rehearsing at this point, but what do I know? They'll be amazing."

He nods, eyeing me.

"I'm not a man who beats around the bush, Beckett."

"Neither am I, sir."

He nods, then sips again. "I got the full report on what happened last week, but I want to hear from you how she's doing since you seem to be closest to her. She puts on a brave face for us. Always has. She doesn't like to be a burden even though we're her family."

"She's handling it far better than she did LA," I reply with a sigh. "I think it's because it's over. He's gone. She doesn't have to look over her shoulder or worry that he could pop up somewhere. Yeah, it was scary as hell, and it's a moment that I never want to relive. But I'm glad it happened, and he's done. Otherwise, I would have taken him out myself."

His eyes narrow on me as he examines me, and then he blows out a breath and leans back in his chair.

"I've had plenty of frustrating moments in my life. In

business, of course. In my marriage. With my babies." He clears his throat. I expected Patrick Gallagher to be ruthless and cold, so I wasn't expecting this family man. Right now, he's a father concerned about his daughter.

And I don't think I've ever respected him more.

"But," he continues, "I don't think I've ever been more fecking frustrated than I was in LA."

I nod as I turn my glass in a circle. "I can only imagine. I didn't realize before that night that Skyla hadn't told you about him."

"Did you know?" he asks.

With my gaze on his, I say, "Yes, sir."

"Stubborn kids," he mutters, shaking his head.

"Had I realized that you *didn't* know, I would have encouraged her to tell you," I continue. "Because you shouldn't have been in the dark on that."

He sips his drink. "Are you thinking about marriage, then? With my Skyla Maeve?"

My stomach clenches at the idea of her wearing my ring.

"Eventually, absolutely." I smile at the other man. "You raised a brilliant, kind, loving woman, Patrick. She's everything I never knew I needed in my life. That I didn't know I was waiting for. Yes, someday soon, I'd love to marry her and start a family with her. For now, for right this moment, I can't wait to get her home and start growing old with her."

He doesn't smile back. If anything, the few lines on his face seem to deepen as he watches me over the rim of his glass.

345

"A father's greatest hope is that his children find where they belong. Whether that's a place or a person. I figured that New York City and ballet were that for my girl, but I can see that I was wrong. She loves being in Montana, and I know she loves you."

My brows pull together. "How do you know?"

"Aside from the forty times she said it today alone," he says with a chuckle, "it's in the way she looks at you and you her. I have that with her mother. Money can't buy it. It's a connection, a feeling that sets up root in your soul and doesn't let go. You know you'd do anything for them, no matter what."

I take a deep breath. "You're right. I'd do anything for her. Even meet fucking royalty."

Patrick laughs at that and shrugs. "You'll survive it, son. It's the price you pay for being with someone extraordinary."

"She's everything." My voice is soft. "As far as I'm concerned, she hung the moon."

"Good. When the time comes, there will be an iron-clad prenup. It's nothing personal."

"I don't want anything from you, Patrick. I do fine on my own."

"I know." He grins. "I checked you and your business out."

"Of course, you did."

He shrugs. "I'm her father, and I have unlimited resources. It's par for the course."

"And if I hadn't passed the test?"

"You wouldn't be here. But I do like you, and your

346

family, and it's pleased I am that you've all welcomed my girl into your fold as if she's one of your own."

"She *is* one of us."

"And now, you're one of us," he replies, clinking his glass to mine.

"I'll stretch with you," Birdie says. It's just past noon the next day, the day of the event, and everyone is in our suite. The energy is electric. Taylor Swift is shaking it off through the speakers, and Birdie mimics Skyla's stretch moves.

"You're a wonderful partner," Skyla assures my niece, earning a wide grin from the little girl.

Skyla sits up, and her eyes scan the room, looking for me. They warm when they find me, and she blows me a kiss.

I cross the room and take her hand, pulling her to her feet, then plant my lips on hers.

"Yuck," Birdie mutters, making me smile.

"Not yuck," Skyla whispers. "I'm so nervous."

"You're beautiful," I reply and push my fingers in her loose hair, loving the way the smooth strands feel against my skin. "And talented and amazing. You have no reason to be nervous, Irish. You're ready for this. You're going to smash it."

"Gosh, that's romantic," Dani says with a happy sigh, and I smile but don't look away from my girl.

"What do you need, baby?"

"I know what she needs," Billie says, patting me on the shoulder. "Let her go, lover boy."

"No."

"Jesus, Beck, stop being so needy and let the poor girl go."

With a laugh, Skyla steps away from me and turns to Billie. "And what do I need, then?"

"You need to dance it out." Bee nods, and the music changes to a P!nk song that Skyla's played in the house before. Suddenly, my sister, Dani, Birdie, and Skyla start to *dance*.

I step back, giving them more room, and feel Connor walk up beside me. Mik and Benji join the girls, jumping, shaking their heads and arms, moving their shoulders with the beat of the song.

God, she fits. My girl fits into my family like a missing puzzle piece. As if she was supposed to be here all along.

Billie sticks her butt out and gives it a shake, swinging her dark hair around in a circle, and Connor growls next to me.

"Hurt her, and I'll end you," I say quietly.

He doesn't reply.

But he also doesn't leave.

When that song ends, another begins, and the dance party continues. Blake even moves into the mix. He takes Dani's hand, and they start to do the jitterbug.

I had no idea he knew how to do that, but he's surprisingly good at it.

"Me too!" Birdie exclaims, and Blake twirls her around, making her giggle.

After the second song, everyone's out of breath and laughing. The tension in the room has dissipated.

"Okay," Skyla says, accepting a glass of water from Benji, "that was fun. I think any time I'm nervous, I'll simply dance it out."

"Spontaneous dance parties are the way to go," Billie agrees. "Sometimes, it's more fun than"—she gives Birdie the side-eye and then whispers—"*sex.*"

"Then you're doing it wrong," Dani says with a laugh, and now Connor *does* leave.

Interesting.

"How do you feel now?" I ask Skyla.

"Better. But I have to get dressed soon. We have the royal reception in two hours."

"You get to meet the king and queen of the freaking commonwealth," Bridger says, shaking his head. "That's wild to me."

"I think it's wild to everyone," Benji says with a shrug. "It's new for me, and I've been a dance husband for a decade."

"You've met celebrities before," Mik reminds him.

"Not royalty. This is new. Even I'm nervous."

"And Benji *never* gets nervous," Skyla informs us all. "Okay. I really have to start my hair and makeup. After the reception, we have to come back here so I can do it all over again. Stage makeup is different."

"We're here to help," Billie reminds her.

"And I love you for it," Skyla says, bringing both

Dani and my sister in for a group hug. "But now it's time I have a private freak-out."

"That's our clue to clear out," Brooks announces, gesturing for everyone to leave. Mik and Benji head for their suite so they can also get ready.

And when we're alone, I take Skyla's face in my hands.

"Stop being nervous, Irish."

"I will. Later tonight when it's all over. Now leave me alone so I can get pretty."

"You're already pretty."

"*Beckett.*"

I laugh and back away. "Okay, okay. I'll go check in with Brad."

"Your Majesty." I tip my head down in the bow I was taught before we walked in here. I'm the last of the four of us to meet the royal couple, and I'm nervous as fuck.

But King Frederick smiles and shakes my hand.

"Mr. Blackwell, it's a pleasure," he says. "I hear you're from Montana."

With a surprise, I nod. "I am, yes, sir."

"My brother, Sebastian, and his wife have a home there in Cunningham Falls."

"That's a beautiful area," I reply. "It's about four hours from Bitterroot Valley by car. Have you been?"

"Oh yes, many times to visit. Thank you for coming all this way. Skyla is exceptionally talented."

I smile and look her way. She's chatting with King Frederick's wife, Queen Catherine.

"She's been looking forward to performing for you," I reply. "And it's an honor to be here, Your Majesty."

We chat for just a few more moments, and then we're led out to the waiting cars to take us back to the hotel.

"All of that nervousness for less than thirty minutes," I say, pressing my hand to Skyla's thigh as we ride through London.

"Honestly, the hardest part is over. I can block out who's in the audience and just dance."

"Our Skyla has always been good at that," Mik agrees with a nod. He looks handsome in his tuxedo. "No matter who was in the audience, malishka can focus on the performance and block everything else out. Not everyone can do that. She has nerves of steel."

"Or a bad memory." Skyla laughs.

I lean over and kiss the top of her head. "You're halfway there, baby."

Our family has excellent seats in the auditorium where tonight's celebration is taking place. King Frederick wanted a show, featuring not just Skyla and Mik with their ballet piece but other artists as well. Music, drama, comedy. It's been a fun evening of live theater so far, and my girl is up next.

The lights dim after the applause dies from the last act, and as the live orchestra begins to play, Mik and Skyla walk out on stage, hand in hand, their posture regal.

This is the first time that I've *really* seen her dance, and my heart begins to race.

The emotion of the piece isn't conveyed only in the dance or the body language. It's also in their facial expressions and the chemistry between them. To say that it's a moving experience is doing it a disservice.

It's nothing but pure love on that stage—between the characters they're portraying and the two dancers. I can see the emotion in their eyes as the music swells, and she wraps her arms around his neck in a tender embrace. They're pure magic as they seem to float over the stage. How do they make it look so effortless? I know for a fact that it's anything, but with all the hard work they've put in leading up to this.

The way he holds her, carries her, and cups her face makes my chest hurt. Not in jealousy, but because I know, I can *see*, how much they love this.

Skyla fits with my family like a puzzle piece, but she fits here, too.

She should be on a stage with Mik.

She was made for this, for dancing with her best friend and making an audience believe every step, every smile, every move is just for them.

Skyla takes my breath away.

When the performance is over, Mik and Skyla take their bows to a standing ovation. I see people wiping tears from their eyes, and when I look up at the royal box, I see that the whole royal family is standing and smiling as well.

Yeah, she belongs on a stage as much as she belongs in Montana, and now I have to figure out a way for her to have both. Because I won't give her up. But I can't ask her to walk away from this either.

Chapter Thirty-One

SKYLA

The applause is deafening.

In the heart of my career, I never would have said that I danced for the applause, but standing here, holding Mik's hand, trying to catch my breath as we smile at the audience, and then bow especially for the new king and queen, I can honestly say that I have missed the ovations since leaving my career.

We bow once more, and then the curtain falls, and Mik scoops me up in one of his amazing hugs, lifting my feet off the ground and burying his face in my neck.

I can feel the emotion rolling through him, just as it's rolling through me.

This was it.

Our last performance together.

"I love you," I tell him as he carries me off stage and into my dressing room, where he shuts the door.

He hasn't let me go.

"I don't want it to be over," he admits, not pulling away.

"I know." I rub my hands up and down his back. "But it's not over, *a stór. We* aren't over."

"The magic is." His voice is so rough, so full of tears, and it fills me with sadness. I hate disappointing him. "What will I do without you?"

"Well, you won't be able to yell at me anymore." I smile against his shoulder, and he slowly lowers me to my feet, but we don't pull away from each other.

"He's gone now. You don't have to be afraid to be in the city. You could come back, malishka."

I'm already shaking my head. "I have loved this time with you, and I'll always cherish it. But, Mik, it's just not who I am anymore. It's not what I want."

"You want to live on a farm, feed chickens, and have babies?"

Babies.

"I do." I can't help but laugh when he scowls. "I really do want that, and it's okay that *you don't.* You have years left in your career, and you need to take them. I'll come to every new performance. Beckett and I will fly out for each opening night, and I'll be in the front row. You and Benji will come to Montana for the holidays and vacation in the summer."

"Benji does love it." He tips his forehead to mine. "I know we've been through this, but I had to try since the bastard is gone, and you're in such good shape. You're so talented."

"You always yell at me."

"Of course, because you are lazy, and you keep dropping your left shoulder."

I laugh as I cup his face. "Exactly. What do you want a lazybones like me around for, anyway?"

"Because you are my soulmate," he says, serious now. "You and Benji, you are my heart."

"I know." I brush his hair off his forehead. "But we're not saying goodbye. You will never be rid of me. I'll call and harass you every day."

He swallows hard and nods once. "Fine then. It is decided. I will retire and move to Montana."

I laugh and jump into his arms again, hugging him close. "You're so co-dependent, Mik. You're not retiring yet. I forbid it."

"You have no say. I will buy your house, and Benji and I will move there, but I will not have babies."

"I don't think that's physically possible anyway. You can't retire yet. You're not ready. Besides, I won't let you buy my house."

Mik scowls. "Why not? If it goes up for sale, I will buy it. You cannot stop me."

"I can, too. Because I'll gift it to you." I smile when his jaw drops. "I never did get you a wedding gift."

"You got us an espresso machine."

"That you regifted, so it doesn't count. I don't want your money, Mik. I don't need it. But I do need *you*, so if you want the house, it's yours."

He sighs before stepping away from me. "I am proud of you, malishka."

"I'm proud of both of us, *a stór*."

There's a light knock on the door, and Beckett pokes his head in. I feel the smile spread over my face as I rush over, and he crushes me against him.

"You were incredible," he says against my lips.

"It felt incredible."

Benji walks past me to greet Mik the same way, and I love how happy my dear friend is. *And that he wants to move to Montana.* How did I get this lucky?

"Do you want to stay for the rest of the show?" I ask him.

"It's over. The last act just finished, and the auditorium is emptying. I wanted to give you and Mik a minute."

I rub my nose against his, then turn to see Benji kissing Mik's forehead as my best friend wipes away a tear.

He's so emotional. It's one of the things that I love the most about him.

"Let's go back to the hotel," Benji says. "Everyone can get comfortable. You were both amazing out there, and I'm so proud of you."

"We didn't do too bad." I smile and link my fingers with Beck's. "I'm going to change my shoes, then we can get out of here."

It's much later by the time Beckett and I are alone again. When we returned to the hotel, we changed clothes and met with everyone in my parents' suite for food and champagne. We laughed and talked, and I was reminded once more just how much I enjoy having my family around me.

My *whole* family, whether they be a Gallagher or a Blackwell.

I love them all.

But now, Beckett and I are alone in our suite. We've had a shower, and he's just finishing with removing my makeup.

I'm a spoiled woman.

And I love it.

"That feels so much better," I murmur after he finishes rubbing the moisturizer into my skin. "I don't think I'll wear makeup for a while after this. I don't like it."

"You don't need it." He kisses my nose, then leans his hands on the counter on either side of my hips. His face is suddenly so serious, it makes me nervous. "We need to talk, Irish."

"All right, then talking is what we'll do. Let's go sit in the living room."

For a moment, I don't think he's going to move, but he kisses my forehead and steps back, giving me space to hop off the vanity. With my hand in his, we move into the living room, but he doesn't pull me onto his lap.

And that makes my heart kick up a notch and not in a good way.

Beckett sits next to me and turns on the cushion with one knee bent to face me. I mirror the pose, resting my hands on his thighs, and it helps my anxiety a bit when he takes one of my hands in his.

"I've been thinking..." He frowns as he looks down at our hands. "Watching you tonight was fucking incredible. I knew you were talented and had a successful career before I met you, but I have to tell you that seeing you on that stage with Mik was—" He shakes his head and looks blankly across the room as if he's searching for the right words.

I have to take a deep breath to calm myself down.

"It was spectacular," he continues, smiling softly. "And I think that it occurred to me for the first time just how much you deserve to be on that stage with Mik all the time."

"Whoa." I hold up a hand, stopping him before I have a stroke. "Beckett, are you *breaking up with me*?"

His eyes widen, and he immediately tugs me onto his lap, wraps his arms around me, and buries his face in my neck.

"Fuck no. Jesus, not in this or any other lifetime."

A tear runs unchecked down my cheek. "You scared me."

"No, baby." He leans back and brushes the tear from my face. "I'm so sorry. I should have led with that."

I sniff and brush another tear away. Now that the floodgates have opened, it's hard to close them up again because the thought of him ending this is just ... *no.*

"You're *mine.*" He cups my cheek, staring deeply into my eyes. "Do you understand me?"

I nod and bite my lip. "Okay. Now that that's settled, what were you trying to say?"

"Fuck, hold on." He hugs me again and drags his hand up and down my back. "I need a second because just hearing you say those words fucked me up."

"I'm sorry, I—"

"No. No apologies. That's on me." He kisses my cheek, then my lips. "I just think that you should dance, baby. Now that The Asshole is gone, and you don't have to be afraid anymore, you should be free to dance. I'll commute to New York for the next few years. And you'll come to me when you're between projects. Your chickens will miss you, but we'll figure it out."

I'm already shaking my head, but he keeps talking.

"I want you to have everything you want. I'm so proud of you, Irish. And I know Mik misses you. You're too young to retire. We'll work it out."

"No." I take his face in my hands, loving how his whiskers feel against my palms. "No, *a ghrá*. My life is in Montana at the Double B Ranch. I have chickens to take care of. They're my responsibility. You said so yourself, and I can't just abandon them."

He starts to speak, but I press my hand over his lips, and he narrows his eyes at me.

"I love our home. Our mountains. We're turning your cabins into a special retreat for sick kids."

He kisses my fingers, then takes my hand away from his lips. "I can still do that, baby."

"Not without me, Beckett Blackwell." I frown at him, shaking my head. "I want to be a part of it. I love my studio and my students, and I want to add yoga classes, too. I *love* Bitterroot Valley. It's my community. People smile at me and know me when I walk down the street. Jackie knows I want a huckleberry scone when I walk into The Sugar Studio. Millie knows my coffee order."

"Millie knows everyone's coffee order."

I press my hand to his mouth again.

"I have my Spicy Girls Book Club, and Billie and Dani, along with Alex and the others." I straddle him now and wrap my arms around his neck. "But most of all, I have *you*, and I don't want to live away from you for even a day, Beckett. I'm finished with dancing professionally. Mik and I said goodbye to that tonight. Never to him or our friendship, but the dancing is done. My life is with you. My home is with you. Whether at the ranch, on a beach, or on the moon, as long as I'm with you, I'm home."

"Fuck, I love you, Irish."

Beckett moves quickly, laying me on my back on the sofa and kissing me. He licks my lips until I open to him, and then he sinks into me as if kissing me is as essential as breathing.

He tugs my robe open and kisses down my chest as he nudges his sweats down his hips. Then he's inside me, buried so deeply that I don't know where he ends, and I begin.

He's still kissing me, cradling my face, and not moving.

"*A ghrá*, I need you to move."

"In a second." His hand grazes down my side to my

hip and then around to my arse, and he holds on tight. "You're *my* home, too. Never forget that."

His hips shift, and I moan as heat spreads through me. He squeezes the globe of my arse, pulling me closer to him, watching me so intently that I couldn't look away if I tried.

Pushing one hand between us, I cover my clit with my fingertip, and my body immediately clutches around him, making us both groan.

"Christ, baby," he whispers. "I need you to go over."

Moving my fingers back and forth, I feel the sizzle course down my spine, and I know I'm *so close.*

"That's it. God, you're fucking incredible. Let go, baby. Let go for me."

His words, his voice, his body.

The way he loves me so much that he'd sacrifice time with me so I can chase a dream so many miles away from him.

I've never been loved like this.

I didn't know I *could* be.

I have no defenses against any of it, and I explode in pleasure, crying out his name as I fall over the edge. Beckett growls as his climax moves through him. He rocks into me and kisses my neck.

"Mine," he says without lifting his lips from my skin. "You're fucking *mine.*"

"Yours." I don't even mind that I can't breathe when he collapses onto me. I'll gladly take his weight.

But he finally leans up and brushes my hair off my face.

"I know you wanted to stay for a few more days," he says.

"I want to go home," I reply. "Take me home, Mr. Blackwell."

We've been home for a week, and I've never been happier.

I had Connor draw up the paperwork to transfer the ownership of my old house to Mik and Benji, and it's ready for their signatures. They tried to put up a fight, but I ignored them.

It's my gift to give, and I want them to have it.

Riley barks, and I turn to see that his tail is wagging, but he's watching something in the woods.

"If there's a wee deer out there, you'll be for leaving it alone, Riley." I narrow my eyes at him, and he whines, but he doesn't run off into the trees.

I go back to feeding my chickens.

I added ten more hens to my little flock, and so far, all of the ladies are getting along just fine, but I notice that Harriet, one of the older girls, seems to have a bit of a limp.

"What's happening with your leg?" I'll have to keep an eye on her, and if she doesn't get better ... well, I don't want to think about that.

I understand it's a farm, but I've grown to love these birds.

After they're fed, I search for eggs, and then Riley and I go back inside.

Now that the chickens are tended to and I've had breakfast, it's time for me to curl up with my book. I have book club tonight, and with only about eleven chapters left to go, I should be able to finish on time.

Riley curls up on his bed for a nap, and I've just sat in the corner of the sectional, where I prefer to curl up with my reading device when Beckett walks in from outside.

"Did you start without me?" he asks.

"I figured you'd be working today." I grin when he joins me, presses me against his side, and takes the device out of my hands.

"We're catching up for your book club," he says, kissing my head. "And you're not finishing this book without me."

"Big Navessa Allen fan, are you?"

Beckett's eyes skim the page, looking for where we left off. "This one is *good*. The guy is super fucked up, though."

"I mean, his biological father is a serial killer. I'd suspect that would feck anyone up."

"Fair point. However, this is about a stalker, and it doesn't seem to bother you." He raises an eyebrow.

"But he's such a golden retriever stalker." I laugh and snuggle against him. "I'm fine with it. Honest."

"Okay, here we go."

"Wait." I press my hand to his chest and smile at him. "You're *really* blowing off work so you can read with me all day?"

"I worked this morning." He sounds only a little defensive. "My chores are done, and now I get to spend time with my girl. It's one of the perks of being the boss."

"Hmm." I lean against him once more. "I do like that perk."

"Good." He kisses my head, breathes me in, then starts to read, his deep voice filling the air, telling me a story. I do love listening to his accent while snuggled up against his hard body, being here in our home together.

Riley's snoring in the corner.

And now that The Arsehole is gone, and the investigation is over, I don't have to be afraid anymore. I can live this beautiful life with the man who makes me feel whole, with no regrets or hesitation.

This life of mine is perfect.

Epilogue

CONNOR GALLAGHER

I'm a goddamn glutton for punishment.

My private jet just landed at the airport after flying for ten hours from Brussels. It was a disappointing trip, and I'm fecking exhausted. I should go home and go to bed. Instead, I'm standing outside Billie's Books because I can't seem to stay away from the pretty wee owner of this shop despite the fact that she can't stand to have me around.

She's made it clear that she doesn't want a repeat of our one and only true sexual encounter all those months ago. I've stolen kisses here and there, but she always stops things before I can take them too far.

And because she's in control when it comes to sex, I always back off. I *will* always back off. I'm not in the habit of forcing myself on women who don't want me.

Jesus, I've never had a problem finding a willing woman to warm my bed at night. But since I had her, I

366

don't want anyone else. There hasn't been nor will there be anyone but *mo rúnsearc*.

I want *Billie*.

I think of her constantly.

I know every inch of her lush, gorgeous body.

And when she snaps at me, my cock twitches.

I drag my hand down my face. No one in my personal or professional life would *dare* speak to me the way Billie Blackwell does, yet here I am, bloody eager to get just a glimpse of her before I go to my cold, lonely house for the night.

Pushing through the door of the bookshop, I pause when I see the group of women sitting in the center of the space. Some are in chairs, others are on the floor, and it occurs to me that it must be their book club night.

In fact, there's my sister, Skyla, confirming my suspicions.

Feck me.

I turn to leave before anyone notices me, but then I hear her voice and it has me stopping in my tracks. My hands fist at my sides. Even her raspy, gorgeous voice turns me on.

"Okay, ladies," Bee says. Her back is to me, but I'd recognize that glossy brunette hair anywhere. "I need some book recommendations."

"What are you looking for?" Skyla asks her.

"I want a billionaire"—I take a step in her direction. *Billionaire. That's me*—"one-night stand"—*Check, did that*—"dirty talker"—*there's nothing I love more than muttering filth in her beautiful little ear*—"a smidge morally gray"—*she doesn't need to know about that side of me*—"but absolutely *no* accents because that might make me spontaneously combust."

"Why this specifically?" a blonde woman asks just as Skyla spots me, and her eyes widen.

I shake my head at her.

"Because I'm not getting it in real life, so I might as well read about it."

"You could have it in real life, but you're too bloody stubborn."

I hear a few gasps, and Skyla grins, but I only have eyes for my bumblebee as she turns in her seat and scowls up at me.

"This is a *private party*."

"And it's over," I reply as I reach down and take her hand, pulling her to her feet. "Come with me. Skyla, lock up on your way out."

"Hey, you can't just walk in here and—"

"I just did." She's jogging behind me, trying to keep up with my long strides, and I should slow down for her, but I don't.

Because the mere thought of her getting off on the fictional version of me is absolutely fecking *not* going to fly with me.

I pull her through the door of what I thought might be her office, but it turns out to be a supply closet.

Close enough.

"Connor, you can't—"

I pin her against the door, cage her in, my elbows

resting against the wood above her head, and my lips cover hers.

I'm pissed. I'm horny as hell. And I can't resist her.

Billie moans against my lips, and she doesn't push me away as I sink into her, urging her lips open with my tongue, and she gives me what I'm after.

She bites my lower lip. Her hands fist in my white button-down just above my waist as if she's holding on for dear life while I plunder her amazing mouth.

"Can't get enough of the taste of you," I growl and boost her up so I don't have to lean so far down to reach her.

I'm a tall man, and Billie's just a wee thing, and I want to feel her against me. I need to feel every curve in my hands. I fecking love her curvy body.

Her arms and legs wrap around me, and before I press her back against the door again, I yank the hem of her pink dress up around her waist, exposing the sexiest fecking lacy pink panties I've ever fecking seen. Billie is always dressed impeccably, her hair and makeup perfect, yet not overdone or too much. She's classy. She's beautiful.

She's everything.

"God, your body was bloody made for me, angel."

She whimpers, and my hand dives under that lace, and I find her soaking wet.

"Good fecking girl," I growl against her neck as my fingers get to work, dancing over her clit, then down into her wet crease before I push them up to circle her hard clit again.

She's wiggling, circling her hips as if she's silently begging me to push my fingers inside her, and I will.

But not yet.

"I want you to come for me, *mo rúnsearc*," I murmur against her skin. "I can't believe you sat out there and told your friends that you want to read about *me*, but you won't let me have this with you. You keep denying both of us."

"Connor," she chokes out, tipping her forehead against my shoulder.

"Look at me." Her hazel gaze is on fire as she follows the order. Her jaw drops as I slide two fingers inside her and press the heel of my hand against her clit and work her over, curling those fingers, making her shiver and come undone against me.

"That's right, give it to me, angel. Don't you fecking stop."

Her orgasm is fierce and rattles me to the core.

I *need* to get inside her.

But before I can, she shakes her head and presses on my shoulders, stopping me cold.

"No." She licks her lips and those pretty eyes fill with tears. "I said *no*, Connor. Put me down."

Immediately, I do as she asks.

"Did I hurt you? Christ, Bumble, I'm so sorr—"

"I won't do this with you," she says, her voice shaking. "No more. No more kisses at dance recitals and family dinners and at the fucking coronation of a king. No more messing with my head, Connor. I'm sure it makes you happy to know that I enjoyed fucking you, that I can't help myself from responding to you when you touch me, but I'm done letting you use me. You don't get to do that anymore."

Before I can reply, she opens the door at her back and marches out of the supply closet, leaving me floundering.

Using her?

I'm not fecking using her. I can't stay away from her. I crave her. I need her.

"Christ." I take my glasses off and pinch the bridge of my nose between my finger and thumb.

"I'm sure it makes you happy to know that I enjoyed fucking you, that I can't help myself from responding to you when you touch me, but I'm done letting you use me. You don't get to do that anymore."

That's where you're wrong, angel.

We will get to do that and a lot more.

I want you sated.

I want you happy.

I want you to be mine.

Are you excited for Connor and Billie's story? Turn the page for a sneak peek of Where We Bloom:

Where We Bloom Preview

Prologue
Billie

Last Autumn

I like him, this handsome *stranger* who approached me at my bookstore right before closing. He asked if he could take me to dinner, and honestly, I wasn't sure. I mean, he's hot as hell at well over six feet tall, with dark hair and the greenest eyes I've ever seen, and it looks like he has muscles for days beneath his white button-down shirt and black slacks.

He's sexy.

And did I mention his glasses? Yeah, he has the nerve to wear black-rimmed glasses that might have made my vagina salivate.

But he's ... broody.

I'm not a broody person. And yes, I read enough

romance novels to know that the grumpy-sunshine combination can be hot, but that's fiction. In real life? I've never been attracted to the grump. And this guy has *intense* written all over him.

However, despite that, I said yes, and two hours later, here we are, finishing dinner at my favorite restaurant in Bitterroot Valley, Ciao, with the handsome stranger sitting across from me. We shared the appetizer of Italian nachos, a *huge* entrée of pasta, and tiramisu for dessert. I'm not afraid to eat in front of a man. Yes, I'm a curvy girl, and I know how to dress my body, and I'm not ashamed of it.

I like to eat.

But the portions here are so large, I suggested we share, and I think it was the right call.

The best part of this dinner, though, has been the conversation. This guy—I didn't get his name—is intelligent, and he *listens.*

Which, in my limited dating experience, seems rare.

"I might be in a food coma," I admit as I sit back and sip the last of my after-dinner coffee, watching him. "That was delicious."

"Everything about this evening has been delicious," he replies, holding my gaze through those sexy-as-fuck glasses, and I feel the warmth from his words spread through me.

He may be broody, but he's charming. And he's hardly taken his eyes off me all through dinner.

"May I be blunt?" he asks, his light accent coming

through. I don't know where he's from in Europe, but I know he's not American.

"Of course, please do."

"I'd like you to come back to my suite with me. Stay the night with me."

The hand lifting my water glass to my lips pauses halfway as I stare at him, and then I slowly lower it to the table.

"Is that so?"

"Yes."

"Why do I feel like you're a man who usually gets what he wants?"

His green gaze holds mine as he waits quietly, his finger tapping the side of his wineglass, watching me as I decide what to do. He's sexy, there's no doubt about it. He held my hand on the way here from my shop, and it made my whole arm tingle.

I'm not an impulsive person. I certainly don't have sex with someone on a first date.

But I like him.And a chance to have sex with a man like this one may never present itself again.

And did I mention that he's sexy?

"Where are you staying?" I watch his lips twitch, and his face relaxes as if he were worried I'd say no.

"At the ski resort."

I nod slowly, take one last sip of my water, and ignore the butterflies currently doing the Macarena in my stomach.

"All right."

His eyebrow wings up. "Just like that?"

"It seems so."

He pays the check, then offers me his hand and guides me through the restaurant. I like walking next to him. He's such a big man, I feel perfectly safe when I'm next to him, which is an odd thought, considering that I don't typically feel *un*safe.

When we're standing on the sidewalk, I turn to him.

"I can meet you up there. My car's parked behind my shop."

This tall, hot-as-hell stranger steps closer to me, and with his finger under my chin, he lifts my face so he can look into my eyes. Did all of the air rush out of Montana just now? Because it's suddenly harder to breathe.

"I don't want to let you out of my sight in case you disappear on me. I'm only here for one night, and I plan to take full advantage of that. I'll make sure you get back to your car safely in the morning."

Wow. After swallowing hard, I simply nod, and he kisses my forehead before leading me to a massive black SUV parked across the street.

My stranger opens the passenger door for me, makes sure I get my seat belt secure, closes the door, then circles the hood to the driver's side.

"You know," I begin as he backs out of the parking space and heads toward the road that leads to the resort, "we talked all through dinner, but I never asked you where you're visiting from."

I'm watching his profile as he drives, so I see it when his lips tip up at the side, and I wish he'd give me a full smile.

I saw his eyes light up when I said something funny, and those lips tipped up too, but he has yet to grace me with a full grin.

I bet it's devastating.

"Perhaps we shouldn't divulge too many personal things tonight." He shoots me a glance before he reaches over and sets his hand on my thigh, then gives it a little squeeze.

Just that simple touch makes my nipples pucker. I bite my lip.

We had great conversation at dinner, but we never talked about anything too personal. Obviously, I discussed my bookstore a bit, but never my family or friends. He asked me questions about the store, about the town.

But really, we've kept things quite surface, and I don't really mind. He's only here for this one night, and if he wants to keep things mellow, I'm down for that.

I stare at his hand, then cover it with my own and glide my fingers over his, enjoying the way his skin feels against mine.

"As long as you don't have a wife somewhere who assumes you're being faithful to her and your six children, that's fine with me."

To my absolute shock, he laughs. *Laughs.* And it lights me up inside. It's the kind of laugh you give when you're tickled with someone.

And his smile is as devastating as I expected. It makes my heart speed up into hyperdrive.

"That's not exactly a denial."

He shakes his head and glances at me again. "No. I'm not married, and I don't have any children. Certainly not six."

"Great. I don't either."

He leaves his SUV with the valet and takes my hand again to escort me into the lodge and to an elevator. After riding to the top floor, he leads me to the suite at the end of the hall, opens the door, and gestures for me to walk in ahead of him.

This room is *fancy*. Or set of rooms, I should say. A wall of windows in both the living area and the bedroom gives a view of the ski mountain and the beautiful trees beyond.

"Great room." I immediately kick off my shoes, because that's just habit, and the next thing I know, I'm spun around, back against the window, and he frames my face in his hands and kisses me.

Not a tentative first kiss. No, this man *consumes* me, as if he's wanted to do this to me since the moment he first saw me, and I'm not sure that I've ever felt so wanted.

So damn sexy.

His mouth is *amazing*. Not too hard, not too wet. He growls against me, those hands drift down to my ass, and then he *lifts me*.

I let out a yelp and wrap my arms around his shoulders. I'm not a little woman.

"I've got you," he says against my lips as he carries me to the bedroom. "And as much as I'd love to fuck you against that glass, I'd have to kill anyone who got a look at you, so we'll take it to the bedroom."

I smirk. I can't help it.

He's not going to kill anyone over a one-night stand.

But it's an amusing thought.

And then all thinking goes out those windows as he sets me on my feet. My hands dive for the buttons on his shirt, and he unfastens the belt I have around the green dress I'm wearing.

"You're fucking gorgeous," he says as the belt hits the floor.

With a grin, I push his shirt over his shoulders, and when it joins my belt near our feet, I let my eyes roam down over smooth skin and those muscles that aren't for days. They're for *years*. His abs are so defined, I want to lick them.

I want to nibble them.

And my hands are all over him.

"Lift your arms, beautiful girl," he says, and I comply, letting him pull my dress over my head. He discards it, and I'm standing before this Greek god in just my pretty purple bra and panties, my many flaws on display for him. "Christ Jesus, you're gorgeous."

We're not touching now, just staring at each other, taking each other in. His chest heaves. His hands fist at his sides.

"Your pants," I whisper, meeting his eyes. "Please."

His jaw clenches.

"I like it when you ask nicely." He steps out of the

slacks, along with his boxers, and *Oh. My. God.* "My eyes are up here, angel."

Angel. I'm going to die tonight. I feel it coming.

I swallow hard.

"And you have nice eyes, but holy shit, have you seen *that*?"

I'm scooped up again and am lying on my back in the middle of a soft island of a bed, and he's hovering over me, kissing up my chest toward my chin.

His hands explore me everywhere. Over my sides and hips. My thighs. And then his palms skim up to my breasts, and his thumbs brush my nipples over the bra, and I arch into him.

"Every fucking inch of you is perfect," he growls against my ear. "If there is anything that I do that you don't like, you just say so, and it stops. Got it?"

I nod, biting my lip as I watch his lips move.

"I need your words, angel."

"I understand. Same goes."

He gives me that smile again before twisting me onto my stomach. He unfastens my bra before he pulls my hips back, so my ass is in the air and my face is against the bed. Then his mouth is *right there.*

I hear him inhale, his hands ghost over the globes of my ass, and then he swipes his tongue through my slit, from my clit all the way to the back door, and I moan.

"Look at you," he murmurs before doing it again. "Already so damn wet."

It starts out gentle, and then it's anything *but*. He licks and then sucks on my clit, and pushes a finger inside me, and I push back against him, needing so much more. I feel like if I don't get him inside me *now*, I'll spontaneously combust.

"You like that?"

I nod, and then there's a smack on my ass.

"Words, angel."

This is going to be the best way to die.

"Yes, I like it."

"Good."

He pushes in another finger, stretching me, and I moan again, still pushing back against him, wanting so much more than his fingers.

Just as I'm about to come apart with the most intense orgasm of my life, he stops.

And I frown back at him, but then I realize he's rolling on a condom. He flips me back over, braces himself on his hands beside my shoulders, and pushes the crown inside me. I grip his sides, my nails digging into his skin.

"Take a breath, angel." He brushes his nose over mine so gently, I take that breath.

Why do I love it when he calls me angel so much?

With my eyes on his, I inhale, and then he slides all the way in. My legs are hitched on his hips, my hands slide to his back, and to my surprise, he lowers his forehead to mine.

"Christ, you're snug," he whispers. "Your pussy fits my cock perfectly."

I feel like I've just been given a gold medal.

He covers my mouth with his, then he starts to move,

and I can't help the whimper that pushes through my throat.

"Are you okay?" he asks as he tucks his hand under my ass, tilting my pelvis up.

"Never better. Don't you dare stop."

He cups my cheek and jawline, and picks up the tempo, making my spine tingle and every muscle clench around him.

"Oh fuck."

"That's right. Come for me. God, you're so bloody gorgeous."

His accent is thicker when he's aroused, and before I know it, I'm shattering into a million pieces, holding on to him for dear life as I'm thrown off the sexiest cliff *ever*.

With a roar, he follows me over, cants his hips into mine, and shivers with his own climax.

He lowers to his elbows, bracing himself. Pushing his hands into my hair, he brushes his nose down my jawline, making me shiver.

"Are you okay, angel?"

"If I die because of the best orgasm of my life, please tell my family it was worth it."

With a proud grin, he kisses me, softly this time. Leisurely. As if we have all the time in the world to lie here, in this opulent bed and soak each other in.

This man, this stranger, is a grade A kisser.

Finally, he rolls to the side, disentangles himself from me, then takes my hand and pulls me from the bed.

"Where are we going?" I ask with a laugh.

"Shower," he replies. "I'm going to clean you up and then get you messy again."

Well, yes, please and thank you, hot stranger. Sign me up for that.

Connor

I jolt up out of a dead sleep and pull air into my lungs, taking in my surroundings.

Waking up in a strange place is nothing new to me. It's part of my job.

I'm in Montana. I was supposed to leave yesterday, but my plane had a problem, and we had to postpone until today.

And then I met the most beautiful woman I've ever seen in my bloody life.

I glance down and frown when I see that the bed is empty, and a brush of my hand over the sheets tells me she's been gone for a while.

I push the blanket aside and walk to the living room, and find my dark-haired angel curled up in one of the leather armchairs by the windows, a blanket tossed over her lap, watching the snow outside. She's wearing my shirt from earlier, and it's sexy as hell on her.

I don't know when the snow started, but the trees are already covered in white, and the flakes falling from the sky look like they're the size of my fist.

"It's the first snowfall of the year," she says without turning to look at me. Her voice is raspy, her beautiful long hair tangled, and I need to get my hands on her again more than I need air.

"Have you slept at all?" I ask and scowl when she shakes her head.

"I don't sleep much. But I won't say anything else because we're not sharing personal things." She grins over at me, and her whiskey-colored eyes go round when she sees that I'm naked.

I want to ask her a million questions. *Why* doesn't she sleep well? How does she want her coffee in the morning? When can I see her again?

What's her bleeding name?

If I was a man who did relationships, I'd claim this woman as mine.

But I'm not.

However, I plan to enjoy the hell out of her while I have her, so I kneel in front of her, pull the blanket off her lap, and spread her legs, hooking one of them over the arm of the chair.

"Uh, you don't have to—"

Before she can finish that thought, I lean in and wrap my lips around her clit, flick the little bundle of nerves with the tip of my tongue, and grin when her hands twine in my hair and *pull*.

I love that she's not gentle.

That she's not fragile.

And with a growl, I push my tongue inside her and lap at her juices.

"Ah, shit," she moans. "God, you're so damn good at that."

With a growl, I pull her out of that chair, sit, and straddle her over me. She immediately takes my cock inside her, sinking down until I'm completely buried inside her. She circles her gorgeous hips before she starts to ride.

I unbutton the shirt, lean in and suck on her nipples, tease them with my teeth, and with my hands planted on the globes of her bloody phenomenal arse, she rides me until I feel the orgasm gather, lifting my balls, and I press my thumb to her clit, making sure she comes with me.

Her movements falter as she cries out, coming apart on my lap, and once she's finished, I lift her and pump my cock until I come in thick ropes all over her stomach and tits.

"No condom," she whispers, grinning at me. "Good call."

Still catching my breath, I stand with her in my arms and take us back to bed.

"Come on, we're going to work on that sleep."

"You know, I'm not a small person," she says as she wraps her arm around my neck, still catching her own breath as she presses her sweet face to my neck. "I'm not used to being carried around."

"You're small compared to me," I reply. I don't want her to think she's anything but perfect, just the way she is.

I *love* curvy women.

"I won't sleep," she informs me, dragging a finger down my neck. "And I don't want to keep you up. I'm fine in the chair."

"You're fine in the bed, and you won't keep me up."

She starts to protest, but I silence her with a kiss.

"I want you with me, angel."

I lay her down, and once I've fetched a warm cloth from the bathroom to clean her up, I curl up behind her, tucking her back against my front. We lie like this for a while, watching the snow through the windows. But then, to my surprise, she wiggles around and presses her face to my chest, wraps her arm around my waist, and sighs as she loops one leg through mine, snuggling into me so tightly, as if she's worried I might get away from her.

I kiss her head and hug her close, breathing her in.

I've never felt this kind of instant connection to someone. I don't remember the last time I was this attracted to a woman. I'm not in the habit of keeping someone in my bed overnight, and I'm not a cuddler.

That's too personal.

But this girl had me trapped in her spell from the moment I saw her.

I glance at the clock. I'm leaving in five hours.

And I spend every minute of those holding her. She was wrong. She fell into a deep sleep and relaxed against me. I washed her face in the shower earlier, so she's free of makeup and even more stunning.

The snow stops at around six, and it's time for me to get ready to leave. My angel is sleeping so well, I don't want to wake her.

Okay, the truth is, if she wakes up, I won't want to leave her.

And I have to go.

So I cross to the walk-in closet and dress, grab my already packed bag, and carry it through to the front door of the suite. Then I return to her and watch her for a few moments. She's still in my shirt. She can keep it.

I wonder, briefly, if she'll hang on to it or discard it.

"Take care, angel," I whisper before I leave the suite, shutting the door quietly behind me. I stop at the front desk and ask them to send up coffee and everything on the breakfast menu in two hours, then have a driver take her to her car whenever she's ready, then I leave for the airport.

Although I know I'll be back in Bitterroot Valley often to see my sister, I also know that I won't repeat this night with that glorious, stunning, and witty woman.

Because I'd lose myself to her, and there's no room for that in my world.

Chapter One
Billie

This is my very favorite day of the month.

One Monday a month, I leave my bookstore in the capable hands of my two employees and drive the four hours to Big Sky, Montana, to shop. The only time this doesn't happen is when it's too snowy and the roads are treacherous.

But it's summertime, which means that for the next few months, I'll be able to come to this resort town and buy clothes on my usual schedule.

I'm a self-professed fashionista. I love clothes, especially expensive, high-end labels, but I don't have the budget for that when it comes to buying brand new.

That's where Big Sky comes in.

This ski town isn't so unlike Bitterroot Valley, except it's where the richest come to vacation and own vacation homes. Mega celebrities, billionaires, you name it, and these wealthy women send their hand-me-downs to the local thrift store.

A little secret I discovered by mistake a couple of years ago, and I'm so glad I did. I find a place to park, then walk down the block to the little boutique-style thrift shop and push inside.

"How are you, Martha?" I ask the owner, who's hanging what looks like a red wool coat on a hanger.

This store is the cutest. It doesn't look or smell like a thrift shop. It looks like an adorable fashion boutique, and I always feel fancy when I come in to browse through the racks and hunt for amazing finds.

"Oh, no complaints here. How's the bookstore life treating you, Billie?"

"It's the best. I brought that series you requested and a couple of bags of donations as well."

Not only do I buy from this thrift store but I also donate back anything that I've grown tired of or just didn't work for me.

Because although I'm a clothes horse, my little house can't hold all the clothes I'd keep if I had the space.

"Oh, that's great, thank you," she says with a smile. "I held a few things back for you because I knew they'd sell fast, and I wanted you to get first dibs."

Those magical words make my tummy flip, and I've already pulled two dresses and a pair of slacks from a rack to try on when Martha returns, pulling a rolling rack of clothes behind her.

"That's not a *few things*." I quickly twist my long hair up into a knot. It needs to be out of my way so I can try on clothes.

Martha laughs and takes my finds from me so she can start me a room, and I immediately hurry over to the rack to comb through it.

"This is a Gucci blouse," I call out to her as my adrenaline spikes. "And it's in my size! That never happens."

Unfortunately, not all fashion houses offer their ready-to-wear clothes in larger sizes, but every once in a while, I find something.

In fact, this whole rack is full of designer pieces in my size.

"Who donated this stuff?" I ask as Martha joins me.

"A governor's wife," she says with a shrug. "I swear, she must have brought me half of her closet. These are last year's pieces."

"Who cares?" I laugh and step back. "I'll try it all on."

"I figured you'd say that. Let's get started."

Every piece fits me like a glove. A Dior shift dress, a Louis Vuitton blouse. Chanel, Hermes, and Valentino. Some of the items still have tags on them.

"I'm going to give you everything for three hundred," Martha says.

"There's easily ten grand in clothes here, and that's on the conservative side," I reply, shaking my head. "I should pay you at least one thousand."

"*Used* clothes, and besides, you'll bring them back to me when you're finished with them."

"This might be the best day of the whole year. I feel like I should buy a lottery ticket," I inform her as I pull on the long maxi dress I wore here and follow her to the counter where we dig in, folding everything and gently placing it all in the two totes I brought.

"Billie?" Her voice sounds tentative.

I raise an eyebrow at Martha. "Yes?"

"I'm thinking about selling the shop."

I feel my eyes go wide, and my heart stutters.

"Oh, why? It's such a great place."

"My parents are in Arizona, and my dad's not doing

great, health-wise. I feel like I should be there with them, you know? I have a serious case of daughter guilt."

I bite my lip. "I get it. Mine moved to Florida a few years ago, and if my dad wasn't well, I'd want to be closer to him, too. It's a tough decision. Is the shop struggling?"

"No. Actually, I do well, and I love it so much," she replies. "You're not my only client who comes from far away to pick through rich people's castoffs. I stay really busy. Why, do you want to buy it?"

She giggles at that, but I'm not laughing with her.

I can't really *afford* to buy this shop, and it's four hours from where I live, so I really shouldn't entertain the idea.

But I get 90 percent of my wardrobe here. And the day trip over each month is so good for my mental health. It's really the only day that I *don't* work. I don't stop by the shop to restock, or shoot an email, or change the display window. I listen to music or audiobooks in my car and empty my mind. Not to mention, my favorite restaurant is here in town, and I always treat myself whenever I'm here.

"No, of course not." I shake my head. "But do me a favor? Please give me a heads-up before you sell. I love it in here."

"I'll keep you posted. I'm not convinced that selling is the right move, but I've considered it. I know it would be a stretch for you to own two businesses in two very different places."

"One is hard enough, as you know."

Martha helps me load the totes into my car, then I

hug her goodbye. I'm hungry and have a long drive ahead of me, so I walk down the block to my favorite restaurant, which happens to be inside the cutest boutique hotel I've ever seen. Because we're in the mountains, you'd think it would have a rustic lodge feel, but it doesn't. It's classy, with beautiful sage green and burnt orange colors. The lighting is moody, and it makes a person feel ... *luxurious.*

Not that I've seen many boutique hotels. It's not like I travel the world often or anything, but this place is adorable. I wish I could afford to spend a long weekend here.

But, given that this is the playground for the ridiculously wealthy, I'm quite sure I can't afford the nightly rate.

I can, however, afford to eat in the restaurant.

I'm shown to a table by the windows, and once I take a seat, I pull out my phone to check my messages. I have a group text thread with my Spicy Girls Book Club girls that always has some activity.

Starting that book club is one of the best things I ever did. Not only did it bring me closer to my best friend and now sister-in-law, Dani, but it also brought my other bestie, Skyla, into my life. Add in the other ladies, and I have a kick-ass group of women around me.

I never take it for granted.

Millie: *Did you make it to Big Sky, Bee?*

Oops, I didn't see that earlier. Millie owns the coffee shop right next door to my bookstore, and I've known her all of my life. She's the best.

Me: *I did! Sorry, I didn't see this message earlier. I'm having lunch before I get back on the road.*

Skyla: *Did you find some fun things this time? I want to see everything!*

I grin and look up to thank my server, who just brought me some warm bread and water.

"Hello, miss. I'm Travis, and I'll be helping you today."

"Thanks, Travis."

"Have you had an opportunity to look over the menu?"

I don't need to. I know exactly what I want.

"I have," I reply with a smile. "I'll have the whipped feta dip because it's absolutely addicting."

Travis grins as he writes on his pad. "It really is. What else can I bring you?"

"I'll have the grilled chicken Caesar salad, no anchovies."

"I can do that. Anything to drink?"

"Just an iced tea, please. And also, for dessert, I will have the huckleberry crème brûlée."

"You're living your best life, my friend," Travis says with a wide smile before he walks away to put my order in. Travis is cute. He's tall with blond hair and one hell of a smile, complete with dimples.

Adorable.

Not nearly as sexy as Connor Gallagher. My stranger. The man who not only fucked my brains out one night late last year but has found ways to corner me and kiss the hell out of me at every opportunity since then. He's

Skyla's brother, a detail that I didn't know until I saw him at my niece's dance recital several months after that night, where he dragged me out back and kissed the fuck out of me.

And ever since then, it's been the same. Family dinner? Stolen kisses. Trip to Europe to watch Skyla dance? All the fucking kisses. He even stormed in on a book club meeting several weeks ago and dragged me into a supply closet, where he proceeded to give me an orgasm in three-point-seven seconds.

He's *everywhere*. And because he's my best friend's brother, it's not exactly possible to *never* see him, but I can be an adult when he's around.

I can be civil.

I can keep my hands and my lips to myself.

Because as much as Connor makes it clear that he's attracted to me sexually, he's *never* indicated that there's anything else there. I don't even have the jerk's phone number, for God's sake. And I'm through with meaning-less sex. When I'm with Connor, I lose myself to him, but in a good way. I feel safe. I feel … *content.* God, I slept the best I have in years when he took me to bed with him that night, and I haven't slept that well since. But the last time, when he kissed the hell out of me in that closet, I told him he didn't get to do that to me anymore because I feel used. Even if I *love* the way he towers over me, making me feel petite for the first time in my life. And even if I *love* how he treats Skyla, and I know that's the extraordinary way he'd treat his partner.

I don't *just* want sex with him. There, I admitted it. He intrigues me, and I know he's a good man.

I want more. Just like Dani and Skyla have recently found with my brothers. I want that for myself. I deserve more.

And he won't give me more.

If he wanted more, he'd have asked for my goddamn phone number. I'm done feeling used by that ridiculously sexy Irishman.

Newsletter Sign Up

I hope you enjoyed reading this story as much as I enjoyed writing it! For upcoming book news, be sure to join my newsletter! I promise I will only send you news-filled mail, and none of the spam. You can sign up here:

https://mailchi.mp/kristenproby.com/newsletter-sign-up

Also by Kristen Proby:

Other Books by Kristen Proby

The Wilds of Montana Series
Wild for You - Remington & Erin
Chasing Wild - Chase & Summer
Wildest Dreams - Ryan & Polly
On the Wild Side - Brady & Abbi
She's a Wild One - Holden & Millie

The Blackwells of Montana
When We Burn - Bridger & Dani

Get more information on the series here: https://
www.kristenprobyauthor.com/the-wilds-of-montana

Single in Seattle Series
The Secret - Vaughn & Olivia

ALSO BY KRISTEN PROBY:

The Scandal - Gray & Stella
The Score - Ike & Sophie
The Setup - Keaton & Sidney
The Stand-In - Drew & London

Check out the full series here: https://www.
kristenprobyauthor.com/single-in-seattle

Huckleberry Bay Series

Lighthouse Way
Fernhill Lane
Chapel Bend
Cherry Lane

The With Me In Seattle Series

Come Away With Me - Luke & Natalie
Under The Mistletoe With Me - Isaac & Stacy
Fight With Me - Nate & Jules
Play With Me - Will & Meg
Rock With Me - Leo & Sam
Safe With Me - Caleb & Brynna
Tied With Me - Matt & Nic
Breathe With Me - Mark & Meredith
Forever With Me - Dominic & Alecia
Stay With Me - Wyatt & Amelia
Indulge With Me
Love With Me - Jace & Joy

Dance With Me Levi & Starla
You Belong With Me - Archer & Elena
Dream With Me - Kane & Anastasia
Imagine With Me - Shawn & Lexi
Escape With Me - Keegan & Isabella
Flirt With Me - Hunter & Maeve
Take a Chance With Me - Cameron & Maggie

Check out the full series here: https://www.
kristenprobyauthor.com/with-me-in-seattle

The Big Sky Universe

Love Under the Big Sky
Loving Cara
Seducing Lauren
Falling for Jillian
Saving Grace

The Big Sky
Charming Hannah
Kissing Jenna
Waiting for Willa
Soaring With Fallon

Big Sky Royal
Enchanting Sebastian
Enticing Liam
Taunting Callum

Heroes of Big Sky

Honor

Courage

Shelter

Check out the full Big Sky universe here: <u>https://</u>
<u>www.kristenprobyauthor.com/under-the-big-sky</u>

Bayou Magic

Shadows

Spells

Serendipity

Check out the full series here: <u>https://www.</u>
<u>kristenprobyauthor.com/bayou-magic</u>

The Curse of the Blood Moon Series

Hallows End

Cauldrons Call

Salems Song

The Romancing Manhattan Series

All the Way

All it Takes

After All

Check out the full series here: <u>https://www.</u>

kristenprobyauthor.com/romancing-manhattan

The Boudreaux Series

Easy Love
Easy Charm
Easy Melody
Easy Kisses
Easy Magic
Easy Fortune
Easy Nights

Check out the full series here: https://www.
kristenprobyauthor.com/boudreaux

The Fusion Series

Listen to Me
Close to You
Blush for Me
The Beauty of Us
Savor You

Check out the full series here: https://www.
kristenprobyauthor.com/fusion

From 1001 Dark Nights

Easy With You
Easy For Keeps

No Reservations
Tempting Brooke
Wonder With Me
Shine With Me
Change With Me
The Scramble
Cherry Lane

Kristen Proby's Crossover Collection

Soaring with Fallon, A Big Sky Novel

Wicked Force: A Wicked Horse Vegas/Big Sky Novella
By Sawyer Bennett

All Stars Fall: A Seaside Pictures/Big Sky Novella
By Rachel Van Dyken

Hold On: A Play On/Big Sky Novella
By Samantha Young

Worth Fighting For: A Warrior Fight Club/Big Sky
Novella
By Laura Kaye

Crazy Imperfect Love: A Dirty Dicks/Big Sky Novella
By K.L. Grayson

Nothing Without You: A Forever Yours/Big Sky Novella
By Monica Murphy

Check out the entire Crossover Collection here:
https://www.kristenprobyauthor.com/kristen-proby-crossover-collection

About the Author

Kristen Proby is a *New York Times*, *USA Today*, and *Wall Street Journal* bestselling author of over seventy published titles. She debuted in 2012, captivating fans with spicy contemporary romance about families and friends with plenty of swoony love. She also writes paranormal romance and suggests you keep the lights on while reading them.

When not under deadline, Kristen enjoys spending time with her husband and their fur babies, riding her bike, relaxing with embroidery, trying her hand at painting, and, of course, enjoying her beautiful home in the mountains of Montana.